THE CHANGELING CURSE

Cursed Ones Book Two

DANI KRISTOFF

Australian Speculative Fiction

To the Canberra Romance Readers
Thank you for being there during the plague and inspiring me to get the book done

CHAPTER 1

Abbie pretended her nose didn't itch as she read from the autocue. "And that is the news round-up for today. This is Abbie McGregor for the Canberra News Network. Thank you and good night."

She smiled into the camera until the light flashed off, signalling the end of the broadcast. Wrinkling her nose, she rubbed behind her knee, attacking another annoying itch where her pantyhose rubbed against the chair. "Thanks, Abbie. Same time Monday." The producer's voice sounded in her earpiece. She scooped the device out and placed it in its protective casing.

She exited the studio and walked up the corridor. Dave, the producer, put his head out the recording studio door and gave her a nod of approval. "Nice work on that defective construction piece. A Walkley for you."

Abbie laughed and waved goodbye. It had been a good piece and the research into the substandard building practices for the swathe of new apartment buildings had been rewarding. Night after night reading through plans and chasing reports had left her exhausted. A Walkley Award was not likely, but it was something she hoped for in the future. What journalist didn't? Being a journalist and newsreader in

Canberra, a small city, was the next step on the ladder of her career. *Better than nothing!* Canberra local news was not the national politics and the big headlines one would expect from working in the political capital. It was the 'Today a kangaroo caused havoc on State Circle as it bounded down the road into traffic' type of thing.

Abbie checked her watch and sped up. She needed her make-up off and herself out of the studio in time to catch a movie with her best buddies, Ruby and Bella, who were visiting from Sydney for the weekend. Pushing the door to the dressing rooms open, she high-fived Jenny the make-up artist. "I didn't melt."

"That's good news," Jenny said and peered closer. "No sweat. Excellent. Damn hot in here today."

Jenny helped her out of her trendy blazer and blouse and hung them up for cleaning on the rack with the other clothes used to dress the 'talent'. Being from Wagga Wagga, a smaller, inland city, which was hotter and drier than Canberra, Abbie could cope with the heat the capital dished out in the summer months. That was the only advantage she'd discovered so far from being from a country town.

In the make-up chair, Jenny helped her get most of the gunk off her face. "You got plans tonight, Abbie?" Jenny asked as she gently drew the wipe over Abbie's eyelids to remove the eyeliner and mascara.

"Just meeting the girls. They're down from Sydney."

"Sounds like fun," Jenny said as she quickly removed the last of the face paint. "I bet you're going out on the town. Maybe you'll meet Mr Right."

Abbie scoffed. "Mr Right?" She looked at her reflection in the mirror. Was there such a thing? She certainly understood attraction and passion, but the destiny side of things? She wasn't too sure. "Maybe."

"You want me to do your eyes? This copper shade will go well with your amber-coloured eyes."

"Sure, thanks. You doing anything?" Abbie asked in return as Jenny turned to load a brush with colour.

"Nah, late shift. I've gotta hang around." She applied the eyeshadow and pencil, then some mascara. Not heavy, just enough for a night out.

"That stinks. I hope time goes quickly for you."

"All done. I'll let you apply the rest. Your eyes look great."

"Thanks," Abbie said and then she sat forward to peer in the mirror to apply some pale pink lipstick.

After checking her face, Abbie climbed out of the chair, grabbed her handbag and jacket. "See you Monday, Jen.

"Sure." Jenny waved, then set about wiping the chair down for her next client. Jenny had a book to read to help pass the time, so Abbie gave up worrying about her.

As Abbie made her way out, she bumped into Fleur Bellenose in the corridor. "Great work on the autocue, Fleur."

Fleur leaned in close, "I think you fumbled a line."

Abbie laughed. It was a running joke between them. "Not me. Must have been you."

"Never! I'll be sacked." Fleur smiled and elbow bumped her gently. "You were great. I'm going to get your job one day." Abbie knew Fleur was keen and smart and was currently researching a story that would get her noticed.

"You definitely will. I just hope I've got a better one lined up before you do."

"But I'll never have that red hair and freckles," she pretend pouted.

"You could try. I have my Scottish father to thank for mine."

"Have a good one. See you Monday?"

"Sure will. Bye."

Out in the car park the wind whipped up Abbie's hair, so she grabbed it and slid a band around it, pulling it into a ponytail. It was time to meet the girls. She wasn't far from Civic, the city centre, where she was meeting her friends. In the trunk of her car, she found a short jacket and a decorative head band. She put these on, hoping it made her different enough from her on-screen image. She'd been on air for six weeks now and as yet had only been recognised a couple of times by members of the public. She was happy being *Canberra famous*, but tonight she wanted to hang with Ruby and Bella, both of whom had driven down for the weekend just to be with her.

"So, Abbie, what keeps you in this place?" Ruby asked, hugging her mugaccino as if her life depended on it. Ruby had lovely, tanned skin, which she owned to her Maori grandfather. Her hazel eyes roamed about the restaurant and the streets outside. It was reasonably busy for Canberra, as it was Friday night. The clubs were rocking, the cafés packed and the good restaurants full to bursting.

"Yes, what?" Bella near screeched. "I mean it's cold—" Bella was part Malaysian-Chinese, with creamy skin, dark eyes and hair, and a wide smile. She was a smart woman, currently working in academia.

"—hot," interjected Ruby, fanning herself.

Winters were cold and summers were hot, that was true. "The temperature difference between night and day is often more than ten degrees due to Canberra being high up and inland," Abbie commented. "It's pretty, though."

"Pretty confusing," Ruby quipped.

Bella gave her a sideways glare and took a swig of her gin and tonic. "It's small," she continued and then raked her gaze around the room meaningfully, before adding. "And where are all the hotties?"

Sitting across from Bella and seeing her serious pout nearly made Abbie burst out laughing. "I'm not here to get a man, Bella. I'm here to get a career. Have to start somewhere, don't I?"

"I suppose." Bella took another sip and managed to look unconvinced.

"It's just that we miss you." Ruby said, reaching over to pat Abbie's hand.

Abbie smiled and nodded. "I know. I miss you, too. One day I'll be back in Sydney. But right now, I'm working hard. I don't notice the absence of ..." she waved her hand out to the street "... decent single men."

Both Ruby and Bella gasped. "But how do you get by?" Ruby asked.

Bella elbowed Ruby. "Perhaps she has supply of vibrators handy."

Ruby covered her mouth with a menu, barely disguising her snort of laughter. "Yes, I hear there are sex shops galore in Canberra."

"Great! Day trip ... or is that night trip?" Bella asked, leaning in close and waggling her eyebrows.

Abbie leaned on the table and cradled her head in her hands. *Sex shops? Really? They wanted to visit them?* "You're incorrigible. Getting laid isn't the be-all and end-all." Abbie sat back in her chair, flicked her ponytail with a hand and feigned seriousness. "Besides it's none of your business." She wasn't about to discuss her personal bedroom habits in a restaurant in Garema Place. Her cheeks did burn though.

"I'd love to see those sleazy places." Bella was at it again, whiney voice included.

Abbie shook her head and checked the time. These two were out of hand and Abbie had had enough. "Nope. I can't be seen in those places. I might be recognised. You two are welcome to go out there yourselves. I'm not sure if they're open at this time of night, though."

Her friends laughed hysterically. "You are so weird," Ruby said, calming enough to take a sip of her drink.

"Night-time is when it all happens. Business booms!" Bella added.

As Abbie gave them a severe look, she narrowed her eyes and pursed her lips.

Ruby was the first to acknowledge that Abbie was being serious. "Nah, it's okay." She flapped a careless hand, lifted her glass and sucked the last of the gin from among the ice.

"We're only teasing," Bella said, swirling the remains of drink and sending Abbie a wink.

"We're happy to do the pyjama thing in your apartment tonight," Ruby said. "That's what we came down for. Only razzing you. Tomorrow night, though, we're hitting the town."

"We saw you on air tonight. It was very cool. We were in the pub down the street there." Bella pointed down the road.

"She told everyone we knew you." Ruby laughed as Abbie cringed. She had to bite down on the questions she wanted to ask. *Did you tell anyone about my private life? Did you blab about the old school days, who I dated?* But she held her tongue. What was done was done and she didn't want to fight with them.

Without seeming like too much of a party pooper, she managed to get her friends back to her apartment and their sleeping arrangements sorted. There Abbie was able to let her hair down, accepting a couple of glasses of bubbly, while they sat on the floor, listening to nineties music and swapping bawdy stories. Abbie fell asleep on the double mattress she'd made up on the floor for her friends. When she woke the next morning, she was sprawled half on the mattress and half on the carpet. Ruby's butt was aimed at her face and Bella had her limbs dangling from the couch.

"Ow," Abbie said when she moved her head. She had one hell of a hangover. She didn't know whether to dive for the painkillers first or lurch to the bathroom to throw up.

There was no response from her friends. Suffering mightily and moaning loudly, Abbie crawled to the bathroom, dry retched in the toilet bowl, then fumbled for painkillers and slunk into the shower. It took her a while to register that she was still wearing her underwear. Groaning, she climbed to her feet using the wall for support, resting her forehead on the tiles and peeled her wet undies off and undid her bra. It took a further ten minutes to wash and get out.

Bleary eyed, she gazed into the mirror. The painkillers hadn't kicked in yet and she wasn't up to taking her friends sightseeing feeling like this. Zombie-like, she shuffled past her friends, still obliviously asleep on the floor, and headed to her room where she flopped on the bed and crashed out.

The tantalising aroma of coffee teased her eyelids open sometime later. Ruby sat on the bed, resembling the smart-looking businesswoman she was. With a grin, she passed over the mug. "Bella is nearly ready. Time for the tour. First the museum, a ride around the lake on a Segway and then dinner, followed by a night club."

Abbie groaned. "That's a lot to pack in."

Ruby nodded. "Yep. You gotta live a little. Even in Canberra."

❧❦☙

So it happened that later that night Abbie sat perched on a stool in a nightclub in Civic, watching children—well they were children to her —gyrate drunkenly while she did her best to have fun.

Ruby ordered drinks. The first thing Bella did was check out the hunks in the joint. Her dark rag bob framed her face and her trim figure excelled in the tight black number she wore as she surveyed her surroundings.

"There aren't any men over the age of twenty-one in this club." She focused on Abbie. "I may have missed one. I'll double check." Bella arched her eyebrows, and then strolled away to do another reconnoitre.

The drinks arrived and Abbie clinked her glass with Ruby and took a couple of mouthfuls. She zoned out, not quite sure if she was enjoying the music or ignoring it. Ruby had been one of the first people to befriend Abbie when she'd headed to the big smoke from the country. "You look nice tonight, Ruby," Abbie said, feeling her mood lift. She looked at her glass. *That could be the booze.* She met Ruby's dark, assessing gaze. Her friend moved so that her thick single plait swayed with the motion of her head. She was a nurse, capable and reliable. Abbie always felt safe when she was around.

"Thank you, gorgeous," Ruby replied. "I don't know what you've done to your hair tonight, but I have serious, serious hair envy."

Abbie laughed and grabbed at some of her hair, which hung past her shoulders. She'd washed it and let it dry naturally and now the ginger waves fell untethered down her back. The subject of her hair was how they met in the first place and they'd been friends ever since. Ruby excused herself, waving her phone. She had to make a call to her mother, no doubt. They were very close.

Abbie sat there on the stool, taking sips of her gin and tonic and staring into space.

Bella sidled up to her and bumped her out of her reverie. Startled Abbie met Bella's eyes. Her friend lifted her head, pointing with her chin to a tall, striking man with a goatee and a build to die for. "What about him?"

Having finished her phone call, Ruby came up alongside. "Nice work, Bella."

Abbie cast her gaze in the man's direction and he turned her way in slow motion, lifting his gaze from the bottom of her feet to the top of her head. Riveted, she couldn't look away. A sizzle of sexual attraction kicked her heart rate up. When their eyes met, it was as if he'd zapped her.

"Close your mouth, Abbie," Ruby whispered in her ear. Abbie did, then turned to take a drink and the urge to fan the heat from her cheeks was overwhelming.

"Wow, baby," Ruby commented as she picked up her own drink. "He's not bad. Not bad. At. All. I thought you said there were no decent men."

Abbie coughed after swallowing a mouthful of Dutch courage. "The decent ones are married with two-point-five children." She continued to survey the club, the small crowd on the dance floor, a bunch at the bar trying to get served and, in the farther darker shadows, the shape of a man. A sense of wrongness passed over her and then it was gone, along with the shadowy shape. She shivered as goosebumps spread along her upper arms.

"If you aren't interested in fetching that one over, let me know, I'll be there." Bella said, her dark eyes glinting in the light from the dance floor.

"Do you think he's married?" Ruby asked, then took a sip of her champagne cocktail while barely keeping her drooling under control. "You better go find out."

Abbie shook her head. "Not me."

"Oh, yes, you." Ruby said, stabbing her finger into Abbie's chest. "We don't live here. No good to us ... unless he's a one-nighter." She peered around Abbie and bit her lip as she sized him up. "Actually a one-nighter has appeal, but it would be such a waste. He looks like he'd be good for several weeks."

Bella bumped Ruby with her shoulder. "None of that. It's Abbie who needs to get laid."

"How do you know?" Abbie was appalled.

Bella grinned. "Well, I didn't find a stash of dildos and vibrators at your place, so I'm figuring you're way too needy."

Abbie threw up her hands. "You went through my bedside table?"

Bella snorted with laughter. "Actually ..."

Abbie wasn't game to hear it. She lifted her hands in a sign of defeat. "Stop, stop."

Ruby stood there eyeing them both, her mouth an impatient line. "Well, are you going to at least try? I agree with Bella. It's for your own good."

Bella did a three-hundred-and-sixty degree turn. "If he doesn't appeal, we'll ask that guy there."

Abbie leaned around her friend and swallowed. *Not that one. Eww!* She wasn't sure if that one was a football head or a couch potato. But it didn't matter. No sizzle. She would only make an effort for the sizzle factor. And the tall, mysterious, sexy stranger definitely lit her fuse.

"Come on, before someone else gets lucky." The guy's attention had swung away, but not so the heat he'd generated—that instant attraction. Her heart thumped just looking at him. Licking her lips, she tried to get her imagination under control, because images of them both naked flooded her mind—the touch of skin on hot skin, the thrill of the touch, kisses dragged from the very soul.

A young blonde woman who looked about sixteen if a day, wearing a very tight miniskirt and midriff lace top gyrated in the sizzling hunk's direction. Abbie held her breath as she watched, but the guy didn't even move or give any indication that he noticed the girl. The dancing girl span and boogied for a few minutes, flinging her long hair for effect and wiggling her butt. He didn't even twitch. He could have had that girl on the spot, she was that keen. Abbie considered this. The man had taste, apparently, but did his taste tend to someone older, more experienced, with a generous head of red hair?

Abbie sighed when the girl bounced away to giggle with her friends. "Go on, Abbie. Now is your chance," Ruby said in her ear.

Abbie stared at her empty glass. She did want to make a move. How much had she had to drink? Was she seriously considering going up to this guy and chatting him up? Another gin and tonic might give her more courage, but that was cheating. Sliding from the bar stool, she eased a crick out of her neck, then smoothed her skirt and swished her hair over her shoulder. Taking a deep breath, she ordered her thoughts and headed over.

There wasn't enough distance for her to order her thoughts properly. She was a bit rusty on the chatting up procedure. Usually, she was fending off men. "Hi," she said, using her professional smile. "You waiting for someone?"

Those eyes drifted to hers. In the dim light of the club, she couldn't see what colour they were, but they stirred her all the same. "No," he replied, his voice smooth with deep tones.

Her breath hitched. What was going on with her? She'd come this far, so she may as well go for it. "Hello. My name is Abbie. Abbie McGregor." She put out her hand for him to shake.

He spared it a glance. "No."

Her head jerked up at his words, the deep voice slicing through the fog of her senses. "No?"

He turned slightly toward her, towering and broad. "We don't do the name thing, or the phone number thing."

"We don't?" She was slow on the uptake. "What do we do then?"

A smile lit the corner of his mouth and his eyes narrowed. Gently, he grasped her elbows, drawing her closer. Her hands glanced against his chest, a hard wall of muscle. Mesmerised by the feel of him and the shadowed eyes, she gasped and stared at him.

His gaze narrowed, and his forefinger brushed some hair from her face. "You're a rare one," he said, his voice soft and so full of growl her knees weakened.

"I am?"

"Yes." The finger dropped to her bottom lip and it was as if he was imprinting himself on her skin. Heat and electricity spread out from his touch. She sucked in a breath, just as he lowered his mouth to hers. Firm lips and a hot tongue had her blood pounding in her ears as they kissed. She forgot to breathe as she rested her hands against his broad chest, meeting his kiss like for like. It went on and on, until she felt like she'd merged with him, not knowing where he ended and she began. Then, like a bell had rung, he stilled. Hands pushing gently against her shoulders, he edged her back.

Her gaze was glued to his face. What had just happened between them? She wanted answers.

"I'm sorry," he said, lowering his head like a bow. "That's all I've got time for. Gotta go."

He eased her away from him, giving himself room, then turned and strode out the door of the club.

Abbie stood there gaping, not even able to speak. Hormones that had been running rampant cooled. He was gone. Just like that. People were looking at her. Her anger hardened like a fist in her gut. How dare he do that? He'd snubbed her and made it obvious to everyone. Especially to her. She didn't even know his name and she'd just snogged him in a bar. For god's sake, was she a teenager? But it had moved her. God, how it had moved her to her soul. Yet, it had meant nothing to him. She didn't understand.

Her mouth was still opening and closing when her two friends came up to her, demanding to know what happened. Abbie was mad. If she had extendable claws, she'd scratch his eyes out. He'd ruined it. If a man could kiss a woman like that, if he could excite her and then walk away, then nothing made sense. It must be bullshit. Love and attraction were bullshit. She thought they had a connection, something that was indefinable, but it was crap. It was her imagination. It made her want to howl.

Bella grabbed her. "Abbie? What's going on? Where did he go? Is he coming back?" She shook her hand, fanning her face. "Man, that was some hot kiss."

"I don't even know his name." Her voice caught and she looked to her friend for help, her face crumpling. "Ruby?"

Ruby nodded and turned to Bella. "We need to take Abbie home, right now."

Bella opened her mouth to speak. "Can it," Ruby said and then took them both by the arms and led them out to the street. Abbie looked for him, but he wasn't there. Why did he do that? Was he out to get her? Don't be stupid, she thought. He doesn't know you. Can't possibly know you. They passed a café as they headed to the car. Her earlier news broadcast was repeating on the television that hung above the bar. Maybe he did know who she was. Maybe he was a psycho fan.

❧

Rolf exited the club, pausing on the threshold. A shadow loomed and then dissipated. Then he was outside among the pedestrians and the lights, searching for his illusive quarry. Dane had signalled that it was time to move. Which sadly meant it was time to forget about the gorgeous redhead. He was a werewolf on the hunt. She wasn't for him.

Humans were too fragile for werewolves, and they generally asked too many questions to make good sex partners. Damn. Something like regret pounded through his veins. He'd been zapped just by the look of her. The kiss? He'd lost himself in there. If not for Dane's hail, he'd still be there, annihilating all her defences like she'd done to him. Hell, he'd have taken what she'd offered and more, despite his personal prohibition on fraternising with humans. Bad timing. Their quarry was making a move. He surged across the road and bounded along Bunda Street.

Thoughts of Abbie lingered, like the scent of her perfume, as he jogged past the intersection. "Where?" he thought. Rolf should have been able to pick up Dane's location from that thought. Their connection from Dane's time as a werewolf still held true. Not as well as it used to do, but at moments like this it could, boosted by Dane's magic. His friend hadn't been a real werewolf, rather his change was caused by a spell, one that threatened his very existence.

He couldn't stop his mind wandering back to the woman. There had been a hint of fuzziness to her mind, the lowering of inhibitions. She wouldn't have normally approached him. He was certain of that. It was alcohol, attraction and sexual need. Maybe something more. He was certainly strongly attracted to her. A bit above the normal register.

"Park," came Dane's thought. Rolf closed his eyes momentarily and then cleared his head as he sped up. Up the street and into the park he went, following the trail of the out-of-towner, the one with the scent of magic trailing behind him.

Glebe Park was eerily quiet with pockets of shadow under trees. Tall apartment buildings loomed above, stark and surprisingly quiet. Rolf inhaled, searching for that sickly scent of magic. The wind rustled the leaves. Still no sign of his quarry. He stepped softly, sniffing the air for any sign. *Thunk!* He spun, but it was a garbage bin blowing over. Yet there was something else, a scent, a presence. As he turned slowly back, a powerful surge of magic took him by surprise and shoved him up and back, lifting him up and slamming him into the dirt, his landing ripping up the grass. Dazed, he shook his head and sprang to his feet, crouched and ready for attack. Nothing. There was nothing. Whoever had attacked was gone.

A familiar tingle in his mind alerted him to Dane approaching with Annwyn. Dane, a blond, powerfully built man, himself a strong sorcerer, had been saved from the werewolf curse by Annwyn. Annwyn had been the victim of a rogue sorceress called Nira, who had stolen Annwyn's body and life. She was left existing in Nira's body, but luckily the exposure to so much magic had ignited her latent magical talents, leaving her a powerful sorceress with a unique talent. However, Annwyn was plagued with some remnants of the sexually insatiable sorceress, which at times overpowered her sense of self and made her provocative. Rolf, Dane and Annwyn had a close relationship as a result of that previous event.

Rolf ran his fingers through his hair, dislodging blades of grass and then sniffed for a trace scent in the shadows beneath the trees. The dark magician they'd been tracking had given him the slip. Again.

"What happened?" Dane asked, his normally blue gaze darkened by the night.

Rolf shrugged. "Knocked me flying with magic. Didn't see it coming."

"Are you hurt?" Annwyn asked, reaching out to brush dirt from his shirt.

Rolf stepped back out of reach. "No. I'm fine." He had to be careful with Annwyn. He could never be sure it wasn't Nira trying to come on to him to stir up trouble. It paid to be wary.

"Don't you think it odd that they left without doing anything?" Annwyn asked. She sniffed the air and looked about her. "No spells here."

"Are you sure?" Dane asked. Annwyn's special gift was seeing spells —the weave, the weft and the curls and coils of them. She could even tell who made them sometimes. Dane had explained to him that it was a rare gift among sorcerers.

"Whatever they used on Rolf didn't leave any residue. Someone is being very careful."

"Because they know you can see spells and maybe recognise their work," Dane said, rubbing her on the back between her shoulder blades. "The knowledge of your gift was meant to be known to only a few."

Annwyn's face tensed. "I think we should stay in town, rather than head home to the farm. I feel that whoever it is, they're here for a reason, some sort of mischief. We need to be close." She pointed to the Crowne Plaza Hotel that stood next to the park. "Why don't we see if they have any rooms?"

Dane scanned the park and then nodded. "Yes, you're right. They wouldn't have come all the way to Canberra for nothing. They'll stay until it's done. Rolf?"

"Makes perfect sense," Rolf replied. No one from the magical world came to Canberra, or even Australia, without reason. Dane lived in the country because he wanted to be out of the mainstream. As a sorcerer he could travel anywhere on the planet with a spell, so it was hardly an inconvenience. Rolf liked the isolation. He and his pack had enough space to roam without getting embroiled in larger were politics.

Rolf scanned the park, the streetlights, their illumination interrupted by swaying tree limbs. Something wasn't right and that made him uneasy. Until he knew what he was dealing with, he'd rather stay near at hand as well. Pity he hadn't asked Abbie to wait. A room in the hotel would have been ideal for an encounter of the sexual kind. He shook his head, realising he was playing with fire with that one, and not because of the red hair. The attraction between them was strong and not easily ignored. Why there was an attraction, he didn't have time to think about. If she'd been a were then it would have made sense, but she was one hundred per cent human. Not that unions with humans didn't happen; they did, but tended to be messy. Rolf wanted to avoid that sort of complication. As alpha he needed to lead by example. Hard to do that when you have to hide your true nature from a human. As pack leader he would have to conceal the whole pack's activities and intrusions. Then there was Dane and Annwyn, resident sorcerers. Just as difficult to explain and conceal. Best he didn't take that delicious Abbie to bed. Certainly, the wisest choice.

After falling in behind Dane and Annwyn, Rolf continued to study their surroundings, inhaling the different scents and using his other senses to search for that dark presence.

Australia was well out of things due to distance, small population and a general lack of involvement in political wrangling. Why would enemies of the Collegium of Sorcerers strike in Canberra of all places? It made no sense, unless Dane and Annwyn were the targets. While Canberra was Australia's capital city, it wasn't big and who really cared about the politicians anyway? Only other politicians. Rolf grinned. The collegium represented the supernatural races. There was a hierarchy of course, with sorcerers at the top. Vampires were a close second. There just weren't enough supernaturals in the country to warrant even a chapter of the organisation. Rolf repressed a shrug. He didn't care for any politics, human or otherwise, and not least because werewolves and other were came in pretty low in the scheme of things. He liked his freedom. It was only his friendship with Dane that had him consider any sort of interaction with the collegium.

"I'll fetch the car," he said to Dane, who nodded and led Annwyn inside the hotel. His friend held his woman close, fitted her nice and easy under his protective arm. Since Dane had been cured of the werewolf curse, Rolf had never seen him happier. He was happy for them.

Rolf's memories of that last encounter were mixed. Nira had made him fuck Annwyn up the arse, made him hurt her, and Rolf didn't hurt women. But Annwyn had saved herself, and him, and rid them of Nira. Well, they were free of the sorceress most of the time—except when she occasionally surfaced, providing Annwyn with an insatiable desire for kinky sex. Hence, the need for established ground rules for dealing with Annwyn when Nira surfaced.

It didn't take long to retrieve their car and Rolf drove it into the car park beneath the hotel. When he checked with reception, Dane had booked him a room next door to his. At least he'd get some privacy. In the elevator up to their floor, he again regretted letting the redheaded woman go. He was in the mood to show her a good time, human or no. He could be a gentleman, when he chose to be. He keyed his way into the room and when he saw the smoothly made king-size bed, memories of that kiss returned, making him hard. That had been something. He moved to the bathroom, peeling off his clothes. Even as pellets of hot water hit his skin, he wasn't sure what had happened with the woman, but the feeling was more than sex. A psychic connection?

He grabbed the soap and scrubbed. A thinking connection with a human? Weird.

⁂

Sunday morning and Abbie and the girls were up early. Brunch at Gus's was on the agenda for the day, then a girlie shop before Ruby and Bella headed home. Abbie still smarted from the snubbing she'd received the night before. She was tired, too. She'd tossed and turned, body on fire with the recollections of that kiss, and the way she'd moulded herself to that body of his. She clenched her fists. She didn't even know his name. Why she kept thinking about the encounter she didn't understand. It's not like she'd even had a conversation with the dude. He wouldn't recognise her in the cold light of day.

It had to be her pride. She'd made a move, something she'd not done before, and been snubbed. Royally and painfully snubbed, after having all of her senses put on high alert. Usually, it was her avoiding attention, steering the flirts away from her. Abbie was quite good at keeping unwanted attention at bay. Some might consider her aggressive. She didn't agree. She just didn't like bullshit or wasting time. So to be snubbed was too much to be borne.

Her dear friends had commiserated and said he was a slacker who wasn't worth it. "He probably goes around doing that in all the bars, just to piss women off," Bella had surmised.

Ruby had agreed. "It's probably all he can do. He probably can't get it up so he wants to bring everyone down."

Even after having a good laugh, Abbie couldn't shift the hurt. The memory of his searing gaze and the brush of her hand on his chest and that kiss that had burned across her skin, her mind and her soul. Her failed attempt at chatting up the stranger had essentially ended their night out. They'd gone home, watched *Love, Actually* and eaten a full box of chocolates until two am, along with imbibing three bottles of bubbly.

It had rained overnight and the street still had puddles as they walked along. Sunlight peered between a break in the clouds and Abbie pulled her short jacket close around her neck. A chill had crept up her spine. A quick glance to her friends showed they looked perfectly comfortable in T-shirts, when usually the Sydneysiders complained about the Canberra cold, even in mid-summer. Was she coming down with something? A chill? She had a function that evening and couldn't afford to get sick and miss it. She straightened her shoulders and quickened her step, leading the way into the café. She was not going to get ill. No way and no how.

They ended up taking seats outside, watching the Sunday shoppers walk past. A police car revved its engine. The noise was deafening, and they weren't even going anywhere or pursuing anyone, just being noticed. A man's shadow passed by; she saw it out of the corner of her eye. When she turned he was gone, but the image was there in her memory. The black shape of a featureless man.

"So, Ruby. You driving all the way back to Sydney, or are you letting Bella behind the wheel of your new car?" Abbie asked with false brightness. Saying goodbye was not easy. Watching Bella hug her morning coffee, as she squinted through bleary eyes, reminded Abbie of the old days when they shared an apartment while studying at university in Sydney. Bella didn't even blink.

Ruby scoffed. "No way. I'm driving. It's not that far you know. You should remember that and visit more often. Once you're on the highway there're no lights until the eastern suburbs. Two-and-a-half hours max."

"I'd like to, but there always seems to be something on, some event ... like this evening. I have ..."

Ruby laughed. "But I'm a nurse and work shiftwork and I'm always so tired and I manage it. Not often mind you, but I do ..."

"Argghhhhh," Bella moaned, holding her head as if she didn't have the strength to keep it up.

Ruby tut-tutted and rubbed her back.

"Poor Bella. You will indulge," Ruby gibed.

"In what. Booze or chocolate?" Abbie asked.

Ruby grinned. "Too much of both will make you sick. I think the chocolates she ate had liqueur in them, so pow!" She smacked her hands together. "Double whammy."

Ruby waved the waiter over and ordered another long back for

Bella, and then waved her fork at Abbie's plate. "Why aren't you eating those pancakes?" she asked and speared one for herself.

"I don't know. I'm off my food for some reason."

"Sad to see us leave, I expect," Ruby said around a mouth full of pancake.

Bella groaned agreement. "I want to go home. And I don't want to go home. It's a bloody paradox."

"Them's big words," Abbie replied. "You've actually been reading those theses you've been editing, haven't you?"

"Some of them."

Ruby nudged Abbie. "She's been dating one of the professors. I think it's serious."

"Really?"

Bella's moan was cut off by the arrival of her coffee. "Nothing wrong with brains." She lifted the mug and inhaled theatrically.

"As long as he's good in bed," Ruby said sagely, as if she'd had this conversation before.

"Yep," Bella agreed. "And we have something to talk about after."

Abbie smiled, feeling a twinge inside. Thinking about Bella with a man made her see her own lack of partner starkly. That brought another flashback of the bloke last night. What amazing sex they could've had. Who knew where that could lead? Nowhere. He'd more or less stipulated that first up. Now, she didn't have a name to fixate on, or grumble about.

They continued eating breakfast. Abbie let Ruby and Bella's chatter soothe her and tried not to think about how she was going to cope without them. While she dissected the remaining pancakes on her plate, she tried to calculate when she could next get a day or two off to go visit them. She only ate a few bites. The small pieces of pancake ended up on the edges of her plate, pretending not to be there.

By the end of the meal, Bella was looking improved. "Headache better?" Abbie asked.

"Yes. I'll be fine. Ruby here nursed me. Fed me some 'Hairy Lemon' potion, when you were in the bathroom."

Arm in arm, they headed to the Canberra Centre, which was across the street. Abbie experienced a heavy feeling in her middle and her skin was layered in sweat. She shook her head, wondering if she'd picked up a virus.

Ruby narrowed her gaze. "Is everything all right? You've gone a little grey."

"Yes, I'm fine."

People walked past them, giving curious looks.

Bella tugged on her arm. "Abbie your lips are white."

"They are?" Abbie squinted at her friends, not really seeing them.

Ruby put a hand on her shoulder. "Abbie, what is it?"

The world was spinning slowly around her. Her stomach heaved and punched. She tried to walk on, but her step faltered. Her mouth opened but her words came out jumbled.

"Abbie?" Ruby said again. "Look at me. Tell me what is wrong."

Nothing, Abbie tried to say but her mouth didn't work properly. A garbled sound, ending in a growl came out. The world shifted around her. Smells leaped at her, rammed into her nose. Vomit raced up her throat as she heaved onto the pavement. Bella squealed as she leaped away and Ruby deftly sidestepped.

"Abbie. Can you speak to me? I'm going to call an ambulance. Can you sit on the ground over there?" Ruby tried to steer her out of the way of the other pedestrians to near the plate glass window of a store.

Lights flashed, blinding Abbie, and pain knifed through her body making her cry out. A scream fought its way up her throat and sounded like a howl.

Ruby got her to sit on the ground, but Abbie could barely take it in. What was happening? The various scents around her exacerbated her feelings of nausea. Her own perfume made her vomit once more. She tried to get to her feet but her hands weren't obeying her commands. Bella started screaming hysterically.

"Quiet!" Ruby said. "Something is terribly wrong ..." Ruby's voice dissolved into a meaningless jumble. Abbie could no longer understand the words.

Sounds like breaking glass razored through Abbie's skin. She opened her mouth to scream. What came out wasn't her voice. "Wha ... grrrr ..."

CHAPTER 2

Rolf stood in the lobby of the Crowne Plaza Hotel while Dane took care of their bill. Annwyn sat in a lounge chair by the window, her straight blonde hair glistening in the sunlight. She flicked another page of the newspaper, but her attention was on what was going on outside. She looked relaxed to a casual passer-by, yet she scanned the streets looking for signs of the sorcerer they were tracking. Her ability to see spells was essential to their mission. Rolf wasn't a sorcerer and only knew spells had a smell, a different kind of scent.

Rolf yawned. He'd not slept well, not with all the lust and sex vibes leaking out of Dane and Annwyn's room. Maybe hunting wayward dark mages turned them on. They were at it for hours. Rolf had lain there wishing he'd been able to pick up that redhead. Imagining licking her soft white skin all over until she screamed had made his own solitary endeavour at sexual release a tad more satisfying. It wasn't often a human made such an impression on him.

Rolf stilled, drawn out of his reverie. There was something thick and strange in the air. Rolf frowned over it, not quite sure what he was sensing until Annwyn's head snapped up, her gaze centring on the outside. Dane stiffened, then detached from the flirty receptionist. A quick glance in Rolf's direction and his sorcerer friend was striding toward him. "Where?"

"Not far," Rolf replied as he headed for the front door.

Annwyn responding, picked up her purse. "Back down in the city centre," she said. "Close."

Rolf felt rather than heard a gut-wrenching cry and knew without a doubt that the dark sorcerer had struck. Rolf listened with his being, felt the magic like it was attacking his own skin. This attack was close to home. He darted out the doors, following Dane and Annwyn.

"Can you see anything?" Dane asked.

Annwyn studied the air. "Not from here I can't."

"What kind of attack is it?" Annwyn turned to Rolf, her eyebrow raised in question. Dane followed suit. "Rolf?"

Rolf couldn't answer. Whatever was going on was knifing into his mind, his body, his were essence.

Annwyn closed her eyes and shook her head. "He can feel it. That's not a good sign."

The scream came again. Something earthy in it kicked off his werewolf instincts and he couldn't hold off the change. He bolted for the road, peeling his shirt off as he went and undoing his jeans, shoving them down and off. The change was on him.

"Rolf?" Dane called after him. Rolf couldn't answer. He was too busy embracing the change, forcing his body into its were shape.

Rolf heard Annwyn talking to Dane. "I can't see the magic, but he's reacting to it. I don't understand."

"It's magic targeted to weres," Dane replied. "Someone is being forced to transform for the first time. Rolf is the alpha and close by. He's changing because he has to."

Then Dane and Annwyn faded from his notice. The knife edge of pain was brief. Years of practice had inured him to it. Transforming into a wolf while running, Rolf bounded down the street, leaving Dane and Annwyn behind him. They followed at a run. He hoped they could fudge people's memories, because it wasn't every day a werewolf went bounding through Canberra's centre.

More screams, louder and increasingly guttural, drew him to the spot. A group of people standing around someone or something crouched on the ground. He growled, hoping to scare them out of his way. No one took any notice. He pawed the ground, made more noise and a threatening sound that couldn't be ignored.

A man turned, saw him and jerked back with a yell. He banged into the woman next to him and she swung around and let out a yell. Hand in hand, they edged sideways and then ran away. An old woman standing opposite happened to look his way. She pointed and backed away. Another person noticed her odd behaviour. A young man in a hoodie looked up, shook his head slightly and walked away as if he hadn't just seen a werewolf baring its fangs.

Familiar scents reached him. The women from the club. The dark-haired one, face in her hands, sobbing uncontrollably. The Asian one was speaking into a mobile phone, possibly directing an ambulance to their spot. Rolf growled, hoping to get her to notice and stop what she was doing. He didn't see the redhead.

Rolf paced back and forth, snarling at the onlookers, who took fright and scattered. A form writhed on the ground. Someone was going through the change; someone was shape changing into a werewolf. The process was partially complete, but not progressing normally. Rolf sniffed the air and detected something amiss. Magic. Who was it? Rolf's wolf mind recalled the scents of the girls, who hadn't retreated very far, and realised the partially transformed were was the woman. The redhead from last night. Abbie, she said her name was. The scent was all wrong though. Muddled and hazy. Could that be the dark magic?

Rolf neared the fallen figure, ignoring the shouts of her friends who tried to guard her. He nosed the loose pieces of clothing, licked a section of matted fur. Magic was thick on her. Was the sorcerer weaving a potent spell to transform a human into a wolf? A changeling curse? The horror of such a thing made him reel. To be born a werewolf had its challenges and rewards. To willingly inflict the change on a non-were was cruel beyond imagining. The risks and the pain were great at the first turning, even for those born to be were. When they had first met, Dane had been cursed to become a werewolf at the full moon. While he had transformed into a wolf, it was never a perfect transformation. Dane wasn't able to keep his conscious self while in wolf form. He'd lost himself to the beast during the change. If they hadn't broken the curse, Dane would have been a mindless beast now, lost forever to dark magic. Rolf would have been forced to put his friend down.

Was this what Abbie was destined for? Rolf's mind revolted at the thought.

Dane and Annwyn came up behind him, panting with exertion. In the blink of an eye, everyone in their near vicinity began staring vaguely at nothing. Some moved off down the street as if nothing unusual had happened. Dane was good at that. He'd mesmerised them, blanked their memories.

"Annwyn, can you see the threads of the spell?" Dane asked.

"Yes, but it goes deep. The weave is different. Complicated. I can't unravel it."

Dane turned to Rolf. "Can you change back?"

Rolf let out a howl. He was stuck. The magic of Abbie's change had speared him. He couldn't turn back, not while she was mid-transformation. He was werewolf until she completed the change or died trying.

Dane frowned as Rolf whined at him.

At a whimper from the transforming human, Rolf went up and licked her snout. The were bitch tried to bite him. Her teeth were sharp and he let out a yelp. Her legs were bare skinned and warped. Human ears sat on a half-transformed head. The jaw and teeth were well-developed as were the front paws. He couldn't read any coherent thoughts from her. Her mind was a mass of confusion and pain. He also got little sense of her inner beast or her human mind. Her consciousness was hung in mid-transformation.

The sound of a siren approaching grew louder. Rolf cringed, the blaring noise biting deep into his skull.

Dane glowered and lifted helpless, fisted hands. "Emergency services. I can confuse them. There I've sent them down the wrong street. Annwyn we need to leave."

"Right. I'll get the car," she said. "This barrier you've erected will only last for a short time." Annwyn looked over her shoulder as she strode away, "Can you manage?"

"Yes, but make it fast." Dane ruffled Rolf's ears. Rolf growled and then lifted his head to howl.

Dane knelt by Abbie, trying to move her malformed limbs. "This is a damn mess if I ever saw one. Let me see if I can help."

Dane tried to apply some magic but was soon cursing and shaking his head. "I can't stop the transformation. I can't help her by easing her pain either. She's resisting this herself." Dane rubbed his chin. "Actually, it's not her, so much, but the fact that it's not natural. She's not a born werewolf."

Rolf sang a sad whine in agreement. He'd met her last night and there had been no were twinge when they'd met, kissed.

Abbie continued to transform and, as Rolf looked on, he could sympathise with every stretch of bone, every moment of remoulding of her flesh. The first transformation was the worst. Rolf snarled at the two girlfriends, who weren't leaving. They sat huddled next to each other on the ground. No longer able to see Abbie, but not moving away. Pity for them welled inside him. They had a strong bond with each other. They could cause problems later on, when Abbie failed to surface. If she failed to surface. Looking on, he had his doubts. Whatever Abbie's life had been, it was never going to be the same.

Dane noticed the two friends and shook his head. "Those two are very loyal. They aren't easily fooled either. I'm going to have to play with their minds a bit more than I ought."

With a light chant in the air, Rolf watched as the two friends jerked upright and walked away, their movement stiff like robots.

Rolf whined and pawed at Abbie, because she'd gone quiet and, for a moment, he thought she had died. Then, a small whimper escaped from her mouth. Her chest heaved, looking like all her ribs were broken and the bones looked to be at the wrong angles. Agony radiated off her form, and Rolf could only sympathise and recall his own first transformation.

At least she was alive. First transformations could be brutal. Unnatural transformations could be deadly. This was definitely unnatural, given the lingering dark magic in the air. They'd had limited experience with unnatural transformations, though. Apart from Dane, the latest ones had been geographically isolated. And all fatal.

If she survived, would Abbie be destined for the same problems that Dane'd had? Or was that Dane's specific curse? They had to stop the sorcerer who was doing this. Sniffing at Abbie, he could tell the transformation was not going well, not following the normal course.

It was probably a good thing that Rolf couldn't revert to human form while this close to Abbie, as he could better communicate with her while wolf.

A growl served better than any explanation at this point.

A screech of tyres heralded the arrival of Annwyn, followed by a thump as she steered the car onto the sidewalk, nearly knocking Dane and Rolf over.

Rolf saw Dane shaking his head at Annwyn's driving as she hit the gutter, which was bound to mess with the suspension and steering on Dane's precious Lexus.

He watched as Dane lifted Abbie's tortured body gently, using magic to keep her still and not increase her pain. Half her body was stuck between human and wolf form, her midsection was a globular mass of bloody flesh and tangled organs. Normally, it was best not to move someone mid-transformation, but it couldn't be helped: weres did not normally transform without warning in public places either.

It was imperative that they get back to the farm, safe from prying eyes and where he could help her. A normal werewolf was detected well before the change. He had the bloodlines of those in Australia and definitely those in his territory. He even owned a register of latents, details of those who carried the genes but were unlikely to become werewolf themselves. They could interbreed with a werewolf, but usually they were ignored like the general populace.

Dane held her with his strong arms and magic, yet still she let out a low moan when she was lifted. A pitiful sound that made Rolf whimper in sympathy. Watching Dane place Abbie's form on the back seat, he noticed the care the sorcerer took. As Dane had experienced life as a werewolf, he seemed to understand how to proceed.

Abbie snapped and fought Dane as he tried to arrange her. Rolf yipped and howled, trying to reassure her. Dane wrapped threads of power around her, holding her snout and claws still to avoid injury.

"Settle down," he said as he slid the limp wolf into the back seat. "You too, Rolf."

Annwyn, who had been maintaining the spell on the onlookers while Dane was occupied, slid behind the wheel and Dane backed out, signalling to Rolf to jump into the rear seat.

Rolf leaped in, stepping carefully so as not to hurt Abbie. Dane still had her bound in power, so she couldn't snap or snarl, but the aggressive vibes rippling off her let him know he was in for a bit of a brawl when she completed her transformation.

After Dane climbed into the passenger seat, Annwyn sped away, leaving many bemused onlookers shaking their heads and wondering what was going on. "Can you see the magic now?" Dane asked as he studied the surroundings.

Annwyn bit her lip and then shook her head. "No. It's gone and I can't trace it."

"Then why isn't she reverting to human form?" Dane asked.

Annwyn glanced at him sideways and shrugged. "I don't know. When Rolf turns back maybe we can ask him. He seems to have an understanding of magically induced were."

Dane harrumphed. "I don't like this. Why here? Why turn someone into a werewolf in Canberra of all places? What's the point of that?"

Annwyn sighed as she turned onto Limestone Avenue. "I don't think this is personal like the attack on you. This is more general." She glanced to Dane. "You know, chaos causing. It threatens to expose supernaturals to the general populace. We've had reports of similar instances in other places, like Poland, Siberia and Nigeria."

Dane shook his head. "I'm not sure. I don't know any of the details of the other unnatural transformations ."

"Do you think it's directed at you, at us?"

Rolf howled and Dane glanced over his shoulder. Abbie moaned, but it came out like a whine. "I don't know. I don't like coincidences. This seems different to the curse that affected me. I turned on the full moon. It's not full moon yet for another week."

"So we have to wait and see if there are more." Annwyn sped up, pushing the speed limit.

Dane rubbed his forehead and slumped a little. "Yes. It will mean trouble if there are more in Australia."

Annwyn steered the car onto the Monaro Highway and floored the accelerator. "It's not the same curse as yours. You were a sorcerer. The spell that you were hexed with had to take into account your power and it had to subvert it. This is different. I won't know until I can examine ... it's a she isn't it?"

Dane looked back. "I think so. The voice when she screamed, sounded like a woman, so I think so."

"And Rolf?"

"I don't think he can turn back right now, or he would. There was either spillover or there's some alpha werewolf thing going on. A new cub needs an alpha to help them the first few times. That's how Rolf found me, despite me not being a real werewolf. It's some instinct in him."

"A new female werewolf? Interesting."

Dane shook his head. "We don't need any more complications in our lives. We have enough on our plate as it is, finding out who this dark mage is."

"Well, you didn't need me complicating your life, but some good came of it."

Dane laughed softly and reached out to twirl the ends of her hair in his fingers. "Definitely some good."

They continued to drive, with Dane suggesting that he make a report to Rafael at the collegium after they settled Rolf and Abbie at the farm. "I should also call Rolf's second to let him know Rolf will be unavailable for a bit."

Rolf yipped in agreement. Definitely a good idea.

"May as well put him on alert in case there are other incidents."

Dane groaned out loud. "Don't even suggest the possibility."

Annwyn flicked her gaze toward him and then back to the road. She sucked her bottom lip before responding. "Look, it's just a precaution."

Rolf growled. He agreed. It could be disastrous if more people turned, particularly if they were random and they happened in public places. It could expose them all.

"You seeing or sensing something you aren't telling me about?" Dane asked Annwyn softly, as if afraid of the answer.

Rolf tilted his head and studied Annwyn. She shook her head. "No. I told you. Whoever it was, they were gone."

Rolf sniffed. As far as he could tell, Annwyn was telling the truth. If that inner, evil sorceress, Nira, was calling the shots then it would be a different story. Fortunately, there was no sign of her.

Abbie whimpered and Rolf licked her shoulder along the line of perfect russet fur that had sprung up there. He was better off in wolf form at the moment, despite the inconvenience to the greater mission. He needed to establish a mental link with Abbie. It was the best way to provide support and encouragement.

Right now her mind was likely to be full of fear, pain and confusion. The miasma of pain and fear he detected only confirmed his supposition. It was going to take time. He also needed to work out what exactly had happened. Whatever had set off the transformation, it was different than Dane's curse. It was more organic, more intrinsic to Abbie's make-up. This thought had Rolf worried. Until he settled her down and she'd safely completed the transformation, he wasn't going to be able to investigate.

The ride to the property seemed to take forever. Rolf alternated between counting off the landmarks until they reached home and licking the top of Abbie's head and nibbling on her ears just to hear her whimper and whine so he knew she was alive. Annwyn drove like a fiend and soon they were heading up the drive with the crackle of gravel echoing around them and dust kicking up behind.

As soon as she skidded to a stop, Rolf saw Dane leap out and race over to the small flat they used for lock downs. Sometimes, werewolves had to be secured if they couldn't hold their shit together. Usually, one of the newer ones. They didn't have to use it often. Occasionally members of the pack used it as a place to mate. Rolf was sure Dane didn't mind. Even though he wasn't a werewolf anymore, the pack was still part of the family.

Next thing Rolf knew, Dane was back at the car, yanking the door open, once again wrapping Abbie up in magical bonds to hold her still so that she didn't injure herself writhing and contorting in agony. Her body was still rearranging itself in such a sickening way as if it was being forced, rather than a natural process.

Rolf's stomach clenched, remembering his first time. The red heat of agony that had cloaked his mind and flesh. Always there was some pain when he transformed. These days his body remembered where to go and bones and flesh slid easily into place. The transformation was second nature to him now. The sound was always what got to him—the crunch and crack as bones broke and reformed. The jaw particularly was the most painful, even now, after many transformations. For himself, he didn't have to worry that it would stop part way through. That could happen to the new ones, though. They usually died horribly, unless they were euthanised and put out of their misery.

Dane slid his arms underneath Abbie's partially transformed body and eased her out of the rear door. Rolf bounded out of the car, chasing his heels. It pleased him that Dane took such care. Dane and he had been through a lot together and the trust bond between them was strong. He didn't think he could have let anyone else touch her.

Annwyn stood leaning on the driver's side door, watching with those green eyes of hers, a fleeting frown on her forehead. Casting his head back, Rolf didn't like her expression. His wolf sense told him she was worried. Her mind was raking through the possibilities and, from the look on her face, none of them appealed.

Rolf was concerned too. There had been no hint of werewolf about Abbie last night. He entertained the thought that his senses were wrong, that he'd made a mistake. That kiss had been something after all. There had been a kind of elemental connection. He wouldn't know if she was a latent until he looked at the register, but he couldn't do that until she was stable and he was able to revert to human form. A late transition wasn't unheard of, but late twenties or early thirties? He had a dossier on the resident werewolves and their direct family lines. He doubted she was in that.

Dane placed Abbie on the mattress, arranging her limbs carefully to minimise hurt. Her midsection was still realigning and one foot was still partially human. If she didn't complete the transformation soon, she would die. Rolf whined. She'd been stuck in this final stage for too long and was too quiet.

Dane scratched him between the ears. "I don't like this new play by the renegade sorcerer. I'll hail Rafael and tell him about the nature of this attack." He backed up to the door. "I'll check up on you regularly. Use the intercom if you're able to transform back and I'll let you out. Fresh meat through the door flap. Okay?"

Rolf growl-barked his affirmation. Breakfast seemed a long time ago.

❦

Rolf sprawled next to Abbie and licked her muzzle. She was small compared to him, even though her transformation wasn't complete, he could see her general wolf shape. The red of her hair was represented in the russet of her coat. A fine-looking wolf, she'd be. If she survived, that is.

Abbie was still quiet. Rolf dozed to pass the time, pressing his body along her spine so he'd wake if she stirred. With a jerk, he awoke to the scent of Dane approaching. His friend spoke from the other side of the door. "Hey, Rolf. I hope you're doing okay. I've spoken to some of your pack—Mick, Trevor and Rhonda—and put them on alert. We think there's a risk of further transformations, so they've gotten the word out to other packs and are setting up patrols in the major shopping centres and at any major events. Anywhere they'll be crowds. They're going to check in regularly. I'll pass the word on to you when I hear something. I've sent a message to Rafael, but I've not heard from him yet."

Rolf howled in answer. Dane tapped on the door in acknowledgement and strode back to the house, taking a call on his mobile phone. Rolf listened until he heard Dane close the door as he went into the house.

To examine the still form beside him, Rolf climbed to his paws. The utter stillness of her body had him worried. Had she died? He licked her head and then her still misshapen foot. Her chest rose fractionally. Rolf yipped and then panted in her ear.

She breathed again, then stopped. He watched as she took another breath but otherwise didn't move. Not a good sign. Rolf grew desperate. His gaze travelled along her body searching for a twitch. He nudged her with his snout, careful to only touch those parts of her that appeared fully wolf. Still, she didn't move. He was losing her.

A moan filled his mind. She had lost the battle, unless he could make mental contact with her. He stilled as the thought crystallised. Her consciousness was most likely overwhelmed by the transformation, but he had to try to reach her. He'd only met her that one time. She'd been vibrant and bright. He had to try. She needed moral support and his mental strength to pull through.

He positioned himself on all fours, his head close to hers. Would she even understand him? With a shake of his head, and the snap of his ears, he put doubt aside. She would hear him. She had to.

Abbie?

No response.

Abbie, can you hear me?

Nothing.

Abbie? Listen to me. Please.

Still nothing. It was like dropping a stone into a bottomless well.

He rested his head against hers, trying to see into her, trying to make that connection. There had to be some essence of her in the maelstrom of pain he could sense. He thought about her suffering and recalled his first change. The difference was that he'd known who he was, knew what he would become. It was the pain that had held him back. He drew back from Abbie as if burnt by flame. Abbie had no idea what was happening to her. He had to fix that gap in her knowledge. If it wasn't too late already.

Abbie. You need to embrace the change. Embrace it. Accept the pain.

There was no response from her, no sense of her as a person, just a confusion of pain and fear.

He sent encouraging and soothing thoughts her way, knowing that her sense of self was severely challenged. He knew nothing about her, other than that fleeting contact the night before.

Accept your fate, Abbie. Embrace the change. Don't let this kill you.

A whine escaped, so faint he thought he'd imagined it. A sliver of excitement lit his heart.

Yes, Abbie. Soon the pain will be over. Push through. That's it. Keep going.

He didn't add *push through or you'll l die. You can't exist like this, half one thing and half another*. Although the thoughts crowded his mind.

The whimper came again. It was even fainter than the one he'd almost imagined.

As he lay there nuzzling her, licking her ears and muzzle, Rolf tried to understand why this woman, why this random stranger had attracted him within moments? The only thing he could come back to was that fleeting contact in the club. The kiss that had stirred and then seized hold of him. A strong attraction between were and human was uncommon. Could that dark sorcerer have seen the attraction and chosen her as his victim? Or was Rolf somehow contagious, infecting innocent bystanders with his DNA unknowingly? He mentally shook himself. That was too difficult to even entertain. He was not contagious. This was an attack and he had to remember that.

Yet fear that he was responsible kept coming back to plague him. He shouldn't have gone to the club. He shouldn't have kissed her. Could he be the one cursed as Dane once was, but in his case cursed with changing ordinary people to werewolves? Rolf prowled around Abbie's inert form, shoulders tense, mind seething in anger.

Abbie was not on his list of possible werewolves. She was past the age of normal transformation. What if that was it? What if this was his fault? He circled Abbie. Suddenly, her chest gave a mighty heave. She was losing the battle. Her internal organs were not reshaping, reabsorbing to the shape a werewolf's form dictated.

He stalked away and then came back, refusing to give up. He noted her foot was marginally further along, but still had human toes and heel. He sniffed and licked her foot, sending more encouraging thoughts to her. Maybe on some level he was getting through, even though her sense of self was buried in the change.

Night sounds intruded as darkness fell. Alert, Rolf paced around the room. Abbie became more animated, moving her limbs and bending her spine as she threw her head from side to side, but he didn't know if that meant she was living or dying. Her laboured breathing dominated everything in Rolf's perception. Every hitch or hesitation on the inhale and Rolf paused, waiting to see if that was the last one.

The sound of the lock turning alerted him to Dane. He leapt up and pattered over to the door, embarrassed he hadn't caught the sorcerer's scent earlier.

"It's all over the news." Dane said as he placed a red-brown paper bag on the counter beside the door. "I figured I may as well bring the meat in with the news."

Rolf tilted his head. *What specifically?* Sometimes Dane could understand his thoughts.

Dane continued. "Her name is Abbie McGregor, local newsreader, reported as missing. Last seen in Civic, before being kidnapped. Not much detail about us. Thank the deities.

Rolf growled. He knew her name, but ... *A newsreader? A local celebrity? Fuck. Just what we need.*

Dane rubbed at his chin and studied Abbie's form. "I know. Talk about being indiscreet. Let's not worry about it now. Focus on getting her through this." Dane turned to the paper bag and opened it. "I figured rib eye should keep you happy."

The smell of fresh meat filled Rolf's nostrils. His hunger was wild and immediate.

Dane tossed a slice of steak, which Rolf caught in his jaws and gobbled down hungrily, and then another. Rolf was still licking his lips when Dane shut the door.

Feeling energized by the meat, Rolf returned to studying Abbie. The mass of organs in her midsection looked slightly smaller. He hoped it wasn't wishful thinking. He just had to keep vigil until the process ended.

Although Rolf could think and reason in wolf form, he was smarter in human form. Even so, he knew there were going to be issues, given that Abbie was well-known locally. People had seen her face. He didn't know much about television life, but he guessed that whatever career she had, it was in jeopardy. That was something to worry about once they had moved through this crisis. If she lived.

He studied her form. He'd shied away from examining her midsection, not quite able to lick that mass of malformed flesh. It was not only queasiness, but also concern in case he hurt any vulnerable organs. Abbie needed encouragement to accept those misshapen organs inside herself. He nuzzled her gently, telling her mentally how beautiful she was, describing her russet fur and sleek figure. He licked tentatively at her face and heard her breath catch.

Looking up, he regarded her midsection. It was working. The final mass of organs and tissue were moving, reabsorbing. There was movement beneath the near-transparent flesh. Another convulsive movement and Abbie cried out, a whine that near tore his ears to shreds.

Just a bit more, he thought at her. Using his muzzle, he nudged her encouragingly. *Come on.* She struggled away from him, the pain making her flinch, and her whine becoming shrill.

Well into the night, when the sounds of foxes, frogs and insects filled the darkness outside, he thought she'd make it. He circled her body, stopping occasionally to run his tongue along the top of her head or nip at her encouragingly.

Once more he assessed her transformation. She was very still, her chest barely rising and falling. One pink toe still stood out from her rear paw and there was an unsightly bulge still in her middle. There was a chance she'd stall at this stage. Rolf had hope, though. He stretched out beside her, his fur meshing with hers. He was exhausted now and all he could do was be there for her, hold her close until fate decided whether she lived or died. He whined and placed his head on her shoulder, dropping into an exhausted sleep.

❧

Early bird call woke him the next morning. Light seeped through the shuttered window, locked until Abbie's transition was complete. He sprung to his feet, pacing around Abbie, his claws clicking against the linoleum floor. Her physical transformation was complete. Yet she lay so still and quiet; if not for her warmth, he would have thought her dead. Perhaps, she finally slept.

A whiff of Dane approaching had him pawing at the door excitedly. He was pleased to have Dane see the progress and also nature called. The door opened and he slipped out. Dane stuck his head in, saw the sleeping wolf and closed the door. "She made it," he said. Rolf smelt the fresh meat. Dane had brought breakfast.

A satisfied feeling accompanied the emptying of his bladder. After finishing taking a piss, he raced back. He needed to be with her when she woke. Then the difficult work would begin. *So far*, he thought at Dane. *Now we need to see if she can exist as a wolf. Not much sign of a personality surviving yet.*

Dane rubbed his forehead. "Let's hope there aren't more transformations. Your team are monitoring police broadcasts. Can you shift yet?"

Rolf growled. He hadn't tried until then. It didn't work. He was still linked with Abbie's transformation. If she died, he would be free. But he thought she was going to make it and until she was through to the other side, he would remain in wolf form. His job as alpha was not done.

Slipping back through the door, he prowled up to her and nudged her shoulder with his snout. Nothing. He nipped her on the shoulder to get her attention. Still no reaction. He tried to reach her mind and bring it forward so that it didn't get swallowed by the beast. There was nothing there. No beast. No Abbie. What the hell was he to do now?

He'd have to wait it out. Something had to happen soon. Good or bad, he'd have to deal with it.

Dane tossed him some more fresh meat, before heading back to the house. It was obvious Dane was worried too. This attack of dark magic could spell big trouble for all of them—exposing supernaturals to the world at large and forcing humans and non-humans to deal with each other.

It wouldn't be pretty.

CHAPTER 3

Abbie was lost in a sea of pain. Confusion swelled around her. She had no idea what had happened, or what was happening. Her sense of self was still there, even though it had been battered and torn by whatever accident had befallen her. Her mind latched on to that idea. She'd been hit by a car. That was it. She was in a coma and trying to wake up. She was in a dark space and every time she tried to reach out, angry beasts snapped at her, teeth snarled, howls filled her ears and she cowered.

Pulling her consciousness into a tight ball, she stayed out of the reach of the beasts, even though their hot, fetid breath washed over her skin. As her control slipped, tongues lapped at her feet, her stomach, her face. There was no escape from the incessant reminder that a beast was looking for her, seeking her out, preparing to gnaw at her, rip and shred her. The howls were deafening, the teeth long and sharp, the savagery overwhelming. Yet, if she stayed very still and quiet it would go away. It would fade.

While she stayed cocooned, nothing seemed to change around her. Every time she put a mental foot out of her special quiet space, the howls would erupt, the onslaught would begin. It was like there was a raging beast in the room with her. She couldn't move without its say-so and she was too afraid to take it on, too afraid to fight her way past it.

For a while she slept, curled up into a ball, safe, comfortable, warm. A presence surrounded her. It was a wall of calm—reassuring, quiet and aware. Abbie wanted to touch it, but the beast was there, laying low, growling, salivating, waiting ...

It wanted her and she couldn't give in. It seemed that the coma was going to go on forever. But she really didn't know how long it had been. Did one experience time when you were in a coma? It could have been hours or days. Then something she recognised imposed itself. Hunger burned in her gut. Her whole body craved fuel. The essence of her was stretched thin. The need for food was clawing its way up her throat. If she didn't eat, she'd die and if she didn't move, she'd die. She had to choose to live or die. She had to face the beast to live. But she was so afraid.

The hunger punched and pounded inside. She had to face it—the beast. What about that presence? That warm, caring presence. The one with a hint of frustration and more overlays of worry. This safe zone she'd created was going to kill her. She had to move or die. It was time to fight the beast.

In her mind, she stood and shook her shoulders and scanned the darkness surrounding her. The growls came, as did the sweep of claws and fangs. Using an arm block, she stopped the slash and it bypassed her. She crouched ready for the next attack. Teeth ravaged her calf. She screamed and kicked out. Her nails shredded flesh and her teeth gnashed and tore. The mind beast retreated a little. She stepped clear of her hiding place and it retreated another step. Defiant howls filled her ears and wet flesh caked her claws. Her claws? Puzzled, she studied her hands and they were paws. A scream ripped through her, driving her up and out of the darkness.

❧

Rolf had almost given up. There'd been no movement, no sign of life, no hint of personality. It had been nearly forty-eight hours since she'd started the transformation. Rolf was sprawled next to her when a paw jerked, her snout lifted.

Alert, Rolf scrambled up to study Abbie closely and was just about to give her a lick to nudge her when she jumped up, standing shakily on all fours. Rolf backed up, wary and alert. With sickening speed, Abbie lunged, teeth sinking into his neck, immobilising him. Her claws came up to rake down his vulnerable belly. Rolf acted, dropping his weight to cause her to unbalance. They rolled along the ground, growling as they bit and clawed each other, each trying to get the upper hand.

Rolf tried to hold back, to be gentle, but Abbie's ferocity denied him that. He was bigger, brawnier and had greater skill. Abbie fought like a rabid animal, like she was possessed, like she was fighting for her life. She was not really aware, not quite in the moment.

Abbie! he thought frantically at her. *It's okay. You'll be fine.*

Lips curled over fangs, she snarled and gave no sign she'd heard him. Rolf backed away, leaving her slavering and growling in the centre of the room.

He thought words at her. The words an alpha would use to calm a newly turned werewolf. *I'm here to help you, Abbie. I won't harm you.*

Rolf panted as he waited. Blood dripped from two separate bite marks and deep scratches from her claws itched along his flanks. She wasn't answering him, but he sensed that she'd heard him. He needed more evidence that she'd survived intact. A rabid, out-of-control animal had to be put down. If she didn't respond to him soon, he'd have no choice. It was up to her to prove herself.

Abbie lunged for him and he sidestepped. *Abbie? Speak to me.*

A wall of fear swamped him. It was Abbie. It was her fear.

Fight it, Abbie. You can conquer the beast.

She leapt high, landing on him before he could get away. Her jaw was locked hard on his throat. He thought at her, trying to make her understand. Wanting to protect her meant not hurting her. The pressure of her jaw increased. This was getting serious. A sharp shake of her head sideways and his throat would be ripped out.

It was now a fight to the death. Rolf had to fight her and win, yet he hesitated. Too late, he started to get dizzy. She'd cut off the blood supply to his brain. Rolf's forelegs buckled. Consciousness slipped away.

A loud bang split the air, stunning him.

Abbie fell off him, a dead weight. Rolf's tongue lolled as he fought for air, his throat burned. Red lights flamed in the darkness of his vision. What had happened? Through his blood-filled gaze, he saw Dane standing there, rifle in his hand.

Shock and sorrow rocked Rolf and he howled in frustration.

"Sorry, Rolf. I had to put an end to it."

Rolf snarled and then clambered to all fours. Dane had killed Abbie was his first thought as he glimpsed her prostrate form nearby. *No. No. Nooooo!* He howled and readied to spring at his friend.

Another sharp report filled his ears and the world went black.

CHAPTER 4

Rolf had a massive headache when he came to. Memories surged at him from all sides. A thumping terror drew him to unsteady feet as his attention zoned in on the spot where Abbie lay still and quiet.

Dane was gone, but there was fresh meat left out for him. Rolf smelled the meat, the blood-ripe odour of it. He shook his head. How could he think of eating when she lay dead, just a couple of metres from him? He sniffed the air and noticed something. There was no human or wolf blood in the room, other than his own wounds.

Padding over to Abbie to investigate, he sniffed and nuzzled her body, prodding and investigating. There were no bleeding wounds. Her chest rose and fell. Then Rolf noticed the dart. Dane had tranqed her, not killed her. Dane had drugged him too.

A wave of relief washed over him. At least she was alive, and while alive she had a chance to beat this. She could wake up rabid or she could wake up with a glimmer of her human self. He just had to wait and see. He licked her muzzle and rubbed his face against hers. Bringing her gently to wakefulness might help. Dane was unlikely to use tranquiliser darts next time. Next time the remedy would be permanent.

Upon examining her, he was satisfied that her transformation was complete. Now she was no longer in the throes of transformation, he should be able to revert to human form once more. Only he was reluctant to while she was mentally absent.

A change in the melange of odours nearby alerted him that Dane was on his way. Rolf could scent Dane's air of anticipation, the spice of excitement. Something had happened.

The door opened. Dane sent his gaze toward Abbie's unconscious form. "Feeling better?" he asked.

Rolf let out a yelp of agreement.

"There's been another one. A butcher cutting meat in the north of Canberra. He didn't make it. He died mid-transition. Mick found him too late."

Rolf growled. Frustration made him shudder and shake with rage.

"The press are reporting it as an accident. I think Mick got inventive with the partially transformed body. I'm not sure it will stand up to scrutiny. Here's to hoping they don't link the two incidents." He nodded at Abbie's inert form. "We're running out of time with that one."

Rolf trotted over to stand protectively over the she-wolf and growled.

Dane nodded and studied her. Rolf guessed Dane was checking her over to assure himself the physical transformation had completed. A further glance at Rolf and Dane rubbed his chin and then nodded. "I see where you're coming from. I'll give her one more day. Let's hope she finds her way back. If she attacks you like that again, we won't have a choice."

Rolf looked from Dane to Abbie and whined.

Dane sighed loudly and slipped out the door, locking it before he went to the house. Rolf tried not to let the fresh meat that was waiting for them distract him.

❦

Abbie's eyes snapped open. The world looked different, skewed. Scents assaulted her, weaving a pattern in the air that told stories of places, of emotions, of people. Then there was that presence again. It was close. Strange emotions boiled inside her and she fought against them. There were two presences. One exterior to her and one interior.

Abbie? the outside presence said, whispering the words in her mind in a way that made her doubt her sanity. People didn't speak directly into minds. *Can you understand me?*

Yes? Abbie whispered in response. The words were in her brain. A sort of bark came out of her lips. Her tongue was too big and loose to form words anyhow. What? Abbie tried to rub her face, to work out what was wrong, but a clawed paw slapped her snout. Her snout? Mother! I have a snout.

A whine issued from her mouth, communicating panic.

It's okay, the voice whispered in her brain. *You're all right. Just stay calm.*

Calm? Are you shitting me? Abbie sent thoughts like barbs.

No, I'm telling you the truth. It's important to stay calm right now. Then you can shift back.

Shift back?

You've undergone a change. You've survived it. You will be able to revert back.

A scream was fighting its way out of her throat. Her head shifted and there was a wolf in the room with her, or a very large dog from a breed that looked like wolf. The eyes were citrine-coloured and intelligent. Abbie turned her head, turned around, searching for the owner of the voice. The wolf was the only other living thing in the room ... she glanced around ... shed with her. She looked down at her paws, looked behind and saw a fluffy thing that waved about and disconcerted her. After a few turns she realised it was her tail. The other wolf gave of signs of amusement.

Do you think this is funny? She thought angrily at him.

I think it's a joyous moment. You're whole.

I'm a godforsaken wolf.

A beautiful, russet-furred werewolf.

Abbie's legs wobbled and her hindquarters dropped to the ground. *Werewolf?*

Yes. That means you can resume your human shape. Do you want to shift back?

Shift back?

Is there some strong force binding you into that shape?

Look, whoever you are, and I'm not even agreeing I'm having this conversation, I have no idea what you're talking about.

His tongue lolled. *Do you feel the presence of the moon?*

Moon? I don't know. How can I tell?

Can you feel a power in the sky, like someone stroking your back?

Abbie shifted her shoulders, looked up to the sky, which she couldn't see because she was in a shed. The only window was above the sink at it was shuttered. There was something there. Like a tickle in her mind. She tried to listen to it and then she detected the slight strokes of fingers, maybe electricity or something, along her spine.

I think I can sense the moon.

Is it binding you to this shape?

I don't think so.

Good. Then watch me, then try it. Think yourself back to Abbie.

The wolf then grew, shedding his coat like lifting a blanket. His jaw shortened with a crack as it took on the shape of a man. Legs thickened and hands grew from paws. The man who stood there flexed his shoulders and a bone made a cracking sound. He rubbed his chin, which had beard stubbled on it. He had a magnificent body, naked and full of allure. Her eyes tracked up. The face was familiar. It was that guy.

"Come on, Abbie. Remember me. I'm Rolf. You try it now. Remember who you are."

Confusion made Abbie stumble. It was that guy from the club, the one she'd kissed. What was he doing here? Had he drugged her? Was this some kind of dream?

"Abbie? Don't get lost on me now. Remember. Remember who you are."

Abbie whined and lolled her tongue, anxiety making it hard to breathe. Who was she? This couldn't be real. She should just give up and maybe she would come round. She lowered her tail. She couldn't do what he'd just done, couldn't transform to a human shape. It was ridiculous. There was too much going on. Abbie bent her back legs and lowered her stomach to the floor. She rested her head on her front paws and whined some more.

"Damn," the wolf guy said. He made to lean over and touch her head. She was inordinately angry and snapped at him, a whisker away from crunching on his fingers. "Now that isn't nice. I'm trying to help here."

Pissed, a growl escaped her mouth.

۞

Sometime later a scent woke her. Lifting her head, a few things surprised her. She'd been sleeping. Rolf stood at the door of the shed, as if waiting. The scent grew stronger.

Rolf turned around. "Now don't get excited. It's Dane and he's bringing food. Dane is a friend, understand? No attacking him."

Abbie growled, not liking Rolf dictating things to her. Who did he think he was, her boss? As soon as she thought it, she realised that she did want to obey him. She had to fight that compulsion. Standing, she shook out her coat and lifted her lips over her fangs. It was a general warning, not only to Rolf but to this Dane as well.

The door unlocked and Rolf stepped back, blocking her path to the door. How did he know she was ready to escape? A large man came in, a covered platter in his hands.

"Success!" he said, putting the platter down and then vigorously slapping Rolf on the shoulder. "She made it. The first of the changeling cursed to make a full transition."

"Yes. She is whole. She cannot as yet resume her human shape."

"Oh?" Dane said, staring down at her. Abbie snarled.

"There's more to come before we're through this."

Dane looked up. "You mean the urges?"

Rolf rubbed his chin and then inclined his head once. "Her first full moon approaches. It will be a powerful urge." Abbie listened. She could understand their conversation but not the urges Rolf spoke of. She had the urge to rip his arm off, maybe a leg.

"Even with her transition not being natural?" Dane asked,

rubbing the back of his neck as he surveyed the shed, then her. She met his gaze, trying to see into him, and inhaled his scent. Her eyes shifted to the meat, along with the blood aroma that drew her attention more and more. Her gut churned with hunger. A growl escaped.

Rolf half turned and looked at her. "Now she has transformed, she appears a normal were."

Dane dropped his hand and jerked his head up in surprise. "Really? We need to check if she has were ancestry. Even a latency might explain her survival. Same goes for the ones that didn't make it. Do you want the register?"

"Yes. I need to check it thoroughly. I thought I knew most of the lines here in Australia." He shook his head. "Now I'm not so sure."

"I'll bring the names of the two other victims."

"Two?"

Abbie's attention focused on Rolf, at the surprise in his voice. She didn't understand the talk of registers and ancestry, but she detected the alarm in his voice.

"Yes, there was another fatality. It was reported in Melbourne. It was in Southbank, and the man threw himself into the Yarra River before he could be helped."

"Verified?"

"Yes. Mac has seen the body, half-transformed. He managed to pass it off as some deformed sea creature. Good thing he's in the force. He was able to pass on the man's name."

"Shit!" Rolf said, running a hand through his hair and shaking his head. Three victims, including Abbie. It was an escalation, a pointed threat to them all.

"You could say that. I've brought more meat. It's raw. You want me to cook yours?"

"No. I'm going to change to wolf again. You better go. Abbie needs to eat to keep up her strength. Then I'll see if I can get her to try to transform."

Dane turned to leave. "Anything I can do?"

"Yes, can you play some of Abbie's broadcasts to the set here? I think it might help her remember who she is."

"I'll see what I can get. Give me an hour or two. I need to make a few calls." Dane left, locking the door behind him.

Abbie drew her head back. Broadcasts? What did he mean?

Rolf put the platter on the floor and lifted the cover. Abbie focused on the food and pounced. Hunger took over her mind, just like a snap of fingers. A whole steak was in her mouth, warm and bloody. She chewed and chewed and gulped. When she snatched the next steak, another muzzle was in the way. She growled, low and long. Rolf the wolf was back. He let her take the steak and while she was busy chewing he took the last slice for himself. Waves of happiness seemed to emanate from him. Abbie wasn't sure what was making him so happy. Being in wolf form or the meat? The meat was very good. Straight away, Abbie grew more alert and felt stronger. She was no longer distracted by hunger, or the desire to rip Rolf's throat out. She didn't care that he was bigger. Him being bigger just made her angry, made her want to hurt him more. It was a blind kind of rage. She tried to engage that thought, but other emotions, fears and thoughts invaded her mind.

Rolf's mind voice penetrated her consciousness again. *Abbie?*

Abbie didn't want to respond, as she was still enjoying the food, the last morsels of steak clinging to her teeth.

Abbie? There was a sense of annoyance there, disappointment maybe. His scent changed and teased her nostrils.

Go away. I'm busy eating.

Rolf didn't respond, but she got the impression he was smiling. *I'm glad you like the food. Now you're done, I want you to try and turn back to your human form.*

I can't.

You don't know until you try.

Abbie growled, increasing the volume so he'd understand she didn't want to try or discuss it.

You're strong minded. I liked that. But you're resisting me. You need to trust me now, listen to me. Turn that strong will of yours on yourself.

Maybe later, when I'm not so tired. She made to turn away. She wanted to curl up and sleep now that her belly was full of delicious, red meat.

No. Abbie. You will do it now.

An invisible force squeezed against her. At first she was puzzled, then recognised the wave of compulsion washing over her. It stank of Rolf. She resisted, then with a heave of her will, shrugged it off. It was hard to fight against. She had to put some distance between them, so she turned around and padded over to the door. *Let me out.*

Don't turn away from me, Abbie. Come here.

Abbie pretended to ignore him and continued to fixate on the door. If she focused hard enough, she could continue to resist him. A blow caught her on the side of the head, making her stumble. He'd knocked his head against her. In retaliation, she lunged at him, teeth seeking flesh, angry growls filling her ears. She and Rolf grappled and growled and then broke apart.

Abbie panted, fear and anger shrouding her mind in red. She hurt, too, grazes from his teeth and scrapes from his claws, throbbing and stinging as they made themselves known.

Pay attention. This is important. Transform now.

I said I'm not ready. Fury was building up inside her brain. She couldn't understand the feelings, the base needs coursing through her.

Abbie. Trust me. You must transform now, or you will lose the ability. Understand? You'll forget who you really are and stay a beast.

Abbie growled, her teeth wanted to bite down hard on his throat. *You are so annoying. Leave me alone.*

Abbie try it. Picture yourself. Picture who you really are.

As if summoned by his words, the image of herself formed in her mind. She tried to keep the picture there. Smells and noises distracted her. There were other people here, other wolves, too. She wanted to explore, to find them, sniff them. She wanted to know all the smells and all the grass and ground and the water.

Abbie! The mind shout was accompanied by a sharp wuff.

Her mind came back to the shed, to Rolf, whose fur was now bristling with anger.

Pay attention. You had her in your mind. Bring her back.

Abbie tried again, just to shut him up. *Who would have thought that hunk would be such a nag.*

I heard that. Concentrate. Picture Abbie.

The vision of herself formed in her mind again. It was appealing.

The red hair, the pale skin, the soft, full mouth, dewy skin, luscious curved breasts and round hips and slappable butt. Abbie shook her head. That wasn't her memory. *Is that what you saw?*

Sorry. I was trying to help. His mind voice grinned.

Abbie paced away, trying to clear her mind. What was he thinking? *You're a wolf?* She thought at him.

Yes and a man. A werewolf.

Abbie tried again to transform, this time without help from Rolf. She could almost picture herself, could almost picture being in that shape. The effort, though, had her panting and left her feeling weak. She couldn't do it. She lay on her belly with her head on her paws, defeated.

A short time later, a monitor came on. Rolf bounded up to his feet and came over to nudge her shoulder. She snapped at him, not really wanting to hurt him, but to let him know she didn't like being bossed about.

A voice sounded from the monitor and a girl appeared on the screen. Abbie strode over to get a better look. The girl was familiar. Abbie tilted her head. It was her. A whine issued from her lips.

Yes, that's you. Go back to you. Reclaim yourself.

The image in her mind was easier to form with the vision coming through her eyes. The voice filled up her ears, penetrated her mind. This time when the image formed, her body moved. A scream issued out of her mouth. Muscle ripped from bones as they broke and reformed. Her head split from the pain and her howl was swallowed by a scream.

The pain went on and on. Abbie's mind focused on the screen, on the vision of her talking and the words. A wall of black slammed into her.

Next thing she knew, she was on the floor. She pushed herself up and lifted her head, wiping at the drool dangling from her mouth. Naked, she panted with barely the strength to push into a sitting position. She'd done it. She was human again. Exhaustion made her body heavy, her eyes droop. She was on all fours, facing the screen and the image of herself.

Rolf stood behind her. She turned her head, knowing without

seeing that he was equally naked and human. In her eyes, she beheld him, well-formed muscle, proud cock, not erect but holding the potential. A strange power wafted off him. She could taste it, feel it, even sense it with her mind. *What was it?*

"Well done, Abbie," he said. There was no smile, but a bright light shone in his eyes. He was pleased. He nudged her foot. "Get up now."

Emotions roiled inside her, as anger swatted away her tiredness. She wanted to smash his face in with her bare hands. She wanted to fuck him, too, rut on him until he cried for mercy. A strange mix of anger and desire, rage and fear drowned her. What was happening to her?

She stood, the world spinning around her. She met his gaze and fire burned through her, like liquid lava through her veins, her muscles, her tendons. Skin tender, ready to rip apart. Smells stampeding, invading her nostrils, her sense of taste, her mind. Bright light slashed into her eyes like sharp blades. Abbie fought these competing sensations, whimpers leaking from her lips.

"Abbie?" Rolf said.

Abbie screamed.

CHAPTER 5

Rolf caught her before she hit the concrete floor and stared down at her, bewildered. She was whole. She was through. Why then had she succumbed to this faint, this seeming overload of the mind.

"Abbie?" he inquired and brushed her hair out of her face. Then he shook her. Nothing.

Rolf lifted her and placed her on the bed in the corner, gently placing her feet, her hands, and arranging her hair. She breathed deeply, as if in sleep.

Rolf could sense the wolf in her. Moving a hand along her torso, he could feel the pull of her wolf to his. She was strong, powerful in her own right. He frowned as he studied her. She should not be. Not new like this, not a cursed one and a woman to boot.

He lifted his head. Dane was approaching. He quickly covered Abbie's nakedness and went to the door. Dane came in carrying the register.

"I brought this. How is she?" Dane asked, his eyes centring on the bed.

"She's whole, but ..." Rolf also let his gaze linger on the still form on the bed. "Something's not quite right."

"Is she in danger?" Dane asked.

"I don't think so. Not right at this moment." He gaze dropped to the register.

Dane caught his eye. "Is she a danger?"

"No, that's not what I mean." He nodded at what Dane held. "Let's check the register."

Loose pieces of paper dislodged as they opened it. "That's a copy of her birth certificate and those of her parents. I had them hunted up."

Rolf chewed his bottom lip as he studied them. Abigail Leslie McGregor the birth certificate stated. He ran his finger down the lines of names in his register and shook his head. He checked for her father and mother, and then the grandparents as listed. "There's nothing direct."

"Latent?" Dane asked.

Rolf flicked the pages over and searched the names and birthplaces of some latents. "There was a McGregor way back. The hereditary lines don't match, though. I'll search the other names: Vincent, Ross and McGrath."

"That sort of explains the red hair. She must be 100 per cent proof Scottish."

"You'd be surprised." Rolf had out his phone and accessed the internet. "A French connection here, and Spanish. Still no direct line to a latent or a ..."

"What?" Dane asked.

Rolf flicked to the back pages. "Adoptions." Werewolves needed to keep track of those so the records were fairly accurate. Rolf caught a name, then read the corresponding entry. "Maria Palmer Guest had a male child, Duncan, father unknown. Adopted by Felton Smythe. See here—Duncan turned were during puberty."

Dane squinted over his shoulder. "It says Duncan was killed. He would've been too young to have fathered a child."

"But look here see the address. Same village, same street. The Ross Smiths were neighbours to the Smythes. Amelia Mary Ross Smith died age fifteen. Then here, a birth entry. Isabelle Ross Smith the same year, same month. It could be that Duncan did manage to reproduce before being killed."

Dane looked up. "They dropped the Smith?"

"Yes, and that could be where the latency occurred. Isabelle Ross, Abbie's maternal grandmother."

"Which could be why Abbie survived the transformation."

Rolf rubbed his goatee. "Yes. It wasn't a natural transformation, though. A lot of magic was used to force the changeling curse." Rolf thought of the havoc the black sorcerer would cause, if not stopped. He considered what he'd just witnessed and bit his lower lip. "Mmm ... It could be why she survived when others didn't. She had enough of the wolf in her to make it. Genetics are like that. Some descendants have more genetic material and some have less, and some genetic material doesn't survive down the line."

A moan interrupted their conversation. Abbie writhed on the bed. Waves of rage and sexual desire rolled off her. Her heat was upon her. Rolf lifted an eyebrow as his body responded to her need. An erection so sudden and hard he had to force himself not to move.

Dane smirked. "Duty calls, I see. I'll leave you to it."

Dane gave Rolf a wink as he left, smirking again as he shut the door behind him.

As alpha it was Rolf's duty to see to her needs, to help her through this and ensure her safety, as well as that of the pack. Running wild also helped with the urges, but it wasn't full moon yet and, as such, they could not shift and run to the energy of the moon. They could not let all that were energy out through exertion and then sex. No, not yet. It wouldn't be long, but still a few days yet. Right now, Abbie had a newly whelped were's desire for sex or blood. He hoped she wanted sex rather than battle.

Abbie's sexual need screamed at Rolf. Already his rock-hard cock throbbed, as he responded to the desire she was communicating to him. Like other newly turned werewolves, the sexual need was intense and, if not dealt with, could harm her recovery and adjustment to life as a werewolf and with the pack.

A growl came out of her luscious mouth as her amber eyes focused on him.

"Abbie?"

She came off the bed in a surge of power and lust, rage dripping off her like water as if she had just come from a shower. Distracted by her divine, naked beauty, he didn't duck when she punched him hard in the jaw. He reeled, not expecting the strength behind it. He ducked away from her next punch and put up his hands, eyes fixed on her. "Abbie?"

"You bastard," she growled at him. "What have you done to me?"

Rolf blanched. She blamed him?

Wavering a little, her eyes held fear and uncertainty. Her gaze flicked to the door, probably thinking of escape. Dane had locked them in.

Rolf let his hormones react to her, knowing that hers were rampant in her system. Her naked body was gorgeous—neat, tight breasts, narrow waist and flared hips. Pale skin like rich cream that he wanted to lick every inch of so badly. Her thatch was light brown and sparse and her legs were lithe and athletic looking. Right then, she was panting hard, her face flushed, her lips plump. A pink tongue licked out as she tried not to make it obvious that she was thinking about heading to the door.

Rolf tried to quell his powerful reaction to her. He wanted to fuck her so bad right now, but he had to be a gentleman and a protector. "I didn't do anything. I'm here to help you."

Abbie stared at him; her apparent confusion didn't dissipate but the fear did a little. "Can't trust anything." Her knee bent like she was going to fall down but he could see her fighting the dizziness. "I feel strange," she said, brushing her hair off her face. "So much anger ... so much ..." she said, breathing hard. Her breasts rose and fell, and Rolf supressed a moan of his own as his arousal notched higher and gave him a physical ache low in his belly. Just looking at those creamy globes of perfection with their hard and dark nipples made his mouth water. Her thigh muscles rippled as she adjusted her stance. Abbie kept herself fit, obviously. A runner, maybe.

Her eyes travelled from his eyes, to his lips, down his body to rest on his groin.

Another growl emitted from her mouth, along with a psychic blast of lust that rocked him back on his heels.

"I want to fuck you," she said in a hoarse voice, eyes lifting once again to his face, tongue moistening her lips. "I want to fuck you like there's no fucking tomorrow." Then she doubled over and wailed.

"What the hell! What am I saying?" she struggled upright again and balled her fists. "I want to smash your face in for doing this to me!" Then she writhed as the opposing desires clashed in her mind. She thumped the side of her head. "God, I'm confused. What is going on?"

Rolf moved a step closer, hand out, voice soft. "It's normal at this stage to feel both of those things."

Her head shot up. "Normal? Nothing is fucking normal." She swung around with arm outstretched. "I'm locked in a shed with a total stranger, totally naked. I'm naked. You're naked. Yet, I want to take your cock in my mouth and suck on it until you scream." She staggered then. "I don't usually say these things ... or think them." Tears fell then and she wiped at them and regarded him with pleading eyes. "Help me?"

"That's what I'm here for. Part of what you feel is normal and as the only alpha here, it's my job to see you through this, to protect you, to help you and meet your desires for sex and violence."

"Alpha? Like the boss man ... wolf?"

He nodded. He knew she needed to fuck. It was the only way to decrease the energy inside her. That and fighting, but he wasn't sure she was up for that yet.

On the other hand, Rolf was not going to let her teeth anywhere near his cock, not until she had the warring energies of her new were self under control. "How about you let me put my hot tongue on you?" he asked softly. "No penetration, just something to relieve the pressure."

A smile lit her face. It was rather ferocious. "Sounds like a deal," she said in a voice with a hint of purr. She didn't move. She didn't lie back on the bed. She just stood, hands balled as if waiting to pounce on him.

It looked like it was up to him to give her what she wanted and, even then, he sensed a fight on his hands. Abbie was not submissive at all. She wanted the edge taken off that great wall of desire inside, but she wasn't making herself weak to get it. If anything, she came across as an alpha female, a good mate for an alpha male. Able to stand up and protect her mate, her children and her pack.

Rolf stilled at that realisation. Could she be his mate? He normally didn't think in such a way. There was too much magical interference in the world to believe in fate or destiny. Yet opportunities, chance meetings, serendipitous happenings, he could relate to and take advantage of.

Well, if she wasn't going to cooperate or be submissive, he'd take the lead. The sooner she let off some of that sexual desire, the safer they would all be. "Get on all fours," he said.

Her eyes blazed and her fists were tight, held just a little in front as if ready to take another shot at him. "Make me," she snapped back.

Rolf saw that her body was taut and ready to respond to any action he might take. Rolf heard a growl and then saw her slow smile. She wanted him, but he was going to have to fight for the privilege of helping her, of slaking that build-up of sexual need.

He moved and so did she. Their bodies collided with a slap of flesh on flesh. She had led with a punch in the gut, but he was ready, and it bounced off firm muscle. He used his weight and tipped her onto the bed. He dived after her, hoping to pin her. Before Rolf could blink, she'd twisted away and was on her feet, while he was sprawled on the bed. Her eyes were locked on his erection, glittering with something like greed. Danger alarms were going off in his head. Being ravaged by a new werewolf was not his idea of fun. He liked his cock too much to risk it in those jaws.

Rolf moved quickly, rolling off the bed and along the floor to trip her up. She fell to her knees. He pushed her forward so that she was on all fours, arse aimed in the air, luscious slit waiting for his tongue. Before he could get near her, she dropped her front end and kicked out at him. He grabbed her foot and pulled her closer. She used the other foot that he'd lost hold of and kicked. Rolf rolled away, dodging the foot.

She dove after him and landed astride his chest. He paused. In this position he could help her bleed off some of that lust. She pinioned his hands at the side of his head, moving herself further up his chest as she made the movement. "Lick me now if you dare."

His line of sight showed him a luscious sight. He licked his lips. "You need to move closer and let go my arms."

"No!" Her voice was feral. "I'm not letting go. My way or no way."

He lifted an eyebrow. "Impasse?"

She moved her knees to his arms, shifting herself close to his mouth. Oh god, Rolf thought. This is seriously hot. Such a blatant act of need and domination turned him on. How much harder could his cock get? His tongue shot out and he got his first taste of her. A shudder ran through her body. He stroked again, lifting his head to get more strength behind the stroke of his tongue. Again, he licked, finding the nub of her clitoris. She moaned and pushed herself closer to his mouth. She was rocking against his mouth and Rolf lost himself, licking, sucking and devouring. He thought he'd lose his load as she screamed and shook as her climax hit. So quickly. He'd barely begun.

At her weak moment, he pushed against her weight, shoving up with his torso and tilting so that she fell sideways. He rolled with her, landing on top of her, lips to lips. "Like that did you?"

She growled and tensed her body, trying to throw him off.

"I deserve a kiss for that nice deed, yes?"

Her eyes lowered and he brushed his mouth, still gleaming with her juices, across her lips. Her response was immediate and intense, meeting his hunger with her own. They rolled this way and that as they kissed with lips and tongue and fervour.

Her hands grabbed his cock in a firm hold. "I want to fuck you," she said when he broke off their kiss.

Rolf panted. "I want you to fuck me, babe. More than anything. But let me go."

"I'm not your babe." Her growl preceded a jerk on his cock, a strong, sharp movement that hand him panting with fear and excitement. He could not trust her, not yet.

His hand shot out and clasped her hand, pausing her movement. "Let it go."

Her lips curled. "No." He held her as firmly as she held him.

"I don't trust you," he admitted.

Her lips widened into a smile, revealing white teeth, not quite perfection but close. "I don't trust you either."

He frowned. "Didn't I just lick your most vulnerable part until you screamed? If that's not trustworthy I don't know what is."

Her face was expressionless, but a fire burned in her eyes. "I could've stopped you if you did something I didn't like." Her voice was level, emotionless. She was doing a damn fine job of showing that she was in control of herself, or was doing a damn fine job of pretending to be. It was surface layer. He could taste her desire, feel the currents of her rage and confusion and lust.

Her hand tightened, reminding him she still had him in her grip.

He tilted his head. "Fair enough." He didn't like his chances of separating her teeth from his cock if she had a mind to chomp on him. Yet he knew a challenge when he heard one. Would he be able to stop her if she did something he didn't like? Maybe not without injuring or killing her.

"Let me. Trust me," she said, voice softening on the last syllable. Her amber irises glowed with lust and were energies. Rolf looked too deeply and lost himself in there. A connection snapped into place and he gasped. He wanted her so badly that he abandoned caution. He removed his hand from hers and she stroked him. Nothing gentle in the touch. He inhaled sharply, body tensing. She paused and removed her hand.

He gave her a slight nod and they separated, crouched and facing each other as if they were about to wrestle instead of having sex. As they circled one another, he knew that she was going to do this her way. Nervous, he didn't know what her way was, but he was up for it.

Her gaze shot around the room and fixed on a spot behind his right shoulder. He didn't turn. He knew exactly what she'd spotted. They often had to bind newly whelped were. He was going to refuse, but something stilled him—an image of himself tied up while she sucked him off. He nearly keeled over with the fantasy of it, panting as just the thought took him to the brink. What if she wasn't going to go there? The moment hung suspended.

Her expression grew thoughtful as she strode across the room and took down the length of rope.

He turned his body and watched as she faced him, rope in hands, a sexy smirk on her face. Their eyes met. "Chair," she said.

She was shaking, obviously excited, and scared. Rolf could almost taste it. In that state she might revert to wolf form and right now he didn't want that. He'd revert as well and that would be problematic with the rage and lust in this shed right now. In wolf shape they'd fight it out rather than slake the beast with sex.

After rolling his shoulders and silently considering the situation, he pulled the chair out and sat down. "I'm going to tie your legs and your torso. Your arms too. Can you cope with that?"

He nodded, not quite willing to talk, or able to more like. His throat was tight and dry. This was pushing the boundaries for him.

She wrapped the rope around him, including his upper arms. He had his hands free but there wasn't much he could do with them, unless driven by self-preservation. He couldn't help assessing the rope's strength, looking for a way out.

After tying the ends and testing the knot, she grinned savagely. She leaned close to his ear and hissed with a breath laden with moist lust. "Thank you."

His erection had waned somewhat. She really knew how to take the floor out from under one.

Stepping back, she eyed him from the top of his head to the tips of his toes. The hunger in her eyes rekindled his own. Leaning down, so that her long hair brushed the skin of his thighs, she drew a forefinger along his cock. His breath hissed in and his erection hardened as if she had commanded it. So hard and fast was his reaction, it left a tightness in his belly and a throbbing ache in his balls.

An appreciative growl escaped her mouth as she slowly licked her lips and knelt between his legs. Her hot mouth enveloped him. She started sucking hard, stroking his length with firm fingers.

He hissed in a breath and squeezed his fists. This was no gentle stirring. His skin was on fire, his mind almost blinded by lust. Fear and desire wove deep into him. He resisted and fought the need for release but the determination with which she worked him broke down his defences. His ragged breaths filled his ears as he fought for control, to hold on. Could she know how close he was? His skin was alive from her hot lips and strong tongue. Soon that was all he could focus on.

His cock throbbed. His body jerked and he strained against the bindings. He wanted to shove himself inside her. He wanted her screaming his name as he gave her the full length of his cock, but she held him. She was in charge. And he held on, resisted release to make his point. Then she changed tactic. She shoved him deeper in her throat. Rolf couldn't stop watching her, the image undoing him faster than the feel of her tongue. He wasn't going to last. Then she used her other hand and cupped his balls, broke off long enough to take them into her mouth and tongue them. The chair was in danger of tipping over. His thigh muscles tensed, hips thrusting as she drew him into her mouth. He was going to come.

"Stop! I'm close," he said, panting as if he'd run a marathon. Sweat dripped from his brow and moisture dripped down his back.

She paused and looked up, resting the tip of his cock just below her lips so that her breath swept over him. He caught his breath as he met those eyes. "Come in my mouth," she said and paused. She swept her lips over his tip. "It's a fantasy of mine."

His eyes rolled up. Jesus Christ. He was supposed to be the one in charge, but she had reversed that, just smacked him up the side of the head. *Come in her mouth. Her fantasy.* Christ it was his own fantasy.

He didn't get a chance to respond. She shoved him into her mouth, sucked and sucked and worked him, up and down his shaft. With each repetition, she swallowed him deeper. With a yell, he spilled into her throat, his whole body jerking as she licked every last drop from his tip.

He'd died and gone to heaven. Exhausted, sated, he sat limp in the chair. He must have zoned off or something, because next he knew she'd undone the ropes. He just sat there, not quite able to process it all, not able to move. She could've killed him, and he wouldn't have reacted. He was an open book. He'd trusted her with his most vulnerable organ. She'd repaid him with a touch of paradise.

Stepping back, she looked him up and down, lips pursed, eyes dark. Then her mouth twitched into a smile. She leaned down, hands resting on the arms of the chair, her breath fanning his face as she whispered to him. "I think I can trust you now."

Rolf opened his eyes and studied her face. Smooth pale skin, a smattering of freckles on her nose, full moist lips and fine arches to her eyebrows. She stood back, her stance relaxed. Rolf could taste the rage simmering beneath the surface, but it was noticeably less. Lust light still filled her irises. A spark was all that was needed to ignite her passion.

His recovery time was usually pretty good. This time it was phenomenal. Just looking at her had the blood flooding back into his cock. Maybe this time, she'd let him do some of the fucking.

He pushed out of the chair, and she retreated to maintain some distance between them. She was canny this one. Some weres gained from the transformation, but some just changed—personality, tastes, habits. He hadn't known her well before the curse, but it seemed to him that she had gained as well as changed. Her demeanour would settle eventually, he hoped. Right now, she was out of control. No restraint. Unbridled lust. Fierce aggression.

Before he could blink, she had assumed a fighting stance—fists up defending her body and face, knees bent, one a little in front of the other. He realised she was inviting him to spar, when she launched a kick at him. He had to be quick so as not to hurt her with his deflection. He swept the floor with his foot, bringing her down. She twisted and landed easily, with a wolf's grace, and charged again, this time with fists. He grabbed those and held her, but she lifted her knee and he had to let her go or risk being kneed in the nuts. She charged again and he grabbed her and tossed her on the bed. He followed quickly to pin her with his weight but, damn, she was gone.

She had rolled and dived off the bed and came back at him with a blow to the back of the head. He landed face down on the bed and she followed, her moist sex on the small of his back, her breast pressed between his shoulder blades, her breath damp on his neck.

She rubbed her body against his, the friction of their skin exciting him further. "You are so fucking gorgeous," she said with a sensuous growl. "I knew I wanted you the first time I laid eyes on you."

Rolf didn't try to dislodge her. Her hands ran down his arms, fingers finding every curve of muscle and every hollow of flesh. Her touch burned and sizzled and thrilled. His cock was paying attention. It was screaming for a fuck.

This was not normally how these sessions would go. He would help a newly whelped were release tension, help them get grounded, teach them he was their alpha.

Mentally, he found this reversal of roles hard. He was the alpha, it was his job to help a newly turned werewolf, to initiate them, to help them come to terms with their new life and teach them respect for the pack and him as alpha. Abbie wasn't about to be dictated to. He'd never been in this situation before.

Her hot sex rubbed against his buttocks. He could picture her mock thrusts as she rocked against him. "Tell me. What the fuck is going on!" Her voice was low and authoritative.

The command in her voice rocked him. Before he could even formulate a reply, her hands reached between his legs and cupped him. It was distracting. He was so caught in the moment of her touch, her audacity, her damned hotness, he couldn't reply.

Her grip changed, grew firm. "What happened to me?"

"It has something to do with magic." His breath was quick and light, his manhood in a precarious position.

Letting go of his balls, she levered up to slap him between the shoulder blades. "Don't give me that crap. I've been drugged. I'm hallucinating."

"No. You were hit by a curse. It transformed you into a werewolf.

"Nup. More bullshit."

He let out a sigh and shoved back. She clung harder. He let out a growl low in his throat. "Someone cast a magic spell on you, cursed you so that you turned into a werewolf."

"No!"

The weight of her body was suddenly gone. He turned and watched as she prowled around the room. She was twitchy and scared. He admired how her muscles moved and as she began to hyperventilate, he sat up on the bed.

"I helped you complete the transformation. You're a werewolf. There's more to learn."

Silence. Stillness. A hitch in a breath.

"Abbie?"

She closed her eyes, drew in a deep breath, and then opened them again. She seemed in control, but it was surface level. She was trying very hard to be brave, to be strong. It made his breath hitch. "Even if what you say is true. Why? Why me?"

"I don't know. I really don't know who is doing it, or why. We're trying to find out. You're not the first one to be cursed, but you're the first to make a successful transition."

There were wet drops in her eyelashes. "What happened to the others?"

He shook his head. "They didn't make it."

"They died?" she said, and sank down onto the bed, her bare arse on the sheet. All the rage seemed to have left her. He edged closer, reached out with fingers to brush her shoulders. She didn't pull away. Tears glistened on her cheeks.

"Yes." He nuzzled her hair, the scent of her filling him up.

She turned to him, face close to his. "Couldn't you have stopped it? Made me stay human? I feel different, out of control, not me anymore … I'm scared by this thing inside me and …"

"We couldn't stop it happening, Abbie. But you're strong, a fighter. You'll be a great werewolf and in no time it will feel natural and normal to you." He stroked her hair, dug his fingers into her scalp to release the tension there.

Abbie squirmed. He pulled back to study her. She grimaced and embraced herself as if trying to stop the urge to move.

"What's wrong?" he asked, touching her hair lightly.

She drew in a breath through her teeth. Her eyes focused on him. Intent. "I want to fuck you!" she blurted. The words seemed to surprise her, to shock. She covered her mouth, eyes wide.

He grinned, her audacity a delight.

After a moment, she removed her hand. "I can't stop saying that. Thinking it. It's not who I am. Who I was. But I have this urge, this fire that wants to …" She gulped and focused on him. "What is wrong with me?"

"Nothing is wrong. It's your wolf. She will take time to tame. She's very strong, very powerful. I can feel her, taste her." Her eyes widened, panic-stricken. But there was no point in sugar coating it.

"Every full moon your change will come upon you. Your wolf will take over, but each time you'll learn to control her more and you'll be aware, rather than mindless …"

Her eyebrows furrowed, questions building up inside. "But ... but will I be normal again? Is there a cure? Will I ever be me?"

He shook his head. "This is your new normal and as far as I know no cure. You'll adapt and the wolf inside will integrate with your human side. In time you may be able to resume your old life, if that is what you want."

Her eyelids shut, closing him out. He thought she might faint at first, but then her eyes snapped open, fury and intelligence bright in her irises. "So I'm always going to want to fuck, growl and rage?"

He nodded, then nipped her nose. "Probably. For a few months for sure. Your wolf will always feel things strongly, more intensely. The upside is you'll be stronger, your reflexes will be quicker and you'll heal faster."

A snarl slipped out of her throat. "It couldn't get any more intense than this." She pushed him back, rolled onto him and ground her sex into his groin. His cock twitched, then grew hard. He'd been anticipating sexual need.

"I have to fuck you now!" she stated. "Before I give in to the urge to punch you in the face."

"Kiss me," he ordered.

She smashed her mouth to his. She leaned back, a puzzled frown on her face.

Rolf grinned, leaned up and leisurely licked her bottom lip. "I'm the alpha male, the head of the pack and you obey my commands."

She shook her head. "Not bloody likely."

With a growl, she lunged toward his neck and nipped. Rolf grabbed her head and held her, then kissed her with all the dominance he could muster. She met him as an equal. Her hands grabbing for him, trying to control.

He responded like for like and aimed his mouth at a nipple, while his hand ploughed her already moist and willing sex. Pleasure ripped out of her. She screamed with release as he sucked on her nipple, her body writhing as his fingers brought her pleasure to a peak. She started to fuck his hand. He switched nipples and she grabbed a handful of his hair and pulled as she lifted her breast to his mouth. The sounds she made were more wolf than human, as he held her breasts tightly. She bucked against him. "Fuck me you bastard! Fuck me now!"

They grappled as they fought for a position. In the end, Rolf had to position her doggie style as she kept trying to bite him. Once he pushed his cock into her, she froze and let out a growl so loud he blinked. Then she wiggled her butt and he began the magic dance: in slow, out slow, in fast and shallow, almost out, then down deep until she shuddered and then he lost his control as she reached around and hit him on the thigh. "Faster! Harder!"

Rolf just went for it, not giving a shit who was in control or who obeyed who. They rutted and grunted and yelled. She came so hard he nearly lost hold of her and then he came right after her. He let her go and she lay face first on the bed. He flopped down next to her, exhausted. She had her eyes closed, her breath panting out of her, her face flushed.

Rolf tried to calm himself. They had fucked like there was no goddam tomorrow. There was only one problem. He wanted more, even though he was totally wasted. Tendrils of sleep took control of his mind. His eyes closed and he was out.

He woke later to her hot mouth reviving his already hardening cock. He closed his eyes to revel in the sensation of her tongue on him, thinking it must be a dream. Then she straddled him and shoved down on his erection. He nearly leapt from the bed, suddenly awake and horny as all hell.

"Steady," she said, correcting her seat. Then she lifted her body up and lowered it down, lost to the moment, if the sheer pleasure on her face was a gauge.

Rolf rolled his head around on the mattress, not sure whether he'd died and gone to heaven or he was hallucinating. She rode him mercilessly. He rose to meet her, thrusting up and smiling as she moaned and threw her head back.

They must have dozed, as the next thing he knew they were at it again, rutting as if their life depended on it, fingers grasping, teeth nipping, arms clenching.

Trying to take control, he pushed up into a sitting position, but she was on him, sliding down his length. With his hands around her waist, he thrust into her. Her red hair whipped around her head, driven by the force of his movement. She had her eyes closed, face filled with ecstasy. Rolf was absorbed in the moment, loving it, loving the feel of her heat on him. Then, a sliver a fear crept up his spine. His heart leaped and quivered. The thought that brought cold fear to him—he could lose himself to this woman, this wolf. Then the thought and the fear slid away as more bodily urges took over.

The shed echoed with their cries and pants and shouts and the sounds of flesh hitting moistly against flesh. He came so hard he thought his cum was draining his soul.

Foreheads resting against each other, they breathed exhaustion into shared breaths. Abbie's hands ran through his hair and her bottom wiggled on his lap. He responded to her movement, growing harder by the second. Rolf tried to fight the arousal. He was spent. He could not fuck again. He needed a break. Having none of it, Abbie drew his head back by the hair and slammed her mouth against his again. Her other hand teased his balls. He might be too tired to continue, but his body, and Abbie, had other ideas.

CHAPTER 6

Abbie woke, every muscle in her body stretched and sore, as if she'd run a marathon. Her face was lying against a firm, slightly furred chest. At first her memory was blank. Then the memories rushed in, every single moment. She closed her eyes against the images that flashed into her mind, the primal sounds that bore into her brain. It was Rolf.

She made a move and winced. Her body felt like it had been pummelled and used, yet there was no bruising, no twinges. She recalled Rolf had mentioned healing.

Memories of their rutting flooded into her mind. The way she spoke and acted. Denial hit. She could not have done that—taken the sexual lead. And all those feelings of rage and lust—where had they come from? It just wasn't possible. It must be drugs or hypnosis. Or worse she'd lost her mind. She sucked in a breath ... no ... she remembered ...

Being a wolf.

The incredible pain of transition, as if a new shape had been carved in her flesh. The crest of pain, the moment when she decided to push through urged on, encouraged by a voice in her mind.

Inhaling, she breathed in his scent, the maleness of him and of sweat and more. Rolf was awake now. But he lay still beneath her.

Easing off him, she rolled into a sitting position. Her legs folded up so she could bury her head in her knees. She couldn't look at him. She'd sucked his cock. Oh god! Her behaviour had been outrageous. How could she look at him, speak to him?

"Abbie?" he whispered. She wasn't sure if she heard it with her ears or in her mind. It was as if there was some link between them and, try as she might, she couldn't fight it. She stayed huddled, unspeaking, not quite able to form words. The memories of what had passed settled in a kind of chronological order. Although some moments were large and bright and full of something fierce, others were hazy, like half-forgotten dreams.

Fear should rule her. This was all so out of this world. Who were these people? What was she doing here? Yet, there was an anchor inside her that kept her from taking flight. A nodule of calm that spoke of being safe. Was this the bond? This alpha thing that Rolf had mentioned? She didn't want to leave him. Just entertaining the thought set alight a torch of panic inside. She didn't think she could leave him right now. Maybe later, when she knew more about the situation. But the memories, oh the memories.

A knock at the door. Her head jerked up and Rolf stiffened. He got up and tossed a blanket to her, which she grabbed and draped over her naked form. She frowned. She'd not been comfortable naked previously. Now, it didn't seem to matter.

The other man—Dane, Rolf had called him—came in and gave Rolf a nod, his eyes focusing on her. He was tall and blond and big. He wore an expensive-looking pale green sweater and well-fitting jeans. Tan ankle boots beneath the cuffs. She watched him through slitted eyes, noticed that there was a bit of the wolf about him. It might be the shape of his face, the way he moved, his scent or just intuition. She didn't know for sure which, or even if she was correct.

His gaze was fixed on her. With a nod to Rolf, he came forward. "I'm Dane. May I?" He motioned to the edge of the bed.

She glanced from him to Rolf, who nodded. "Y-ye-yes," she replied in a voice croaky as if she'd been screaming for days. Her gaze flicked to Rolf. He was naked and that didn't seem to bother either of the men. He made no move to cover himself up. His nakedness was distracting. Her gaze kept sliding to his cock, sitting in its dark matting of hair, waiting for her to call it to life.

"Rolf tells me you're feeling better," Dane said. Her gaze snapped back to his.

Anger and embarrassment sent heat to her skin. "Better?" Her gaze flicked up to Rolf who stood behind Dane. "He means you've transitioned to wolf and back again and can hold human form."

Dane smiled a little smile, just a friendly gesture. She didn't feel like being friendly, though. A surge of distrust burned from her gut to her brain. "I need to ask you some questions." Her voice was tight, her hands clenched into fists.

"Questions?" His eyebrows rose and he half turned to Rolf and then faced her again. "You have questions? I have questions. Important ones that need answers right now."

"Me first," she almost growled the words. Abbie blinked, shocked that she'd been so aggressive, so outspoken, so rude to a stranger.

Rolf growled at her in warning. Immediately it felt as if she'd been doused with cold water. Rage and anger fled. She wanted to obey. She fought against it, even as she nodded and lowered her eyes. "Sure," she said in milder tones. "Ask your questions."

Dane let out a breath, and nodded, as if acknowledging her sudden willingness to talk to him. "Before you started to change, do you remember experiencing anything strange? Or seeing anyone unusual?"

She lifted her head and stared at Rolf, fighting to keep the smile, or snarl off her face. "I met Rolf at the nightclub. He's the only strange thing I remember."

Rolf didn't change his expression and kept studying her. She wondered what he was thinking.

Dane continued and Abbie dragged her gaze away from Rolf. "You were with friends. What did you do before you went to Civic and had breakfast?"

Her heart leapt. Belle and Ruby. What must they think? "How did you know that?" she replied, suspicion once again pushing to the forefront of her mind.

Dane tilted his head to the side, studying her. "Your friends gave statements to the police and the press," Dane replied. "We were able to see them."

"Oh, I see." Abbie frowned as she tried to remember. It was difficult. So many emotions. So many disconnects. Details were a little hazy, as it seemed so long ago, awash with the fading of time. "We stayed inside my apartment, I think." She unclenched her fist and clenched it again, noting the whiteness of her fingers. "The night before we ate pizza and drank champagne." She looked Dane in the eye. "Terribly hungover."

Dane let out a breath and nodded reassuringly. "You said you met Rolf at the nightclub. Did you notice anyone close by, someone who might've given you a queer feeling, a look that you thought odd?"

Abbie shook her head. "I don't think so ..."

"Try to remember. It's important," Dane urged.

"I'm trying," she said, shaking her head, starting to come apart.

Rolf moved to sit next to her on the bed and squeezed her shoulder. Then all her thoughts centred on him, as if he was a magnet. It was as if he'd suddenly become the centre of the fucking universe. "We all noticed Rolf."

"You and your friends?" Dane asked, a smile lingering, softening his features.

Abbie fought the compulsion to just stare at Rolf and forced her gaze back to Dane. "Yes, but it was my friends who said I should go up to Rolf, introduce myself. I wouldn't have normally ..." She shrugged. "Done such a thing?" The memories came again of what she'd done and how and her skin heated again. She'd gone way beyond bold. Way beyond embarrassment.

"Were there other people in the club?"

She licked her lips, trying to focus on Dane and his questions. "Yes. It was early, but there were younger people there ... and ..." Her memory tickled, just a flicker. "And an older man standing in the shadows."

Dane straightened. "An older man? What did he look like?"

She shook her head. "I can't tell you any details. It's just a shape in the shadows, the stance, the hint of a light beard, the hunch of shoulder that tells me he might be older than the usual crowd. I think that's why I noticed. It's not a place for old people. Hell, I was considered too old for that place."

"Would you know him again?" Rolf asked softly against her cheek. All her senses were on high alert. When did he draw so close? His breath on her cheek made her sex throb. What the hell was going on with her? He was so deliciously close that her restraint was unravelling. She wanted him, whether Dane was there or not.

Control yourself, she thought. Her resolve gathered and she focused on answering the question. "I don't know. Maybe ... at least the hint of him." She wasn't sure what she meant by hint. Had she seen more, noticed greater detail?

Dane stood up and tugged his sweater down. "Thank you for that. It helps. I don't know if Rolf has told you what's happening." Her head jerked up, her lip curled as she growled low in her throat. Dane backed off, hands out in a placating gesture. "I'll give him some more time to ... um get you sorted. Later, I'll drop some clean clothes down and you can join us at the house, if Rolf thinks you're ready for that."

Rolf glided off the bed in a smooth movement that had muscles flexing deliciously. He slapped Dane companionably on the shoulder.

"What do you mean if I'm ready?" she asked both of them.

Dane quirked an eyebrow at Rolf and made for the door. He paused before opening it and turned back. "A new werewolf can be unpredictable. We need to be sure of you." Then the door thumped shut. Her gaze met Rolf's. She wanted to complain, but the moment their eyes met pure lust flamed. She lunged off the bed, launched at Rolf. Her mouth latched on to his hot lips, tugging at them, begging for his tongue.

Rolf met her advance like for like. It was less of a battle and more like a ballet. She used her tongue all over his body and he let her. His breath only caught when she took one of his balls in her mouth. He tasted delicious: sweet, musky with a hint of spice. Then he was hard and ready, and she was wet and ready. Their bodies merged so hard and fast, Abbie had to remember to breathe.

By the time they were through, they had tried just about every position under the sun and licked and sucked all that could possibly be licked and sucked.

It was dark outside when they finally dozed, flesh against flesh. When the moon rose and peered through the unshuttered window, she experienced it like someone brushing an electric current against her skin. She sat up, suddenly horny again. "God!" she gasped, desperate to have him inside her.

Rolf still slept on oblivious. It wasn't good enough. She wanted a quickie—a hard and fast fuck. She fondled his cock and straight away it jerked to life. "Come on, Rolf. Fuck me. Quickly."

He didn't respond, so she leant close to his ear. "I need you, right now," she said, voice dripping in frustration and need.

Instantly he was there, powering off the bed. With a quick assessment of the situation, he grabbed her and pushed her against the wall, where he impaled her at the same time. He was pumping as madly and as wildly as she wanted. She wondered how he knew instinctively what she needed. She slapped his shoulder. Faster. *Faster* she thought at him, and he complied. Within a couple of minutes, they were spent, sagging against each other, disentangling limbs.

"Oh, that was good," she said, sagging against his shoulder and liking the feel of being there.

He slapped her bottom lightly. "We need to get showered and dressed. Dinner is ready."

At first annoyed because she didn't want to move, she growled and then stopped as she caught the aroma. "Is that roast lamb?"

"Yes, medium rare. Very bloody close to the bone." She saw eagerness in his eyes and heard his belly rumble. He was as exhausted and as spent as she was.

Her mouth watered at the thought and her stomach heaved. Her hand went to her middle and the hunger gnawed.

In the shower, Rolf scrubbed her down, exploring while he cleaned every part of her. The water ran cold when he stopped to lick her. Luckily, she was so hot she came before she grew too cold.

When they came out there was a pile of clean clothes on the table by the door. Dane had been in and out and she hadn't even smelled him. That thought made her blink. She could smell him?

Her gaze went from the clothes to the bed.

He slapped her bottom again. "Later," he said and then shoved his head into a T-shirt.

She blushed at being so transparent. What the hell was wrong with her? She'd just been fucked senseless for more than a day and a half and she wanted more. Donning the gifted underwear, a pair of tight-fitting track pants and a T-shirt that hugged her breasts, she was dressed and ready. A rumble in her gut made her head for the door. It was like the need for sex. Her hunger became her focus. She had to eat. No negotiation. She struggled to control herself. This naked want, this drive to fill her needs, felt so animal and basic that logic didn't seem able to control it. She needed to get her equilibrium back. Rolf caught up and put his arm around her waist as they walked up to the house that loomed over them in the dark. It seemed like a romantic gesture, but she knew it was to stop her running.

The almost full moon topped the house and she paused, realising it was tingling her skin, like the feel of an ultrasound at the physiotherapist. She cast a worried frown at Rolf, who stood illuminated by an outdoor light that showed them the path to the house.

"It's the moon's call. Soon your body won't be able to resist."

"What will happen then?" she asked, disturbed by the thought. The inside wolf was scary and different. Her whole inner landscape had been radically altered. How would it be when it came out again? She was revolted at the thought.

Rolf grinned and opened the door for her. "We change. Our wolf comes out and we'll run and hunt together with the pack."

"The pack?" She gulped.

"Yes, my pack of werewolves."

A pack of werewolves? More new things to adjust to. She wasn't sure she could. She was glad she felt sane now, as there had been madness in the dark space when she went through the transition. Yet she feared that it could come back again and hold her prisoner.

"You'll meet them soon." She stepped inside into a short hall. She didn't want to share Rolf or meet other people, other werewolves.

"Inside you'll meet Annwyn. Dane's other half. She's a sorceress, like Dane is a sorcerer. There's some history there that I'll tell you about later, but for now know that sometimes Annwyn's personality may change. She has the essence of an evil sorceress inside her."

Abbie frowned, suddenly wary. "Should I be careful?"

Rolf smiled. "Always!" Then he leaned in close and spoke quietly. "The evil one was into kinky sex and sometimes Annwyn doesn't realise that she's under the influence."

Abbie drew back. "So you're saying that she might come on to me?" Abbie cast him a look, wondering if he was having her on. Magic and sex? Werewolves and sex? At least some of the werewolf predilections were in popular culture. Who knew they were true?

Rolf's eyebrow lifted. "I suppose she might. It was more how she reacts to me sometimes that I wanted to warn you about."

"Oh?" Abbie said, not liking the sound of that by half. She wanted to ask more, but a vision of loveliness opened the door: blonde, beautiful with a sweet smile.

"Hi, you must be Abbie," Annwyn said, opening the door wider. "Do come in. Dane is carving the roast right now." She smiled at Rolf, touched his forearm in a friendly gesture. "Bring her in. You know where everything is."

Abbie followed Annwyn down the hall and into a dining room that was wide and long, with full-length windows providing a full view of the night. The table was set with a white and gold dinner service, fine linen napkins.

"This is lovely," Abbie said with a smile, knowing it was polite to make such a comment, but feeling weird at the same time. After all she'd been through, this elegance was unexpected. Then she blinked. There was a mountain of food on the table and a platter of lamb in the centre that smelled so divine she couldn't speak. Pink meat in a pile had her heading for the table and growling.

Rolf grabbed her hand as she tried to snatch some of the meat. "We will eat like civilised people," he said, pushing her into a seat. "Get a grip on yourself."

He sat next to her. Rocked by emotions and embarrassment, Abbie tried to control the urges, the desire, the hunger. All these things swirled in her gut, and her anger at Rolf and his domination brewed and boiled. She tried smiling, but if the look the sorceress cast her was any indication it must have looked feral rather than feminine.

Annwyn took a seat and began to chatter pleasantries. Abbie just sat there staring at the food, fighting the urge to gorge. She imagined leaping onto the table and wolfing down the meat and sending crockery and glasses smashing to the floor. The sight of pink bloody juice had her mouth watering. Hunger so primal in her gut that she couldn't think of anything but the meat in front of her. She wanted to snap and bite and rend Rolf, Annwyn, Dane when he came into the room with more meat to tip onto the platter.

"Hello, Abbie," Dane said.

Abbie ignored him, as she couldn't stop obsessing over the meat. A pinch on her leg jerked her around to snarl at Rolf. "What?"

"Answer Dane politely. You're a guest in his house."

Abbie stared at Rolf's throat. She wanted to rip it out. A snarl escaped her mouth and she covered it and her eyes widened. "Did I do that?"

"Yes," Rolf said. "Control yourself or you can go back into the shed."

Her eyes lifted to his, doing her best to appear sorrowful. "I'm sorry. I'm so hungry. And the moon, it's bothering me."

"Control it. Concentrate on being sociable and polite. Now sit there and wait until I say you can eat."

Abbie gritted her teeth and fidgeted. "Hello, Dane. Thank you for inviting me."

Dane acknowledged her words with a smile and took a seat.

Rolf chatted companionably to Annwyn and Dane and put items of food on her plate, spinach in cheese sauce, roasted vegetables of all kinds, peas, gravy and then the meat, piece after piece piled up high.

"Abbie?" Rolf asked.

"Yes," she said, not taking her eyes off the food.

"You can eat now."

She lifted her hand to grab several slices of meat to shovel into her mouth, but Rolf intercepted it and shoved a fork between her fingers.

"Use it," he said, picking up his own. "I know you're hungry, but try to be civilised."

Abbie stuck the tines into a piece of meat and shoved it in her mouth. She swallowed without chewing and jammed another one in there. She was so hungry. The meat was so delicious. She swallowed and sighed, swallowed and sighed.

"Slow down," Rolf suggested. "Chew your food first."

She responded to his suggestion and slowed down. The pile of meat on her plate was down by a half. She was feeling full, but couldn't stop wanting the taste of it in her mouth, the texture of the meat on her tongue. It was as if she had no control.

"At least she likes the food," Annwyn commented.

Rolf gave a small laugh. "I don't think it matters. She's so hungry, and her wolf senses are in high gear. I'm sure she wouldn't mind me apologising on her behalf. She really can't help it."

"No," Abbie said. "It's delicious. Really, the best lamb I've ever tasted." Noticing her plate, she saw it was empty. She looked up at Dane. "More?" she asked in a pitiful voice. She belched loudly. Rolf pinched her leg and their eyes met. Then she grew aware of her surroundings again. "May I have some more, please?" she asked, bringing her manners to the fore.

"Are you sure you can fit it in?" Annwyn asked as she pushed the platter of meat toward her. "Gravy?"

"Yes, please," Abbie said, taking the gravy and layering over the smaller pile of meat. "Is there going to be any dessert?"

Annwyn laughed. "Of course, if you have room for it."

Abbie tucked into the meat, chewing each piece before she swallowed, while casting glances at Rolf. Her craving for meat was now equal to her craving for sex. With Rolf so close it was hard to divide her attention. She tried to smile at Dane and Annwyn, even if she couldn't converse with them. They just smiled in return, although Annwyn had an eyebrow raised as if she thought Abbie was going to grow two heads or change into a wolf at the drop of a hat.

Dane chuckled to himself and tossed his napkin on his plate. "I'll go get the dessert, shall I?" He stood, picked up some plates and went into the kitchen area.

Abbie was feeling fuller now, more replete. Some kind of sweet would do well to round out the meal. Again, she burped loudly. Rolf looked at her and Annwyn laughed.

"Nothing wrong with how her insides work, I see," the other woman commented.

Rolf replied, "Yes, she is perfect."

Her nose caught the aroma before her vision did. Cinnamon spice and apple with a bowl of whipped cream and some swanky rich ice cream. Abbie sat back in her chair, patiently waiting to be served. It unnerved her how focused she was on the dessert, watching as each piece was served up.

"Feeling better now?" Annwyn asked as she scooped ice cream into a bowl.

"Yes, thank you. Much better."

Annwyn looked up expectantly. Abbie continued. "I'd say I was feeling human again, but that doesn't quite cut it."

"I'm sorry for what's happened to you," Annwyn said and handed over the dessert. "I can't see any magic around you now. I imagine you were very distressed. I understand the disorientation you might've felt."

Abbie straightened and cast her gaze around the table. "You can see magic?"

Annwyn grinned as she surveyed the table. "Oh yes. It comes in handy when you're hunting a rogue sorcerer." Seeing that everyone had their dessert, Annwyn sat back down and picked up her spoon.

"Rogue sorcerer? You mean the person who did this to me?" Abbie asked.

The bowl in front of her was distracting. It was difficult to focus on the conversation, instead of the food. The food was it. The centre of everything. She may have whined.

"Don't worry. It will settle in a little while," Rolf commented, as if understanding her dilemma.

Her head jerked around to Rolf. "What?"

"The intense food reaction. Soon that will only be a full moon side effect."

Given the aroma of the food drawing her back to her bowl, Abbie didn't bother engaging in further conversation. She ate her way through two heaped bowls of dessert. Rolf slipped the second bowl in front of her without her even asking, or growling. That elemental desire satisfied, she found the scent of Rolf next to her intoxicating. She wanted to return to the shed and rut some more.

Much to her disappointment, Rolf stood up and helped clear off the table. Annwyn stood close to him, smiled up at him and touched his hand and her fingers lingered there. "Thank you, Rolf." The scent of the other woman's arousal reached Abbie. Immediately, Abbie was on her feet, chair flipped over and a growl in her mouth. "Take your hands off him."

"Abbie?" Rolf said, surprise and concern in his voice.

"What?" Annwyn said.

Abbie took a step in Rolf's direction, keeping Annwyn in full view. "Step away from him," Abbie's voice was laden with menace.

Dane came into the room, as if he knew what the problem was without explanation. "Annwyn come over to me, will you?"

"Why?" the sorceress asked. "I'm not doing anything. Nira isn't here."

Dane took a step, hand out to her. "It's a wolf thing. You're getting too close to her mate."

Annwyn took Dane's hand and looked up into his face. "Mate? She's not his mate. They're just fucking, like most new werewolves with the alpha or betas."

Rolf turned to Abbie, citrine eyes glittering. "Abbie." His voice was low, chiding.

Abbie was lost in a sea of base feelings. She wanted to attack Annwyn and wanted to bite Rolf's neck and fuck him at the same time. Yet his command reached her. She gave a frustrated growl and then shook herself. "What's happening to me?"

Rolf come over, ran his hand down her back and soothed her. "It's all right," he said in a gentle voice. "It's just that you're still so new to it all. It can be overwhelming, impulses hard to control."

That soft tone of voice undid Abbie. She burst into tears and started sobbing. Rolf pressed her face into his chest and held her, rubbing her back in a soothing motion. She calmed a little, but still felt emotionally rocky.

"I'm sorry," Annwyn said from behind her. "It's a terrible thing to happen. And your poor career, your life."

Abbie jerked around and took a step. "What happened to my career?"

Rolf sighed loudly. "Annwyn," he near groaned. "Not now."

Annwyn put a hand over her mouth. "Oh!" She walked to the table to pick up the empty plates. "Was I not to mention that? I just thought with being a werewolf and all that ..."

Hot emotion writhed in Abbie. She fought against Rolf's hold. "Calm down," Rolf hissed. "You need to focus on maintaining control. The danger isn't over yet."

She fought his hold. "Let me go. I'm fine."

Rolf studied her and released her. Abbie's gaze flicked to the clock and then to Dane. "Put the news on. Please."

Dane nodded his head at the large TV in the next room and sound blared. Abbie went straight in there. It took a few moments for Abbie to digest what she was seeing. It was Fleur reading the news ... "The disappearance of Abbie McGregor remains a mystery. Police advise that they're continuing their enquiries. A hotline has been set up to take calls from the public. If you know anything about Miss McGregor's disappearance, please call the number below."

Abbie didn't realise she was shouting at the TV until Rolf, grabbed her to him, muffled her mouth in his shoulder and patted her head and shoulder. "I'm sorry," he said in a soft crooning voice. Part of her were nature was soothed by his ministrations, but a deeper part of her was outraged. Fleur took her place, and not because Abbie had climbed the ladder. She'd stepped off it completely.

"My career!" she wailed. "Do you know how long I've dreamed of getting somewhere. Now it's over."

"It can't be helped," Rolf reiterated.

"Can't be helped? I moved to Canberra for that job and I was going to go places. Now this happens! It's not fair." She pulled away from him, slapped his hands away when he tried to soothe her further. "No, stop it. Leave me alone."

"Abbie, please," Rolf said, concern in his voice. "It's not that bad."

Hot wet tears travelled down her cheeks. "Not that bad? I can't be a newsreader if I'm a werewolf!"

"For the moment, yes." Dane said, coming forward, his tall blond personage like a Viking of old.

"What do you mean *for the moment*?" she asked with a small hint of hope. Rolf slid his arms around her waist and she let the feel of him soothe her.

"Until we can find out who is doing this, it's too much of a risk you being in the spotlight. There's too much mystery over what happened to you as well. How can we explain your disappearance without risking the exposure of all of us?"

"Who cares if there are sorcerers and werewolves?" Abbie said, without giving much thought to the problem.

"We care," Dane explained. "The collegium cares."

"What is the collegium?" Abbie asked.

Dane leaned forward. "The governing body of supernaturals."

Rolf interrupted. "Sorcerers are the most powerful and dominate the triumvirate, which is a group of three that makes decisions. Vampires are the next most powerful—"

Dane sighed. "There are issues ... werewolves are not as valued as the should be."

Abbie blinked. "Are you telling me I'm now at the bottom of the supernatural pecking order?" She turned to Rolf and looked at him expectantly.

Rolf's cheeks pinked and he gave a Gallic shrug.

Dane continued to explain. "As I was saying, the collegium cares. Whoever is doing this is trying to provoke wide-ranging exposure of our kind and an ultimate confrontation between humans and supernaturals. We aren't ready for that. Humans aren't ready for that."

"I take it humans will come out worse off?" Abbie asked.

Annwyn put down her glass. "We aren't sure." She studied her glass and then looked up and met Abbie's gaze. "There are many more humans than supernaturals and we know from the past that humans will attack and root out difference. Not only supernaturals, but their own kind. What we do know is that there could be suffering on both sides and it's important to avoid that."

"But my life. You can't expect me to give up my life, my everything?" she wailed some more, realising that it is exactly what they were asking.

Dane's expression was sad. "For now, at least. Werewolves do integrate well with humans. Many live and work alongside others, without humans knowing about their true nature. You might be able to as well, in time."

"Might," she said, with rising hysteria. "Why do I not like the sound of that?"

Dane frowned. "You were in the public eye. News of the incident is out in the world; the police are involved. For now, your career is definitely on hold, because we can't reasonably explain your disappearance."

Rolf cleared his throat. "Maybe we should head back to the shed. There's been enough excitement for one night. With the full moon coming within the week, it's going to be hard for Abbie to control these new urges."

"As well as dealing with selfishness," Annwyn added, crossing her arms across her chest, and glaring as if it was her life that had been taken away. Abbie narrowed her gaze at the other woman, rankled. There was an odd spice to her scent. Rolf flicked his gaze to Annwyn and then to Dane.

Abbie went to open her mouth, but a pinch on her thigh from Rolf stopped the words. She turned to glare at him. Something in his look cooled her anger. She turned back to Annwyn, recollecting that she'd lost her life and her body, her humanness she supposed. "Thank you for the delicious meal."

Rolf's shoulders lowered and he sighed.

Dane nodded. "You're welcome. I'll talk to you in the morning. Mick is out looking into another report. I should know more by morning."

Rolf nodded. "Come on, Abbie."

He took her by the arm, guiding her outside and along the path. Annwyn could be heard murmuring to Dane as they left. Feeling a bit numb about the news about her career, she went willingly. Her desire to continue the hot sex with him was dampened for the moment. "Another report?" she asked Rolf as he led her to the shed.

"Another unnatural transformation. You weren't the only one affected. I told you that you were the first to survive."

"I see ... and will you have to fuck them, too?" She hated how pitiful and needy that comment sounded.

"I'll explain how things work again when we get to the shed," Rolf said.

"I want to know now." She stood still, resisting the pull of his hand.

He gave a grunt of frustration. "It depends on the situation."

"Oh, so you'll fuck them and what else does it depend on?"

"The need. Who else is available."

"Bullshit!" She got in front him and stopped him with two hands to his chest. "If that's the case, what gave you the right to be there with me?" She was smarting and hurting and confused on top of it all. She was connected to him, even before this curse or transformation thing. If he was doing it out of some kind of duty, she wasn't going to put up with it and didn't want to examine her feelings about it either. At the same time, if he'd been doing it to others, too, well she didn't like where that took her. She had never experienced murderous rage before: it was a scary feeling.

He lowered his head, meeting her gaze directly. "The situation, the need ... and the desire."

She stepped back. "You desired me?"

A growl was all the reply she got as he opened the shed door, and he was on her before she even drew breath. She made a low sound in her throat.

CHAPTER 7

Later, as she lay in his arms making circles with her fingertip around his nipples, she asked. "So, what if it's a guy that's transitioning?"

He sighed and turned his head to meet her eye. "Again, depends on the situation. Natural transformations usually take place within the pack. We know who is ready to transition and their family supports them. As alpha I have some involvement."

"So you fuck men, too?"

"No necessarily. I mean, I have done when it was required. But that's maybe twice ... Often the females of the pack help relieve the sex urges. I help with the fight urge. My pack must recognise and respect me as alpha. Sometimes teaching a wolf who is boss means I have to beat them in a fight and make sure they obey me. Our safety depends on that."

This was food for thought. "Have I acknowledged you as alpha?"

He turned to her, tipped her face to his with a finger under her chin. "No, you have not. There will be a formal ceremony. I'm sure you will submit to my will then."

"Do I have to?" she asked.

"If you want to stay in my pack, yes."

"Can't we just fuck and hang out instead?" She liked that idea.

He chuckled. "I'm afraid there's more to being a werewolf that hanging out and fucking. Although there's nothing wrong with that." He rolled on her and demonstrated.

In the morning, Abbie came awake feeling slightly sore and tired from over exertion. Grey light filtered in through the open door. The air smelled of rain, rotting leaves and dogs. Rolf and Dane were talking quietly, standing huddled by the door.

All night she and Rolf had been at it like rabbits. Rolf had said it was the moon that gave them the stamina and the energy to keep going. Her sexual experience with Rolf was the first time in her life she liked it a tad rough. It was also the first time she'd aggressively pursued her sexual partner. Despite the rough play, mostly initiated by her, she was feeling pretty good about the experience. It was as if all of the self-restraint and long-held inhibitions had been ripped away. Sex with Rolf was liberating. Being a wolf was liberating. Her strength and new-found aggression were as surprising as they were exhilarating. It was as if the wolf inside her pushed her to the edge and she had to be careful not to fall off.

A sheet covered her. Rolf must have tossed it on her when Dane came calling. She wanted a few more hours sleep. Instead, she rolled over and listened to their conversation.

"I'd much prefer to see Abbie through her first full moon before we go off on some mission," Rolf said. "It's important to me that she be ready and there are still risks, as you know. She has little control."

Dane leaned in closer, hand out as if pleading. "Can't your second do that for you? There are two more instances in Sydney."

Rolf's back stiffened. "There are three packs in Sydney that can deal with it," Rolf said flatly. "I'm not passing the care of Abbie to another wolf." He shook his head. "No way."

Abbie realised they had been discussing it for some time. Dane stepped back and straightened. "I can see this is your last word on this."

"It is. Pack comes first. Abbie is my pack now."

Dane's eyes shifted to hers and he acknowledged her with the briefest of nods and left.

Rolf stood there staring at the door for some minutes before he went into the kitchenette. "Hungry?" he asked with his head in the fridge.

Abbie sat up. "Most definitely. What's on the menu?"

He pulled his head out of the fridge. "I have steak, steak and eggs, steak and bacon and maybe bacon and eggs if you want to be a puss."

"A puss? Is that meant to be insulting?" She tossed a pillow that landed at his feet. "You'll pay for that insult."

Rolf grinned and pulled out a plate of steak. "I hope so ... well?"

The gas flared to life under the frypan. Abbie took herself off to the bathroom.

"Not too cooked, please," she said, poking her head out of the bathroom door.

He nodded. "Of course. Trust me."

Abbie had the strange urge for rare steak. She peed and had a quick wash. She'd hold off on the shower until Rolf could join her. She stepped back out, still naked and happy to be so. Rolf grinned as he warmed two huge steaks in the pan, searing the outside a light grey. He appeared to enjoy cooking. The aroma had her pacing the room, salivating. She was ready to pounce on Rolf or on the steak. "Why am I feeling like this?" she asked Rolf, coming to a halt in the centre of the room, clutching at her upper arms as if cold.

"Sit," he said.

She sat down at the small table by the window. He slid the steaks onto a plate in front of her. She cut into the meat and on seeing the red flesh, she wolfed down the first mouthful and had the second piece by her lips before she'd swallowed.

Rolf took a seat and, as he was busy eating down his own steak, he didn't answer her question straight away. Cutting up steak was taking too long. Abbie dropped her knife and picked up the steak with her hands and bit into it, licking the blood from her lips. She took another bite and another. Nothing had ever tasted so good. All her thoughts centred on the food, just as they had previously centred on sex. She knew in some part of her mind that there was more to life than this, but somehow couldn't keep that thought in her brain. It was like all her self-control had fled in the path of the wolf and her brain had run off to Hawaii for the summer.

When they had finished eating, Rolf looked at her, gaze intense and one eyebrow raised. With that one look Abbie was ready for sex again. She got up from her chair as Rolf did the same. She shook herself and put a hand to his advancing chest, which took a lot of self-control. "Why am I feeling like this?" she asked, already shuddering from his closeness, the feel on his hot skin under her fingertips, the scent of him in the air between them. She thought all the sex would take the edge off. Instead, it was worse. She was petrol and he was the naked flame.

Rolf's lips shifted into a smug smile. "Full moon," he said. "First full moon. That's not to say the moon change isn't always intense, but the first time is powerful. All your senses on high alert, all your passions riding you ... just like I'll be riding you." She dropped the hand that was holding him at bay. "And you also find me eminently fuckable." He leaned down and nipped at her neck. Electricity rushed through her, enlivening every cell. "Then," he continued, his breath hot on her neck. "We transform tonight into our wolf form. We run, we hunt."

"And then after that?"

"We change back," he said as he began to nibble on her ear. "Maybe we fuck again."

"Maybe?" she asked, challenging.

"Most probably," he said before his mouth closed over hers and she engaged his tongue in play and then going deeper, smashing her lips against his. They didn't even get to move from where they stood. She was in his arms, legs around his waist, fucking him for all she was worth. There was so much power in her body, her muscles, that she was doing most of the work and still she had energy. Being a werewolf was exhilarating. After a couple of long fuck sessions, they napped on the bed through the afternoon.

After that, she was tense and fretful as the moon made its presence known. Her skin was itchy. She felt hot and bothered and fractious. To distract herself she snuggled into Rolf's shoulder and asked, "Tell me what you were arguing about with Dane this morning?"

"We weren't arguing." He ran his fingers through her hair, loosening the tangles he'd made.

"Discussing then."

"Let's walk and talk. If we stay here, I'm going to want you again."

They dressed in jeans and T-shirts. As they stepped outside scents assailed her, little sounds in the bush had her on alert. It was hard to focus on what Rolf was saying. Perhaps Rolf was doing this on purpose. He must know what being outside was doing to her. It was as if her nose had never smelled before and her ears had never heard, so crisp were her senses, so alive to the life around them. Then the intensity of the moon gnawed on her essence, threatening to pull at the tendrils of her mind and body and tug them away.

Rolf came to a stop and turned to face her, his eyes bright like a cat's. "I'm helping him track down the rogue sorcerer who is casting these spells. There were more transformations in Sydney yesterday. Dane wanted me to go with him to investigate."

"And you didn't go because of me?"

Rolf eased his neck to first one side then the other. "Yes."

"Dane said someone else could look after me. Is that true?"

Rolf grimaced and avoided meeting her eye.

"Well?"

He met her gaze. "Technically, yes. My second, Tim."

Abbie didn't like the idea of letting Rolf out of her sight and of having another male being close to her.

"What does that mean? He gets to fuck me?"

Rolf's face tensed and he didn't answer. She was right then.

"Are you here with me for duty or preference?"

"Both."

That was an ambiguous and annoying response. Abbie growled in frustration and the sound, quite loud, surprised her.

Rolf laughed.

"That's not funny and you're avoiding the issue."

"I'm not. It's true. I am alpha and I'm seeing you through your first full moon as is my right and my duty."

"But you acknowledged a preference." Her gaze was intense, her mouth tight with the potential for rebellion.

He stepped closer, hands on her elbows. "I did. I don't want anyone else in my pack fucking you." Rolf froze after uttering the last word.

She suspected he hadn't meant to say that. "Do you mean I'd have to?" She threw out a hand as if someone else was there. "Fuck some random dude?"

Rolf shook his head. "There is no compelling you. No one will force you. You would want to, if the moon's need was on you. If I wasn't here, you'd fuck any available wolf or human, I suppose."

She made a vomiting noise. "That's so not true. I'm no slut." She had the urge to smash him in the face for saying so.

"It is true and no human labels, if you please. Non-mated wolves can fuck whoever they like, and often do."

Rage trembled under her skin. "I want to fuck you! I don't want to fuck anyone else."

"You say that now, but tonight with your first full moon it will be different. You think these last few days have been intense. That doubles, maybe triples, tonight. You will fuck anyone after we transform back into human form, because the wolf will still be riding you."

Abbie nodded, her mind calculating, thinking it through. "Then you can't stop me from fucking other werewolves?" His eyes widened fractionally, unable to mask his surprise. A smile twitched her lips. "I can fuck them all if I want to? Every single one?" She sensed the increased tension in him, the wave of anger rolling off him, and revelled in it. He was not just performing his duty. He wanted her. She turned out of his embrace, but he jerked her back.

"Try it," he said, his voice revealing a savagery that Abbie responded to on a deeper level. Heat flooded her loins. She wanted him right there under the white ghost gum tree.

"I might just do that." She didn't laugh, but sent him a saucy smile and started to walk off.

"That tears it." Rolf growled.

Too quick for her to react, he lifted her up and threw her over his shoulder. Abbie was half-laughing and half-screaming. "What are you doing?" she asked as he carried her, slapping his back and wriggling to escape his hold.

"Taking you back to the shed."

"Why?"

Obviously, she wasn't the only one on edge due to the full moon. In a few minutes, he kicked open the door and threw her down on the bed. His T-shirt ripped as he tore it off with a roar.

"Take off your clothes," he barked.

"Ask me nicely," she said with exaggerated sweetness, even while she was shaking with raw need. A girl had to take a stand, exercise some restraint, and maybe control the situation. His emotion slammed into her like an avalanche. She realised he'd been hiding his feelings from her these last few days. She could not name all that she could sense from him: passion, possession, lust. This situation was ripe sensual danger. Not just to her body, but also her mind and her heart.

A disgustingly handsome, sexy male towered over her, muscles quivering, need pouring off him in waves. She could tell that he was close to this moon shift, that it was playing with his self-control.

"Take off your clothes, please," he barked.

With a yelp, Abbie had her jeans down to her ankles in no time, but she barely had time to kick them free of her feet before he was on her.

"Do you want to fuck?" he asked hoarsely, tearing her T-shirt off as he bit down on her shoulder.

"God yes! Fuck me, damn it," she said then screamed as he entered her.

Rolf was a virile male and he had stamina plus. Her wolf revelled in the rutting and so did she.

Her mind whited out for a moment, taken away on a river of lust and sensation. Rolf was so good. He felt so good. Lust and power rolled off him and into her. She rode the sensations as he rode her. She came fast, but he was still going hard. "Again," he demanded as he flipped her sideways, her right leg on his shoulder and he surged deeper. Abbie dutifully came again, so quick it felt like a minute. He turned her again, taking her doggy style. She had to hold firm to the bedhead against his onslaught. A big powerful werewolf. There was no mistaking him.

Sometime later, she lay sprawled against him, limbs wrapped around him, their sexes touching, and sighed. Maybe life as a werewolf wasn't that bad after all.

Before moonrise the pack gathered in the ranges. Rolf introduced Abbie to the other members of the pack, though her mind was so full of moon energy she could barely remember their names. Rolf kept hold of her, literally keeping his arm around her waist, while they ate barbequed meat and chatted. Abbie started to shake, dropping the remains of her food to the ground. "Rolf?" she said a might shakily.

"I'm here," he said, giving her a reassuring squeeze. "Don't worry. It's the moon. The change is coming."

Abbie looked to the horizon where a pale-yellow glow blushed over the edge of the ranges. Her mind sank into that light. Sharp pain seized her and the cry in her mouth sounded strange. It was the beast coming for her, coming for her mind. A voice in her ear urged her to relax, urged her to accept the beast, but she chose to fight.

"Abbie!"

With bone cracking sounds in her ears, she moaned and tasted blood. She wanted to rend flesh with her claws. Then she was off into the bush, to the smells, and the noises and the animals, the prey. Another ran with her. A large wolf with yellow eyes. He nudged her with a shoulder and directed her down a path. She snapped at him and then aimed for his throat. Rolling together, jaws gnashing, teeth biting, they struggled.

Abbie didn't want to give in. She wanted to hurt him, to allow her rage free rein, and the larger wolf gave a great heave, flinging her off. Landing on her side, she jumped to her feet and away she ran, free of pursuit, free of him. She forgot about him, become lost to the wolf who invaded her mind. Lost to the call of the wild, she breathed in the scents and sought warm, bloody flesh.

Later, as the moon continued to ride the sky, she sensed the others in the pack. Each beast's mind had a different flavour. She knew them better in wolf form than in human. One mind was large and strong. It was him, following her but keeping his distance. Rolf. The alpha. Abbie was drawn and repulsed by him. It was a war in her mind, her heart, her instinct.

I will not submit. I want to submit. I will not!

Across a creek bed, the luscious water dampening her paws. She lapped, washing the blood from her mouth. She ran up to the ridge, in the direction of the road. Her shadow wolf followed but did not intercept. She'd had his blood on her tongue. She would not be dominated. Refused to be dominated. She wanted to dominate him.

A track loomed out of the shadows and the scent of fresh meat lured her onto it. Tongue lolling, she tasted the aroma on the air. Hunger. It grew in her mind until she could not control the desire for that meat. She had to have that food. No one else. She ran, faster and faster.

Through the haze of her hunger, the emotions and impulses in her brain, she noted that someone lingered nearby. A human, but their scent was strange, somewhat tangy. They were near the source of the meat smell.

Abbie's instinct to protect her right to the food made her put on a burst of speed. Bursting out into a clearing, she stopped abruptly, her hind legs not quite getting the command, so that she bunched up. *Danger!* The word filled her mind. Nose sniffing, she definitely smelt the meat and something else.

Her eyes darted, trying to make sense of the turmoil in her mind and the way the images were conveyed to her mind. A light shimmered and flashed. Someone had been waiting. For what? she wondered. Edging out into the clearing, the smell of meat distracted her. Why had someone waited with the meat? Were they still there? Abbie fought her need to eat the meat—the bloody flesh smell teasing her nostrils, baiting her tongue. She waited, suspicious, cautious and then she could no longer sense the human.

It was uncanny how her caution overrode the hunger she felt gnawing at her. Abbie sniffed some more, checking that the human was indeed gone. The meat was still there. She snarled, even though she was trying to smile. Her shadow touched the food before she did. If she wanted the food, she needed to get it now before he came. Before he ate it. Before he took it from her. *Rolf!*

Stepping further into the clearing Abbie drew closer to the meat. The scent was divine. Drool formed and dropped to the bare earth. As she neared it, she caught the other scent again, the human one. Certain the human was gone, she stepped closer. A whole side of lamb lay in the centre of the clearing. A few flies hovered over the stump of the neck. *Meat and bone!* The beast inside her wanted to rip and tear and gulp. But the other her was there and she questioned. Why is the meat there? Rolf didn't mention that someone would leave meat for the pack. She circled the meat. It could be a test. It could be poisoned.

Rolf, her shadow wolf, drew near. He had her scent and maybe that of the carcass. He was close now, still on the track. Abbie whimpered as instinct and intellect warred. *Eat! Eat! No. Wait!* The temptation was winning. She took a step closer, tail down.

Suddenly, a bright light blazed. Her head jerked up, eyes dazzled. A spotlight? Powerful, bright. She froze. *Danger!* The impression was of a man standing there, a flavour and sight familiar but unlabelled. He held something long, something that he aimed in her direction.

A whine leaked from her mouth. The smell of the raw meat filled her head. She should run. Must run.

The rapid click of claws scrabbling against the rocks approached. A growl. A howl, one that summoned the others.

A loud bang pierced the night.

A sting to her hindquarters. The impact made her legs buckle. She was on the ground. Abbie lay in the dirt, a cry leaving her mouth. Something had happened. She'd been hurt. She'd been shot!

A wolf form straddled her prone body. The spotlight went out. No more shots rang out. No other sounds. No cars leaving the area. Just a hint of spice in the air. Abbie filed it away. She had to remember that smell, these details. The beast had to remember.

Rolf stepped away, his body no longer sheltering hers. He whined and licked her face. Abbie twisted upright and tried to stand. Taking a step, she limped and whined. There was pain and blood. She could smell her blood.

Small holes in her fur, blood leaking down to drip onto the dirt. Pellets, she thought. A shotgun.

Turning her head, she licked at the wound, tasted blood. Why had someone shot her? Her skin shook as she trembled. The knowledge of what had been done to her had taken her over. She'd been shot. On purpose. She must remember that. The meat was a trap.

Rolf let out a howl that made her stagger. Around her, wolves converged. The moon set as she whimpered in pain.

Rolf growled and paced and she realised he was struggling for some reason. He was pushing and pulling mentally at his form. A kind of magic that only he could wield. It was like the rest of them but he had more of it and was strong enough to manipulate it. She could taste it and him on her tongue. Then he changed into human form, effort etched onto his features as he fell to his knees in the dirt next to her. He panted, struggled to right himself.

Next thing she knew, he knelt on one knee, strong hand stroking her ruff. She sniffed at him. It was definitely Rolf. *Rolf. Lover. Alpha. Dominance. Fear.*

"Abbie! Let me see," he said.

He pressed along her flank until she nipped at him when he touched the wound. "It's all right. Just a flesh would. You caught a few pellets."

"Stay here. The pack will look after you. I'll fetch help."

He sent a message to the gathered wolves. *Guard. Protect. Kill any who mean harm.*

Orders understood, he let out a strangled cry as he returned to wolf form and bounded into the bush. A wrench tore at her gut when he left her. *Rolf!*

A female wolf lowered to her front paws and approached, making whiny noises. She licked at Abbie's wound. A younger male came close and licked Abbie's face. She let him for a short time and then nipped at his muzzle to make him back off. The other males in the pack circled around her, sniffing the air, watching her. Their yips and whines rose into the chill night air.

None approached the meat that still sat there. Abbie rested her head on her paws, suddenly feeling sick and low. Her vision grew blurry, her heartbeat erratic. The female whined and another male licked the back of her neck.

A car approached on the road above. Her ears pricked up and her nose caught familiar scents. The wolves around her stood alert. Rolf howled as the car door opened and he bolted out of the car. The sound of his passage echoed in the night as his claws clicked on the track, scraping rocks and skidding on dirt and leaves. Dane made his way down the side of the hill from the road, following Rolf's path. He carried a little box in his hand. A first-aid kit, Abbie thought. He also had a lantern.

Rolf returned to human form and held her head in his hands. "No biting, okay?" he said to her, grabbing her by the ruff. But Abbie couldn't bite anyone with Rolf holding her like that. She kicked out when pain hit her flank as Dane tried to probe the wound. Dane then leaned on her so she couldn't scramble away. The other wolves stepped back so that they ringed the clearing. None were going to interfere and stop these two from hurting her, from helping her.

"Hold her a bit tighter," Dane said through clenched teeth. "I'm about to dig these pellets out."

He turned the lamp on and turned it up bright. The rest of the pack faded from view. Only their panting breath could be heard over the frightened beating of her heart. "Thank the lady that you're able to revert to human at full moon," Dane said as he used tweezers to remove a pellet. The wound burned. Abbie whimpered with the pain. Dane held up a small piece of metal. "These pellets are silver."

"What?" Rolf growled out. "Then it was deliberate? Aimed at us?"

Dane dug into her wound again and then again. Rolf held her firm: she couldn't bite Dane or Rolf, no matter how much she wanted to. The pain of his probing tugged and burned. She wanted it to stop, but feelings of weakness swamped her, making her thoughts fuzzy.

Dane made a noise of disgust. "Looks like it. No other reason to use silver bullets." He dabbed disinfectant on her wound and Abbie struggled as it stung.

After packing up the kit, Dane stood and stared down at her. "I think we should get Annwyn to look at that carcass. It might be spelled." He walked around the side of lamb and then came back. "Let me see if I can speed the healing up."

Dane laid his hand over Abbie's wound. She experienced heat and her head cleared. "Put her in the car. I'll bring the meat."

Rolf picked her up. She was a big wolf, but he was strong. He buried his face in her neck fur. "Abbie!" It was an impassioned plea, as if he really cared for her. She tried to keep that thought for later, but the wound and the excitement zapped her strength. Dane helped him carry her back up to the road. Then he went back for the meat, slamming the boot lid, before getting into the driver's seat.

She had her head in Rolf's lap, while he scratched behind her ears. "Why would someone suddenly try to kill one of my pack?" Rolf asked.

"I don't know. What effect would the silver have on a wolf, a newly whelped one?"

Rolf stiffened. "With the silver in her system, if the pellets hadn't killed her, she wouldn't be able to revert to human form. Without treatment, she'd sicken and die over a number of days."

"Hmmm," Dane said.

Rolf tensed. "You think they were after Abbie specifically?

Dane made a noise that Abbie couldn't quite understand. "Yes. She's new. She's different. She has been cursed and that's exactly why I think they're after her. Abbie is the only successful changeling from this curse. Obviously, the goal isn't creating more weres but the exposure, the disruption and panic that would ensue should our world be laid open to the human one."

"Abbie is a powerful wolf," Rolf said. "She's alpha. Maybe she's a danger to this rogue sorcerer, but I don't know how. Even as a powerful werewolf she couldn't hurt this person, this sorcerer, could she?"

Dane was silent for a few moments. Then he said, his voice low and thoughtful. "Maybe she can recognise him. I'm pretty sure it's a him."

Rolf stared down at her. "Yes, but only if she can revert back into human form. It's always a risk on the first full moon, even with pure weres, that they don't shift back, that we lose them to the wolf. With a cursed one, it is hard to say. She did lose herself tonight. She forgot who I was. And then she's powerful. I found it hard to contain her. With silver in her system, the risk of staying wolf is greater. She may never come back to me ... us."

Dane cursed under his breath. "If she's as strong as you say, she'll find a way. Until then, it's back to the shed."

Rolf nodded. "I'll stay with her. She's my responsibility."

Dane chuckled. "I won't argue with you. Will you be all right? The pack?"

"They'll be all right. Tim will look after things."

Tyres ate gravel as the Dane slammed on the brakes. The car door opened, and Rolf lifted her into his arms. Dane helped him to carry her the short distance to the shed. The sensor light flicked on, illuminating the door. Strands of night lingered around the shed. Branches rustled in the light breeze.

That room, that shed. It was where they were taking her. Abbie found she didn't mind. She would be safe there. Rolf would look after her.

It wasn't long before she was back on the bed, being stroked by Rolf. Abbie was smiling on the inside. Rolf's fingers where sure and strong and each stroke made her more and more relaxed.

Dane stopped by the door. "I'll go wake Annwyn and get back to you if she finds anything."

Rolf farewelled Dane and then got up to pull on jeans and a T-shirt. Abbie wanted to object. She didn't mind his naked form so close to hers. His heat reached through her fur to her skin. His scent filled the air around her.

Abbie closed her eyes, trying to sublimate the throbbing in her flank. Rolf re-joined her on the bed, and he cuddled close to her, stroking her, and soon they were both asleep.

Voices woke her a short time later. A woman's voice. It was Annwyn.

Abbie was instantly alert. Beast and human occupied the same space. Morning sun filtered in through the blinds. She'd been asleep for a while then.

"The meat had a death curse," Abbie was saying.

Rolf stood close to her. Annwyn was touching Rolf again. Abbie's lips lifted from her fangs.

"Do you recognise who the caster is?" Rolf asked, standing very still.

Something weird was happening with Annwyn. Abbie could taste it. It was Annwyn and not Annwyn. "It's him," she hissed, then she reached out and feather-touched Rolf's bulge through his jeans. There was no mistaking it. Annwyn was coming on to Rolf.

"Nira?" Rolf said, stepping back.

Abbie shot to her feet, wavered and then growled. *Hands off! Mine!*

Annwyn and Rolf turned toward her. Annwyn had a triumphant grin.

Annwyn's eyes were funny; her scent strange. "Down girl. I'm only playing. Rolf and I have an arrangement."

"Abbie," Rolf said, a grating sound that was almost a growl. "Wait."

Abbie growled again and took a step closer, hackles high.

"Just try it and I'll transport you to the pound," the not-Annwyn said.

Confused, Abbie yipped at Rolf. A question.

Rolf eased his shoulders. "It's Nira. The sorceress. Sometimes she surfaces. It's not anything I can't handle. I'll explain later."

Abbie had the sense that there was more to this *handling* than she liked. Stuck in wolf form, she couldn't do much about it. But in human form, she could rip the woman's hair out and maybe cuff her. And she could bonk Rolf to within an inch of his life, so he'd have nothing left for this Annwyn-Nira.

Rage surged up inside. How dare this Nira touch Rolf, her mate.

Nira's feather-touch to Rolf's equipment grew more assertive. "Just a little bit, where I like it. You know Dane doesn't mind if you do the anal."

Abbie's vision grew red. There was magic in the room. It swirled and insinuated itself in her nostrils, her mouth. Along with the moon's energy that still surrounded her, there was power building in her, under her skin, on her tongue. It combined with the jealous rage in her mind. There was no way she was going to watch a little bum party while in wolf form. There was no way she was letting whoever that was have her Rolf while she stood around watching. Pulling all her energy forward, she pictured her own human form.

"Don't Nira," Rolf was saying, trying to keep out of reach. "Annwyn pull yourself together."

"It's the magic," Annwyn said. "It's from him. It's made Nira stronger. I'm trying to fight it." Annwyn's voice was distant.

Pain filled Abbie's body, her mind, her soul. Ripping, tearing, searing and she kept the agony in. She had to be quick and quiet.

Rolf held Nira away from him, his muscles bulging with the effort. "I can't control you and Abbie at the same time. Stop it."

Abbie stepped forward, grabbed Nira's shoulder and swung her around. "Keep your hands off my man."

Nira's eyes widened. "Your man? Hardly," she said and laughed. "Rolf belongs to no one. Know your place."

Nira turned to Rolf, anger moulding her features. "Go on. Show her she's nothing but one of your wolf bitches. *Fuck me*."

Abbie didn't really know what happened next. A blanket of rage surged through her. When she was aware again and shaking her head, Nira was sitting on the ground against the wall, out cold.

Abbie's fist ached and she stood there panting as the red rage lifted from her mind and she came back to herself.

"Abbie?" Rolf's surprise was almost comical. He went directly to Annwyn to check on her.

She towered over Rolf as he bent to make the sorceress more comfortable. "If you ever fuck that bitch, I'll know. You understand? I can taste that weird sorceress's scent on my tongue."

Rolf blinked. "You can scent her?"

"Yes. And if you do, we are through."

Rolf's gaze hardened. "I think you have this way out of proportion. We fucked. That's it. You don't own me. I'm not your mate."

Abbie's eyebrows lifted. "Is that so? So, I'm free to fuck whoever I want?" She turned her head to the ranges where the pack still ranged. Some were even fucking at that moment, she supposed. "I can head back to the range ..."

Rolf shook his head. "No. That's not happening."

"Game, set and match."

"What?" he asked, skin blushing red from anger.

"You are mine," she said.

"You can't act like we're mates. It doesn't work like that."

"I think you'll find you're wrong about that. You're reasonably intelligent. You work it out."

Abbie went into the bathroom, looking for some clothes. Rolf came up behind her. "You're crazy, you know that?"

"If I'm crazy then you're the whole looney bin in one." She shut the door in his face.

She could sense Dane coming and wanted to face the repercussions of punching his wife out fully dressed.

"We're not mates!" he yelled at her through the door. "I don't submit to anyone."

Abbie got dressed, whistling to herself. She broke off when she had a thought. "If I can't fuck anyone else and you can't fuck anyone else, what does that make us? Priest and nun?"

There was no answer, but a few things were being bashed about in the kitchen. A pan or two. Breakfast, she thought when she smelled the gas ignite. She was quite certain when the aroma of bacon wafted into the bathroom. She inhaled and realised that her sense of smell was still acute, even in human form.

Raised male voices reached her. She decided to finger comb her hair until the argument quieted a bit. Annwyn had woken up and yelling started.

Abbie came out. Dane had Annwyn in his arms and was checking her bruised face, maybe healing it. Rolf stood rigid and angry with a frying pan in his hand. Dane's head shot up as she walked in.

"You do not get to assault Annwyn and get away with it," Dane said.

Abbie tensed. "She had her hands on Rolf's cock. She doesn't get away with that."

Dane stiffened slightly and angled his head to Rolf. "Rolf?"

"Bloody Nira. Something in the meat brought her out. She was pretty nasty to Abbie."

Dane stared down at Annwyn again. "You all right? Nira hasn't bothered you in months. Was it the spell?"

"I'm good." She turned to Rolf. "Sorry, Rolf."

Abbie waited. No apology coming her way, looked like.

"I think Nira has been here more recently than that," Abbie said, drawing out a chair and sitting on it.

Three sets of eyes turned to her. She shrugged. "I smelled Nira at dinner. Was that the night before last?"

Dane's head jerked up from examining his wife. "You smelled Nira?"

Rolf put another pot on the stove and shoved some eggs in there, whisking them like they had been misbehaving.

When Abbie didn't respond, he turned to Rolf. "Something you need to tell me?"

Rolf banged the pot and shoved at the bacon with a pair of tongs. They waited and then he turned to face them. His fists were clenched and the muscles in his jaw bunched.

"What is it?" Dane asked.

"Dammit. She can smell sorcerers."

Dane let out a loud sound and turned to her, leaving Annwyn to come up close. "You can smell sorcerers?" the sorcerer asked.

"Yes, can't everyone? I mean all werewolves?"

Rolf and Dane shared a look. "What do I smell like?" Dane asked.

Abbie didn't want to answer, sensing there was tension there and something she didn't quite understand. She shifted focus to Rolf, only he was back at the stove, killing the eggs and the bacon, his back stiff. No help there. Smoke rose from the pan. Abbie breathed and faced Dane. "You smell a bit like cinnamon."

"And Annwyn?" Dane's blond eyebrows arched.

"Normally, a bit like vanilla. But the other one, Nira, she's more like a chili-capsicum blend."

"And the man who shot you?"

Abbie tried to recall the scent of him. In the bush there were competing aromas. Rotting vegetation, a decaying bird, wombats and kangaroos; scents filling up the tracks between the trees. "Not sure. It's more the shape I remember. Half-vision. Half-scent."

"Excellent!" Dane said and smiled.

Rolf smashed a plate and stood there with the jagged piece in his hand. "No. I forbid it."

Abbie frowned. "Forbid who what?" She came forward and stepped around Rolf to peer in the pan. "Can I have those two pieces of un-cremated bacon and a double helping of eggs? Let me put some toast on."

Dane laughed. "Oh, Rolf. You have a lot to look forward to." Rolf tossed the broken piece of plate into the bin, drew out a fresh plate from the cupboard and dished up Abbie's breakfast.

Dane passed Abbie the butter from the fridge and then a knife. "Abbie. Would you be interested in a trip to Sydney? I need to sniff out a rogue sorcerer."

"Sure. I love Sydney." Then she thought about it. Rolf's stiff back, his apparent anger. "So, this ability to sniff out sorcerers isn't common among werewolves?"

"They can recognise them, but you're the first to tell them apart by scent," Dane said as Rolf put a French press full of coffee on the table. Rolf's lips turned down.

Annwyn poured herself a coffee and sat at the table opposite Abbie. "It must have something to do with the changeling curse. Perhaps part of the taint is this ability to smell sorcerers."

"Taint?" Abbie bristled. "Watch your mouth."

Annwyn blinked. "I'm sorry. I didn't mean to be offensive. This is all a bit weird. I meant that a residue of the sorcerer or his spell is inside you and is now part of your natural abilities. You're the only one to have survived so far, you see. Partly that is your bloodline and maybe Rolf's presence."

"Bloodline? What do you mean?"

"You're latent, apparently. Didn't Rolf tell you there's a werewolf in your ancestry?" She shrugged. "He also used his alpha powers to help you survive. And you're obviously very determined and stubborn, too."

Abbie's gaze flicked to Rolf. So, she owed him. That didn't give him rights over her, not unless he was prepared to grant her the same rights over him. Fair's fair. Belatedly she acknowledged that Annwyn had paid her a compliment.

Dane stood up, heading to the door. "I'll contact Rafael and let him know we're on to something."

Abbie put a hand out and touched Dane's arm. "One thing: Rolf comes too."

Annwyn looked at Rolf and at Abbie. Rolf was still in a grump. "I'd better get ready for the trip myself." She went to the door, looked at them both again. "See you later then."

Dane followed her. "Me too. A few things to do before we leave."

Alone with Rolf again, she watched as he ate the food, stabbing here and stabbing there, the fork clinking against the ceramic surface.

Abbie savoured her bacon, while watching the blackened bits on Rolf's plate break into smaller and smaller pieces.

Silence interspersed the sounds of eating. Abbie finished her meal and waited. There was a wall of something oppressive coming off Rolf, possibly this alpha-vibe thing, because it was familiar to her, like the smell of toast or the aroma of coffee well after they had been consumed. It was pushing against her resolve, and she chose to ignore it.

Rolf shoved the remains of his breakfast aside. Abbie noted that he hadn't eaten much, just smashed it down to tiny fragments with his knife and fork. He breathed heavily, shoulders rising and falling as if he was controlling a great rage.

She winced, while she waited, wondering if she should break the ice. As soon as she moved to put her plate away, Rolf surged out of the chair. "You're not going."

Abbie took a wide berth around him, continuing to take her plate to the sink. She held it out in front of her like a shield because he moved in front of her blocking her path.

"I said I'd help."

Rolf shook his head. "You aren't going? That's it."

Abbie narrowed her eyes. "You can't tell me what to do."

"I can. I'm your alpha. You're my responsibility."

"That's all a little new and weird to me. You need to come up with a better argument."

That wall of oppression grew stronger. "You will obey me or face the consequences."

Abbie tilted her head. "Is that your alpha power trip you're throwing at me? It's not working."

Rolf growl-shouted. "You will stay here. You're too vulnerable. Not ready. There could be complications."

Abbie flinched and then set her jaw, shaking her head. "That's why I'm not going anywhere without you."

"Stop trying to trap me."

He came for her then, knocking a chair flying. She dropped the plate in the sink, and it cracked in half. She sidestepped to the door. His hand came down on hers where she held the handle. "You do not walk away from me."

Abbie sneered. "I don't do this macho bullshit." And she body shoved him and slipped out. She turned and faced him. "Either you come with me or shut the fuck up about it."

Rolf slammed the door and didn't come after her. She jogged down the drive and lingered by the gate. Even though the wound on her thigh was healing quickly it still pinched. After all the excitement, she needed to chill. A nice piece of shade opened up for her, so she parked herself there and stretched out. Let Rolf calm down a bit before she faced him again. The thing was, she wanted to obey him and that whole wall of oppression thing did intimidate her, but she knew she had to make a stand now or she'd lose this battle for good. Rolf was used to being obeyed, particularly by members of his pack. She didn't remember much of her first full moon, but she'd seen the looks, the envy from more than just the female members.

She wasn't stupid. All of his pack would obey him and die for him. So would she, if it came down to it. But she wasn't going to let him know that. If he didn't respect her, if he didn't value her, then she was just another pack female, available for fucking and nothing more. She wasn't going to settle for that. No, she wanted more than that. Needed more than that. Besides, something powerful within her wanted to dominate, to give the orders as well. She knew in her bones that she was meant to do more than just take orders. She was meant to lead. And she knew he knew it too. If their sexual encounters meant anything at all, it was to teach her that. She was his equal. She was his mate. He just needed more time to let that fact settle in, then perhaps a bit more to accept it.

Looking back, it had been obvious in that kiss in the nightclub, when she was just Abbie McGregor, TV journalist. Now she was Abbie McGregor, investigative werewolf and mother-fucking sex queen. A smile grew as she snuggled into the crook of her arm. *Rolf, alpha werewolf, you can suck it up.* Her smile widened when she thought of the ways he could make it up to her.

CHAPTER 8

The twisted corpse made Abbie's eyes hurt and her head spin. She wanted to vomit, but to do so would seriously jeopardise her status as an investigative werewolf. That could have been her. Those mangled remains could have been her body. *What sort of sick fuck does that to strangers, to random people who haven't done any harm?*

They were standing in a warehouse, dark and dank; it made the smell of decay worse. "Is it the same?" Dane asked.

Her eyes flicked to him and to the brooding presence of Rolf behind him. The slovenly, bearded alpha of the Penrith pack, Joe Stubbings, stood beside her. Short, plump, but muscled, he'd already rubbed up against her twice, luckily out of Rolf's sight. Sergio, the North Sydney alpha, hadn't been as smart when he touched her and now had a broken arm thanks to Rolf. Dane had lost patience with his werewolf buddy. Annwyn just kept her distance from Rolf and Dane. Nothing dumb about her.

She'd confirmed it was the same spell. Abbie had to tell them about the scent. Was it one sorcerer or were they dealing with many?

"It smells like the same guy," she said, licking her lips to check the taste of him.

Dane let out a long breath. "So just one rogue sorcerer? That's a relief, but also a puzzle. How could this one do so much harm? How is he targeting his victims?"

Annwyn came forward, avoiding looking at the corpse. "Why don't you summon Rafael? Perhaps he can advise us where to from here."

Dane bit his lip and shook his head. "Rafael said he has a lead in the northern hemisphere and doesn't have the time to travel here."

"Does that mean we go to him?" she asked, a twinkle in her eye. "I'd love to see his castle again."

Dane shook his head. "He hasn't invited us." He shared a look with Rolf. "Beside, Rolf doesn't like to travel by magic."

Rolf coughed. There had been a huge discussion about how they would travel to Sydney. In the end they flew on a commercial flight and picked up a car at the airport. "I didn't exactly say that, but we don't know how Abbie will react. She's still new."

Stubbings grinned at Rolf. "You could always leave her here. I'll take good care of her. She won't even know you're gone."

Rolf exuded tension, jaw clenched, shoulders hunched, fists balled. She wondered if the Penrith alpha knew how close he was to getting his throat ripped out. Abbie stepped closer to Rolf, put her hand on his forearm and squeezed. "I wouldn't stay without my alpha," she said in a smooth, purring voice, which was a direct imitation of Nira as expressed through Annwyn. The sorceress's eyes widened and Dane frowned. Rolf just harrumphed.

"Annwyn, do you recognise the pattern of the spell?" Dane asked.

Annwyn took another look and shook her head. "It's been too long. There isn't much left. I think it's designed to decay quickly."

Dane's head shot up. "You mean that whoever has done this knows you can see spells?"

Annwyn shrugged. "I don't know. It's been a few days. The spell could have dissipated naturally, I guess." She squeezed her bottom lip between her forefinger and thumb, her eyes lingering on the corpse. Meeting Dane's gaze, she said, "I think that designing the spells to disintegrate is a good tactic." She shook her head. "I wouldn't discount it."

"You need a fresh one then," Abbie said.

Annwyn sniffed and didn't look in Abbie's direction. "What she said," she replied to Dane.

Abbie detected that spice again. Was that Nira making Annwyn so bitchy? Dane turned to Stubbings. "Contact the other Sydney alphas and pass on my phone number. At the first sign of one of these curses in action, you get them to call me. Got it?"

Stubbings nodded, then caught Abbie's eye and winked. She wanted to smash his face in and took a step, but Rolf was ahead of her. "You respect my ... um, Abbie."

The grizzly alpha smirked and tucked Dane's number away in his top pocket. "I'm paying her a lot of respect." He winked at Abbie again and dropped his gaze to her breasts. "She could have my cubs if she wants."

"We don't have time for this, Rolf, Joe." It was Dane who interposed himself between Rolf and the other alpha.

Rolf lifted a fist. "You're mated, you jerk," he hissed at the sloppily dressed alpha. Abbie thought that meant off limits to other females.

"I know. I can but dream." Stubbings grinned a feral grin. "And I can poke you in your pompous ass."

Dane leaned on his shoulder to hold him back. Rolf backed down and shook his head. "Let's go."

Abbie stuck close to Rolf, tasting the scent of his anger in the air. It was crisp and clean and cutting. She looked back over her shoulder at Stubbings and some of his pack, who were now dealing with the remains. If Stubbings could taste Rolf's anger, he had a lot more balls than she gave him credit for. She rubbed at her arms, feeling goosebumps rise. She couldn't help reacting that way. A thread of Rolf's anger scent scared her, made her want to obey; she had to consciously fight against it. It was irritating to always be on alert for his silent influence, always trying to fight it.

After they climbed into the car, they sat there in silence. Suddenly, Dane smacked the steering wheel. "Dammit!"

Annwyn caressed his arm. "We should wait in Sydney, in case there's another attack."

He glanced at her and nodded. "Then we should find a hotel."

"Not in this hole," Rolf said grumpily. He sat as far away from

Abbie as he could and the waves of displeasure rolling off him were giving her a headache. She'd done nothing wrong. She squeezed her fists, wanting to punch him hard in the face, but quelled the desire.

"Amen to that," Dane said. "Harbour views, it is." He put the car into gear and headed off.

Annwyn turned around to talk to them. "It would be easier if we could travel by magic. Are you sure Abbie isn't up for it, Rolf?"

Rolf stared out the window and chewed his lips.

"I'm willing to try it," Abbie said. "Sounds like fun."

"Shut up," Rolf snapped at her. To Annwyn he said, "It's too risky just now."

Abbie twisted in her seat, lifted her foot up and kicked him in the thigh. He grabbed her foot, his expression half surprise and half anger. "Stop!"

"Right, I will. But listen to this. First, don't tell me to shut up. Next, how do we minimise this risk you perceive? I don't want to be the one to jeopardise this hunt. What do I have to do to prove I can do this?"

Rolf glowered at her and pushed her foot away. "You dare challenge me?"

Annwyn faced the front hastily and whistled quietly. Abbie hadn't missed Annwyn's widened eyes when she'd kicked Rolf.

Abbie smiled lazily, not letting her tension show. "Yes, I do dare. Either speak to me properly or shut up."

Rolf grabbed her hand and tugged her towards him so that they were nose to nose. "You do not get to speak to me that way."

"You do not get to speak to me that way," she responded in the same way.

"Cut it out!" Dane said and braked suddenly at a set of lights. "You do not do this in my car. Can it!"

Annwyn chuckled. "Don't book them a room near us, for god's sake."

Dane glanced at her before setting off again. "Agreed."

Rolf gave Dane a sharp nod, their eyes meeting in the rear-view mirror, then he continued to glare at Abbie. She turned her face away and ignored him. They kept up their silent warfare until they were at the hotel.

"I want a separate room," Abbie said to Dane.

"No," Rolf replied and took her hand, dragging her a few steps away from the check-in counter.

She turned on him. "Why? Is that because it's too risky? I think you are full of bullshit. You just want to control me, and you know what? I won't be controlled." She'd been whisper-hissing at him and then stopped, hoping that no one had noticed. She shouldn't be making a scene. What if she was recognised?

Rolf seemed to understand, for he also stopped talking and just glared at her.

Dane tossed a key and Rolf caught it. "Come along, sweetheart," Rolf said, not bothering to try to touch her. Abbie followed him obediently, not willing to make a further scene in public. A few people looked in their direction and she noticed the security cameras. Definitely time for good behaviour.

Rolf exited the lift and she followed. Dane and Annwyn stayed in the lift and continued up to another floor. Sensible, Dane had got them rooms on a different floor. Rolf swaggered down the corridor with Abbie trailing behind. She found the view of his ass quite satisfying and figured that if she said so he'd be even more pissed at her.

He swung open the door and gestured for her to enter before him. Abbie sucked in a breath. The suite was gorgeous—muted beige tones, huge bed, large television on the wall. When she inspected the bathroom, she saw it contained a deep bath and a double shower. Quality toiletries littered the top of the vanity unit. Abbie mentally booked herself in for a long bath.

Through the open curtains, Abbie saw there was a balcony too. She stepped out onto it to a view of Circular Quay and the white sails of the Sydney Opera House perched on Bennelong Point. To the left she caught a glimpse of the struts of the Sydney Harbour Bridge. The breeze was warm and soft; overhead, white clouds cast shadows over the water.

The low murmur of Rolf's voice ordering room service reached her on the balcony. Abbie realised she was starving again, craving red meat and something else. She was hot again. Desire damn near burned through her skin. Thoughts of Rolf's naked form rubbing against her titillated her mind. Oh god, she was horny again, even though she wanted to smack that dominant bastard to hell and back. Damn him. Damn her.

She stayed on the balcony until the food arrived. Even then she hesitated, until he lifted the covers and the scent of red meat overpowered her will.

He looked up when she entered and held herself still by the curtains. He was cutting up the meat into bite-sized pieces.

"When's dinner" she asked.

"When I say so" he said, his shoulders jerking as he continued to cut the meat. "It's time you learned to submit."

That's going to be interesting, she thought. The wolf change had made her stronger; not just her sense of smell, but physically too. She might look small, but she packed a punch. She wished he'd take off his clothes so she could rub herself against him and fuck him senseless. The aroma of the meat caught her, drew her forward. Her focus was on the meat and the demanding growl in her belly.

"Take off your clothes," he said without looking at her.

She grinned. That was exactly what she wanted to do. She stripped off her jeans and tossed them on a chair. Her T-shirt ruffled her hair as she ripped it off. Her undies followed and then her bra.

"Kneel," he commanded, still not looking at her.

She knelt, tilted her head and studied him.

"Come closer on your knees," he said again, arranging the pieces of meat on the plate in little rows.

She shuffled forward, hoping not to get carpet burn. Not that she was a wuss, but she'd rather get carpet burn while rutting, not crawling meekly.

"Bow your head," Rolf said, his voice giving away nothing.

Abbie tried to stop herself laughing. She was not humouring him, as such, more like seeing where this were going.

She heard movement. "Keep your body still, but lift your head."

She did and he held a piece of meat out to her. "Eat this," he said and their eyes met. His yellow-tinted eyes seemed to glow. Abbie reacted like the fire in his eyes was in her belly. She opened her mouth, capturing his finger in her mouth and sucked and licked it as she took the meat from him. Rolf didn't move, didn't react.

"Bow your head again," he instructed and picked up another piece. He held the next piece of meat in front of her, the smell driving her nuts. Wouldn't he be surprised if she bit it taking the meat without his say-so.

"Lift your head."

She did and waited.

"Open your mouth," he said. When she did as she was told, he popped the meat in. She chewed.

"You're doing very well. Submission to your alpha is important."

Abbie lifted the corner of her mouth in a smirk. He held out another piece of meat. "Eat," he said. She took the meat and captured his finger in her mouth, licking and sucking it and she worked her way down to the soft skin between his fingers and caressed it with her tongue. He didn't pull his hand away. The fire in his eyes kindled further.

He withdrew his finger from her mouth and picked up another piece of meat. "If you don't learn to submit, you can't be a part of my pack."

She took the proffered meat and rubbed her face against his hand, her lips finding his thumb and took it into her warm mouth. The piece of meat was swallowed whole. He'd made them rather small after all. His breath hitched, but he did not remove his hand or his thumb from her mouth.

"You need to take this seriously."

She let his thumb go and licked her lips. "So, I'll be free to join another pack, if I can't be in yours?"

Rolf growled. "That's not the point of this exercise. I'm trying to teach you to submit to me. It's important for trust. The members of the pack won't be able to trust you, either, if you don't respect me, obey me."

"But I'd be free to leave and join another pack, if you don't want me?"

"Yes," he replied and picked up more meat. "But you'll have to submit to any alpha if you join their pack."

She took the meat and his hand lingered. She licked his palm, a big swirl of her moist tongue. She sat back on her heels and stared up at him, no trace of submission in her posture or tone. "What if I don't join a pack?"

That startled him. His eyes widened. "Not join a pack? You have to."

"Why? What if I create my own with me as alpha?"

The look on his face was priceless. Wide eyes, slack mouth. "A female alpha leading a pack?"

A small smile lifted her lips. "Yes. I'm up for it."

Rolf stilled, seeming to calm himself and, after a deep breath, took another piece of meat and held it out. This time she ignored the meat and licked his wrist, working her way up his arm. He didn't move. She stopped at the elbow and aimed for his mouth, catching his bottom lip.

"You have clothes on," she observed breathily.

He met her lips, kissed her hard, leaving her breathless. "You're impossible. I can taste your arousal. It's so potent I can't concentrate."

"I apologise for being so transparent." Her gaze dropped to his white T-shirt. "Are you taking that off, or do I have to go for a stroll to have my needs met?"

His response was a growl. He pushed her back, ripped his T-shirt off and dropped his jeans. He was wearing no underwear and his erect cock sprung free. She lifted one eyebrow in challenge. She wasn't the only one aroused.

He grabbed her by the arm and near tossed her on the bed. She rolled and he landed on her as she came face up. "Point one to me, I think," she said.

Rolf growled low in his throat and her sex responded, throbbing and wet. The steak was foreplay, as far as she was concerned. "Get in me now, you brute."

Rolf positioned himself and drove into her, capturing her gasp with his mouth. He moved in her, slow at first and then increasing the rhythm. "You're not going anywhere else. You will learn to submit to me. I am alpha."

"Shut up and fuck me."

And he did.

⁂

The call came early in the morning. They were downstairs and ready to get into the car within ten minutes. "It's Bondi, Waverley Park. Eastern Suburbs pack."

Rolf nodded. Abbie wondered at the exchange and looked to Rolf. "We've been in the area before," he answered her silent question.

Abbie looked away, detecting some undercurrent. The trip was relatively short, considering the traffic. Dane found somewhere nearby to park the car and they climbed out. Cars swished past the oval. As they strode away from the curb, the rest of the park unrolled before them like green carpet. Smells assaulted Abbie's senses—grass, trees, people, rubbish, and sea spray. The sea air was cleansing and uplifting. She wished they could go to nearby Bondi Beach and plunge naked into the water. Her skin was always so hot these days.

A nudge from Rolf had her focused on the task at hand. Annwyn looked a picture in designer clothes. Abbie was in jeans, a T-shirt and runners. A bit dowdy in comparison, but Abbie was so sexually satisfied after multiple orgasms with Rolf, she didn't care that the other woman looked picture perfect. Rolf sure knew how to satisfy a woman. When he was done rutting, he'd started licking and Abbie had screamed until a neighbour thumped on the adjoining wall.

A woman appeared in front of them, sneaking out from behind a tree. She was thin and willowy and her long cotton dress floated around her in layers. Her scent was strong, interesting. Abbie couldn't quite identify it. "Canberra people?" she said. "I'm Layla. My father said to bring you over."

Her eyes danced over them and settled on Rolf. "Good to see you again, Rolf." Her voice held a soft purr.

Rolf dipped his head in acknowledgement. "And you."

Abbie was instantly on alert. This woman was sending sexual lures to Rolf. There was history there, too complex for Abbie to parse, but she knew that Rolf had fucked the little she-wolf.

Abbie squeezed her hands into fists as she followed along behind the others. The raw, untamed emotions threatened to derail her. The urge to smack the woman down, to stake a claim on Rolf, roiled in her belly and filled her brain. The wolf was trying to take over and Abbie had to try to hold it back. She was in danger of losing herself all over again.

Layla was full of sexual promise, if the way she rolled her hips was any indication. Rolf followed along behind but made no move on the other woman. Abbie wasn't sure who she wanted to kill first: Rolf or Layla. The strength of these urges was hard to ignore. Surprising and different, it was a struggle to control them. Is this what Rolf meant about her being too new, too unpredictable? She had to be on alert, suppressing the urge to attack the other woman or Rolf. Her urges and emotions cut through her control like a mill saw. She breathed deeply and put her claws under her control. She had to fight this.

Soon they came upon a bunch of males, who had the feel and scent of werewolves about them. They parted to reveal a body on the ground. Annwyn went forward and knelt by the corpse. Blood leaked onto the ground, staining the grass black.

One man detached himself and shook Dane's hand. "Kaylen, pack leader." Dane introduced them and then stepped closer. "What happened to the body?" Dane asked.

"A dog found it and had a go at it," Kaylen replied. He nodded to Rolf but there was underlying tension there in both the males. If Rolf had been in wolf form, his hackles would be up. The other would be gnashing his teeth. Yet they held it together and passed as normal men. Abbie was surprised how much her sense of smell had opened up her world. Things normally unnoticed were big and bold like billboards.

"How long?" Rolf asked.

"A few hours since we were notified. Layla found it on her way back from the beach." They turned to stare at the woman. "My daughter has a good nose."

The woman was the alpha's daughter. Abbie guessed that Rolf had fucked the girl last time he was in town. The issue was whether he wanted at her again. Abbie did her best to control the feelings filling her up. Jealousy, anger, the need to protect her own. Rolf was hers, no matter that he denied it. What if he did throw her out of the pack, though? Her thoughts shamed her. She was acting like some crazy stalker chick. Relationships only worked if both sides agreed to be together. She couldn't force herself on him, just like he couldn't force himself on her. He hadn't forced himself on her. She'd been consenting, demanding even.

The situation with Rolf and this wolf business was confronting and difficult. She bit down and tried to focus on the body, on the scents around it.

Annwyn stepped forward, peering at the remains that had been half savaged. The throat was open, the soft skin jagged. Normally, Abbie would have barfed at such a sight. Now, the smells were more important.

Annwyn touched the fabric of the dead man's shirt. "There's a pattern here," she said. "Some aspects are familiar and others not. It's like whoever did this tried to hide their signature."

Dane knelt beside her. "They definitely know you can identify them."

"Only some inside the collegium council know that I have that skill," Annwyn said.

Dane's gaze centred on Abbie. "What can you smell?"

She knelt down and inhaled. "Too many scents. Step back all of you."

Rolf shepherded them away as Abbie closed her eyes, trying to discern the sorcerer from the tangle of scents in the air. It was there, beneath the scent of the dead man, beneath the scent of the pack members who had been conducting a search of the area, beneath Annwyn's perfume and the were-bitch's smell. Rolf's scent was on her own body, too, and she tried to filter it out. "Lavender, shoe polish, spearmint and hairspray."

Dane knelt beside her. "Is it familiar? Anyone you've smelt before?"

"No. Not so complete as this."

"Good. Will you remember it?"

She looked at him. "Yes. Why?" She knew she could. The scent was better than a photograph.

"We're going hunting."

"No," Rolf barked. "She's not going anywhere. Not without me."

"Then you have some compromising to do, mate, because car travel or conventional air travel is not going to cut it."

Dane turned to the local alpha. "Thank you for this. Dispose of the body now as you choose. We have what we need."

"Sure," Kaylen replied. "Where are you going?"

Dane met the alpha's stare and then turned his gaze on his pack members. "It's time to take this to the collegium itself." He nodded to Abbie. "This new wolf has a talent for scents. She's going to help us find the callous bastard who is doing this."

"Is she the one who survived?" he asked.

"Yes," Rolf answered. "We think she completed the transition because there's some wolf in her line, and I was close by early and was able to help with her transition."

"And the last full moon?" the alpha asked his eyes assessing Abbie.

"She managed quite well, but there was an attempt on her life. Poison meat put out for her to find."

"Just her? Not the pack?" he asked.

Rolf nodded. "We believe so. The bastard shot her, too, with silver bullets."

The alpha's eyes widened. "That does seem targeted." He moved closer to Abbie. Rolf tensed, but held still. Abbie noticed this, but calmed as the alpha came forward. His scent was strong, like he was upset and angry, yet he was successful in hiding the visible signs. Although not from her.

"I'm glad you survived the transition. If you have this gift, then use it well to find the person responsible. People shouldn't be dying like this. The whole community is nervous and some in the general population suspect it's not natural. There have been too many partially transformed bodies. Yesterday a detective we know and work with sometimes came to see us. He knows us, knows about the pack. He said it's getting harder to keep it quiet. Anymore and our world is going to split open like a big fat melon."

He lifted his arm, then slowed the movement when Rolf reacted. He laid a hand on Abbie's shoulder and squeezed lightly. "Good luck."

"Thank you," Abbie said. "I will do my best."

Kaylen nodded and turned away. They took that for their signal to depart, heading back to the car.

No one spoke. What could they say? They had feared that these continuing incidences were going to reveal their existence to normal people. That was obviously the motive.

"I don't understand," Dane said as he pressed the remote to open the car. "No sorcerer in their right mind would do this. There's nothing to gain. Only chaos."

"Maybe they aren't in their right mind," Annwyn replied.

Dane nodded. "But they are aware enough to cover their tracks, to change the weave of their spells. A twisted, clever, sane mind then."

Annwyn sighed as she slid into her seat. "Just what we need after the Nira business." She shut the door and put on her seatbelt.

Rolf bundled Abbie into the back, as if he thought she was about to run off. Abbie bit back a snarky comment as Rolf slid in next to her.

"Where do you want to do this?" Dane asked Rolf, meeting the other man's gaze in the rear vision mirror.

"Back at the hotel. We won't be long, will we?" Rolf said.

Dane shrugged. "I don't know, but I'll extend the booking for the week. That way the car and our belongings will be safe. We can just ask housekeeping to stay out of our rooms until we get back."

Rolf nodded once. Abbie studied his face, saw the displeasure etched there. His scent, though, was obscured by too many conflicting emotions. Anger, fear, desire interlaced. Nothing offensive in the aroma of his emotions. Abbie found she liked Rolf's scent, whatever the configuration. Her mind headed down a lustful route and she pulled herself up. There was important business to attend to and fucking would have to wait.

CHAPTER 9

They gathered in Dane and Annwyn's room. There was no time to slake Abbie's pent-up lust. Rolf could taste Abbie's desire in his nose and on his tongue. She met his look of concern with a challenge in her eyes, which then softened to something he couldn't quite categorise. Such a strong werewolf. Who would have thought it? She was a challenge indeed. He had to hope she was in control enough to cope with the magical transition to a new place. Rolf hated that method of travel and preferred conventional transport. He had, when required, travelled that way, but it took a lot of self-control to not get spooked. The magic did something to his lupine senses, stirring his inner wolf.

He took Abbie's hand and squeezed it gently. She looked up at him, widened her eyes and grinned as if she was a child on a trip to an amusement park. "Breathe deeply. The transition can be unnerving. Just remember, I have you."

"Okay," she replied, squeezing his hand back. "I've got you, too." He widened his eyes at the comment, because she was completely serious.

Dane initiated the transfer, taking them all at the same time, even though Annwyn was quite capable of transporting herself. The ground solidified under Rolf's feet and his senses went on high alert, heart thumping, head spinning and nostrils flaring at the assault of strange, new odours.

"Easy," Abbie said and squeezed his hand.

Astonished, he blinked at her. She was smiling, calm and looking around. Rolf didn't like that the magical travelling upset only him. He had thought it a werewolf thing, but now with Abbie being so calm—so smug and calm—he realised that must not be the case. Slightly rattled by this insight, he let go of her hand and ran his fingers through his hair, trying to keep hold of the array of feelings swirling inside him. Anger, embarrassment for himself and pride in Abbie also.

The office block they had materialised in was firm underfoot. After slowing his breathing, his olfactory senses grew accustomed to the smell of the place: dust, pollution, humans and other creatures, cleaning substances and something else. A new place in Denver, Colorado, USA.

Abbie smiled. "Hey, Dane, that was fun. Can we do it again?"

Dane patted Rolf on the shoulder. "You okay?" he nodded to Abbie. "She seemed to cope with the transition just fine."

Rolf growled his annoyance.

Abbie sniffed. "Oh, nice aroma. I smell food. Is there a banquet or something?"

Rolf inhaled, savouring the smells on the back of his tongue. Abbie had been quick to pick that up. Rolf shook his head. Abbie was a smart one. He had to keep on his toes.

Dane's gaze went blank, and Rolf sensed he was communicating with someone. "A celebration we're belatedly invited to. Rafael's birthday apparently." He checked a wall sign. "We're in luck—it's on this floor in the function room come ballroom."

"I didn't think he'd go in for that kind of thing," Annwyn said. "A bit ostentatious I'd have thought."

Dane grinned. "The man lives in a Scottish castle. I can't see how you can get more ostentatious than that.

Annwyn frowned. "But he's ancient. I don't think I'd celebrate my hundred-and-forty-seventh birthday."

"Is that how old he is?" Abbie asked.

Dane shrugged. "I don't know, but I don't think he has that many years on him. Annwyn is trying to be funny." He turned and gestured with his arm down the corridor. "This way, if you please."

Abbie tugged on Rolf's arm so he slowed and leaned down for her to speak in his ear. "I'm not exactly dressed for a fancy dinner, although I am hungry."

Rolf sniffed. "You're always hungry." He lifted his head. "Annwyn?"

Annwyn turned back, still with her arm tucked into Dane's. "Yes?"

"Any chance you can fancy us both up?"

"Sure, but Dane's not dressing up."

"He doesn't look as rough as us, though." Dane wore a clean white shirt, unbuttoned at the neck, and beige slacks.

Annwyn stared at them and then lifted a hand, flicking a finger at a time. Rolf felt the change in his clothes, the adjustment to the weave. His collar grew tighter, and he stood straighter as the more formal attire fit around him. His feet were enclosed in leather. He glanced down and saw he was now in a black suit that fitted him like a glove, complete with black patent leather shoes and a black bow tie. His eyes fell on Abbie and his mouth dropped open. Her hair was now coiled on her head in an elaborate hairstyle with dark red curls kissing the pale skin of her cheeks. The fabric of the cream-coloured dress she was wearing was flimsy as a cloud and seemingly always in motion. On her feet, a pair of strappy shoes, in gold lace and glitter. Abbie scrubbed up very well. She was adorable in jeans and a T-shirt; in this dress she was divine. His mouth watered just looking at her.

Abbie grinned at him, her lips slick with gloss. The sorceress had done her make-up too. Abbie bowed her head to Annwyn who stood admiring her handiwork. "Grateful, thanks, Annwyn."

"You're welcome." Annwyn gave a quick wave and turned to catch up with Dane who was waiting for her a few steps further down the corridor. Dane had changed his clothes after all. He was dressed in a dinner suit with a red bow tie. Annwyn's dress changed as she walked. The dark red satin flowed around her waist like some southern bell. Her hair curled up and into a bun and then a few coils disengaged from the bun to coil in ringlets to one side.

Rolf shook his head. Annwyn certainly had flair. She'd grown in skill as well. He remembered how she'd been when they first met. Once shy and crazy in love with Dane, now she was powerful and confident and still very much in love with Dane. They'd had a love spell thrown at them, but very quickly it gave way as they fell deeply and passionately in love. Rolf held his elbow out to Abbie, a romantic whim stirring his mood. "Care to accompany me to the banquet?"

Abbie gave him a sly smile. "Oh yes, please. You look dishy in that suit. I could eat you." An almost-growl vibrated in her throat. Rolf caught his breath at how just those words made him want her. He became hard just in that moment. If they didn't have a mission, he'd have her flat on her back an instant after such a blatant invitation. With a certain amount of embarrassment, he checked himself. Seriously, how was he expected to lead the pack when one look or one word from Abbie had him forgetting everything except her smile, her scent and the feel of being inside her. He was the one acting like a new wolf, full of lust and appetites. These urges and thoughts did not reconcile with his view of what an alpha was. The previous alpha had been a hard wolf, a tough foe, and he'd kept them all in line. Rolf tended to be easier on the pack, but still he faced up to the challenge when needed. A quick glance around made him glad that none of the pack could see what a cub he was now.

Rolf quivered when Abbie slid her hand into the crook of his elbow as they walked behind Dane and Annwyn. Very soon that feeling settled into a sense of rightness, of belonging. The world felt right with Abbie on his arm. Part of him rejected the feeling. It wasn't him. It wasn't what he wanted with his life. At least that's what he'd thought. Just because the previous alpha was a hard bastard with no mate, didn't mean he had to be the same. Rolf shook his head. This was no time to engage in such reflections.

The doors flung open at their approach and noise assaulted his ears, scents filled his olfactory senses. The aroma of people and food intermingled, and Rolf fought hard to arrange them in order. How else was he to sense danger, if he couldn't keep everything sorted? There was a tremor in Abbie that he detected from their physical contact, which left him wondering if the assault of smells made her nose twitch.

Even with her excellent sense of smell, he bet this lot would be hard to sort through.

They stepped into a large function room with bright, golden lights hanging from the ceiling. Voices competed with each other, as conversations abounded. Shrill laughs, low murmurs merged with the sound of cutlery scraping crockery as the attendees partook of the food on offer. The acoustics were bad, as Rolf's sensitive ears attested. Round tables had been placed evenly around the room, each holding eight to ten people. Rolf estimated that at least three hundred guests were seated, attended by about twenty black-clad waiters, who magically directed huge platters brimming with roast meats, roast vegetables, salads, pink shrimp and huge lobsters to the hungry hordes.

The scent of food went straight to his gut and had him wondering when he last ate. He guided Abbie to the table Dane indicated, where there were four vacant seats together. The other occupants of the table looked up as they pulled out chairs. Dane frowned as he took his seat, then his expression cleared as he greeted the others at the table and introduced them all. Annwyn smiled at them as she took her seat. "Lovely party. I hope there's cake," she said.

Rolf's skin prickled, sensing that Dane was upset about something. They knew each other too well to disguise their feelings from each other. "What is it?" he asked across Annwyn who sat between them.

Annwyn lifted a fluted glass and a bottle poured itself out. Rolf growled at the bottle, and it backed away from him. Abbie, he noticed, picked up her own glass and let it be filled. She narrowed her eyes at him, her smile daring him to say something against her action.

"Rafael's not here," Dane said, waving his hand as the champagne bottle approached him. He picked up some water and took a deep drink.

Annwyn lowered her glass and swallowed a mouthful of wine. "But I thought it was his party ..." Annwyn said, a frown marking her beauty. "Surely he's going to make an appearance."

Dane scanned the room. "It is. It's meant to be. But he's not here and he's not answering my hails. It was his private secretary who issued the invitation."

Annwyn lifted her glass to take another sip, pausing before letting the fluid slide into her mouth. "So many here too. He'll have to put in a grand appearance later or risk offending all these guests. I imagine it's a bit noisy for him. He is getting on in age."

A waiter waved five platters in their direction—roast meats, a mountain of potato salad, piles of peeled shrimp and lobster, a plate of greens, more vegetables. Annwyn used tongs to lift some morsels of lobster mornay onto her plate and also a couple of large prawns.

Rolf asserted his will over his senses, blocking out the scents of food and the noise. He cast a sideways glance at Abbie, but she'd already started ladling food onto her plate. There didn't seem to be any theme to her choices. She was taking from platters that were the closest. Already she had two slices of rare roast beef in her mouth, which she swallowed before even chewing properly. Rolf held his smile in check. There was no point in chiding her for bad eating habits. They were meant to be working, not eating. She was a new wolf, with a new wolf's appetite, so he had to unbend.

Rolf let his gaze roam about the table, which sat eight people. Others he saw seated ten and maybe twelve. They were sorcerers mostly and then his gaze stopped. A chill ran over his skin. A vampire was sitting on the other side of the table. He was pale and gaunt, with short dark hair and largish, sticking-out ears. He smelt like death dressed in black tie. Rolf marked him and continued with his scrutiny. Another three vampires were at the table. They also wore black tie and had a musty smell that Rolf found itched his nose; all were males. One was plump and short, one average height, with big, almost black eyes, and the other rail thin with reddish hair and a goatee. The last one grinned at him, showing his elongated canines. Rolf growled, letting a bit of his wolf come to the fore. Two could play at that game.

The redheaded vampire dropped the smile and dipped his head, after receiving an elbow in the ribs from the first vampire, the tall pale one. Rolf's survey continued, noting another guest was some other kind of creature. Fae. A fairy? Rolf didn't think their kind would be invited to a soiree such as this. Maybe Rafael's reforms had taken effect already. He was trying to make the collegium more accepting of others, or so it was said. Rolf did not feel welcome and, as far as he could smell, there were no other weres in the room. Just him and Abbie, and only invited due to their association with a powerful sorcerer. Rolf tried not to be angry about that. He knew how things were and, while he didn't like it, he'd not actively fought against it. He liked Dane, liked working with him and for him. In Australia, they were far enough away from the collegium and their prejudices, or they had been until these attacks. The changeling curse was directed at exposing werewolves in Australia and elsewhere. Maybe Rolf needed to change his ideas about keeping his distance from the international politics governing supernaturals. As he looked around the room, studying those at the surrounding tables, he realised he was involved. He was smack bang in the middle of the whole shebang.

"A penny for them," Abbie said, nudging him and breaking into his thoughts.

"Just keep alert."

She pushed a forkful or rare meat at him. "Keep your strength up."

He lunged for the meat, taking it straight off the tines and making Abbie break out in a laugh. He grinned, then schooled his expression and stared balefully at the vampires. Abbie wasn't aware of the animosity between vampires and weres and he put that on the list of things he needed to teach her, right after respect and submission to her alpha.

The vampire lifted an eyebrow at him and then looked at Abbie. Despite weres being considered the lowest of the low, he hoped the vampire didn't make a scene and demand that they be fed elsewhere. He didn't want Abbie to be dissatisfied with the reality of being a were in this world. He'd mentioned it, but the reality of it would be stark. Being this low in the pecking order meant that the undead piece of filth they were sitting opposite was second only to the sorcerers, and well above them. Abbie had already lost her human career and he didn't want her disillusioned with the supernatural world as well. Not yet, anyway. It wouldn't be good for her, settling into her new life, and he realised it was important to him that she was satisfied.

Everyone was eating and drinking and talking and the general vibe was light-hearted. Abbie sniffed loudly and licked her lips. She'd stopped eating, even though platters were floating within reach. Rolf turned to see what she was doing, as her lack of movement seemed strange. Her glass of bubbly was still in her grip, but she wasn't drinking. Her plate was empty, and her gaze was riveted on the centre of the table where a large floral arrangement sat.

"Abbie?" he asked, leaning in close to her ear and speaking softly. Abbie didn't even blink.

Dane was engaged in conversation with the sorcerer seated at his other side, but even he couldn't help noticing that Abbie was still and staring.

"Annwyn?" Rolf called to the sorceress, hoping not to call attention to himself by leaning over to catch her eye.

Annwyn lowered the fork full of lobster back to the plate. "Yes?"

"Something is wrong," Rolf said in a quiet voice.

Annwyn smiled, a sort of fake, don't be alarmed smile. "Besides the guest of honour being missing?"

Rolf narrowed his gaze. Rafael's absence was strange, but so was Abbie's behaviour. Only one thing made her like that. He directed Annwyn to look at Abbie with a flick of his eyes. Annwyn's gaze tracked to Abbie and then shifted to the centre piece. "Someone is using subtle magic."

Rolf looked meaningfully at the floating platters of food and the bottles of wine that came over when one lifted a glass. "Should we be worried?" he asked. "Magic is being used all around us."

Dane edged his seat over and returned to the conversation, placing his hand over Annwyn's. "Do you know what it is she's sensing?" Dane's face alerted Rolf that it was serious and that his sorcerous friend was worried.

Annwyn narrowed her gaze as she studied the table. "I can see it, but I can't feel it. That is strange."

"And?" Dane prompted.

"It's not a pattern I recognise. I can't tell what it's meant to do."

Dane studied the invisible spell and then relaxed. "Well then." He picked up his glass and paused while it was being filled by a magic-propelled bottle. He leaned in close to them and spoke in soft, clear tones that they had no trouble hearing. "The spell doesn't appear to mean us any harm. Let's carry on as before," Dane said. He lifted his glass in salute and added, "Just be ready."

Rolf put his arm around Abbie and leaned in to kiss her cheek. "Abbie? Dane says it's nothing to worry about. You can relax now." Abbie sniffed, shuddered. "Abbie?" Rolf said, putting his arm around her to draw her close to their conversation.

"The magic smells funny. Something isn't right. Why is it there if it's not doing anything?"

Rolf sniffed, but he could detect nothing. He had to trust Dane. Besides they were in collegium territory, a guest of a sorcerer, so he was inclined to go along with Dane and be ready. He put his arm around her shoulders and squeezed gently and put his lips to Abbie's ear. "Just stay alert."

Turning her head to him, their lips only inches apart, she whispered. "What does he mean? It's either something or nothing."

Rolf met her open gaze and relaxed his lips. "You're right. Magic is nothing if not contradictory. It can help and it can harm." He wanted to lean in and kiss her hard, ruffle her feathers, make her want him as much as he wanted her. Instead, he leaned back into his chair, sniffed, and picked up his glass of champagne, but did not drink. "Dane is being cautious, nothing more," he said out of the side of his mouth. "There's so much magic in here, it's hard to tell what is going on."

Abbie frowned, her forehead creasing in puzzlement. "Yes, there's lot of magic around, but that," she pointed to the centre of the table, "is odd, wrong, strange. Why don't you take me seriously?"

Rolf reached out and squeezed her head. "It's good you picked up that unusual use of magic. But Dane and Annwyn said it's nothing to worry about. Nothing to do but relax and enjoy the food, but," he leaned in close "we keep alert and ready, like all good werewolves."

"Then I shouldn't be concerned?" She smiled. "That's good to know, because there are other things demanding my attention," she replied.

Rolf turned his head to look her up and down. Abbie smiled, lowered her eyelids and licked her lips. Rolf felt like he'd just been put on the menu. Abbie reached over to the table to pick up her glass and then downed it.

A few seconds later, Rolf stiffened as a firm hand gripped his thigh.

Now she was no longer hungry for food, she was hungry for him. He turned to Abbie. "Now is not the time."

He detached her grip and placed her hand on her own thigh. The surge of lust in his groin made him adjust his seat and tug the trouser legs to ease the pressure on his erection. It seemed to him that he always had a hard-on when Abbie was close.

Abbie grinned, arching her eyebrows. "There's a time?"

"Yes," he hissed at her and then regretted it. She was a young wolf, still full of surges of emotion and primal urges. He was angry at himself, because he wanted her and couldn't have her right at that moment.

"My hunger is satisfied," she replied and then smiled at the rest of the people at the table before leaning slightly toward him, her voice pitched so that only he could hear. "I'm mildly intoxicated." She breathed champagne breath into his face and then lowered her gaze to fixate on his lips. "And I'm sitting next to the hottest man in the room. What more do I need?"

Rolf growled low, covering the fact that he wanted to smile at her audaciousness and had serious ideas about what he'd like to do to her and have her do to him. "Privacy."

Abbie grinned and rolled her eyes toward the table. "These tables have long tablecloths. I don't think anyone would notice if we—"

A loud noise had Rolf on his feet in a moment. Abbie squeaked and turned in her chair. Surveying the room, he saw a table on the other end of the ballroom shoot up high into the air as if blown there by a bomb. Plates and food went off in different directions with glasses smashing and cutlery twanging as it hit the floor. The red-stained tablecloth fell away to the floor. Sorcerers and others went flying backwards with cries of outrage and screams of pain. Onlookers surged to their feet and added their cries of dismay to the furore. A few waved their arms and dematerialised, getting out of there before things got worse.

This was not an isolated incidence of rage; it was an attack. Rolf dashed to the edge of the room, clear of the array of tables and guests, so he could get behind the instigator of this outrage. Even with the way relatively clear, there were servers darting about in confusion and some of the guests who had left the table headed to the wall, to better keep watch. Another table punched upwards as if a rocket had launched beneath it, the food and wine meeting a similar fate to the first table. Bodies blew up and out from that table, caught in the force that had smashed the table into the air.

Sorcerers picked themselves up, gaped in horror, and then disappeared. The panicked vibrations filled the air and the scent of fear cloyed in Rolf's nose. Chairs now darted as if shot in all directions, smashing against walls, the ceiling, the lights and into other tables. Those who weren't fast enough screamed as chairs shattered and wooden shards and splinters pierced vulnerable flesh. The tang of blood was in the air, joining the fear and panic. Rolf growled as his wolf grew impatient, fighting at the self-imposed restraints he placed on it. It wasn't time for the wolf yet.

Rolf sensed movement behind him and recognised the light scent. Abbie had moved in right behind him. Her hands held the skirt of her dress and she'd kicked off her shoes. She was poised, ready to attack, her upper body lowered as if waiting to sprint. Rolf could taste her tension, feel her focus as she watched the chaotic scene unfold.

"There!" she said and pointed, her long arm darting out, forefinger accusing. A dark shape moved to another table. Smallish, it was wearing a black robe with a cowl covering the face. Given the dark shadow of the hood, Rolf could not identify them. He tasted magic too, as if the attacker had magically disguised himself. In the crowd of frightened attendees, he lost sight of Dane and Annwyn. In their panic, some of the guests were pushing out through the doors, swirling in lines like a many-headed hydra fighting for a way out.

"Wait here," Rolf said and half-turned to motion to her to wait. Too late. Abbie was already gone. At first, he couldn't see her in the press of bodies, but then he saw that she'd shifted into wolf shape. Her lithe russet form bounded through the press of people. Her howl sent more people screaming, thinking they were being attacked from both sides. Sorcerers and others threw themselves sideways as Abbie cut a direct path to the attacker.

"Vermin!" one shouted. Others had their mouths agape at the horror of having a were in their midst. "Who uses vermin here?" The accusation ripped through the air, before each made a gesture and fled into a puff of air.

Rolf would've liked to have known who had been calling them names at a moment like this, when they were trying to help. He would've liked to take a nip from their flesh. Rolf growled, his wolf once again fighting to get out. To protect Abbie.

Rolf hesitated to change. He thought he could do more in human form, particularly communicate. Dane appeared beside him. "I'll go to the other exit, but whoever that is, they can dematerialise. I doubt we can catch them physically. We need a spell and time to prepare one and we just don't have any. Is it the same sorcerer who's wielding the curse, or just some sick prank?"

Rolf shook his head. "It's no prank. People are getting hurt. Sorcerers and witches are fleeing. Blood has been spilled. There will be death this night if we don't put a stop to it."

Dane frowned as he tried to keep an eye on the attacker, while searching. "Where's Abbie? She should be able to tell if it's our cursemaker."

A scream and Dane's head jerked around. A table flew up and landed smack on top of another. People had already vacated it, but food and drink went everywhere. Magically controlled bottles of champagne took off like rockets, hitting the ceiling and smashing into tiny pieces that fell with the liquid like rain.

Abbie's growls could be heard over the screams of the wounded partygoers. Dane yelled directions to those willing to assist. The injured and the dead were being lifted in the air and directed out of the doors. The crowd had thinned out. Dane, Rolf and Annwyn assisted the injured as best they could, as they moved closer to Abbie. The young she-wolf's luscious russet fur caught the light and Rolf could tell her hackles were raised. She wasn't trained for combat. All she had was instinct.

In a small space between the attacker and the next table, Abbie squared off against the robed figure. Piles of broken furniture lay behind the attacker.

. . .

"Abbie!" Rolf called. Dread filled him seeing her potentially vulnerable like that. She was strong, but not aware enough when wearing fur, and her reaction indicated that she didn't like the smell of the attacker. He thought that meant the attacker was the rogue sorcerer they were looking for. Then it dawned on him that Abbie had shifted at will. She was very new to her skin to be doing that. Her wolf was very strong, so maybe that accounted for it. Pride and fear mixed in his chest.

Before he could decide what to do, she darted forward, going for the attacker's cloak. As soon as her jaws connected to the hem of the robe, Abbie was thrown back with a whine and yelp. The rogue sorcerer had blasted Abbie with a spell and then vanished, the dark robe collapsing in on itself.

Rolf had eyes only for Abbie. He raced over to where she lay sprawled, out cold. Rolf checked her over. She was breathing, nothing appeared broken, but despite shaking her and calling her name she wouldn't wake. That was some powerful spell to knock out a werewolf. "Abbie!"

Dane strode over to where the attacker had been, nothing was there except the discarded black robe. He'd fled before they could even identify him. Annwyn came to check on Abbie, freeing Rolf to check the areas around where the robe lay. There were many competing scents in the air and the attacker had done something to disguise his trace, so that Rolf was at a loss to identify the attacker, other than he was male. Abbie's keen sense of smell had been put out of commission, probably on purpose.

Dane was still cursing when Annwyn came up. "That happened quickly," she said, taking in Dane swearing. "Did anyone see who it was?"

Dane stopped cursing and shook his head. "No dammit. He disguised himself and fled before he could be caught. Is Abbie all right? Damn fool thing for her to do, going after him. Now he's escaped."

Rolf drew Abbie into his arms. She was still in wolf form and still out to it. Her head lolled when he lifted her. Rolf wanted to howl, but that would serve no purpose other than to let out his grief at seeing Abbie so vulnerable. He'd nursed her through the curse-forced change, he'd been with her at her first full moon. They had sated their lust in each other's flesh. She was part of him; she was pack.

Rolf gritted his teeth and almost growled at Dane. "You don't know that. He could've taken himself off at any time. We weren't prepared. We needed a plan, a trap. We had nothing. Abbie said there was something wrong, but we didn't bloody listen."

Dane nodded. "Yeah, you're right. Maybe we should've acted when Abbie first detected something. It's just this is the collegium itself. Why attack here, unless they wanted to attack someone specifically?" Dane shook his head. "Now I'm being paranoid. We need to see Rafael. He might've avoided the party, but he's not going to avoid us now. He's going to help us catch this renegade sorcerer." He turned to Annwyn. "Let's go find Rafael. We'll try his office first."

Annwyn stood there elegantly, as if there wasn't mess and chaos surrounding them. Her red satin dress folded down to become a pair of dark blue slacks and short-waisted coat, complete with short boots. A better wardrobe for hunting rogue sorcerers. "Give me a minute. I want to check on Abbie." She knelt down next to Rolf and stroked Abbie's head. After a second or two, she spoke again. "She hasn't been knocked out. It's a hex, Rolf. I can see it."

Dane squatted down next to them. "What?" Dane studied Abbie and touched her head and her jaw. "Interesting. It's not quite a sleep spell, more like an amnesia curse. It's like she's been put to sleep and made to forget. I don't think it will harm her or kill her. That would take a lot more power."

Annwyn pursed her lips, tracing a pattern on Abbie's forehead. "This was targeted. That spell was meant for her and that takes preparation. It will take a while to shift, the fit is so good. Somehow the rogue sorcerer knew we were here, why else would Abbie be targeted like that?" She peered back at their table and nodded slowly. "That spell Abbie smelt, I think it was a monitoring spell. A bug. A way of listening in. He was on the lookout for us, and we walked right in."

Rolf's head shot up and his eyes narrowed. "You mean it was a trap?"

Dane stood up and dusted off his knees. "Looks like it. We can't prove it with Abbie out of it. We were meant to be hunting him and now the tables have been turned. It also marks an escalation. It's almost crazy to attack here, to advertise his presence so blatantly."

Dane narrowed his gaze. "Do you want to stay with Abbie, come with us, or should I send both of you back to the hotel?"

Rolf looked between Abbie and Dane. It was a hard choice. He couldn't leave Abbie unprotected, yet he had a duty to Dane too. He clenched his jaw. "She's vulnerable."

"There's no need to move her." Annwyn touched Rolf's arm. "I can put a barrier around her. It should keep her safe for half an hour or so. No one will be able to touch her. If she wakes up it will fall away. She'll be able to find us with that incredible nose of hers."

Rolf considered this. It did make the decision easier. "We aren't leaving the building?" he asked Dane.

Dane shook his head. "Rafael's office is here on this floor. Hopefully, when we find him, we'll find some answers. In fact, I'm amazed he hasn't come along to investigate. Surely he heard all the commotion."

Annwyn grimaced. "Or heard reports from those attacked."

Rolf didn't like that comment as to him it indicated that there was something wrong, more wrong than this attack. "Very well, do it," Rolf said to Annwyn. Rolf arranged Abbie carefully to ensure she was comfortable, and stepped back as Annwyn stood to cast her spell. At first Rolf tasted it, a vibration on his tongue and then there was nothing, just Abbie lying there. Annwyn reached out a hand and the invisible barrier sprung into effect. Rolf wanted time to test it, but his companions were already on the move.

Dane edged around the debris along the wall. Annwyn and Rolf followed his path and copied where he stepped around broken furniture, crockery and glass, and piles of food. Occasional splatters of blood left splotches on the floor. The smell tantalised him, even with the scent of sorcerer and magic mixed in. They headed toward the far side of the hall, where the door was situated. "Did he enter through that door or did he materialise?" Rolf asked.

"I don't know," Dane said. "A lot of magic in use would serve to disguise a materialisation, and we didn't have a line of sight to the door."

Rolf sniffed the air as they passed through the double doors into the hall. He could detect nothing unusual. There was too much food, fear and blood in the air for him to discern anything.

"Let's go," Dane said.

They pulled up short as a vampire shifted out of thin air in front of them. It was one of the vampires who had shared their table. The tall and thin one, with the big ears. He was still wearing black tie and had red lips. Reeking of age, he hissed at Dane, his old worldly accent pronounced. "What in hell's name is going on here? First, you bring animals in to dine with us and now this outrageous attack within these sacred halls. It is clear the magi are no longer fit to lead."

Rolf clenched his fist, wanting to grind it into the vamp's face. Dane spread his feet in a defensive stance. The vamp didn't look like he was stupid enough to attack, leaving Rolf unconcerned by the undead's bluster. The sorcerers were powerful and could counter the vampires easily, which is why the sorcerers led the collegium. The vampires didn't have to like it, though. Considering the chaos in the banqueting hall, the vamp did have a point. "I don't have time now, Finsk." Dane gestured to the hall. "This attack is on all of us, threatens all of us."

"That may be, sir," Finsk replied. "You sorcerers and your magic are chaos barely constrained. Look to your own ranks for the instigator of this. We do not stoop to such measures. We value our privacy too much to let the humans advertise our presence. This chaos is of your doing and it must be checked before we lose everything."

"What do you know?" Dane asked, his spine stiffening. Rolf tensed readying to act, looming behind the sorcerer's shoulder.

Finsk lifted his top lip, revealing sharp fangs. "Sufficient! Several of our enclaves have been invaded by human police. When questioned they refer to 'tip offs'. As none of my kind would risk themselves this way, we must look elsewhere for the culprits. Who would benefit from exposing our world?"

"Not us," Dane replied quickly."

The old vamp drew himself up, the extra height making him look even more gaunt. "We've tracked this debacle to the sorcerers. Why else do you think we were here tonight? Not only are we not normally invited, we wouldn't normally deign to attend. However, we needed answers."

"And what is your deduction?" Dane asked carefully. Rolf gave him a side eye as it seemed pretty clear.

"The rot in your ranks is obvious."

"But who?"

The vampire disappeared before answering. Rolf caught a whiff or rose oil and rot. No wonder weres couldn't stand the living dead, there was no way to hide the stink. And they tasted bad, too. And for a beast who ate carrion that was saying something.

Dane turned and lifted an eyebrow at Rolf. "Great. Now we have cranky vamps to deal with. Let's head to Rafael's office." He grabbed Annwyn by the elbow and they all jogged down the corridor. Rolf thought of Abbie lying there vulnerable and then pushed the thought away. He had to trust that Annwyn's barrier would keep her safe. The sooner they solved this mystery the better. He had some serious business to sort out with Abbie. Like doing as she was told for starters. He'd told her to stay back, but she barrelled in and got knocked out. No, she'd already transformed when he told her to stay back. Even so, she should have looked to him for direction, as going off half-cocked nearly got her killed. Anger brimmed and Rolf had to push it away. He had no time to sort through his feelings, because right now he couldn't discern whether it was disobedience that bothered him or the fact that Abbie could have been killed.

They ran down the corridor, turned left, and then ran down another. All the doors were nondescript grey-green as if this was a boring public service building and very few bore signs. The sorcerers could tell when another of their kind was near, so signs were superfluous for them, and their non-magic servants would presumably know their way around. Rolf didn't like running around blind or being ignorant of what was behind those doors. On high alert, he sensed danger on all sides, around every corner, within every shadow large enough to hide someone. Then a powerful wall of scents barrelled up the hallway, making him uneasy—blood and death and magic. "Beware!" he said.

Dane slowed, caught his eye, and nodded. Slowing down he approached a door. "This is it." Dane opened it and darted inside, followed by Annwyn. After checking the corridor, Rolf stepped in after them. Rafael's office was a mess. Documents smouldered on the desk with thin wisps of smoke curling to the ceiling. Wooden cabinets gaped, their drawers smashed and splintered. Dented steel filing cabinets looked as if they'd been bashed by a heavy force. Dane moved behind Rafael's desk, bent down and held up the old man's red, ceremonial robe, which had been on the floor. Dane tossed it to him.

Rolf lifted it to breathe in the scents. It mostly smelled of Rafael and maybe a hint of vampire taint. That made sense, given they had been invited to the birthday function. "No hint of blood," Rolf said, dropping the robe onto the desk.

"That's something at least. I'm going to hail Rafael." Dane stood erect and closed his eyes.

Dane stood there quietly. Annwyn watched Dane's face, looking for a sign from his expression. The sorcerer's face was serene while mind questing. Dane opened his eyes and shook his head. "I can't raise him."

"That's not good," Annwyn said. "Do you want me to try?"

Dane scowled and then nodded. Annwyn meant no insult to Dane when she suggested such a thing. She had a close relationship with Rafael, as she was his protégé. Annwyn could not raise the elderly sorcerer either.

Rolf paced the room, sifting through the various scents. "He was here not long ago." Without any hint of jealousy, he wished Abbie was there with her keen nose. "Maybe an hour ago."

Dane reached for the robe and clenched it tight. "I can understand him not attending his birthday celebration, but this disappearance is not like him. As a member of the triumvirate he has a lot of duties that would leave little free time. He would not make his staff and anyone at the collegium worry unnecessarily. I fear he has been kidnapped. It's the only thing that makes sense."

Annwyn turned around after examining the destroyed furniture. "You think the attack at the banquet was to disguise a kidnapping?

That's one very big distraction." She frowned. "It makes very little sense. There are too many prongs of attack: the changeling curse, the attack on all the supernaturals at the banquet, the police raids on the vampire enclaves and now Rafael being kidnapped.

Dane frowned. "Why attack without purpose? If Rafael had been here, he would've put a stop to it. He's powerful. Stronger than me. I didn't even get close enough to decide what could be done to counteract the attack before it was over. Now he's not here and there's this," he said, gesturing to the ruin of the office. "Were his assailants looking for something?"

Rolf frowned. "I can't detect anyone else's scent other than Rafael, maybe a bit of vampire, but that scent isn't strong enough to convince me that a vampire was in this room. More like they had a meeting and not in here. You make it sound like there was more than one assailant, yet the scents in here don't match that theory."

Dane shared a look with Annwyn. "Can you see any decaying spells? Anything?"

Annwyn lifted a shoulder and spun slowly as she examined the room. "There are some spells in here certainly. That's to be expected. Decaying? You think our mysterious attacker?" She turned slowly, her expression hinting that her mind was elsewhere. She gestured to the wall. "There's one over the safe. It shows up as a shiny, glimmering square. There's one on that drawer," she pointed to an unopened draw in the desk. The only part of the desk that hadn't been attacked. "That will probably incapacitate anyone who tries to break into it. I think whoever did this knew about those spells and hasn't tried to tamper with them."

Annwyn looked around the room. "Wait! There's one behind the door." She shook her head as she neared it, squatting down to inspect it. "I can't tell what it was intended for, and it's decayed so the pattern is indecipherable. All I can tell is that there was a spell there recently." She stood up again and checked the door. "I'd have to guess it was a spell to announce visitors."

Annwyn glowered at the destruction in the office. "There's no way of knowing anything for certain. What about his secretary? Surely

Bruce would know about Rafael's appointments, who came to see him, who went away again."

Dane nodded, his eyes bright. "Let's go find him." In two long strides he was out the door. When he didn't come back immediately, Rolf and Annwyn exchanged a look and followed. The door to the room opposite was ajar. It was the same grey-green as the one to Rafael's office, but had a half window. Dane was in there, as they could see his shadow through the window and Rolf could trace his scent trail. They entered and Rolf smelled the blood and death straight away.

Dane had the desk lamp on and was leaning over Rafael's secretary's body. The rather young looking, smartly dressed man was sprawled on the floor, legs splayed and hands lifeless by his side. A gaping wound ran from chin to groin. He'd been gutted. Blood was splattered on the wall behind, over the bookshelves and all over the man's dark clothes. Rolf dampened his reaction to the scent. Blood and shit and so many other things besides. A fragrant oil burner's contents spilled over the desk and the perfume of lavender, patchouli and lemon filled the air. Rolf sniffed around, his heart rate increasing, his palms sweating. Danger lurked and he concentrated on distinguishing the different smells. An old dead smell, pungent, acrid drew him to the small round refuse bin. At its base was a large, very dead rat. He let out a breath. It seemed to be deliberate to confuse the scene, and it was working. Abbie might've found more. He inhaled again and detected cigarette smoke and the aroma of sexual intercourse. Male to male.

Judging by the way he was dressed, Rafael's secretary had been intending to go to the party. All that was missing was the tie. Rolf spied a bright blue, polka-dot concoction curled up in the in-tray.

Annwyn leaned over and pulled back quickly. "Bruce?"

Dane nodded. "He's been gutted. I don't think magic was involved."

Annwyn moved closer and shook her head. "I can't see any spells. Another misdirection, do you think?"

"Rolf?" Dane asked, looking up from contemplating the deceased.

Rolf stroked his goatee with his forefinger and thumb, eventually shaking his head. "There's been an attempt to thwart a were's nose." Dane ran his fingers through his hair and let out a long breath, but before he could speak Rolf continued, pointing out and explaining all the scents in the room. "He had it off with a bloke recently."

"I take it you can't tell who that was." Rolf shook his head. "I'll try hailing Rafael again."

Rolf went to the desk and ran his eye down the open page of an old-fashioned diary. There was no computer in the room. Through the blood splatter on the page, he could see that the last appointment had been two hours previously. The party was written on the page with four whole hours blocked out and shaded in red ink. From the looks of it, Rafael had intended to go the party. Rolf bit his lip. It didn't look good for the old gent.

Dane closed his eyes and then opened them about thirty seconds later. "Nothing. Rafael is still not responding."

"But you contacted him when we arrived?" Rolf asked.

"No. That was Bruce. He told me about the party and said Rafael wanted us to be there."

Rolf moved out from the desk, careful not to step on Bruce's body. "That means Bruce here was alive when we arrived." He looked down at the body. He couldn't tell for sure, but he thought the way Bruce's cheeks had sunken made the death appear older than an hour.

"We need Abbie to see if there are any other scents," Dane said.

Annwyn nodded and, looking pale, stepped back and edged out the door. Rolf didn't blame her. The body and the smell were not pleasant.

Rolf touched Dane on the forearm. "Abbie is out cold. There's not much we can do here. Can the other members of the triumvirate or their staff start a search?"

Dane rubbed his chin. "They should be here already. This is a serious attack at the heart of the collegium. I can only surmise that they fled when the attack happened. I think we should try to wake Abbie. She may be able to give us a clue. I'll try to locate someone to assist."

They followed Annwyn out into the corridor. She turned, face horror stricken, and shuddered once. "What is it?" Dane asked.

Rolf's skin prickled, sensing danger. "Danger," he said before Annwyn could respond. "I can't tell what exactly, only that I can sense it. We need to get Abbie and leave. Now."

Dane nodded. "Let's move!"

Rolf didn't need urging. He was off and running down the corridor, heading back to the ballroom, not even waiting for Dane and Annwyn.

The ballroom was empty of people now. The injured had been transported and the furniture lay where it had been thrown. Abbie had reverted to human form but still lay unconscious beneath the barrier Annwyn had erected. He wanted to scoop her up and run for it. He stepped closer to her and his hackles rose. Danger! A hint of smoke on the air. He looked around, turning full circle. As Dane and Annwyn careened through the door, a ball of flame burst from the end of the room. He was knocked off his feet as a concussive wave hit. He heard Annwyn scream and Dane shout. Annwyn called out. "Abbie! Quickly." She waved her hand, undoing the barrier.

Rolf dove to cover Abbie with his body, as heat and ash washed over him. A sick, gut-wrenching feeling told him that he was being magically transported, and then carpet mashed against his mouth and nose.

He breathed, letting his senses reach out. The danger had passed. He breathed in deep, recognising the smell of the carpet close to his nostrils. When he lifted his head the halo of smoke that had transported with them nearly overwhelmed his senses. They were back at the hotel in Sydney, in Dane and Annwyn's room.

Taking another breath to assure himself that he could, Rolf sat up and pulled Abbie to him, inspecting her for injury. Her head lolled and her mouth was slack. "Abbie?"

No response.

When Dane swore loudly, Rolf remembered he was not alone. His sorcerer friend rubbed his hands through his hair and paced back and forth, anger wafting off him. They all reeked of smoke. Annwyn waved a hand in front of her face as if trying to brush the smoke taint away.

Dane turned, his face incredulous. "Someone just blew up the collegium headquarters. I can't believe it."

Rolf growled. "Yes, and nearly took us with them."

Annwyn ran her hands down her trousers, apparently checking for burns. Her elaborately coiffed hair fell in disarray around her face. Her head jerked up when Rolf spoke and she backed up to the easy chair and sat down heavily, face extraordinarily pale. "This is serious. I don't think the bomb was there before. We would've detected it, or someone would have. I think it was placed there after we left Abbie behind."

Dane patted her on the shoulder. "It could have escaped detection."

"Then why wait to set it off?" Abbie argued. "Almost the whole place was empty. You saw that everyone had evacuated, the wounded taken away for treatment. We were the only ones there and we left Abbie alone in that room."

Dane sat down on the edge of the sofa, shaking his head with a dumbfounded expression. "You could be right, Annwyn. That means that whoever did this, this rogue sorcerer doubled back and placed a bomb to take out Abbie. She must be a great threat to them. If it wasn't for Rolf and you picking up the sense of danger, Abbie would be dead."

Annwyn nodded, reaching over to pat Dane's large hand. "It could've taken us out as well, if we hadn't been quick enough."

Rolf worried over that. "You think we're all targets?"

Annwyn met his eye. "We are targets, yes, but so are many others. It's like this attack is intended to confuse as well as maim. With so many affected, how do we find the motive, the true reason and who is doing it?"

Worry near overwhelmed Rolf. It had seemed clear before. Someone was attacking people, trying to change them into werewolves and that was leading to the exposure of their world. Now the attack was against vampires, and the collegium itself. Rolf checked Abbie over for injury. As she was naked, it didn't take him long. There was nothing visible except for her being unconscious, which was the result of the attack spell. Annwyn's barrier had protected her until it was dropped, when Rolf dove to protect her. "We were sitting with vampires."

Dane turned his head and locked gazes with Rolf. "Yes, we were. Blowing things up is not their style, though. And Bruce? Would they have wasted all that blood?"

Annwyn pulled pins out of her hair and magically brushed the tangles out of it. "It's very puzzling. I don't know enough about vampires to have an opinion. I'm still rather new to the collegium scene."

Rolf agreed with Annwyn silently. She may be a powerful sorceress, but she wasn't born into this supernatural world. Her body may have belonged to a sorceress, but her mind was all human. No one had really been able to explain how Annwyn was able to do the magic that she did: seeing spells was a bit of a lost art. He'd been there, though, when Annwyn had saved Dane from the curse and healed him. Had seen her kill the sorceress, forever losing her own body in that act.

Rolf didn't involve himself in politics, and why would he even try? Weres were shunned, so why stick your nose in where it wasn't welcome? That didn't mean he didn't have opinions. Rolf began to pace, his anger compelling him to move. He didn't like being ignorant, but there was obviously more going on than any of them previously suspected. He returned to crouch beside Abbie and looked up at Dane and Annwyn. "Do we really understand the politics here? There's a fight over power and leadership in the collegium. Last year, Dane was attacked with a curse. Annwyn, your body was stolen, and you ended up exposing Vollos as the traitor in the collegium's midst. We now think Vollos was involved with Tord's murder." Rolf had not met Dane's father, but he knew the loss of his father and the subsequent attempt to smear his name had hurt his friend. Tord had been one of the triumvirate. "Now this changeling curse has hit. I think that Vollos wasn't behind all the machinations, not solely behind them at least. We thought the push to destabilise was coming from those supernaturals the collegium excluded. But it looks like it isn't. Not that we've been able to find exactly who was behind it. Maybe now others seek to lead, to fill up the space left by Vollos, or maybe that was their plan all along. There are plenty of those disaffected by the current state of things. Could they have abducted Rafael? It would be a significant achievement. The most powerful sorcerer captured, kept prisoner ... killed ..."

Dane grunted. "All true. But the most marginalised group is the weres and they're the ones being attacked."

"It's not just us now, though, is it? We aren't the most despised. I think you'll find the fae are more maligned and mistreated. No one takes a fairy seriously. Weres get some respect, at least, and employment, too. Besides, the attack did appear to focus on weres, on exposing us to the wider world and I don't think a were would attack its own kind. Unless they were mad." Rolf shook his head. "A mad wolf would be put down.

"Besides, this whole thing requires subtlety and that's generally not a were thing. We're passion, brute strength and loyalty. The attacker was using magic. While there are sorcerers and witches for hire, I can't imagine werekind paying someone to do this."

Annwyn looked at her fingernails and brushed at them. Rolf could smell the dried blood. Annwyn must have touched something with Bruce's blood on it. She looked up. "Fairies? I can't see it myself. They're a bit lightweight. Vampires—now that I can see. They're second tier, but maybe they want the top job. But you're right, Rolf. This is a puzzling situation. It seemed so clear that the evil was coming from Vollos and things died down after his death. Now this new threat."

Dane shifted his gaze from Annwyn to Rolf. "I haven't had much direct experience of fairies either, but I recall learning that technology is anathema to them. I can't see them using a bomb."

"So we still know nothing and Rafael isn't around to help shed light on anything," Annwyn said. "What about Brun?"

Dane shook his head. "Rafael said he was on holiday and didn't tell me where, just that he wasn't going to be easy to contact. The old man needed a break."

Rolf snorted. The triumvirate hadn't replaced the third member. With Rafael investigating the conspiracy, Brun had been the key administrator. "That's bloody convenient if you ask me. Now the collegium is leaderless in a crisis."

Rolf looked down at Abbie and, seeing no sign that she was waking up, grabbed a coat and lay it over her. He stood up as he needed to work off his frustration. He strode to the balcony doors and looked out on the harbour, the blue of the water turning darker in the afternoon sun. It was beautiful out there, calm. It was deceptive, though. He was full of anguish. A brush with death was bound to make him reflect on his faults. It was an occupational hazard. An alpha had to protect his pack. While his pack wasn't here, he was employed by Dane and that included protecting the sorcerer. Dane did not have to upbraid him for his faults, as Rolf was quite able to do that himself. He'd let Dane down and he'd definitely let Abbie down.

"I agree. That means we have to focus on finding Rafael. We need a lead, something," Dane said. "You look after Abbie. I'm going to search for a trace of Rafael."

"I'm coming with you," Annwyn said.

"Thank you." Dane held out his hand and she launched out of the seat, suddenly immaculately dressed and hair in rolling waves down her back.

"Rolf? Will you be all right here until we get back?"

Rolf nodded. "Yes, of course I'll be fine. Are you sure you don't want me along? It could be dangerous."

Dane gripped Annwyn's hand. "No, we'll be fine." His gaze dropped to Abbie's inert form. "You're needed here."

"I'll take Abbie to our room and keep an eye on her. Just let me know when you get back."

"Wait just a minute, will you Dane?" Annwyn said before coming over to squat next to Abbie. She slowly caressed Abbie's head and then she sat back and looked Rolf in the eye. "She's really deeply under. Let me see if I can unravel this hex."

Although she wasn't asking for permission, Rolf nodded and made some more room for Annwyn, while Dane watched on.

Annwyn closed her eyes, her hand resting lightly on Abbie's head. Abbie twitched, kicked out a leg but didn't wake. Annwyn pushed to her feet. "I got it, I think. A tight ball of blackout. She should wake within the hour."

Rolf smiled and helped Annwyn to stand. "Thank you. Take care of yourselves. Don't make me come looking for you. Send me a text when you can."

Annwyn went to the wardrobe and pulled out a light kimono robe. Tossing it to Rolf, she said, "You can take this with to cover her up."

Rolf barked his thanks, a part-human laugh and part-wolf acknowledgement.

"Keep me updated."

Annwyn flashed a grin and then hooked her arm through Dane's, smiling up at the tall sorcerer. "We will."

"I'll see you when you get back." Dane and Annwyn disappeared.

Rolf squatted to the floor and remove the coat. The robe was a strong, deep pink with white cherry blossoms on it. A bit too girly for Abbie, he thought. Nevertheless, he threaded one arm through it and rolled her so he could slide her other arm through the sleeve, then he made a reasonable effort to tie it around her waist. She looked less vulnerable with clothes on, and damned pretty. The colour of the robe set off her complexion.

Rolf bent to lift Abbie into his arms. "Now my wee feisty one, let's see if we can make you more comfortable."

It wasn't easy negotiating the way out of Dane and Annwyn's room with Abbie in his arms. When he managed to get in the lift, he had to fish out the room key and ended up placing Abbie unconscious on the floor of the elevator to swipe them to their floor. Carrying her to their room and getting in also proved difficult and somewhat embarrassing. A tall trolley laden with sheets made negotiating Abbie past it difficult. A housekeeper squeaked when she looked up to see Rolf holding an unconscious Abbie. At least she wasn't servicing their room.

"Is everything all right, sir?" she asked. "Do you need a doctor?"

"No. No doctor. Too much to drink," Rolf said. "Could you open the door for me?" He held the swipe key in his hand. The housekeeper slipped it from his fingers and opened the door, holding it for him as he placed Abbie carefully on the bed.

Rolf went back to the door and the housekeeper returned the key. "Is there anything else I can do for you, sir?"

Rolf pulled out some notes and handed them over. "Thank you, no. We'll have a nap and then order room service."

The housekeeper backed out and Rolf shut the door, muttering to himself because of the look of suspicion that never left the woman's face. He glanced over his shoulder to Abbie. He didn't think the woman's unease was due to her recognising Abbie, but more to do with a man carrying an unconscious woman into a hotel room, an almost naked woman. He bet she was ringing downstairs to reception to see if there was a woman booked into this room. As there was, he relaxed somewhat, realising that he wasn't going to be called upon to answer embarrassing questions.

Rolf inhaled, smelling the traces of the explosion in his clothes. He checked that Abbie was in a comfortable position and then went to take a shower. At least when Abbie woke up, he would smell nice.

The hotel shower had great water pressure and Rolf rubbed the soap into his body and shampooed his hair. Something about visiting the collegium made him feel dirty. Murder did that, he supposed. And bombs. He exited the shower and wrapped a towel about his waist while he arranged his hair. His discomfort at being at the collegium was because his kind were not welcome, and only tolerated as employees of members. Rolf didn't want to join the collegium and, as werewolves had their own hierarchy and laws, they didn't need the organisation to survive. He paused at that thought.

Was that it? The attack on the weres, exposing them so they would seek the collegium's protection? Why hadn't he thought of that before? He could have told Dane, maybe had that idea dismissed. But then again, maybe not. It did make a queer kind of sense. He soaped up his face to shave and then shunted those thoughts aside. It was too simple to be the real solution to the mystery. He remembered what the vampire had said—vampires had been raided as well, so it wasn't just weres that were under attack. The triumvirate was practically non-existent and, as they led the collegium, it didn't seem to be a good strategy. It was like whoever was behind this wanted chaos for chaos's sake. Clean shaven he stood there and stared at his reflection, still unsure what the answer was. He wrapped a towel around his waist and went to check on Abbie.

She was still out cold. When he went to her, he could detect an aroma on her, the stray scents of smoke and something else. He returned to the bathroom to wet a hand towel so he could bathe her face and clean her hands. He added one of the scented bath gels to it. When he returned to the bed to start to clean her, he noticed the fine layer of dust and ash on her skin, which brought home to him how close a call it had been. If not for Annwyn's warning, her preternatural sense of wrongness, Abbie could have died.

Thank goodness Annwyn detected something. That thought

loomed large in Rolf's mind. It was like the whole attack was focused on Abbie. But that was a strange, perhaps stupid, idea. Yet, the more he thought about it, the more convinced he was that she'd been taken out on purpose. Why would she be a target, though? Was it because she survived the curse? Or for her gifts? Her nose in particular? Rolf thought it was more likely the former. Abbie wasn't meant to have survived the curse and now that she had, she was becoming a strong werewolf with an exceptional sense of smell. That talent could be useful to track down the cursemaker.

He thought he would take off the robe so he could wipe the ash and dust off her skin, hoping he did not draw her ire when she awoke. He may be her alpha, but she was formidable in her own right. He untied the robe and with warm scented water meticulously bathed every inch of her. When he was done, he tucked her into the bed and went out onto the balcony to brood. He had a lot to think about. Was the attacker the cursemaker or someone else? Was it a group, instead of one person? As he watched the bright golden ball of the sun drop behind the AMP building, he tried to think through the different threads of intrigue. It was not easy. Rolf liked things straightforward and the answer to this problem continued to elude him.

CHAPTER 10

A headache that was like a heavy weight throbbed behind Abbie's eyes. A groan leaked out of her mouth, and she sniffed. Something wasn't right. She knew this instinctively, but couldn't remember where she'd been. This was a different place. Instincts on high alert, she breathed again, trying to make sense of the smells that climbed up her nose. Hotel room was her first thought, but hadn't she been somewhere else? A ballroom, a banquet ... She inhaled and savoured a delicious scent at the back of her throat. Rolf. Rolf was close; his fragrance surrounded her. In an instant she knew that she was safe. If only his nearness, as well as providing comfort, could cure the pain behind her eyes.

"Abbie," Rolf whispered so close to her ear that she detected the damp wash of his breath on her cheek. "Are you awake?"

Abbie groaned louder, failed to open her eyelids or move. "Headache!" she whimpered. She tried to take in her surroundings, but it hurt to open her eyes. The mattress moved as Rolf left the bed. Next breath she heard a tap running. A few moments later, a cool cloth pressed on forehead. She dared to open her eyes, just two little slits.

Rolf stood naked by the bed. No trace of injury.

"You're okay," she observed, enjoying the view. If only she didn't feel like a pile of very warm crap. There had been danger, but Rolf was all right. As for the others, she didn't know yet.

She flicked her narrowed gaze to his face, saw his serious expression, the concern apparent in his eyes. Rolf's lips twitched. Not quite a smile but a relaxing of his features. "Yes, I'm well. Although concerned for you."

"Thank you," she replied closing her eyes again and putting her hand on the quickly warming wet towel on her forehead. "I'm all right, I think," she replied dozily. "Do we have any pain meds? This headache is something awful."

"No, nothing like that." He sat on the edge of the bed. "Besides, being a were, I don't think they work as you remember. Let me help."

Abbie opened her eyelids further, flicking her gaze left and right. "How?" she said, unable to hide the suspicion in her voice. She didn't think sex right now would help the headache and, as far as she could tell, Rolf was ready for action. Or was it that he was always fuckable?

Pain jabbed, making her gasp and she shut her eyes with a snap. The cool cloth was taken away and brought back again. Strong fingers then eased the tension from her scalp. The massage was delicious, divine, wonderful. Pain ebbed away and soon she could open her eyes without cringing at the light or the expected wave of pain.

Abbie had noticed that Rolf was naked, but now he had a hard-on to die for. Abbie almost laughed at the irony and the predictability. What was she to expect? He was a very virile werewolf, and she was naked and practically purring under the ministrations of his fingers. She wasn't quite ready to indulge in lustful pursuits just yet, and was interested to see if Rolf pressed her for sex. However, he didn't. "Better?" he asked, sexy, yellow-tinged eyes bright.

"Yes," she replied in a voice almost purring with pleasure. She undulated on the bed to find an even better position. "That was great. I almost feel like new. Thank you."

He leaned down and gave her forehead a light peck. "I'll put some more cool water on the towel, and you can sleep more if you like."

There was something odd in that statement, a lack of urgency, but obviously they were safe or Rolf wouldn't be so relaxed, so she let the mood take her. She rubbed her face in the pillow. A girl could get used to this. "Thank you, I will." She was tired, so she wasn't faking it, but she was definitely not fragile.

Rolf returned with the cold cloth, lifting the covers and sliding along the sheet to join her in the bed. He pressed the hand towel to her forehead, whispered that she would be better soon. He didn't kiss her or attempt to initiate sex. After gathering her in his arms, he spooned her as he drifted off to sleep behind her. A warm feeling in her gut suffused her body and her mind. He cared, she thought, or was he that much of a gentleman? He could certainly command sex when he wanted. That hard-on of his had been spectacular and she regretted that she hadn't been up to enjoying it. Yet his tenderness had wooed her unexpectedly. Abbie drifted off to sleep, occasionally becoming aware of an erection pressed between her butt cheeks, which infused her dreams with hot sexual fantasies. Even in his sleep Rolf exuded arousal. That had to be it, the scent of his lust infiltrated her dreams, sent her own subconscious down an erotic path. The images in her dream could not be physically possible. Coming out of one dream, dozing before sinking down again, she was half tempted to force herself awake and just take him. Unfortunately, that was nothing more than an idle, dream-drenched thought.

A smile came and went. She didn't feel sorry for him—*poor man with a hard-on that won't go away*—instead she was turned on by his restraint, his over-gentleness and gentlemanliness. He'd seen to her needs when she was unwell, controlling his ardour. The concern he had was starting to overwhelm her, because she hadn't expected him to be capable of such consideration and because she was unused to it. No one had ever cared this much for her and she began to wonder if there was some ulterior motive to his behaviour. She could think of none. Was she so jaded that she couldn't accept tender care? Swear to god, if he fed her breakfast in bed, she'd have to jump his bones. That would just turn her on more than she could control. And food was important between them. She recalled the meat game.

Rolf had wanted her to submit to him because he was the alpha of the pack. That just wasn't going to happen. By now she was certain of that. She'd happily play at submission games, if he was willing to play a submissive part when it was his turn, but doing it for real and forever? No. It was something she could not do.

Was all this care and attention some tactic to get her to submit? She didn't think Rolf would sink that low. He wasn't a jerk or a slime ball. He didn't have that kind of manner. There was something very straightforward about him, the way his mind worked, the way he behaved. He was no saint, obviously, but there was little subterfuge in him. He was more the 'I am a man' and 'these are my wants, comply!' person.

That meant that he had genuine feelings for her. Despite him being alpha, and thinking her pack. She doubted he treated other members of his pack like this. But he probably didn't realise his own feelings. That thought perturbed her. It was hard enough to admit how you felt about another person to them. Rolf would be starting behind the eight ball because he hadn't come to the realisation, nor accepted it. Well shoot!

Rolf tossed and turned and woke up. His movement brought Abbie to wakefulness—she accepted that she needed to wake up. Rolf flung off the covers and a few moments later the sound of water running emitted from the bathroom. He came out in pyjama pants, a fact that sorely disappointed her. Abbie feigned sleep a little longer, still interested in what he did next. A knock at the door and Rolf went to open it. It was not Dane or Annwyn, and Abbie wondered where they were but dropped that thought quickly. Who cared? Rolf carried in a big tray. Abbie was wide awake and the tendrils of delicious aromas filled her nose. She could smell crispy bacon, pork sausages and fried and scrambled eggs, Danish pastries, croissants and coffee. Before he'd crossed the room to the bed, Abbie was sitting up waiting for the food. He placed the tray on the bed and reclined next to it. He had given her breakfast in bed and now she was going to fuck him senseless. But first she had to eat.

Taking a big inhale, she said in a voice dripping with desire, "Wow. That smells great."

Rolf grinned, thinking she really did have a good nose. He lifted the stainless steel covers off the plates. A pulse of scented steam wafted into Abbie's face. She might've died and gone to heaven. Her stomach was punching hungry.

He lifted an eyebrow, assessing her. "I thought it might wake you. I've ordered everything. I thought you may be hungry after all that you've been through. You've been out of it for fourteen hours." He assembled a serving for her while she watched eagerly. The salty toasted smell of the bacon made her mouth water.

"What have I been through?" Abbie asked, taking the plate he passed over. It was piled high with English muffins, crispy bacon, beans, scrambled eggs, mushrooms and two hash browns. Using her fingers, she immediately started crunching on a piece of bacon.

Rolf frowned as he took his own plate and rested it on his knee as he sat on the edge of the bed. "You don't remember?"

"Was it a banquet?" she said vaguely. "I remember food and magic."

Rolf nodded. "What else do you remember?"

Abbie relaxed to let the memory flow. "I remember ... danger."

Rolf nodded. "Anything else?"

Abbie stuffed another piece of bacon into her mouth and chomped noisily. She was trying to recollect, but there was a wall of nothing in her mind.

"And after that?" Rolf prompted.

She picked up a hash brown and demolished it, sorting through strange images in her mind that must be memories. "Was there furniture flying?"

Rolf scooped some scrambled egg into his mouth and swallowed. "Yes. And can you remember anything else?"

Abbie ate another hash brown and licked the grease off her fingers. Then she used the fork to spear a mushroom. "The scent of danger."

Rolf stilled, an English muffin halfway to his mouth. "The scent? The one that tried to kill you?" he asked.

Abbie tilted her head and studied Rolf as the memories rearranged themselves. "I transformed into a wolf, didn't I?" Abbie shifted her butt on the bed. She remembered the wolf, the fur and the fuzzy memories of the animal that was inside her.

Rolf nodded. "Yes, you did. Too quick for me to stop you. Then you went for the attacker."

Abbie licked her lips and took a forkful of beans, chewed then swallowed. "I don't remember much after that."

Rolf cut a piece of bacon into small pieces and then looked up at her. "He hexed you and then disappeared."

Abbie didn't like his tone, as it dripped of blame. "You think him disappearing is my fault?"

Rolf forked a small piece of bacon into his mouth, chewed and swallowed. "No, not really. You placed yourself in danger and I do blame you for that. But the rogue sorcerer could've left at any time. We weren't ready for him."

"So, I was knocked out and you brought me back here."

Rolf's eyebrows furrowed. "It's a bit more complicated than that." He went on to explain how they had left her behind under a magical barrier.

"Rafael was kidnapped? Really?" Abbie replied in disbelief. "I've not smelled him, so I can't help you find him."

Rolf lowered his fork. "What did you say?"

Abbie took up her cup of coffee. "I've not met Rafael, only heard about him."

"No, you said you hadn't smelled him." His expression turned serious, his gaze studying her face, mouth a straight, grim line.

Abbie swallowed the coffee, lowered the mug. "I've memorised all the sorcerers we've encountered. I haven't met Rafael, so I haven't had a chance to say hi or give him a sniff." She grinned, trying to make light.

Rolf nodded, lowering his eyes to his plate and skewering a sausage. This he did not bother to cut into small pieces but chomped directly off the fork. Abbie wanted to eat her portion after watching him devour it.

"You said Annwyn sensed danger, and you ran back to rescue me before I was blown up?"

"Yes, we did not expect that. Explosives are a very human thing, you know."

"Yes, I suppose so, but the magic used to disguise the bomb wasn't human." Abbie sat back as her appetite suddenly fled. If not for

Annwyn's warning, Abbie might be as crispy as the bacon she'd been munching. That was rather sobering.

He lifted his gaze from his plate and fixed her with a stare. "You should've waited for my command," Rolf said, as if he'd been waiting longer than fourteen hours to say it. She didn't detect anger in him.

"Mmm," Abbie said by way of response. Finding her appetite returning, she made quick work of the fried and scrambled eggs on her plate. She glanced at him and saw his face was arranged in hard lines. He was serious about her waiting for a command.

When Abbie thought through what had occurred, she was abashed. Maybe listening to Rolf was a good idea. That idea held for about two breaths, then she thought a 'nah'. Rolf didn't know everything, and he couldn't smell that rogue like she could. She'd be cooperative, of course, but he didn't have her nose.

"Where are Dane and Annwyn?" Abbie asked to try to change the subject.

"They went looking for the rest of the triumvirate to help find Rafael." He cut into the last sausage and put a piece in his mouth. She tried not looking at his mouth.

"Triumvirate? That's three somethings? Explain, please."

"Actually, there are only two at the moment, as the one who died, Vollos, hasn't been replaced yet. He was the sorcerer we thought behind the curse on Dane. I think you recall I told you about Dane being changed to a werewolf and Annwyn losing her body to Nira?"

Abbie nodded, concern wrinkling her brow.

"They're the leaders of the collegium. Rafael is one and there's another one, Brun, who appears to be on holiday somewhere and uncontactable."

Abbie frowned as she listened to this. "You don't think that's rather strange? A holiday where no one can find him and now Rafael's missing too? Are there any backup, step-in-and-take-over people?"

Rolf shrugged. "Look, I'm not that conversant with the running of the collegium. I avoid contact as much as possible. It's only because of Dane that I know what I do. I understand, though, there's administrative staff, human and sorcerer, who keep the day-to-day things running."

"And in a crisis?" She shrugged. "Like they're in now?"

Rolf let out a long drawn-out sigh. "I guess that's why Dane and Annwyn have gone off in search of Rafael." He sat forward and speared the last piece of sausage on his plate. "Rafael is a good friend to them both. He looked out for Dane after his father was murdered." He met her gaze.

"And Annwyn?" she prompted.

"Rafael schooled her in magic and they became close."

"Right." She squinted at him. "That explains why they both went, I suppose." She sat back and pushed her plate away at the same time. "Do *we* have anything pressing to do?" she asked.

There was a hint of a smile on his severe face and then he shook his head. "You're incorrigible. I'm trying to get you to understand the danger and the importance of listening to me. There's a lot going on that you don't understand."

Abbie was rather bored with the conversation. "I'm a fast learner. And a journalist. Was." She grinned evilly. "Besides I have all these untamed urges inside me, looking for an escape."

As Dane and Annwyn were away, she had some time alone with Rolf that she didn't want to waste. Even though he'd put on pyjama pants, his naked torso beckoned. Its glorious expanse was there for her to contemplate. "Are you going to just sit there all morning looking pretty?" she said in a low voice.

Rolf's eyes narrowed. He stood and put their trays on the larger table. "You're feeling better I see," he said, turning toward her with arms crossed.

"Why yes, I believe I am." Abbie threw off the covers, revealing her naked body and offering it to the delight of his eyes. "Are you sure you're up for this?" she asked, indicating her body. "I mean you've been running around the collegium looking for dark sorcerers and you mightn't have any energy left."

A scoff slipped past his lips. "That sounds like a challenge to me," he said, voice deep and sexy. "You may be sorry you cast aspersions on my stamina."

Abbie lifted her arms over her head and then stretched her

muscles, moving her legs one by one, and purred invitingly. "I'd be happy to see what you can do. As for me, I'm up for anything."

Rolf stacked their plates and trays and placed them outside in the corridor. She watched this performance with interest. She'd expected that maybe he'd leap on her, but he was playing it cool.

He came back in and went into the bathroom. She heard the water running, saw the steam billowing out the open door and decided it was best to head in there herself. He'd already had a shower, but she was probably a tad rank. A bit of skin on skin and water wouldn't go astray. She like to be clean when being intimate.

Rolf was ready for her when she entered the large shower stall. Soap glistened off his torso in sleek lines and he drew her to him, her length aligned with his. The sting of hot water made her gasp. Rolf liked the water *hot*. His body ran hotter than normal. She tried to back out from the heat, but he grabbed her around the waist, two strong hands encircling and lifting her until her sex was rubbing against his. He kissed her long and hard.

She wanted to attack him everywhere with her tongue. Wanted to have him gasping as she sucked his erection hard. She wanted him inside her now. But Rolf wasn't going to have it. He deftly grabbed her wrists to avoid her touching his long, thick erection and stopped her dropping to her knees to take him in her mouth.

He pushed her against the wall with his hands, lifting her as he bit along her neck, sending wave after wave of sensation, desire and lust licking through her skin and up her spine until she growled in delight. Not to be outmanoeuvred by him, she drew up her legs and gripped him around the waist, anchoring herself there so she could hold his shoulders and kiss and bite him back. It was his turn to growl. Abbie laughed, unable to control her joy in this hunk of a man. He was as addictive as he was deadly. Deadly because it would be so easy to give in to him, to do what he asked, to be submissive, but something in Abbie just couldn't do it. And she knew that her whole future happiness depended on this one thing. She had to stand her ground. She'd lost her career to the curse, but resistance to Rolf's alpha was what would shape the rest of her life. No way was she going to be just 'pack' to him.

"Fuck me and get on with it," she demanded, trying to get him to impale her with his hot cock.

He managed to undo her legs and force them to the ground. With his hands on both of her cheeks, he leaned in close and said, "No."

Abbie leaned up and tried to graze his chin with her teeth and he pulled back. "Not yet."

Well, if that was the way he was going to play it, she was out of there. She dove under the showerhead, letting the powerful, hot spray sluice off the soap, and stepped out of the shower stall, leaving water to puddle in her wake. It was probably the hardest thing she'd have to do, because she was so hot for him and the wolf in her wanted to rut and rut until she dropped from lack of strength. Grabbing a fluffy white towel and draping it around herself, she left the bathroom.

Rolf stayed in the shower a few minutes longer. Abbie searched for clean clothes and had slid into underwear and was pulling on her jeans by the time Rolf came out of the shower, wearing nothing but droplets of water and a towel slung low over his hips. A dark smattering of pubic hair peeked out to tease her eye. He looked genuinely bemused. "What are you doing? I thought we were ..."

Abbie swung in his direction, her wet hair clinging to her neck. "You said, no, so I figured I should find my fun somewhere else."

Rolf was suddenly still; danger and anger wafted off him. Abbie may have gone too far, but she was beyond being submissive. If he wouldn't play then she was going elsewhere. "You forget yourself," he said in a low voice, devoid of emotion.

She was poised, ready in case he attacked. "No," she said carefully. "I don't forget myself. I'm just not playing the submissive game. I'm not doing it your way."

Rolf scoffed and put his hands on his hips, the tension in the room lessened. "There's nothing submissive about you. I was just trying to slow things down so we could enjoy the moment."

Abbie stilled. Could he be telling the truth? She did try to play fast and hard, but then she wanted him more than once. Had she jumped to conclusions?

"I didn't realise. You could've said."

Rolf let out a chuckle. "There didn't seem to be any time or place to talk. It was just all animal lust."

Abbie lifted an eyebrow at him. "That's true."

"It's just that there's so much going on. I wanted to enjoy this moment, this lull, as much as you do. Who knows what's going to happen next with this business with the collegium." He let out an exasperated sigh. "I want you badly." There was emotion and want in his words and tone.

That last part undid her completely. She wanted him as well and maybe she'd read too much into that 'no'. "In that case, take off that towel," she replied, and pushed her jeans down, catching her feet in her haste to be free of them.

A naked Rolf enveloped her and helped her remove her bra and panties. With a laugh, they fell onto the bed, hot mouths joined in a drenching kiss of ecstasy. Rolf worked his way down her body with his mouth, and Abbie barely had the patience to wait, until his hot tongue swept along her sex. Being so hot and ready, it wasn't long before she was screaming out her orgasm, and fuck the neighbours if they heard her. Inconsiderate she may be, but that was one joyous moment.

Rolf barely had time to lift himself away before she was after his erection. Her mouth punished him, made him groan and cry out as she lathed him and sucked. He had to push her away.

"Stop. I want to fuck you senseless. I can't do that if I'm spent before we begin."

Abbie was panting hard, the beast within in control, but just barely. She managed a growl.

"How do you want me?" he asked, yellow eyes almost glowing with lust.

Abbie flipped on all fours and aimed her butt in his direction. His strong hands drew her back against him. "May I enter my little she-wolf?"

"Yes, dear god. Yes. Now!" Abbie cried and then grunted as Rolf drove into her. The world seemed to stop in that movement and then he drew back and drove in again. She yelled and then he was off. She was grunting and howling and enjoying every moment of him deep inside her. She came and then came again. She'd started to tire before Rolf took his own release, his growl echoing around the room.

Somewhat calmer, she flopped onto the mattress, making post-coital mewling sounds as Rolf dropped behind her and gathered her in his arms. He kissed the top of her head. His thumping heart beat against her back, and his laboured breath fanned her hair. That was some incredible fuck. How was she going to live without it? Rolf was just so much more than any man she'd ever met, and she definitely had not fucked anyone as awesome as he was. If only he wasn't deadset on making her submit to him as alpha. She just couldn't see herself doing it. Snuggling closer, she tried not to think about it. Maybe she could put that confrontation off until another day. Even though she knew that each moment she delayed, the issue would become that much harder to deal with. Rolf would be lulled by their extraordinary sex into thinking that she was pliable, drunk on him and that she'd do anything. But that couldn't be allowed.

Later, they made gentle love, full of kisses, soft caresses and running hands down each other's bodies, she revelling in the texture of his skin, and he hers. The feel of muscle beneath taut skin, the way they just meshed in scent, in looks, in feisty characters. Looking into each other's faces, seeing something there in his eyes, a glow, a fire, something that scared her deep to her soul. It would be a risky thing to have this man-wolf love her. Abbie experienced a moment of fear and inadequacy. Could she love this wolf? At times, she felt like she owned him, that he was hers and that she wanted no other to stand between them. She'd behaved that way to Annwyn, when that other mind, Nira, was in possession. Abbie could have quite happily smacked the other woman down, powerful sorceress or no. At other times, he annoyed her, especially when he tried to dominate or get to submit to him.

With everything that had happened, how was she to know what was real? Was it love or lust for this man? She had a wolf inside her and there didn't seem to be any way to be rid of that. It had been in her blood and the curse had brought it forth. It was impossible now to imagine life without that prowling, angry beast within. She was in Rolf's world, whether she wanted it or not.

If she left him, his pack, what would she do? Her human career was stuffed. She couldn't see a way to explain what had happened, the transformation witnessed, her disappearance. That meant she'd have to move somewhere else—Melbourne, Brisbane or maybe even Perth—and take a new name, establish a new life. She knew she could do it. She wasn't afraid, and she had the strength of mind. She'd moved from the country to Sydney and then to Canberra in pursuit of her career. But leaving Rolf for good? Giving up his body, his naked spirit? Taking herself out of his reach? Could she do that? The cold fist of dread in her gut let her know it wasn't going to be easy, but she'd do it if she had to.

Her sleep must have been deep. Although still dark, dawn was close when Rolf shook her shoulder bringing her to wakefulness. "What? What is it?" she said slowly, not quite as alert as she should have been. The dream she'd been having had been good and the threads of it slipped out of reach, the more she blinked her eyes at the glare from the bedside lamp.

Rolf sat on the edge of the bed and turned to look at her. "Dane and Annwyn aren't back yet. They should be."

Abbie elbowed her way into a sitting position and reached for the glass of water on the bedside table. "How long?" she asked and then took a sip.

"You were out for about fourteen hours and then we've been asleep for another seven. I'd say about twenty hours all up," Rolf replied, face glum. The bedside lamp cast an orange glow on his face, making him appear more tanned that he was.

"That's not too long, is it?" she asked, putting the glass back and shoving her hair out of her face. She thought about them leaving when she'd been out of it. It hadn't been a day, but something was worrying the wolf.

"Not overly long, but Dane's not replying to my text messages, and he hasn't contacted me. That's unusual."

Abbie was slowly coming awake and glanced at the clock. Not long until day break. "What do we do about it? Do we even know where they've gone?"

Rolf launched himself off the bed, making the mattress rebound beneath her. "I don't know. I've not been separated from Dane before, not at such a critical moment. He's the brains and the power. I'm the muscle."

Abbie shoved a pillow behind her neck as she elbowed up further in the bed and then stifled a yawn with her hand. "Why didn't you go with him, then?" Abbie asked while studying his body language.

He threw out both hands. "Because I had to stay and look after you."

"I'm sorry you had to stay behind and now we don't know what's going on." Abbie ventured. It was the only polite way to deal with such a statement.

Rolf stilled and stared at her. "It's not your fault." He took a breath and added, "Actually, it is your fault. If you had obeyed my command, you wouldn't have been hexed."

"Command?" Abbie said, her voice tight. "I didn't hear any commands."

"Well, you should've waited for them before acting."

Abbie threw off the covers and searched the floor for her clothes. "You're certain of that are you? The rogue sorcerer could've hexed me if I'd stayed at the table. I might've been blown up too, if I understand rightly. It doesn't change the fact that you chose to stay with me, rather than go with your buddy, Dane. So don't put that on me."

Abbie had located her underwear and her jeans.

"What are you doing?" Rolf barked at her.

Anger surged. "I'm getting dressed. Or do I need your permission to do that?"

Rolf bristled. "You shouldn't be doing this now. I'm worried for my friends and picking a fight is not the way to get on my good side."

"You have a good side?" Abbie scoffed and found her T-shirt on the back of the chair. "You're either bellowing orders or fucking me senseless."

"You don't complain," Rolf responded hotly. "Particularly the fucking part."

"I am now. When you start blaming me for things that I have no control over. And telling me to obey orders."

Rolf growled. "You will learn to submit."

Abbie stood there, feet apart, shoulders hunched, feeling ready to attack. She replied in a controlled voice, low and level. "I won't."

The silence in the room was deafening. Her heart beat loudly. Rolf's heart beat fast, too. They breathed and just glared. When there was nothing more forthcoming from Rolf, she broke eye contact.

Abbie spotted her boots and walked over to them. A shiver went up her back. Rolf looking at her put her nerves on edge. She'd thrown down the gauntlet and she had to face up to the consequences. She's denied him and was leaving. Her overnight bag was within reach. She could buy another toothbrush and more toiletry items if she had to run. She was eyeing her luggage when Rolf spoke again.

"Stay where you are," Rolf said in a low voice.

Abbie swung around. "Why? What do you think I'm going to do?"

"I can read you. And I can smell a runner. I never thought you were chicken-hearted."

Abbie scoffed at that. "I never expected to be a wolf." She walked up to him and poked him in the bare chest as she spoke. "I won't be submissive. Something inside me won't let me do that. The wolf inside me denies your superiority. Get it? It's either equal, or nothing. Right now, I'm thinking nothing is what it's going to be."

The tension didn't leave Rolf's body. When he spoke, though, it was with a clear and even tone. "I need you right now, Abbie. You have a gift and with it we can find this renegade sorcerer. After we're done, we'll deal with your place in the pack, if that is what you want."

Abbie tried not to gape at him. There was so many things going on in what he'd said, and hadn't said. "You need me to help you find Dane and Annwyn if they're in trouble?"

"Whether they're in trouble or not. This changeling curse has to be stopped. You're the only one who has survived. People are dying Abbie. You wanted to be a reporter, an investigative reporter, so use those human skills along with your wolf nose."

"And what about us?" she dared to ask.

He sighed and pushed at his hair with rough fingers. Then he met her gaze. "We have something going on, Abbie. I want you all the time." His eyes narrowed and his breath hitched. "You affect me more strongly than any other. I don't know what it means. I can't think, right now. I just ask you to trust me and to help me. Later we'll settle this dispute between us."

Abbie looked at her overnight bag, a cauldron of emotion boiling inside—hope, despair, love, fear, uncertainty. She had to hold on to what he said, that they would deal with it later. "Where do we start? We don't know where Dane and Annwyn went."

"No, we don't. But there's still the curse." Rolf tapped his phone. "Another victim. Still alive and in pack hands."

Abbie went to the curtains and opened them. Light spilled across the harbour, making the sails of the Sydney Opera House glow. The water was dark and shadowed, but the commuter ferries had started their crossings, bouncing over the choppy surface of the water. The city was waking up. Looking straight down to the street below she could see traffic queued at intersections and people began to spill out of the train station onto the streets. She didn't know what she was looking for, a sign of Dane and Annwyn perhaps. Decision made, Abbie turned back to Rolf. "Let's go then."

Rolf reached for his jeans and oozed himself into them. Then he grabbed a clean black T-shirt and pulled it on.

"How will we get there?" Abbie asked, as she slipped on her runners.

"We walk," he said. "It's not far."

❧

No doubt it would have been faster to catch a cab or transform into wolf form and bound across the intervening streets, but, as it was, on foot it didn't take much longer than fifteen minutes. They cleared Macquarie Street and ran across the wide expanse of green lawn that was the Domain. A high-rise apartment building towered over the expansive lawns, and a nearby road received traffic exiting the Sydney Harbour Tunnel.

They waited for the traffic light to change so they could cross. At the building's imposing front doors, Rolf pressed the door buzzer and, after a brief exchange, they were let in. The lift was small and not very high end, considering the location of the building. When they stepped into the corridor on the fifteenth floor, Abbie winced at the noise. The traffic was loud even indoors.

When they entered the small apartment, a woman who introduced herself as Skye passed over some earplugs. "You'll need them."

Abbie shrugged but after a few minutes needed to insert them. Her sensitive ears couldn't cope with that constant *whoosh* of traffic and horns. It wasn't just her sensitive wolf ears. Rolf stuck them in his ears too.

Abbie glanced out the floor-to-ceiling window to the tiny balcony beyond. It was like the doors were open, even though they were shut. Inside the building the noise still crept in at uncomfortable levels. Seriously the building needed double glazing and some shoddy builder obviously hadn't included it in the design. It was a bit old, so maybe the traffic wasn't bad back when it was built. Abbie let the subject drop away. Maybe it was the journalist in her, always on to something that didn't seem right or fair.

As she moved around the room, the Domain and the harbour sprang into view through the large windows. "This way," the woman said, opening a door. "In here."

On a bare mattress was a writhing body. Abbie squinted, trying to make sense of the shape. A woman, she thought, based on the slight build, but the smell was bad. Blood, dirt, shit and accumulated unwashed body stench. "Where did you find her?" Rolf asked the woman.

"She's a homeless woman who sleeps across the road. I was on the balcony when I saw her talking to someone—a man. Then he disappeared," she snapped her fingers. "Just like that, and Thelma here fell to the ground. I let my alpha know and went to get her with some of my pack buddies. We brought her here to keep her out of view. She's still alive," she looked at the partially transformed body. "I don't think she'll make it. It's been too long and she's weak." Skye wiped at the end of her nose. "Poor cow didn't stand a chance. She was already weak from lack of proper food and housing. This will finish her for sure."

"Keep her comfortable," Rolf said, a look of concern on his face, which Abbie didn't understand. Was it the transformation, the fact that the woman was homeless, or because she wasn't going to make it?

Rolf knelt next to the partially transformed woman and stroked her head softly, whispering to her that it would be all right. Abbie stepped back as if punched. She hadn't expected Rolf to be tender like that, to care. Just a second before she was wondering if he was looking down on a homeless woman and she'd been wrong.

Rolf rocked back up to his feet and met Abbie's look. "There's not much we can do here." He jerked his head at the window and spoke to Skye. "We need to find the bastard doing this. Can you show us exactly where you saw this man?"

Skye led them to the balcony. It was small and uncomfortably noisy. On well-balanced feet, she pointed. "There near that pine tree, the one with the bench beneath it. She was about ten steps downslope from there. That's the best I can make it from here. I can show you in person if you like."

Rolf shook his head. "Please stay with Thelma. We'll be back to check on her as soon as we can. Abbie?"

Abbie jerked as if he'd poked her. "Yes."

Skye stared at her, not in a hateful way, but as if she couldn't figure out just what Abbie was. "Ready?"

"Yes, Rolf." Abbie nodded to Skye, acknowledging the other were. She kept her hands balled into fists at her side. Skye had done her best to hide her attraction to Rolf and Abbie was glad of it. It wasn't time to be bitch-slapping some poor werewolf. Rolf walked between them both, heading to the door. "Abbie!"

"Coming." Abbie jerked, taking her eyes off Skye, and followed.

Rolf left the door ajar. By the time she caught up to him, he'd summoned the lift. The corridor was small and full of odours. The lift pinged and the doors opened with a squelching sound as the rubber seals separated. Rolf entered and stood at the back, hands folded in front of him as if he was standing at ease. "We need to be quick to pick up the scent. If you can't find a trace we'll come back here and see if we can help with Thelma or what's left of her."

Abbie's stomach turned. Thelma was a mess and she smelled so bad from being unwashed and covered in street dirt, it was unlikely that Abbie could pick up any other scents at all. However, she wasn't about to say so, not with Rolf all alpha and determined. Besides, as it had happened less than an hour ago there was a chance that Abbie could pick up the sorcerer's trail.

On exiting to the street, Abbie noticed dark roiling clouds building up like the aftermath of an explosion. A storm hovered, ready to unleash a downpour. The taste of rain filled the air. From the uptick in the wind, it wouldn't be long. "We need to be quick," she said to Rolf. "The change in the weather will kill the trail dead."

He took her hand, guiding her through the line of cars pulling up at the traffic lights. Shaking off the stress of the crossing, they climbed the side of the park and made it to the spot Skye had pointed out, where she'd seen the man disappear. A fork of lightning split over Centrepoint Tower and tickled the tops of nearby buildings. A few moments later the deep rumble of thunder reverberated around them.

Abbie could smell things, conflicting things. "I need to transform," she said to Rolf. "Now, before the rain kills it all."

"Agreed. I'll stay human and watch over you."

Abbie called the wolf forth. It came easily; just a blink and there she was, tongue licking fangs, growls leaking through her mouth. Rolf picked up her clothes and tucked them into a fold-up rucksack he took from his back pocket. This he put on his back. He looked ready to run.

The black-and-white world confused Abbie at first, then the smells assaulted her. She needed to sort through them and decide which were important. Thelma she could taste on her tongue, her trail criss-crossed this area many times in a meandering pattern that seemed to have little design. Fresh scents and stale ones. Abbie sorted through them.

While recognising Thelma in amongst the other smells, the wolf didn't find the homeless woman's scent repulsive, just interesting, like a tale about where the woman had been and what she'd done, what she'd eaten and who she'd hung with.

Sea smells dominated the air as well—gulls, rotting fish, oil on water. The grass was fine and almost like carpet. Her nose picked up a number of other scents. Skye's scent overlaying the other. This she separated to reveal what she suspected. The scent of the one she recognised. Skye had said the man had disappeared, but the scent trail went off through the park as if the man had walked rather than transported himself. Maybe Abbie should have been suspicious at the ease of discovering this fact, only the scent didn't lie.

This was also confusing. Why would a sorcerer do that? Why walk when you could disappear with a wave of your hand. Something didn't sit right, but Abbie had enough of the scent now to follow it in human form. She transformed back as discreetly as possible. Rolf, sensing her move, had dug out her clothes and tried to hide her from view. The main onlookers were the people in the cars below and maybe the werewolf friends in the apartment. Abbie had her bra and T-shirt on and was struggling into her underpants and her jeans when Rolf started peppering her with questions.

"You found his scent?" Rolf asked as he passed her boots over. Abbie sat on the park bench that had been their marker.

"Yes," she said, slipping a foot into the first boot and zipping up the side. She pushed the remaining foot into the brown leather. "He went that way," she said and pointed.

"Walking?" Rolf said, leading Abbie to understand that he thought it as strange as she did. "So it's definitely the same sorcerer?"

Abbie smiled and stood up. "Yes. You coming?" She bolted along the scent trail. It took Rolf a heartbeat to catch up with her, as he was squishing the thin rucksack into his back pocket.

"Did you pick up any other scents?" Rolf asked breathily from beside her.

"Do you mean Dane and Annwyn?"

Rolf grimaced.

"No, not yet. But you think he has them?"

"Yes," Rolf replied. "I can't say why, but I think he's leading you there with his scent. He knows you can smell him. It feels like a trap to me."

Abbie nodded and took the next street, leaving Macquarie Street behind. Scents here were competing and for a minute she thought she'd lost the trail. Then, turning her head, she caught it again. "Down there. It's stronger. No other familiar scents."

Turning down another alley, the scent suddenly got stronger and then faded. Abbie stopped and turned full circle. It was there and then it wasn't. No way was the sorcerer going to lead them here for nothing. "Be careful. The scent is gone."

Rolf growled and swear words funnelled out of his mouth. Abbie sympathised.

"It's a bitch, all right," Abbie said when Rolf stopped cussing.

They were in a dead end. Once-yellow dumpsters overflowed with restaurant waste, some spilling over the sides like a head on a beer. A pile of rotting meat was a feast for flies in one corner in the gutter. A pool of rainwater dimpled as the rain drops fell. The roiling dark grey clouds overhead were ominous. A distant rumble of thunder meant the storm was going to be a big one.

"Have you lost him?" Rolf asked.

Abbie shook her head. "I don't know." Abbie walked in a big circle, sniffing and lifting her head on the breeze. There was just a thin trail of scent, weaving and diving from the direction of a single-fronted, three-storey building between two restaurants. "In there." Abbie pointed.

Lightning lit up the sky overhead. A few seconds later a great clap of thunder scattered the flies and made gulls squawk. They lifted out of the dumpsters and launched themselves to the sky.

"Wait here," Rolf said.

"No. I'm coming with you. You could take a wrong turn."

Rolf shook his head and glared at her. A look that said 'later'.

A steel door with flaky red paint opened when Rolf tugged on it. The rusty hinges sang out their complaint so loudly that no one would miss their entry. The corridor was filled with refuse, and the smell of broken sewer pipes and damp made Abbie recoil and wish her nose was not so sensitive. It was hard to filter out the smells, but there it was, the scent of the sorcerer who had cursed her, tried to kill her. A staircase waited for them and up they went, until they reached another floor.

Walking down another corridor they stopped at the head of a hallway. "Take the left," she whispered to Rolf. Outside, the rain changed from light to heavy. The constant drip, drip from a leaky gutter added to the sound of their footsteps and the scurry of rats. Abbie had never been in such a hovel in her life. A loud bellow of thunder vibrated in her lungs. The storm was above them now—all torment and revenge. They passed a half door, the upper part glass and the lower wood. Graffiti decorated it in fluoro pink and green. They kept moving.

A sound ahead alerted them that they were not alone. A clang of metal or a shout, it was hard to tell with the storm thrashing the building and all the loose fittings beating a drum. "Keep going," Rolf said in a rough voice. He turned his head from side to side, careful of where they were going. The floor creaked badly. Up ahead holes in the floor testified to the rotting wooden boards beneath. "Be ready to shift," Rolf warned.

Abbie nodded. She was less likely to get hurt in wolf form, although unfortunately less able to communicate. Rolf checked the floor, using his right foot to feel his way forward and then to the left. Abbie waited and watched, making sure to follow his footsteps. The floor closest to the wall was firmest. Abbie tried not to look at how far it was to fall. The building had lower levels, basements she thought. The odours rising up from there made her shudder. They reeked of death and rot. Goosebumps rose on the bare skin of her arms and the hair on the back of her neck stood up. Rolf lifted a hand and she stopped, her breath coming in short, hard pants.

Rolf pointed sideways, indicating a closed door. Abbie stepped up next to him ready to enter. The rogue sorcerer's scent was strong, layered thickly all around as if he had marked the place as territory, something her wolf understood.

Abbie closed her eyes and inhaled. There were two other scents here—Dane and Annwyn. That must be what Rolf had detected.

They stood there for a few minutes, waiting. For what Abbie didn't know. It was obviously a trap of some kind. Trouble was, would springing it harm Dane and Annwyn? Abbie didn't know what to do, and Rolf was obviously considering his options. He reached out and tried the door. The handle turned without trouble, without sound. It must have been oiled because everything else in this dive complained when touched, turned or walked on.

The door opened slowly as Rolf squeezed himself against the wall. Abbie did the same. Nothing blew up, came out at them and no one called their name. Was there someone in there? They had to be cautious. The sorcerer didn't just use hexes, he'd placed a bomb at the collegium headquarters.

A smell wafted out the door. "Natural gas," Abbie hissed. Natural gas was impregnated with a pungent smell to advertise leaks.

Rolf nodded. "Not good. Dane and Annwyn are inside," he whispered back. He lifted an eyebrow, the do-or-die challenge.

Abbie nodded. Rolf threw himself through the door, rolling along the floor. Abbie got on all fours and peeked around the doorframe. Rolf was unharmed and darkness near swallowed him. The windows were painted black. The thunder rattled the window panes and tortured Abbie's ears. The smell of the gas was stronger now. She needed to shut the leak off and quickly. Rolf was moving, creeping along the floor as Abbie had chosen to do. She hoped the air was better on the ground. The gas was worrying, though. Could it be used to set off an explosion?

"Annwyn?" Abbie called in a whisper-thin voice, shaking her head as a bubble of gas seemed to coalesce in front of her nose. She waved a hand to dispel the stink of it.

A muffled sound greeted Abbie's inquiry. They were gagged then. Rolf crept forward and Abbie searched for a valve to shut off the gas. There were rusty looking pipes along the wall and some hanging from the ceiling. She needed to find the ones for gas. Her nose told her where it was coming from. She needed clean air, too, as her head was getting muzzy, so she crouched down and scrambled along the floor. Newspapers and other unrecognisable debris touched her hands as she crawled. Lots of fuel for a possible fire. With a potential gas explosion, they didn't need anything else to make matters worse. She felt around for something heavy and found what seemed to be a crowbar or a pipe. She made her way to the blackened window. Once there, she checked behind her. Two dark shapes loomed. Dane and Annwyn tied to chairs, she thought. She lifted the metal implement and swung. A crack sounded and as the impact vibrated through her arms, she dropped it. The black window wasn't glass. It was metal and not breakable. The gas smell was getting stronger. "Rolf?" Abbie said and coughed. "Have you got them?"

No answer. "Rolf?"

Panic reached up and grabbed her by the throat. Was he hurt, overcome by the gas? Abbie fought her way over to a pipe that hissed gas into the room. Feeling around she tried to find a way to shut it off but there was no shut-off valve. The pipe had been severed and the shut-off valve was obviously elsewhere. There was no way to shut it off from inside the room, not in the dark.

There was a sound of movement. "Rolf?"

Nothing. Her voice rose with alarm. "We have to be quick!"

Abbie made her way to where she thought Dane and Annwyn sat slumped. "Dane? Annwyn?"

The bodies felt strange. Her nose told her they smelled like their missing friends, but when an arm fell to the floor, she realised they had been tricked. They were dummies, not bodies, wearing Dane and Annwyn's clothes. "It's not them!" she cried out, now seriously concerned that Rolf had not responded, and she couldn't detect him moving. "It's a trap!"

Abbie went in the direction of where she'd last heard Rolf and stumbled on his inert form. They had to get out of there. How was she going to carry him? He was bigger than her. "But you have the wolf," she said to herself. She didn't have to transform to use its strength. She felt along Rolf's body. He groaned when she touched his face. "Rolf! Help me, we have to get out of here."

She dragged his arm across her shoulder as he tried to stand, fumbling with his feet to get them under himself. Eventually she got him upright enough to put him in a fireman's hold and then staggered for the door. She had to move quickly. The hall was riddled with holes. She leaned over to look at one. She could do it. She could jump down. There wasn't any time to think on it. She leaped, and crashed into something, grunting as it struck her in the gut. She let go of Rolf as they landed and rolled. They had fallen into the basement. She shook his inert body. "Rolf?" At least she couldn't smell the gas anymore, but they were still in danger.

She slapped his face. That didn't do much, so she tried mouth to mouth. He coughed and pushed her off. Abbie landed on her rear and she didn't know whether to laugh or cry. She went to the windows, which were covered in wire grills, testing them one by one. Then went back to the beginning. They were small, so it should be possible to wrench the covering off to escape to street level. Again, Abbie had to call on her inner wolf. With bare hands, she pulled at the grill. Nothing. She focused her will and yanked again, harder. The wire mesh started to shift. She needed more, though. Again, she yanked and pulled, using her feet to give her more force. The grill gave and she fell backwards.

"Rolf," she said urgently. "Get up. We've got to get out."

A slight taste of smoke and ozone in the air, left her dreading what would come next.

Without thinking, she heaved Rolf up from the ground and shoved him through the window space. She growled and screamed and pushed. He fell through into the street and Abbie climbed out after him. A push of air reached her, followed by a fire *thwump* sound and the crack of the building as the force of an explosion tore through it. Looking up, she saw the building's facade start to crumble. Bricks spiralled outward, glass shattered and sprang in all directions. Wood split and metal screamed. All she could do was throw herself over Rolf as the debris rained down. She didn't register pain, just the sense that she was falling, falling into a deep dark pit.

She didn't know how long she'd been unconscious when the pain woke her. A wooden door lay across her head and she pushed at it. Bricks and dust slid down her back. Not a good idea then to try and move, as she didn't know how much debris lay above them. She lay on top of Rolf and he was still. She hoped she hadn't smothered him. "Rolf?" Abbie said and coughed and then froze. Coughing hurt. Something was sticking out through the flesh of her belly and her back hurt. What had Rolf told her? Transforming into a wolf can help with healing? But Rolf needed her in human form to get help. Abbie screamed, hoping that someone was there to hear her. The faint sound of sirens reached her. She could no longer hear the storm. "Help!" she cried, despite the agony of her wound.

Rolf moved beneath her, finally coming around.

"Rolf?" she said urgently, running a hand over his head. "Be careful. We're buried. There was an explosion, understand?"

She felt him move his head. Abbie closed her eyes in relief. She hadn't until then let herself fear that he was dead. Her strong Rolf had been knocked out. She didn't know how and it didn't matter now. They had knowingly walked into a trap. The sorcerer doing this certainly knew Rolf and Abbie, knew their movements, and at least suspected her nose would track him there. It made sense, as she'd been able to follow him. Who was doing this? *Why* were they doing this? Were they crazy as Dane and Annwyn thought? Crazy implied stupid and whoever was doing this was not stupid.

Rolf tried to move again, and Abbie cried out a warning and he stopped. "I'm hurt," she said breathlessly, keeping her breath shallow. "Something is stuck in me. Wood or metal, I'm not sure. Nod your head if you're unhurt."

Rolf nodded his head. Abbie called out again, holding her side to halt the shift of whatever was sticking into her. "Help!"

Debris above them shifted. Her voice was not loud enough, she realised, as the debris reflected her words back, but she had to keep trying and hope someone could hear her. "Here. We're here."

More debris moved. A torch light moving around the debris caught Abbie's eye. Fresh air leaked down to their spot. "Here," she said in an almost whimper. "I'm hurt. There are two of us."

"Hang on, luv," a fireman said. Through the rubble above her, she could just make out a helmet and thick yellow coat. Abbie closed her eyes and let out a sigh of relief.

"Help is here," she said to Rolf.

He nodded his head. Abbie could sense outrage emanating off him. They had been caught in a trap, and he'd been taken out, and that would seriously bruise his alpha ego for sure.

It took another two hours for the rescuers to uncover them. Each piece of debris had to be assessed before it was removed. The bulk of the building hovered over them and each time they removed something they had to be careful to not bring the rest of it down. All the while the man who had found them kept talking to them, attempting to keep them calm and reassured.

Finally, after the last piece of debris was removed, Abbie was lifted onto a stretcher on her side. A piece of wood an inch thick had pierced her back and now stuck out of her mid-section. A medic flashed a light in her eyes, put an oxygen mask over her face and eased sticky contacts onto her chest to monitor her heartbeat. "Rolf," she said, trying to pull the mask away.

"They're bringing your friend out now." He put the mask back over her nose and mouth.

The ambulance trolley jolted as they moved her closer to the ambulance and lifted her into the back. Bright lights blinded her. The press were there and Abbie put her face to the gurney so she couldn't be seen.

Shouts came as more debris fell. She closed her eyes and feared the worst. Pushing up onto her hands, she swivelled her head to see. "Rolf!" she cried.

A medic leaned in closer, squatting down so she could see him without lifting her head. "It's all right. Your friend's out. They're just checking him out now. Anyone else in there that you know of?"

"No ..." Her voice was pain-gripped. "Just ... us ..." The aftermath of her fear response made her heart beat faster and her hands shake. Someone had tried to kill them. Nearly succeeded.

"Headache?"

Abbie inclined her head slowly.

"Do you know what caused the explosion?" he asked, as he attached a pulse oximeter to her finger.

Abbie rocked her head from side to side, fighting for clarity as a wave of nausea hit. "Gas," she breathed out. "Someone ..." she licked dry lips. "Someone cut a gas line. Barely ... barely got out."

He took her wrist. "You're safe now and doing amazingly well." He looked at the smoking ruin of the building. "The electricity had been switched back on, according to the fire brigade. That old place, it wouldn't take much for the old wiring to ignite the gas. Not much left now."

Abbie grimaced. It might look like an accident, but she knew better.

He put an oximeter of her finger. "How are you feeling? Your oxygen levels are good, pulse strong." After wrapping blood pressure cuff on her he took her blood pressure. "How's the pain levels."

She wanted to quip 'How would you feel with a bit of wood in your back and your body pummelled by bits of brick and masonry' but didn't. "Not bad, thanks."

"There's a good girl. We'll get you to hospital soon and they can get that nasty splinter out. And scan you for broken bones and internal bleeding." There wasn't much left of her top and her jeans were now cut down the rear centre seam. The medic sponged at smaller cuts and tried to cover her with a blue disposable sheet.

Abbie groaned. She couldn't let them take her to a hospital. "If it's all the same to you, I'd prefer to just pull it out now."

"What?" The man near jerked out of his seat. "We can't do that. You'll haemorrhage. I'm a paramedic not a surgeon. That injury will require surgery."

Now that the adrenalin rush was subsiding, Abbie was feeling stronger and more alert. "What about my friend? Is he injured?" Abbie started thinking things through, working out possible scenarios for escape. It was imperative that she wasn't taken into hospital and identified. Also, there would be official questions, police. She shook her head, hoping to clear it.

The medic's brown eyebrows drew together over the top of his nose. "My partner is assessing him. He's been knocked out, right? And he has numerous cuts and contusions. He has to be stabilised before we move him in any case. As soon as the second ambulance arrives for him, we'll be off."

"Can't we travel together?"

"I'm sorry, miss. But there's not enough room for two of you."

A siren scream drawing close heralded the arrival of another ambulance. She lost track of what was going on. Next thing she knew the other medic closed the rear door, before climbing into the driver's seat and keying on the engine. The medic attending to her pumped up the blood pressure cuff again.

"Please, I have to be with him," she said, trying to get off the gurney and stifling a grunt when the movement hurt.

A surprisingly firm hand held her still and shoved a green whistle thing at her. "Just breathe into this little tube. It will help with the pain."

"Fuck the pain," Abbie yelled and then grabbed the piece of wood sticking out of her mid-section and yanked, swift and sharp. A scream ripped from her throat as intense pain immobilised her. The medic had tried to grab her hand but wasn't quick enough and just shouted for help. The driver stopped the ambulance.

In the chaos and shock, all Abbie could see was blood all over the white sheet on the gurney and the medic with blood sprayed up his neck and gloved hands as he fought to keep her still. When the rear door opened, Abbie lunged, calling to her wolf as she did so. The remains of her clothes fell away.

The driver stumbled back and Abbie hit the ground on all fours. Weakness nearly overwhelmed her, but the magic of the transformation marched along her veins, beating back shock and fatigue, filling her with energy and healing.

The medic 's shock-filled cry echoed. Abbie clawed the ground, howled at the sky and bolted toward Rolf. He must have heard her, because there were more screams and humans went running as the wolf claimed him.

Abbie raced on, her certainty that Rolf loped close behind confirmed by his howl by her rear flank, giving her a burst of speed. They were out of that little cul-de-sac in less than five seconds and they kept on until they made it to the Royal Botanical Gardens, where they stopped.

The rain had lessened and the lightning dappled the thunder clouds. A cool breeze ruffled her fur, but she didn't feel cold just yet. Taking a deep breath and focusing her mind, Abbie transformed back into human form.

Her naked skin was wet, and she rubbed at the dampness, hoping to ward off a chill. Her wounds were no longer bleeding. With a crack and a growl, Rolf followed suit. Buck naked, he scowled at her, his eyes glittering as he looked her up and down. He was as whole as she was.

Abbie scanned their location and saw that there was no one close. Rolf spoke close to her ear and his rich scent teased her nostrils. "A bit dramatic, don't you think?" Rolf asked. She turned and saw the tenseness in the jaw, his muscles bristling.

Abbie smiled at the view. "Yes, but necessary. It was better than being identified by the press or at the hospital."

Rolf scowled at her for a few more moments and then broke off his gaze and shook his head. "Damn. I didn't think of that. But now we've made a scene."

Abbie lost the smile and frowned. "Okay, so that wasn't good, but with any luck they'll think that it was a hallucination."

"We're going to need clothes if we stay in human form," Rolf commented.

"Can we make it back to the Domain and signal the other weres?" Abbie asked.

Rolf rubbed his goatee. "That should do it. If they trailed us, they may already know our predicament."

The sound of a branch breaking had them ducking behind a tree. Rolf inhaled deeply and Abbie did the same. There were definitely weres out there. No one familiar, though.

Rolf patted her shoulder and bid her stay there out of sight, while he slipped out into the open. "Come out. We know you're there."

Wearing human skin, two males and a female came out into the open. One male had dark, curly hair, pale skin and was tall and broad. He identified himself at Cole, the second was blond and a smaller build, who called himself Nate. The woman was older, with grey hair, wearing a nondescript dark grey leisure suit, who looked fit and healthy. She said her name was Reeva. "You survive that ambush?" she asked in a gravelly voice, which suggested she was or had been a heavy smoker.

"Yes," Rolf said. "You Sydney pack?"

Cole nodded.

"Can you get us some clothes? We had to leave in a hurry."

The old woman stepped forward, used her chin to nod in the direction of the smoke billowing up from beyond the Domain. "We saw. She is reckless this one. Brings danger."

Rolf grunted. "She had her reasons."

The old woman's silver-coloured eyes reflected moonlight. "She's the one that lived." It was a statement.

Abbie acknowledged Reeva with a nod, keeping up eye contact with the older woman.

Rolf came up close to Abbie, half guarding her body with his own. Abbie wanted to jab him in the ribs for his audacious move. Reeva was no threat, so he didn't have to get all alpha and protective. "Will you help us?" Rolf asked.

Reeva shifted her gaze to focus on Rolf. "We will get you clothes, alpha of Canberra pack. Skye said to tell you Thelma didn't make it."

Abbie came forward, hand out to thank her. The old woman backed away and Abbie lowered her hand. Obviously touching between packs was not acceptable; or maybe it was that this older she-wolf was wary of Abbie. Both were possibilities. "Tell Skye I'm sorry about Thelma," Abbie said in a soft voice. "We'll do our best to find out who is doing this and stop them."

Reeva lifted the side of her mouth. Abbie couldn't decide if it was a half-smile or a sneer. "I'll pass on your message to Skye. You did well to survive that explosion. I respect your abilities, but if this *meshugga* doesn't end, all of us will be exposed."

Abbie understood the word *meshugga* meant something like mess or chaos in Yiddish or maybe Hebrew. She wasn't sure how she knew, maybe some popular culture reference. She agreed with the sentiment, no matter how it was expressed.

"We'll wait here while you get us some clothes. Also, I left my personal items at Skye's house. Can these also be returned to me?"

Reeva bowed her head. "It will be as you ask." Cole nodded as if receiving a silent command and bounded off into the night. He was fast as a human and Abbie wondered how fast he'd be in wolf form.

CHAPTER 11

"Is there anything else you can tell us?" Rolf asked the older woman. He was trying to place her and the only thing he could call to mind was that she was the current alpha's mother. Gene Cohen was the name of the Sydney City alpha. He was a property owner and financier, as well as the city's pack alpha. Reeva had a slight accent that spoke of a middle-European origin. It was possible that Reeva knew a lot more about the European scene than Rolf did, as he was Australian born. His only trips abroad had been with Dane. Although Rolf's father had been of German extraction, he knew very little of the country his father had originated from.

Reeva studied him. "Is there something wrong?" he asked the old woman, feeling her gaze burn across his skin.

"You are Georg's son," she stated.

Narrowing his eyes, he studied the old woman. "Yes, but he went by the English version of his name, George, to fit in."

"Don't talk to me about fitting in." She screwed up her mouth like she was chewing glass, paused and relaxed her expression. "I knew him in his younger days."

Rolf's heart jolted, but he held himself still. He didn't know what to say, what to ask. It would seem too eager to blurt out all the questions that rushed into his throat. He took a breath and willed his heart rate to slow. "Did you know him well?"

Reeva stood still for a moment, giving no hint of emotion in her stance or expression. Then suddenly, her face altered, her lips curved up in a smile, and then a grin. She nodded her head slowly, shoulders relaxing. "Oh yes, I knew Georg well. Very well."

Rolf waited, but she didn't elaborate and now wasn't the time to pursue it. The words and how they were said were loaded with meaning, leading him to believe his father and this Reeva had shared intimacy on more than one occasion.

Rolf inclined his head to show respect. The last of the storm clouds blew away and a half-moon skimmed over the sky. Reeva's eyes caught the light and glowed silver.

Abbie stepped forward. "Is there anything more you can tell us about what's been going on? About what this sorcerer looked like?"

Reeva turned to Abbie and Rolf grew wary. There was some hostility there, which he didn't understand. It was strange that Abbie didn't seem to notice it, but Rolf could feel the tension from Reeva like a scrape of a nail along his skin.

"He stinks of age. The scent is familiar to me."

Abbie frowned as she digested this. "You know him?"

Rolf stood up straighter, keen to hear what the old woman said and ready to chastise her for not speaking up sooner. "Maybe I knew him once, long ago. Back there in Europe. He was not one to walk these ancient lands before. Not like this."

"Do you have a name, woman?" Rolf said brusquely, annoyed at the vague reference to someone who wasn't a local.

Reeva turned back to him, thinned her lips tight over her front teeth. "You're a pup to speak to me that way. A name means nothing!" she all but hissed at him. "Names change." He thought anger would take over. Instead, she took a breath and shook her head slightly as if throwing off a bad feeling. "It is the essence of the person that does not change.

Rolf bowed his head. "You're right. I'm sorry Den Mother; I should not have let my frustration show. My friends are missing and that can be my only excuse."

Reeva nodded slowly, her sneer turning to a smile. "You honour me with such a title, young wolf. I accept your apology. Cole comes and then I give you the information that I have."

"Information," Rolf said as Cole came into view with a dark-coloured knapsack on his back. This he swung off and tossed to Rolf. Unzipping the bag quickly Rolf passed the donated track pants and a top to Abbie and took the larger set for himself. He dug out his phone and checked the messages. There were none, nor were there any missed calls. Rolf pulled on his pants and struggled into the sweatshirt. "Thank you, Cole, for your swiftness. And thank the pack for their assistance."

"Reeva," Abbie said, pulling her long hair out from the neck of her sports top. "You mentioned information. Do you have word of Dane and Annwyn?"

Reeva smiled. "I certainly do."

"Then tell us. We have little time." Rolf bunched his arms and bent his knees slightly, ready to take off at a run.

"Trouble comes. We must get out of here. There are people searching for you both. I hope you can run in bare feet."

"Yes, lead the way."

Cole and Nate sprinted away into the darkness. The stars peeked out now that the clouds were almost gone. Reeva turned to them. "We will draw close to the expressway. Take care and follow me. My house is not far."

Reeva took off after the two males and Rolf took Abbie's hand as they sprinted after her. Reeva knew a path through the botanical gardens and leaped fences. The drone of traffic grew louder as they made their way along the shoreline out of the gardens and into Woolloomooloo. The suburb's name was meant to be derived from local Aboriginal words but Rolf didn't know for sure. Here Reeva led them to the Finger Wharf Apartment complex, built on a hundred-year-old wharf, which was a quarter of a mile long. This was prime real estate. Gene Cohen had to be loaded to afford an apartment here. The smell of stale sea and fish was strong. Nearby boats and yachts rocked on the harbour tide.

Rolf checked his surroundings, noting the skyline and the darkness that was the botanical gardens. So close to where they had nearly died. Rolf paused. He hadn't thought of the incident like that before. That it could've been fatal. There had been no time to think about it.

Reeva keyed the security. "Come in and be welcome." The old woman nodded goodbye to Cole and Nate as they departed, retracing their steps along the boardwalk.

Rolf steered Abbie lightly by the elbow and together they followed the old den mother into the complex. "Let me go," Abbie hissed.

Rolf removed his hand. He wanted to touch her, didn't want to let go. He'd been close to losing her and just the thought of that slid cold steel into his gut.

The moderately spacious apartment had views out to the marina through windows that opened onto a large balcony. The obviously expensive furnishings were sedate. Rich cream-coloured couches, warm beige carpet. Dark marble on the bar and in the kitchen. "Take a seat," Reeva said and left the room.

Rolf barely controlled his impatience, but did as he was bid.

Very quickly, she returned to the room in a new outfit after changing out of her nondescript clothing. In the concealed lighting of the apartment, Rolf saw that Reeva was wearing a pantsuit, a one-piece thing in a flimsy, floral material. He thought it could easily screw into a ball and fit in a wolf's mouth. His respect for the old den mother increased.

"Drink?" Reeva asked.

"Yes, thank you."

Abbie said yes too. Reeva didn't specify what was on offer and Rolf didn't care. He could use water or whisky or both together. She passed him a finely cut glass, ice chinking in the swirling golden liquid—scotch on the rocks. To Abbie she handed off some kind of green smoothie. Reeva took a tall glass of water.

Abbie downed hers and smacked her lips when she finished. Rolf took a sip of the single malt, its peaty aroma filling his nostrils as he savoured the taste. From the island of Islay, he thought. Top shelf. "You have information for us?" he said through the burn in his throat.

Reeva sat in the single lounge chair and eyed them over her glass. "Yes. Your friends were seen being loaded into a van down near

Circular Quay. The number plates have been identified and an address found. I'm waiting to hear what the result is."

"You have pack in the police force?" Rolf asked.

Reeva took a sip of water. "We have friends where we need, not necessarily pack."

"Were they alive when they were seen?" Rolf asked.

"Yes, we think so. They were not conscious. I suspect transporting powerful sorcerers would be difficult if they were awake. The driver of the van and the attendant weren't supernaturals. I have that on good authority."

"Humans?" Rolf asked.

"Yes, hired help, I suspect," Reeva said.

Abbie sat forward. "Expendable too, I think."

"Yes, and not good people," Reeva said. "That is why I thought it best to bring you here, until there is more definitive word. And I wanted to get to know you better."

Rolf's nostrils flared. "Get to know us better?"

Reeva grinned, her gaze moving from Abbie to Rolf. "You actually." She nailed him with her unusual eyes. "I was curious about you."

"Why?" Rolf asked. He took another sip.

"Because I can see my son in you."

The scotch went the wrong way. He spluttered and coughed and tried to talk. Abbie smacked him on the back. "Rolf?" she asked, puzzlement evident in the crinkle of skin around her eyes.

Reeva went to get him a glass of water when the choking didn't ease straight away. She sat on the arm of the lounge chair, her movements small and careful.

With tears in his eyes he replied, "Your son?"

"Your brother, half-brother, Gene." Her expression was contained.

"My father ..." Rolf tried to articulate the thought. Sure wolves fucked a lot but they usually only bred with one mate. Then again, Rolf never knew his mother. His father never spoke of her after she died.

"Yes, we were once together. Long story and we don't have too much time to linger on the topic."

Rolf was still trying to sort this out in his head. "Was. George. Gene's. Father?"

Reeva threw her head back and laughed. "No. No, I am your mother."

Rolf went still. For a full minute he couldn't speak and for once Abbie was silent also. "He said you died." Sweat had broken out on his upper lip and the back of his neck. His underarms were wet, behind his knees too. He studied Reeva. He didn't know what to say and he wasn't sure he could form words. He drew in a breath and held it.

"Yes, I asked him to tell you that. He wouldn't let you come with me, so I thought it was for the best. The split was not amicable. The odds of him letting me see you were non-existent."

Conscious of his heart beating, of blood rushing around his system, of his mind being a troubled dark sea, Rolf processed the words Reeva had spoken—he had a mother, a den mother, and a half-brother. Gene Cohen was his brother? Abbie kept still and quiet beside him and that was unlike her. He didn't know if he wanted to look at her or whether he wanted to say anything more. It was such a shock, betrayal, and delight all at the same time.

Reeva stared at him, lips tight. Then she threw up her arms and leapt off the chair, walking away and then turning back. "Well, say something. Scream at me. Growl ... the suspense is killing me."

Rolf cleared his throat.

Abbie got off the couch. "I'll just wait out there for a bit." Rolf didn't see her move and only heard the sliding door open and shut as she exited to the balcony. He was trying to take it in, couldn't move and could barely breathe.

A body sat next to him on the couch. Fingers threaded through his hair. A forehead leaned on his shoulder. "I never thought I'd smell you again, my son."

That undid him. A fistful of emotion pressed into his belly, then clawed its way up his throat. Reeva put her arms around him, held him tight. "I know, son. I'm so sorry."

She held him for a few minutes and when he sat back and disentangled himself, she smiled and touched his head. "What a wonderful wolf you have become. Beautiful and strong and wily."

He turned to face her, still not able to form words. She met his gaze. "I'm so proud of you, so happy to meet you again."

Something broke inside. Rolf sobbed into his mother's hair and held her thin frame against his chest. "I ... this is hard ... it will take time to get ... used to ... having a mother ..."

"For me too. Gene doesn't know. I'll have to break it to him carefully. Not an easy week for a den mother."

Rolf chuckled and wiped at his face. "What is he like?"

Reeva smiled. "That is best left for you to decide. I shall bring your mate inside."

Rolf's eyelids narrowed. "She's not my mate."

Reeva arched her eyebrows. "Not your mate? What is wrong with you? She's splendid. Besides, I think she very soon will be your mate, but that's another conversation."

Reeva got up and beckoned to Abbie to come back in. After his mother's phone pinged, she drew it out of her pocket and took the call. "Mmm, I see. And the trail?"

Reeva listened then nodded decisively and hung up. "They were traced to a house. Your friends were there and then their trail dies. I think he has transported them."

"What does he smell like?" Abbie asked.

Reeva gave Abbie a long look and dug out her phone, dialling a programmed number. "Was Willy with you? Good. Put him on." She sighed. "Yes? Willy great. Tell me, are there any distinctive scents?" Her expression grew attentive. "Mmm, so fear? Undertone of cinnamon."

Abbie stiffened and then nodded. Reeva spoke into the phone. "Thanks, Willy."

She pressed end and put the phone back in her pocket. "Now tell me what you know," she said.

Rolf gave Reeva an overview of what had happened so far.

"You think this trouble is centred on the collegium?" she clarified.

"Yes, although the attacks here in Australia threaten us directly."

"And Dane, your sorcerer friend, lives here in Australia when most others of his kind live elsewhere?"

"Yes, and ... no, " Rolf had to think about it. "Sorcerers do live in various parts of the world and there a few others here in Australia. But Dane's the only one who is very powerful and with connections to the collegium. His father, Tord, was one of the triumvirate. Tord was murdered and then Dane was cursed."

Reeva nodded. "I had heard about the curse. Concerning ... but managed, I understand. Now this new curse ... but a similar theme."

Abbie sat forward on the chair. "Are you saying that Dane and the collegium are the common element?"

Rolf could see where this was heading and liked the clarity that had come to mind. "Rafael is missing and he's also a common denominator. He's close to Dane and the centre of the collegium."

Reeva stroked her chin, and Rolf noticed because it was a habit of his. "Have you been to the collegium in search of your friends?"

"We fled from there, from the explosion, with Dane and Annwyn." Rolf mulled this over. Could the rogue sorcerer have doubled back?

"And has Abbie met Rafael?" Reeva asked. "I've not seen him in many years."

Rolf was about to say yes, but Abbie answered. "No, not once."

"Wait," Rolf said. "You're not suggesting that it's Rafael? He's been kidnapped, his secretary murdered. Besides, he's the one who was cleaning up after the other business with Vollos. He helped Dane when he was cursed. Taught Annwyn"

"You might have missed a few details. Taught Annwyn?" Reeva asked.

Rolf quickly filled her in. Reeva sat still, leaning against the arm of the chair, stroking her cheek and pursing her mouth. "That is some tale," she said after a few minutes. "I dislike bureaucracies at the best of times and hate them at the worst. They have the potential for good, but usually fall short and can be turned evil so quickly and quietly by just a few individuals. I came here to Australia to be free of that kind of evil, and we're far enough away not to bear the brunt of the institutionalised prejudice against our kind. I fear that this is changing. I can no longer stand apart."

She stood up and her elegant floral pantsuit swirled around her lithe frame.

"What are you going to do?" Abbie asked.

"I'm going to call in a favour," she said. "And I'm coming with you."

Rolf pushed to his feet, towering over the two women. "No, you're not. You're not getting involved."

Reeva didn't react, just stared up at him. Then she aimed her finger at him and jabbed the air in front of his chest. "I'm already involved. Someone tried to kill my son."

"That's neither here nor there. I won't have you getting hurt."

Reeva laughed at this. "Spare me the dramatics. You've lived with the thought of me dead your whole life. Besides, you haven't seen me in a fight." She dug out her phone, pressed a programmed number. It didn't take long for to be picked up. "Gene. Yeah. There's trouble. Do you still have the address of that old sorcerer who owes us a favour?"

Wincing she held the phone out from her ear. Rolf heard a raised voice coming through the small speaker and could totally sympathise. That was his brother's voice. His heart beat a little faster, anticipation making him sweat. Abbie rose to her feet and took his hand and squeezed. "It will be all right," she said to him. "She's a tough old boot."

He squeezed her hand back and leaned down to speak into her ear. "That's my mother you're talking about." Abbie's grin widened. Rolf had no time to process the new information that his mother not only lived but was this impressive den mother. Deep in his gut he knew it was good and true and right. He hazarded a look at Abbie and caught his breath.

Eventually, Reeva put the phone back to her ear and demanded the details. "Right. Okay. Thank you." She jotted down an address on a piece of paper from a pad on the side table. "Yes, I'll be in touch."

She pressed end call and put the phone back into her pocket. "Gene is sending a car for us. This guy lives in Glebe. We helped him out a number of years back. He's not that important in the hierarchy, or that powerful. What he can do, though, is transport us to the collegium headquarters."

"I'm still not happy about you coming along."

Reeva thinned her mouth and then chuckled. "I know. Poor baby."

Rolf smiled. No one else could give him such lip, except maybe Abbie. But then she'd pay for it. Reeva, though, could give him cheek and get away with it. Not only because she was his biological mother, but because she was a senior den mother. He knew and respected that.

"You best feed yourself. The car will be twenty minutes depending on the traffic. There's steak in the fridge. I'm going to change my clothes."

Reeva left them alone. Rolf moved into the kitchen, still rattled by what he'd learned about his heritage. Abbie bent down to look into cupboards and Rolf leaned into the fridge to peel six large T-bones off a platter. Abbie took one look at the pile of meat and pulled out another skillet and lit the stove. Rolf assumed that they all took their meat warmed, but Abbie threw in olive oil, garlic and salt. The intense flavours made his mouth water.

He drew out the plates and Abbie made salad.

"Salad?" he asked.

"Heathen," she said bumping his hip with hers. "We need some vitamins. A wolf cannot live on meat alone."

"Yes, he can ..."

Abbie shook her head. "Right, what about a celibate wolf?"

Rolf grinned and slid two steaks onto each plate. "Point taken." He did not think he could live without sex and didn't know a werewolf who could.

Abbie filled glasses with water and he saw the sense in that. There was no point in blunting their senses with wine and they didn't have the time anyhow. Reeva came out and took a seat. She sat and inhaled theatrically. "Just how I like them."

By the time they had bitten the meat off the bones, the door chime rang. "Car is here," Reeva said. "Let's move."

She'd changed from the elegant pantsuit into sturdier clothes in a dun colour, and had a small knapsack on her back. She tossed Abbie some shoes and then frowned at Rolf. Leaving the room for a minute, she came back. "These should fit." They were a fine set of expensive runners, probably about five hundred dollars' worth. Rolf squeezed into them and pressed the seal to enclose his feet.

Then they followed Reeva out and down into the car park. A red coupe with sleek lines waited. When they climbed in, Rolf realised it was a Tesla Model S. Not too shabby at all.

The driver didn't greet them. He had short, dark hair, wore sunglasses and what looked like a bespoke suit in dark grey. There was a whiff of wolf about him.

"Hi," Abbie said on taking a seat. Reeva took the front passenger side, while he slid in next to Abbie.

The driver inclined his head but said nothing. The car glided smoothly to the exit ramp and then shot out onto the street. The speed of acceleration thrilled his senses. The car hugged corners and sped along the straight sections of the road. It was nearing midnight. Rolf thought of Dane and Annwyn and hoped they weren't too late to save them. They must have discovered who the rogue sorcerer was, resulting in them being abducted, and he surmised this meant it was someone with a lot of power to overcome two impressively skilled sorcerers. His gaze slide to Abbie, who watched the streetscape as they sped along. That trap had been set for her; he was sure of it. Abbie and her acute nose were a threat. Anticipation built in his gut. They were drawing closer to the answer, danger was increasing. The car stopped suddenly in front of a tall, Victorian-style wrought iron fence, guarding an even more impressive single-fronted Victorian bungalow. "What ...? No! You aren't meant to be stopping here," Reeva said, clearly peeved.

A broad man looking all of six-foot-five came up to the passenger-side door and tapped on the roof. His gaze fixed on Reeva, who sighed heavily and pushed open the door, slamming it once she was on the street. Immediately they started arguing, arms gesticulating, expressions taut with anger. That was his mother being abused, possibly by his half-brother. Rolf wanted to look, wanted to get out and see what was happening, only his protective instincts did not apply to Reeva. She held her own and soon the larger man's shoulders slumped, his chin dropped as belligerence appeared to flee. Abbie slid her arm through the crook of Rolf's elbow and rested her head on his upper arm.

Reeva got in and swore up a storm. "Of all the stupid, idiotic fuckers."

The driver gaped at Reeva. She threw out a hand, indicating the road ahead. "Get moving, you. You better think twice about countermanding my orders."

They took off again and Rolf half turned and saw they were being followed. "Den Mother?"

Reeva let out a breath that rattled her lips. "Yes, he's coming too."

"I understand," Rolf said, hoping that Reeva knew he wouldn't do or say anything that betrayed their relationship. It was up to Reeva to do the telling. During the trip, Rolf fed her all the remaining information at hand, as she'd be doing all the talking.

They zipped along the streets until they reached Parramatta Road, which was by reputation perpetually clogged with traffic, until they turned off into Glebe. More turns into narrower and narrower streets and the houses grew shabbier—small one-storey workers' cottages.

They pulled up in front of one of them. The windows were darkened in the tiny house. The garden contained plants of the neglected kind. The car following pulled up behind them and a lone figure climbed out—tall, erect and built like a pro wrestler—Gene Cohen. Rolf waited until Reeva exited the car, the door slamming once again, and then he and Abbie alighted. The four of them stood on the street. Eyes like his own glared at him. "Who the fuck are you?"

Reeva pushed between them. "Not now, Gene. Let's just do this."

"Mother. I'm not going anywhere until I know who these two are." Gene sized up Abbie, and Rolf immediately went on the defensive. He didn't like the heat in Gene's gaze.

"I'm Rolf Bauer from Canberra pack. This is Abbie. She's with me."

"Really?" his eyebrows arched over bright eyes quite similar to his own. "Abbie McGregor? The one that lived?" Gene said, nodding his head and biting his bottom lip as he assessed her. "Nice."

Reeva rolled her eyes. "Keep the hormones in check boys. We have serious business to attend to." She poked Gene on the sternum with an angry finger. "Just what the fuck do you think you're doing here?"

He puffed out his chest. "Protecting my investment."

Reeva growled at him. "I don't know if you mean the car or me."

Gene grinned at her and shrugged.

"Very well. Don't get in the way. I need to treat this sorcerer with care."

Rolf was secretly impressed with Reeva. She had balls. Gene backed away as Reeva led the way through the gate, down the garden path and up to the pale-coloured front door. Rolf rolled his shoulders and followed along, with Abbie bringing up the rear.

Reeva stood by the closed door and waited. There was no door knocker, no bell, no intercom. The sorcerer inside knew that they were there. Rolf knew the score: there would be spells to detect intruders and more. No lights came on, yet the door opened by itself. Without hesitation, Reeva walked into the dark hallway. Rolf's wolf eyes gave him an edge to his vision and, coupled with his olfactory acuity, he had a good sense of his surroundings. His nose also told him that there was life here and magic.

"God, what a stink," Abbie said as she trailed behind.

"Shut it," Rolf said, surprised. The smells did not appear that strong to him, just nuanced.

"You shut it. It's awful. It's like a curry that's gone bad. Spices slightly off. Eww."

Rolf rolled his eyes. Now was not the time to try and discipline Abbie. "Just keep it to yourself for now, unless this is the scent of the rogue sorcerer."

"It's not."

Abbie continued to walk along the hall and managed to stay quiet. They came to the end of the hall, which opened to a wide room. Rolf inhaled the scent of food and heard the faint hum of a refrigerator. It was the kitchen-dining room. The light came on suddenly, blindingly bright.

Sitting at a long table was the oldest man Rolf had ever seen. He had a thin smattering of wispy white hair on a patchy bald scalp and on his chin was a long, thin, white beard that had smears of what could only be food stains on it. "Well, well, well," he said in a high-pitched, scratchy voice that almost made Rolf bark out a laugh. "What have we here? Look what the hounds have dragged in. The last person I expected to see here is you, Reeva Cohen."

"Don't get too excited, old man." Reeva said, turning to cross her arms over her chest. "It's not a social call. I need a favour."

The old man laughed, but it sounded like he was dying of asphyxiation. "A favour?" He collapsed with laughter yet again. Rolf saw his thin chest heaving up and down and wondered how the old man had the strength to laugh, or the nerve. These were the two most powerful wolves in Sydney. "From me?"

Reeva lowered her eyebrows clearly unamused. "It's time you earned your protection."

The old man's laughter died. "Why? What do you want?" His rheumy gaze shifted to Rolf and to Abbie, then back to Reeva and Gene.

Gene cleared his throat and inhaled, making himself appear taller. "We need you to transport us to the collegium head office in Colorado. Now."

"No!" It was a cry of despair. "I ... I won't do it. Reeva you can't ask that of me."

"We are desperate, Trent. We would not ask it otherwise," Reeva said. "Dane Archwright, son of Tord, who took sanctuary in Australia, and Dane's wife, Annwyn, have been kidnapped by a rogue sorcerer. Rafael d'Armac, of the triumvirate, is missing, presumed taken. Abbie here knows the scent of the rogue sorcerer. We need to go there to continue the search."

"Tord?" he sat back down in his chair, hands shaking. "He was murdered."

Reeva nodded. "Yes, I believe he was and this might be part of the same business, understand. All we need you to do is transport us. Nothing more."

The old man stood up, his hand holding the edge of the table to support. "Four of you?" His white bushy brows lowered. "How will you get back?"

Gene lifted his chin. "Commercial airline if we have to. You don't need to come with us. Just get us there."

"But they will detect my magic. They will track me. What you ask is suicide."

"The people you fear could be dead. We don't know enough about the collegium to advise you. Gene will leave a guard to protect you. Three of our best wolves."

Trent's old eyes passed over them and back again. "You aren't going to let me refuse, are you?"

Reeva sighed sadly. "Trent we wouldn't be here if there was any other way. We keep our promises. We've never asked for anything in return for protecting you, until now."

"Very well," Trent replied in his high-pitched thin voice. "Who will go first? I can do only one at a time. It may take me a few minutes between transports."

Gene stepped forward, near knocking Rolf out of the way. Reeva spoke up. "Send Rolf first, then Abbie, then me, then Gene. But if you don't have the strength to send my son, then don't worry."

"Mother! You dare," he snarled at her.

"I dare. No one invited you along."

"I'm the alpha here. This is my territory."

With a big sigh, Reeva seemed to weigh up the situation. Then she waved a hand dismissively. "By all means, go first."

She winked at Rolf, which took the edge off the bristling anger he felt at Gene's effrontery. What reason did he have to interfere? Then he looked at Reeva and understood. His half-brother was protecting his mother.

Gene stepped closer to the old man, into the centre of the kitchen. The old man had his head down, his shoulders stooped. He made no elaborate gestures. Did nothing at all. There was just a whiff of magic and Gene was gone.

Reeva took Gene's place. "I need to look after him. He hasn't been briefed, so he has no idea what he's walking into. All pride and balls and no good sense. That's my son."

Trent panted heavily and became more stooped. After a minute or two, Reeva disappeared. Rolf took her place but was worried about leaving Abbie behind. She was crucial. He stepped aside, even though he hated the thought of sending her into danger without him. "Abbie, you go next."

It was hard to let her go first, but if the old man tired before she was transported then they would haven't her nose and they would be vulnerable. Abbie took her place near the old man. She put her hand over her nose, clearly disgusted with the smell of the sorcerer's magic. Rolf could only imagine. He could smell the old man's unwashed body. There was a whiff of magic emanating from him, but to Rolf it smelled like burned toast.

Trent was breathing hard and the hand that had rested on the table for support was now clenched on the edge of it, knuckles white. The old sorcerer bent over double, with his ragged breathing like an old engine, ready to peter out. Abbie was there one second and the next she was transported. Rolf stepped into the same spot and prayed to all the gods and his ancestors that the old man had sufficient energy remaining. He cursed his half-brother for taking his spot on the mission. Clearly struggling, the old man bent his knees and put his hands on the ground. He sobbed, great wracking breaths. Rolf felt a surge of pity. The sorcerer didn't use gestures, nothing to give a hint as to what he was doing. Rolf was ready to smash something and then the old man was gone from view. He arrived outside a large building and turned full circle. The sun was high, the air was thin and Abbie and the others were nowhere to be seen. "Fuck it all to hell," Rolf growled to the air.

Then, when the instant of rage and worry passed, he picked up their scent and ran straight for the entry to the building in front of him. The collegium passed itself off as an ordinary office block in Denver, Colorado. People walked the streets, shopping and chatting. A bus pulled out from the curb. All seemed normal.

He entered the building and saw the other three arguing with a security guard. Relief and something else washed over him. They were safe. Abbie was safe. His mother was safe.

Rolf walked over. "Is there something wrong?"

The security guard looked him up and down. "None of your business."

Rolf smiled and bounced his head as if agreeing. "My name is Rolf Bauer. I work for Dane Archwright and he has requested I meet him here. This party has also been invited."

The security guard sniffed as if smelling something bad. "I'll check the records." The security guard went to a paper register and skimmed the page with a forefinger, narrowing his lips as he did so. He stopped, looked up at Rolf, and then shut the book. "You're listed, but not these people."

"I will vouch for them."

"There has been an incident. The new security protocols do not allow for non-registered members to enter the collegium space."

Rolf let out a breath, clenched his fist as he was ready to lash out. "We were there when the bomb went off. We escaped with our lives. We've returned to find the culprits."

The security guard stepped out from behind his desk and stood with hands on hips and shook his head. Rolf didn't dare look away as he saw that Gene was behind the guard and after a neck chop the man fell to the ground. "We haven't got all day. I'm a busy man, so if you don't mind, let's get on with it."

He picked up the unconscious security guard and folded him behind the desk like he was a bank note. Rolf shrugged and headed for the lift.

Abbie ducked down and retrieved the man's security card and waved it under Rolf's nose. "We'll need this for the lift. What floor?"

"We went to the twentieth floor previously. I'm not sure how much of it is left after the explosion. I don't normally travel via the lift. Dane just plonks us down where we need to be."

Reeva sighed like one who had lost all patience. "Take us to the twentieth. If we can't find what we need, we'll go to twenty-one via the stairs and work from there. I take it you can climb stairs."

Rolf drew himself up, squared his shoulders. "I can climb."

He made a face at Gene who was glaring at him and lifted a lip to bare his teeth. Abbie chuckled and stepped into the lift.

CHAPTER 12

The lift door opened unimpeded on the twentieth floor, although the pungent smell of smoke and other fumes from the ballroom fire knocked Abbie back a step. Black and yellow tape marked out a corridor and the sound of people talking drifted toward them. Rolf nudged her in the back and prodded her out of the door. She hadn't realised she was standing still and blocking the exit. It was the smells. It was too much to digest.

"This way," Rolf said and he stepped in front of her. Abbie bowed her head to acknowledge Reeva's precedence and stepped in behind. Gene was left to bring up the rear. His scent was appealing, and Abbie couldn't help a sneak look over her shoulder. The Sydney alpha had a serious hard-on and it gave her a thrill to think she was the source. While she wouldn't have been able to pick their blood relationship, there were similarities in build and demeanour between the half-brothers. Although Gene was taller and broader, he was austere looking with some serious sex appeal. They passed around the edge of the large room, which had all the ceiling tiles removed. Wires and other fittings hung out. Workmen in yellow vests called out to one another, giving instructions. They were currently removing a wall. The floor was mostly stripped down to the concrete, but there was a serious divot over where the bomb had exploded. She could scarcely believe she'd been so close to the centre of the explosion.

"Hey, you lot," a big man came lumbering over to intercept them. "There's no through traffic here."

Rolf paused. "I understand it's safe along this marked corridor. We have to access the offices through there."

The man pushed back his hard hat and shook his head. "Just be damn careful. You should be wearing hardhats."

He withdrew, stepping back to supervise some repairs and they continued on.

"Keep moving," Gene said to her. Distracted, Abbie had fallen behind as Rolf and Reeva entered a long corridor. She hadn't been this way before, as she'd been left behind. A few steps in and she could smell other things besides the smoke and fire residue. Here there was magic. Little pockets of warmth that indicated sorcerer spaces. They kept moving.

Rolf called out from the front. "Anything Abbie?"

Abbie took in a deep breath, trying to filter out the extraneous smells and focus on the known tang of the rogue sorcerer. There was still too much interference. "No. Not yet. You?"

She figured Rolf should be able to smell Dane and Annwyn if there were close or had walked this way. Rolf shook his head. Reeva turned to look at Abbie over her shoulder, her irises reflecting hints of silver that glowed in the dim corridor. The power looked to be out. Probably due to the repairs being undertaken.

They turned a corner and then there were different smells. "Oh, I remember that rank stink." Abbie asked.

Rolf turned and sent her a grin. "Vamps."

"Yeah, that's it," Abbie replied and heard Gene snicker behind her. It was pretty foul. Like old rancid meat with a hint of bacon and then a thick overpowering perfume with some rot thrown in. She made a face and tried not to inhale too deeply.

Rolf turned into an office. Reeva walked up the corridor further, her head moving this way and that, apparently trying for a discernible scent. Gene stood with legs apart taking up all the available space in the hallway. Abbie stumbled after Rolf. A wave of scents pushed out of the room, and she stood on the threshold sifting through them. Stale Dane and Annwyn. Just a hint of them. She stepped closer to the desk. A robe lay there. Rolf picked it up and tossed it to her. Catching it, she detected the scent and fell back. "It's him!"

Rolf's head shot up. Reeva came in the door, with Gene just behind. "Say it carefully. What do you smell?" Rolf instructed.

Abbie took another long inhale and let the recollection wash over her, the memory of where she'd detected it previously. "There are other scents here ... yours because you've touched it. A faint trace of vamp, but that is evaporating quickly. But imbued into this fabric is the cinnamon spice of the rogue sorcerer."

"No," Rolf said hollowly, disbelief warring with acceptance of her words.

Reeva lifted her hand for silence. Gene stepped in closer to his mother, a protective position by her left shoulder. "Abbie. Let me have a whiff."

Abbie passed the robe over. Reeva sniffed in multiple places and passed it to Gene. "There is one dominant scent. I can't detect the deep spices Abbie identifies, but I would wager it is the owner of the robe."

Gene took the robe, sniffed and looked to Rolf. "This is Rafael's office, right? So this could've been placed here. Are there other things Abbie can smell to confirm?"

Rolf's eyebrows drew down low and his forehead was knotted like thunderclouds. He looked on the top of the desk and picked up a dark blue fountain pen. He passed it over. Abbie took it carefully and sniffed it. "Same scent." She shrugged and handed it back.

Rolf balled his fists until they were white. Abbie thought he might punch a hole in the wall. "I'm assuming you know who this guy is?"

Rolf frowned, eyebrows so low they shaded the yellow of his eyes and made them glow amber. "It's Rafael, the one we thought was kidnapped."

Abbie gaped and then shut her mouth, looking between Reeva and Rolf. "*The* Rafael? Dane and Annwyn's friend?"

"Yes, that's him," Rolf said and his voice slid out of him as if he'd been gut punched.

"That puts a whole new light on things."

Abbie turned to Reeva, eyebrows raised in an expression of surprise. She went to say something, paused and then asked anyway. "You know Rafael d'Armac?"

"Of course I do. I'm a werewolf, not a demon. In Europe, back in the day, weres and sorcerers were on friendlier terms. We helped each other out on occasion." She shrugged. "It has been a while. I don't remember Raf's scent these days, so I can't confirm that it's him."

Rolf came around and shifted his gaze from his mother to his half-brother. "Would he take them to his home, his castle in Scotland? Is that where he has Dane and Annwyn?"

"If he has, we have to find a sorcerer to transport us," Reeva said.

Rolf shook his head. "It's too obvious for them to be there. Besides if we went there we'd be stuck in that old castle without an easy way out."

Gene rubbed his chin and then looked over to Rolf. "You think he'd have them stashed closer to here. Tell me, does the collegium have rooms where it conducts testing or questioning?"

Rolf furrowed his brow, as if that would work loose his memories. "Dane did undergo testing here. The rooms are shielded so magic doesn't escape ..."

"And no one can tell what is going on inside, right?" Reeva said, lifting her eyebrow at Gene. Her younger son looked ready to spit.

Abbie sniffed and then coughed. "How about we ask someone? There are some warm bodies nearby."

Reeva flashed her a grin. "I like you. You may be a redhead, but you aren't a dead head."

Abbie wanted to hurl back a retort, but Rolf squeezed her upper arm in warning. "Thank you."

His mother was a smart-mouth and clever besides. Rolf was the strong silent type. Abbie had yet to work out Gene. The brothers tried to leave at the same time behind Reeva and banged shoulders and blocked the door. Abbie rolled her eyes. "Excuse me boys. Do you mind?"

They sprang apart and she followed the smart-mouthed den mother who had already found someone to speak to.

A young woman, who had maybe just a hint of magic about her, responded to Reeva's query after the den mother had explained who they were and why there were there. She was dressed in a mauve suit and had dark skin and dark curly hair, introducing herself as Jill, assistant day manager of the building. The young woman had some magic about her, but not strong as far as Abbie could tell, but rather someone with limited magical ability, employed by the collegium.

The helpful assistant had produced a map and was pointing out the set of rooms that she said were protected by shielding to prevent people outside the rooms from seeing what was going on.

"Why would you need that?" Abbie asked, genuinely surprised. The woman glanced up and saw her expanded audience and flushed pink. Her eyes widened when she looked Rolf and Gene up and down.

"Um ... for magical experiments. In case something goes wrong. Testing for assessing whether someone can join the collegium, and for a sorcerer to demonstrate what grade they are. That sort of thing. The rooms aren't meant to be used for anything illegal."

Rolf nodded and stroked his chin as he leaned over and studied the map. "We take the lift here down to basement level three and follow this corridor?"

"Yes," Jill replied. "That is the only such space we have. If the people you're looking for are here, and you can't find them, then that's the only place in this building I know of that they could be."

Reeva cleared her throat, bringing the woman's attention back to her. "Does the collegium have other offices in this city?"

The woman cocked her head, sending her black curls tumbling around her ears and neck. "Well, yes. There are two more smaller sites."

Reeva tapped the map. "Can you give us the address for those? If we find nothing here, we'll go to these other sites. Are there any special precautions we need to take?"

Jill frowned as if thinking through possibilities. "Possibly. I'll have to get the key and come with you. My supervisor isn't available at the moment."

She folded up the map and disappeared inside the office. As someone came down the hallway, Abbie squeezed herself against the wall and Gene and Rolf split apart and put their backs to the wall to give the small man passing through room to move. A minor sorcerer by the smell of him.

"Here we are," Jill said as she held up a lapis lazuli amulet on a dark leather cord. She placed it around her neck. "This is the key. It nullifies any locking spells and possibly other spells designed to repel intruders." She handed over a small square of paper. "These are the addresses of the other sites. I'm afraid I cannot transport us there, but they're reachable on foot or by taxi." Jill slid past Rolf and Gene and headed for the lifts. "Come this way and I'll take you down."

Reeva flashed a grin at Abbie and followed Jill. "Thank you for being so helpful and efficient."

Jill turned and beamed at them. "You're most welcome. It's been a terrible business since the explosion. Half the staff aren't turning up to work, they're so afraid."

"I don't blame them," Abbie quipped.

Abbie looked over her shoulder and sent Rolf a sultry look. Rolf didn't make eye contact and Abbie sighed. Damn, why did he look so good?

By the time Abbie and Rolf reached the bank of lifts, Gene had already summoned one and Reeva was inside with Jill. Without a word, Abbie and Rolf slipped inside just as the doors were closing. The tension between Rolf and Gene had not lessened, in fact it had risen during the strange turnabout in the order of who walks where. Abbie didn't care one jot, but obviously Rolf and Gene did, if their little game playing was anything to go by.

The elevator pinged as it reached basement level three. "Here we are," Jill said and stepped out. Rolf was closer to the door and stepped out after Jill. Reeva stepped in front of her son and Gene bowed slightly and indicated for Abbie to go ahead of him.

They walked to a desk that sat in front of four identical doors. The monitor who was seated at the desk, glanced up at them. "Jill what brings you down here? It's been a while."

Jill inclined her head. "Mateo. We've come to inspect the rooms."

"Why?" the monitor ask, casting his gaze as the rest of them. He sniffed and Abbie thought he could tell they were werewolves.

"Dane Archwright and Annwyn Flaydin are missing."

The monitor nodded. "Archwright?" he said and whistled as if he was impressed. He spun his chair in the direction of the doors. "There's no one down here, but you're welcome to check."

Without preamble, they did just that. Reeva and Gene took the first two rooms and Jill, Rolf and Abbie the other two. The scents crossed over one another and Abbie had little luck in trying to decipher them. There was an aftertaste of magic and a hefty helping of fear scent. They met up again in the corridor. Reeva turned to the monitor. "Thank you for allowing us to search."

The monitor bowed and spoke with a Colorado drawl. "Welcome. Dane Archwright is a powerful sorcerer. If he's in trouble then things are really bad." He looked at Jill. "Do you need help?"

Jill shook her head. "We'll check the other two sites. I can handle that."

Abbie took a long draw of air through her nose. The monitor was a were. He shifted his gaze and found Abbie examining him. He flashed a grin, but looked anything but easygoing. "You got a problem there, little lady?"

Abbie lifted her chin. "No, nothing wrong." Abbie would be able to tell this wolf from others. His scent filled up the rooms and the hall.

They returned to the lift and exited the building. In the forecourt, they gathered in a circle, the sound of traffic punctuating the quiet moments. "Which of these two do we go to first?"

"Does it matter?" Abbie asked.

Rolf broke in. "Yes, if we choose the wrong place they might be alerted to our search and evacuate."

Jill coughed. "If I may suggest the closest one. There's no immediate way to contact the other site, unless there's a sorcerer there."

Gene leaned in. "If there's a sorcerer there, they could turn us into dog food. Is there any way to deflect his magic?"

Jill sucked in a breath. "Sir, you are mistaken if you think a sorcerer would harm you."

"No mistake," Rolf said. "I've seen a sorcerer do harm with my own eyes.

Jill crossed her arms. "Well sir, I have a mobile phone and I know how to use it."

Abbie stifled a laugh. Rolf and Gene both kept their mouths shut and Reeva rolled her eyes. "It's good to have backup," Reeva said to Jill. "I hope you'll be able to rally assistance if we need it."

Abbie was downcast because she hadn't even contemplated magical attack. She was not as used to magic as the others were, so perhaps that excused her ignorance.

Reeva pulled out her phone. "I'm calling a car. We'll go to the closest place first, as Jill suggested and then, if we find nothing, we move on to the other one."

"Then what?" Gene asked.

Rolf made eye contact with them all by turns. "We try the castle?"

"I would've felt better having some of that help now," Abbie replied.

Jill lifted her chin. "I can summon help if warranted. The administration may be in disarray but I assure you, assistance will be provided if warranted."

Abbie sniffed quietly and detected the fear in Jill. She was out of her depth, had limited magical ability and was scared. Abbie wasn't about to bank on the assistance Jill relied on. The collegium was in a shambles and its leaders were missing. Part of her felt sorry for the other woman.

Reeva just flashed Jill a look as a dark-coloured limo pulled up. "Our lift. Get in."

CHAPTER 13

There was ample room in the car to accommodate them all. Abbie had to concentrate to avoid being distracted by the competing scents from everyone in an enclosed space. Luckily the trip wasn't long. The first building was just on the edge of the city, in a converted industrial building. Built of red brick, it was double-fronted with white windows set in a five-storey facade, with an attic visible under the arched gable.

Jill stepped up to the locked front door, spoke a few words as she passed the amulet along the edges, where the wood met the building. The door opened and they followed Jill into the darkness within. Lights switched on and inside it was a nondescript warehouse.

Jill shrugged. "It appears empty."

"We need to be sure," Rolf said.

Reeva nodded slowly, her eyes darting around the wide room that was the foyer. Stairs went up and a hallway that lead to the rear of the building opened out in front of them. Jill sat on one of the couches. "Now we're here I think it would be quicker to take the floors in pairs," Reeva said. "Gene and I will go up. Rolf and Abbie you go to the rear and down if there's a basement."

"I'll stay here," Jill said taking out her phone. "I have some messages to respond to." Jill didn't appear to be too concerned about abducted sorcerers. Then again, the organisation she worked for was in near collapse.

Rolf nodded a salute. "Yes, Den Mother." Taking Abbie by the elbow he steered her along the hallway to the rear of the building. The corridor appeared to split the building in half, with doors along both walls, equally spaced. The floor was carpeted and there were pictures along the wall. Not swank, but clean and welcoming. Working quickly, they opened the first set of doors, flinging them wide and looking inside and sniffing. The room had comfortable upholstered chairs and wooden tables that gleamed in the light. Meeting again in the hallway they approached the next set of doors. All these rooms were similarly furnished, empty of people, and smelled of furniture polish with a hint of coffee. At the end of the corridor, they found a door to the basement. Rolf turned the handle and edged the door ajar so he could see behind it. The stairwell leading down was narrow and clean and illuminated by small lights set just above the risers. They started down, and Abbie noted the risers were made of grey unadorned concrete and were very utilitarian. This was not a public area of the building. They reached the bottom of the stairs and had turned right when a familiar scent filled her olfactory senses. The light was dim, but she could see at least three doors. She grabbed Rolf's forearm to stop him. "Get the others," she whispered.

"Tell me," he hissed.

Abbie breathed deeper and detected the scents of Dane and Annwyn. "They're here. That room there." She pointed to the second door along.

"Stay put," Rolf said and bolted back up the stairs.

Abbie had no intention of putting herself in danger, until she heard a scream that tore into her nerves and set her heart racing. She couldn't hear the others coming. They wouldn't get here soon enough. It sounded like someone was in terrible pain. She ran at the second door, calling on the wolf's strength. Unfortunately, it wasn't locked and sprang open on impact; Abbie couldn't halt her momentum and she barrelled straight into Annwyn, who had been standing close to the door, knocking her to the floor and falling on top of her.

Abbie looked up and around. Strapped to a chair in front of her was Dane, jaw clenched, and writhing in obvious pain. Behind him, with his hands clawed as if kneading bread dough in the air above Dane's head, was the rogue sorcerer, Rafael. There was something wrong with the old sorcerer, something that Abbie couldn't place at first. A sick, cloying feeling that something wasn't right. Rafael didn't react to Abbie's entry.

Rolling off the sobbing Annwyn, Abbie saw that the sorceress had her fists bunched under her nose and covering her mouth, as if she'd seen something so frightening she couldn't uncoil her body. The rogue sorcerer didn't take notice of Annwyn or Abbie. Abbie gathered the distressed sorceress into her arms, stroking her back and speaking soothingly. "It's all right, Annwyn. We're here. We can help you."

Annwyn shook her head and whimpered, her gaze fixed on a spot two feet in front of her. Some kind of hex, Abbie suspected. What of Dane? He looked in worse shape.

A noise from outside. "I told her to wait!" A loud curse. Rolf's voice reached her. "Abbie?" Rolf's deep concerned tones reached her.

"Here, quickly."

Rolf came in slowly, legs bent, arms loose, eyes watching and nostrils flaring. Behind him came Reeva, equally on alert, and Gene, whose dark eyes flitted to every corner of the room over and over again. Jill followed.

"Annwyn is petrified, some kind of hex. Dane's not responding to us and Rafael is just being weird," she jerked her head at Rafael who hadn't reacted to their presence.

Abbie was relieved to see her companions, because she had no idea what to do next. If it was up to her, she'd bitch slap Annwyn back to a state of sense and demand the sorceress's help with Dane, along with an explanation of what was going on.

Rolf made a circle as he sidestepped to get to her. "I told you to stay put."

"I tried," Abbie replied out the side of her mouth. "But Annwyn screamed."

Rolf shook his head. She suspected they'd be discussing the incident later.

A hiss sounded. It came from Rafael, whose eyes began to glow in a creepy way. Dane moaned. "Don't approach him. He has a wall of protection up," Jill said, walking sideways as if assessing it.

Rolf looked at Dane, warily at Rafael and back at Annwyn. "We need Annwyn aware."

"Is Rafael always like that?" Abbie asked.

"No, not at all," Jill replied.

Rolf shook his head. "His scent is all off, too. I can smell that spice you mentioned and that's not Rafael's normal scent. No wonder I couldn't recognise him from your description."

Rolf knelt down and took Annwyn by both arms, giving her a gentle shake. "Annwyn pull yourself together. We need you." The only response he got was a high-pitched whine.

"She's not really present," Abbie said.

"Let me try," Jill said, kneeling down beside them. She put her hands to Annwyn's temples and closed her eyes, her lips moving.

Jill's eyes widened. "There's something wrong. There's another presence in there."

"Nira," Rolf explained. "Be careful."

Jill's face contorted, jaw clenched and brow furrowed. Annwyn's body jerked and words came out of her mouth. "Get off me bitch!"

It was Nira! Jill held on, though, moving as Annwyn's body moved. A deep guttural moan came out of Annwyn and then she slumped onto Jill.

Jill tenderly shifted Annwyn and stroked the lose hair from the sorceress's face. "Annwyn?" she said. "Annwyn can you hear me?"

Abbie was impressed. Jill might not be a strong sorceress, but she used what skill she had to maximum effect.

Annwyn's eyelids fluttered open. At first her eyes were unfocused and then finally they focused on Abbie. From the scent of her it was Annwyn and not Nira. It was obvious in the expression anyway. Annwyn was soft and gentle and lovely, whereas Nira was mean, sex-crazed and evil.

"Dane?" Annwyn said at last in a desperate tone, full of worry and fear.

"He's in trouble, Annwyn. Rafael is torturing him we think. What can we do to help?"

"Rafael is possessed, I think. We need witches." Annwyn sniffed and wiped at her tears.

Abbie sat back, surprised. "Witches?"

"Yes," Rolf said as he moved to make eye contact with Annwyn. "Perhaps Salvi?"

Annwyn didn't respond. Her eyes closed and she appeared to be dozing. Curiosity wouldn't let Abbie be. "Why witches? Don't they all use magic? Interchangeable like."

Rolf replied, "Witches deal with nature and spirit. There's some cross over, though sorcerers claim theirs is high magic and witches is low."

While this did not explain everything, it was enough for now. She stroked Annwyn's hair, though the sorceress was unresponsive. "I don't think Annwyn is in any state to transport a witch here."

With a smirk, Rolf pulled out his phone and held it aloft. "Not a problem. I have Salvi's number. I hope he doesn't mind me calling at whatever time it is in Rome." Rolf listened to the ring tone. Abbie could see he was about to give up when it was finally answered. "Salvi?"

A voice responded. Rolf gave Salvi a brief overview of the predicament. "It's up to you, Salvi. We can't reach Dane or Rafael due to the protection circle."

Rolf muted his phone and turned to Jill who was studying the invisible circle around Dane and Rafael. "Can they transport here direct?"

Jill looked up and nodded. "I'll send word to the administration. We've already lowered the wards on this building, so they should be fine.

With a nod, Rolf unmuted the phone. "We'll be waiting." He read off the address. Making eye contact with Reeva he said, "Salvi says it can't be done by one witch, so he has to round up some friends. They won't be long and they'll materialise here. Be warned."

While Abbie ached to know why Rolf had a witch's number in his phone, she decided to find out about that later, sensing a larger story.

She leaned forward and stroked Annwyn's hair and spoke softly to her. "Help's coming. Don't worry now."

This created a response. Annwyn raised her head, eyes open but not really seeing. She cried out. "Dane, oh Dane!" She became restless and Abbie held her closer, trying to give comfort.

Meanwhile, Rafael still had Dane in a kind of mind control. Dane's face contorted with fear and pain.

Reeva spoke up. "I don't understand why he's torturing Dane. Does he want Annwyn to himself?"

Rolf stood up and paced a few steps. "No, that can't be it. Rafael is gay."

Reeva lifted her head and narrowed her gaze. "So he wants Dane then?"

Rolf shook his head. "No, not possible. He has cared for Dane for years and has known him since he was a boy. He was a friend of his father's."

Reeva grinned. "Nothing you have said to me indicates that he does not lust after Dane. Dane's father was murdered wasn't he? Has the culprit been found?"

Rolf shook his head. "No. Rafael promised a more in-depth investigation after the crime was covered up."

Reeva shrugged. "It seems suspect to me. I suggest you keep your mind open to possibilities."

"Annwyn said he's possessed. In that case, logic might not apply." Abbie made this observation, meeting first Reeva's and then Rolf's gaze. Gene grunted as he prowled the room.

Reeva met her gaze. "Perhaps. I was thinking about instincts, rather than otherworldly concerns."

Abbie didn't know Rafael from Adam, but based on his expression and the way he was reacting to the environment, he seemed psychotic —out of his tree and off the planet. Yet there was strength and just a hint of intelligence in the mad eyes.

Gene came up close and hunched down to address her. "Is she all right? No harm done?" His voice was soft and sincere, a contradiction to her first impression of him.

Abbie looked up and met his hazel eyes, more green than brown.

She could see Reeva in him, around the eyes and mouth. His nose, though, was more pronounced. "She seems okay, just out of it."

He nodded. "How about you?"

Abbie narrowed her eyelids, immediately suspicious. "I'm fine. Thanks."

He leaned in closer to whisper. "If you ever get sick of him," he flicked his head Rolf's way and she felt something surround her, urge her. "I will happily take you under my protection."

A little thrill ran under her skin. He was using his alpha power on her, a real dirty trick. "Leave her alone," Rolf said from behind them. Gene shot to his feet. "I'm just offering an olive branch and letting her know what her options might be."

Rolf scoffed. "As if. You just want to fuck her."

Gene leaned in close. They were like two cocks brandishing their chests. "And you don't?"

Rolf snarled. "No, I do. And have."

"Keep an eye on what's happening with Dane, Gene," Reeva said with an angry flash to her eyes.

Gene backed down, cast his mother a look and went to stand by the door to observe Dane.

Reeva chuckled and then looked away when Rolf sent her a penetrating look. When he gloomed at her, Abbie eased back slightly and smiled innocently. Then it hit her. If Rolf wasn't going to accept her as an equal, maybe Gene would. Reeva was pretty powerful and she wasn't the alpha but the den mother.

A vibration rippled through the air. "Someone's coming," Reeva said, just before Abbie was about to.

In the empty space between Abbie and where Dane was held captive, a thin, olive-skinned man appeared. He had a hint of Africa about him. She thought Salvi was a man, but couldn't be too sure. Long dark hair in fine braids was gathered to fall down their back and the skin on their face was so smooth, so unblemished, she thought Salvi might be female instead. A loose linen vest hid what she thought was a flat male chest, while loose-fitting trousers made from similar fabric were tied at the narrow waist. On Salvi's feet were a pair of gold, red and blue beaded sandals. In the next breath another person arrived and then another, similarly oddly dressed.

"Salvi!" Rolf called out as he came forward, both arms outstretched for a hug. He engulfed the newcomer and Salvi laughed. "Still as sexy as ever, Rolf!" Gesturing towards the second person who had arrived, Salvi said, "This is Leo, and Mar," indicating the last arrival. "They have come to assist."

Abbie sat forward, no longer soothing Annwyn who appeared to be asleep. Leo was shorter than Salvi, pale with long black hair in a single braid. Their face was smooth too and had an androgynous look. There was no hair visible on their chest. Mar appeared female at first, their movements were graceful, and they had the same androgynous look. Abbie decided the best thing to do was refer to them as witches.

Salvi turned and visually scanned Dane and Rafael, stepping sideways slowly to get a better view. Leo and Mar did the same, not quite a circle but feeling like one. With eyes shut, Mar appeared to be sensing on another level. Abbie could feel a light humming vibration in the air. It was weird. Not quite a noise, but a feeling that tickled the skin.

Salvi concentrated hard and then stepped back. Leo and Mar kept watch. Rolf stepped closer. "What is it? Can you help?"

Salvi lowered their head. "You were right to call us. It's bad. Rafael is half consumed by an evil spirit. Not a random evil spirit, but one that has designed a means to ride him or has been designed specifically for him. It's probably been there for a while and now has started breaking Rafael down. As to whether I can help, it will be tricky."

"What do you propose?"

"We need to identify the spirit. It's someone recently dead but powerful. Then we need to separate the physical from the spirit."

Rolf nodded. "Right then, you best start your preparations and I'll confirm the name." Rolf strode over to Annwyn and then squatted down. "Annwyn? Wake up!"

Annwyn stirred and groaned.

"Annwyn, I need your help to save Dane. There's an evil spirit controlling Rafael. Do you think it might be Vollos, or something Vollos created specifically for Rafael?"

Annwyn lifted her head. "Vollos? Maybe. But something was controlling him. I remember dark tendrils snaking out or into him." She flopped back. "I'm sorry I can't help. I'm still trying to fight this hex. The more I fight the weaker it makes me. I think I'll be through soon. I just have to keep fighting."

Abbie let out a breath. Action at least. Rolf told Salvi the name.

"Good," the witch said. "It's a name we can work with either way. We need a rope, one we can tie around them once we enter the circle."

"Them?" Rolf said in surprise. "You aren't going to remove Dane first?"

Salvi looked up, soulful dark eyes looking sad. "We can't. If we try, Rafael might kill him. He could strangle Dane. We have to move both of them at the same time. But first we have to prepare the circle to isolate and capture the spirit, then we drag them into it."

Rolf nodded. "Right then, I'll go procure some rope. Abbie behave."

Abbie sat up. "What do you mean? I am behaving." Then she caught a whiff of Gene and understood. Rolf was in jealous mode.

Reeva stepped up to Rolf. "Be careful. I'll watch over them."

"Thank you, Den Mother," Rolf said and left.

The three witches stood together in a huddle, chanting softly. Then they split apart, each armed with a stick of chalk. They lowered themselves to all fours and began etching out a circle. Elaborate symbols grew along the inside and outside rim. Abbie guessed these were spells of protection and other arcane things. She'd read a lot about the occult as part of research for a feature she'd prepared for a university assignment. She cast a glance at Dane. Rafael was anchored to him like a parasitic growth. The old man's hands shook and his breathing grew ragged as they watched. Abbie blinked, realising Rafael had his hands around Dane's throat. The old sorcerer had started to throttle him. Did the spirit inhabiting him know that they were trying to save Dane? Was there a battle of wills inside the old man? According to Rolf, the old sorcerer loved Dane and was very fond of Annwyn too.

A touch on her shoulder had her jerking around. "What?"

It was Gene, looking at her through hooded eyes. "This might take a while. Want to be entertained?"

Before Abbie could respond, Reeva butted in. "Leave her, Gene," she said. "I told Rolf I would keep an eye on things."

Gene looked up at his mother. "What do you care? Your allegiance is to my pack. This female would be a great asset and she's sending off lures that are curling around my balls in ever tightening circles."

"She doesn't know she is doing that. She's new. And Rolf still has a claim on her."

"What gives?" Gene asked. "Why are you so protective of that Canberra upstart?"

Abbie held her breath and watched as Reeva decided.

The den mother straightened and squared her shoulders. "Because he's my son."

It felt as if the room fell silent and no one breathed, but that was not the case. The low chanting continued as the witches drew their magic circle and Annwyn quietly moaned as she fought her hex. Gene didn't move and Reeva stood still but alert, as if expecting an attack.

"Your son," Gene clearly articulated in a flat tone.

"Yes, my son," Reeva replied. "Before I met your father. Before I had you."

Gene stepped back as if pushed. "You mean he's my brother? My half-brother?"

Reeva studied him for a moment and then replied in a soft voice. "Yes."

Gene spun away to walk to the edge of the room and then walked back. "I have a brother?"

Again, Reeva nodded. She wasn't smiling or overly happy, she was just watchful. This unease communicated itself to Abbie, so she stepped closer to the older woman in case Gene lashed out.

Instead, he bent over double as if finding it hard to breath. Reeva locked her gaze with Abbie's and lifted an eyebrow.

There was a bark, a sound that could have been laughter or a sob. Abbie wasn't sure until it was repeated. Gene straightened up and laughed. "*Oy vey*, I have a brother." Abbie relaxed and Reeva exhaled. He rounded on his mother. "You have kept this secret for nearly forty years. Why did you not say something before? Why now?"

Reeva relaxed her shoulders. "Secrets have a way of making

themselves known when you least expect it. I met Rolf tonight. I only knew him as my son from the feel of him, from his scent. There could have been other Rolfs out there. Besides I promised your father I would not tell you until after he was gone."

"Dad didn't want me to know. Why?"

Reeva shrugged. "I can't speak for him. He had his reasons. He hated Rolf's father, so there was never going to be interaction between you. It was a matter of pride, I think, that he kept it quiet. He wanted the pack to think I was a trophy, something to be proud of. And he didn't want trouble with Georg, Rolf's father. A feud between packs is never good. Times were hard and we needed to focus on building a life here. So many reasons, and none of them good on their own. I'm sorry."

"I hate that jerk," Gene said. "He gets under my skin."

Reeva smiled. "I noticed."

CHAPTER 14

Rolf bolted down the street in search of a store to buy rope, but he wasn't familiar with Denver and he had no idea where to go. He hailed a cab and asked to be taken to a hardware store. It took longer than he'd anticipated and, as they drove, he fretted and worried every minute. The cab driver agreed to wait after they pulled up and Rolf flung open the car door and ran into the store. In among crowded shelves and obscure signage he found what he needed among the climbing supplies.

He was worried for Dane, of course, but he found his thoughts centring on Abbie. It was as if he was attuned to her in so many ways—her scent, her movement, the fine play of her facial muscles as her expressions changed. And worse, he wanted her all the time. That Gene had shown an interest only made the wanting worse. The emotional entanglement made matters worse, as Gene was his brother and decisions regarding Abbie were not straightforward and were potentially life changing. He was so twisted up inside, he didn't know if he would see straight ever again. How he wished Dane out of danger, just to be able to speak to his friend, seek advice.

The cab dropped him back to the building and he ran up the short path, pushed through the doors and raced back to the basement. He found that things were still much as they were when he'd left the basement room. The witches were on their knees drawing the circle. Salvi looked up at his entry. "You got the rope. Good. We are nearly ready to start."

"How's it going?" Rolf asked, dropping the rope on the floor and surveying the scene. Dane struggled against the tightening grip of the possessed sorcerer, who was in the same hunched, parasitic position, making Rolf wonder how the old man could keep it up. Then again, he was possessed and it looked like supernatural strength had no bounds.

"We've almost finished the circle. I need you to secure the rope around them."

"Are you sure both of them? I would've thought separating them was the better option?" Rolf said.

"No, this is the best way. You'll see. I will need yours' and your brother's strength." Rolf jolted as if prodded. "How did ..."

Salvi grinned and bumped Rolf with his shoulder. "Your mother has informed Gene about your parentage."

"Oh?" Rolf replied. He hadn't been expecting that, the timing being as it was. Something must have happened to make her 'fess up. Rolf swung his gaze around the room and saw Abbie under the watchful eye of his mother. Ahh, he thought, Gene must have tried to lure Abbie to his pack or his bed. It made perfect sense. If he was in his brother's position, he'd have tried the same thing. He wondered what would have happened if Reeva hadn't intervened. Would Abbie have agreed? They were still at odds about her position in the Canberra pack and he understood her anger about his stance.

"It's time," Salvi said.

Rolf stepped close to the huddled pair, keeping clear of the invisible barrier. Rafael hissed at his approach but did not change posture or attempt to fight him. Rolf went slowly around them to place the rope on the floor and put the meeting ends at the front, close to the witches' circle. Then he took a clip and secured the rope. It was just for placement for now. How to manoeuvrer it to draw them out would come later. For that he'd need his brother's help, or his mother's, and the witches' guidance.

Salvi walked the circle, checking every mark, and when he was satisfied he said, "We're ready."

Leo and Mar took up places around the circle. Rolf summoned his brother and his mother. Abbie stayed with Jill to assist with Annwyn. "First you need to hold the rope at torso level," Salvi said. "The rope can enter the barrier but flesh cannot. We'll commence the ritual as you pull on the rope to secure it, and draw them both into our circle. When Rafael's body passes through, the spirit will not be able to pass. It will put up resistance, so be prepared. Once you have Rafael through the barrier, he should be free of the spirit. We'll hold the spirit in the circle and then banish it to the afterlife where it belongs. I hope then your friend will have peace."

Rolf studied the situation, pointing Gene and Reeva to the rear and sides of Rafael and Dane. As he pulled on the rope the others would guide it around Rafael and Dane and he'd tighten it to draw the pair out. "Thank you. That sounds like a good plan." He'd worked with Salvi before and that had been an interesting but successful job. Salvi was very thorough. Good thing that he'd kept the witch's phone number.

Rolf faced Gene and then Reeva. "Ready? I'll hold the other end of the rope until it you have it in place." To Reeva he said, "Let me know if there's anything untoward. The spirit in Rafael could strike out or kill Dane despite us."

The witches sang low and rhythmically. Rolf stepped to the edge of the drawn circle and picked up the rope so that he could tighten it as Gene and his mother lifted it around the pair behind the invisible barrier. Rolf had to keep out of the receiving circle so that when Salvi banished the spirit he wouldn't be caught up in the spell.

The barrier would slowly build so the spirit wouldn't be trapped until the end. Salvi's plan appeared smooth and innovative. Taking the body from the spirit seemed better than trying to throw the spirit out of the body.

He made eye contact with Gene as he reeled in the rope hand over hand in a steady but slow pace. Gene and Reeva kept the rope at the right height, so it snagged Rafael and Dane. Rolf worked quickly, attaching the carabiner clip to secure the noose and then began to draw them along the floor. Rafael screeched as the rope closed around him and Dane. A force punched into Rolf and threw him back, making him loosen his hold on the rope. Shaken, he tried to clear his vision by blinking and focusing. He was flat on his back and the image of a fire demon sprang to life between him and Rafael. The witches kept on with their mantra and beyond the flames Rolf could see that Gene had run around to take up the rope and keep the tension around the pair.

The fire demon wasn't real, at least he didn't think it was. He climbed to his feet, ready to dart forward despite the flame. Not real, he told himself and then reached out a hand. The flame seared flesh and he tried to drag his hand back, but some force held it to the flames. The agony was immense, and he tried to tell himself it was an illusion. When that didn't work, he summoned his wolf, shrugging off his clothes along with his human skin. The magic of transformation freed his hand from the invisible grip as his body changed. He shrugged off his human form and snarled at the apparition. In wolf form he could see what the demon was, nothing but air and fancy. He was not injured. Rolf leaped and snagged the rope with his teeth to help Gene continue to tug the pair along the floor. It was working. Rolf growled and then pushed back into his human form, scooping up his clothes, he tugged on his jeans.

"I'm getting resistance now," Gene said. The pair were now crossing into the witches circle.

Rolf acknowledged this with a nod and went to lend a hand. Together they pulled on the rope, slow and steady. Rafael's head was rolling about in an unseeing kind of way, his hands tightening around Dane's neck. *Hold on*, Rolf thought at Dane. *Help is coming.*

If they didn't move quickly his friend would be strangled to death. Rafael squeezed Dane's neck and Dane was obviously still hexed as he was not fighting as he should.

"Is there anything we can do?" Abbie asked, tying her hair up into a ponytail. He shifted his gaze to Reeva and Jill as they tended Annwyn, who lay sprawled on the floor as if in a deep sleep.

Rolf chewed the inside of his cheek, trying to come up with something. The witches' mantra grew perceptibly louder. He switched his gaze to the witches. Sweat beaded on Salvi's skin, his eyes moved beneath closed eyelids and tension corded his neck. He guessed the spirit was fighting back. They had to do something to counter it. "Annwyn." Rolf turned to Abbie. "Get Annwyn awake. I don't care how, but we need her."

Abbie nodded and darted over to the inert form of Annwyn, crouched down to converse with Reeva and Jill. The young sorceress tried to rouse Annwyn by touching her on the temple, possibly using magic. When that didn't work, Reeva nodded to Abbie. "Wake up, Annwyn," Abbie said in a loud, commanding voice. "Dane needs your help. Come on!" Abbie repeated herself and as Rolf and Gene paused in their pulling on the rope, Rolf looked over and saw Annwyn sit up. Supported by Jill and Reeva, Annwyn stumbled to her feet. Reeva stood on the other side, holding her by the elbow. Jill shook her head slightly as she didn't quite believe what she was seeing.

Annwyn's face was pale and dark smudges marred the hollows of her eyes as she stared at Rafael and Dane. The sorceress studied the circle and nodded at the three witches. Then she stared at Rafael, mumbling under her breath. "Do it now, I have him distracted." The sorceress's knees bent, making Jill and Reeva fight to kept her propped up.

Rolf and Gene tugged the pair forward and the witches wove their spell, laying down layer upon layer so that the spirit, he hoped, wouldn't guess its fate until too late. The weight of Dane and Rafael grew heavier and he and Gene struggled to pull on the rope.

"Abbie!" Rolf called for assistance but Gene placed his hand over his and they pulled together. Even with their supernatural strength Dane and Rafael only moved an inch. To Abbie he said, "Annwyn needs to do more. He's fighting us."

"On it," she replied.

A tug on the rope signalled a change in tactic. With both of them holding the rope they could barely stop the rope slipping back. "Bastard!" Gene said and bared his teeth at Rolf.

Sweat now broke out on Rolf's back. He couldn't lose this fight. The rope burned the skin of his hand as it fought his hold. Then it seemed to come alive as a snake, its rough fibres becoming scales. Rolf repressed his revulsion and told himself it wasn't real, just an illusion, a trick. They were winning, that was why the evil spirit fought them.

Annwyn was back, wavering as she stood up, flanked by Jill and Reeva. Jill placed her hand in Annwyn's and closed her eyes. Maybe the lesser sorceress was giving her power to Annwyn. Her eyes grew wide as a flame lit her irises. "Feast on this," Annwyn said and flung out her hand. The part of Rafael in the circle erupted in a blue flame. The old sorcerer screamed as the rope slackened, allowing Rolf and Gene to gain ground. Again, the rope grew taut as the old sorcerer recovered.

"We need to keep him distracted, Annwyn!" Rolf called, hoping that she could hear and respond. Rafael calmed, his eyes grew focused, the sneer on his mouth grew bigger. His hands gripped Dane's throat. Dane gasped, the first sound they'd had from him in a while.

"Hold on, Dane," Rolf cried. Dane was aware, he thought. He didn't move, but there was a glint of awareness in his eyes and a coiled stillness about his posture.

Annwyn staggered and threw out her hand again. Rafael grew rigid and started screaming. They pulled on the rope and Dane's torso came all the way through, though his spine was painfully bent as his neck was still firmly in the old sorcerer's grasp. Rafael moved further in, but it wasn't enough. They needed all of him in the circle, needed him trapped and the evil spirit that was riding him contained.

"Annwyn, more!" Rolf cried. Sobbing, Annwyn sagged to her knees and thrust out a hand again. Jill fell unconscious beside her, leaving Reeva as her only support. Rafael grew rigid, his jaw locked in a rictus grin.

"Can't hold him much longer," Annwyn said through gritted teeth.

Rolf caught sight of Abbie crawling along the floor and wanted to growl at her to stay put. Then he realised she was watching for when Rafael was in the circle so she could give the signal. He and Gene pulled again, easing Dane and Rafael along as steadily as they could. Abbie waved them on. "More, just a little more. Be ready!" Abbie called.

The hair on the back of his neck rose, catching on to Abbie's warning. As Rafael's whole body passed through the barrier, the spirit would be forced out. The trouble was he would still have his hands on

Dane before they could get Rafael into the circle, which would give the spirit an opportunity to kill Dane before they could destroy or banish it. Salvi's plan was good in principle, but not easy to implement when a friend's life was in the mix.

Reeva stepped closer. "Is there something this spirit will respond to?"

Rolf frowned and then the idea hit him. "Nira! This spirit was her master."

They turned to Annwyn. She shook her head. "No. I don't think I can do that again. You have no idea what it feels like having her in charge."

Technically it was Nira who had brought Annwyn back from where the hex sent her. What affected one did not necessarily affect the other. Nira had been the spirit's servant. Had cursed and rutted to his command. It made sense. If only Annwyn could be prevailed upon to summon her for Dane's sake.

Rolf didn't even need to beg, as Annwyn spoke before he could even speak the words.

"I can think of nothing else," she said with a wail. Her hair was loose and hung in tangles and her body sagged from fatigue. She was not completely free of the hex that had drained her strength. Who knew what the evil sorceress would do if set free? All that they had in common was Dane. Nira liked to fuck Dane as much as Annwyn did.

Annwyn knelt, chin to her chest. Then something changed. Her body became alive, the movements fluid. Her head lifted and there was a gleam in them. "Free again so soon? What do you want?"

"It's Dane. We need to distract your old master." Rolf couldn't stop glowering. That they had to resort to the evil sorceress galled him.

Nira turned her head. "Oh him. I'm not scared of him anymore. Why should I help you?"

"He's killing Dane," Rolf replied. Frustrated, because all he could do was hold the rope and could think of nothing to convince Nira to help. He cast a look at the witches. All were sweating now, brows creased in concentration. He didn't think they could last much longer. The plan had seemed simple, but it was taking too long.

Reeva came up beside him. "Go. I'll hold this. You're needed."

Rolf nodded and then knelt by Nira and took her hand. "This evil spirt is why you have to share this body with Annwyn. Don't you want to destroy it?"

Nira looked through slitted eyelids and commented, "You presume too much wolf. I am powerful and angry. I could destroy you all."

"You had your chance and lost. Now do something meaningful with your life." Rolf called out to Salvi. "Can you let Nira into the circle to distract the spirit?"

Salvi made a gesture and left his place in the circle. The remaining witches staggered under the weight of carrying the spell. Wiping his sweaty brow, he studied Nira-Annwyn. "If this is the sorceress you spoke to me about, the one with the remnant inside, then there are risks. Once she is in the circle, there's no guarantee she won't be caught in the expulsion."

Rolf thinned his lips and gave a sharp nod. He had to have faith that it would turn out all right.

Salvi stood up. "I cannot guarantee the outcome. You could be risking a life here."

"Oh good," Nira crooned. "I can get rid of Annwyn and get my body back. That's a chance I'm willing to take."

Salvi lifted an eyebrow and shifted his gaze back to Rolf. "You say it's a remnant, but it appears to be more. Are you sure you want to risk Annwyn?"

Rolf looked to Dane, huddled there with Rafael's hands around his throat. "We need to risk it."

Abbie gasped. "That's a big call to make, Rolf."

He turned to Abbie. "I know, but Annwyn would have my balls if I didn't try to save Dane. I'd do the same for your life."

Abbie's eyes widened and then she looked to where Dane sat. "We don't have a choice do we?"

"No."

Salvi bowed. "I will re-join the circle. You must hurry. We're tiring."

As Salvi re-joined the circle, the chanting changed and the invisible barrier became opaque, its edges meeting the circle drawn on the ground.

Nira stumbled to her feet and stripped off her clothes. Nira was taking her delightful body into the circle. Rolf caught the look that Abbie sent the sorceress. When Nira was in control you could tell. It was no mere character quirk. Her expressions were different, the way she walked with so much sexy confidence made it easy to tell them apart. The spice Nira exuded was different too, as there was something exotic in the flow of her magical power. With an exaggerated sway of her hips, Nira walked into the circle. The magical barrier shivered once and then the opaqueness faded, allowing them to see inside. Rolf's breath hitched as Nira swung her head, making her hair sway across her back and she stretched her body like a cat, appearing to revel in the body she now possessed.

Reeva shook her head as she handed back the rope to Rolf. "This is not going to end well. I feel it."

Rolf didn't like how his mother's words echoed his own thoughts. There were risks. He was told but he took them anyway. He tightened his grip on the rope.

The cackling of Nira and her strange gyrations added weight to this comment.

"Come on, Nira! Distract him!" Rolf yelled, not able to control his frustration. He just wanted to go in there and rip Dane from Rafael's grip.

Abbie stood beside him, her hand on his bicep. "Don't go in there."

Rolf nodded but it was killing him inside to risk them, any of them.

Nira leaned close to Rafael but seemed to be speaking to something above him. "You old bastard! You got what you deserved. I'm going to destroy you."

A hiss issued from Rafael's mouth and it sent chills down Rolf's spine. It was so otherworldly. "Slut. You useless slut."

Nira chortled. "If I'm a useless slut then it's your fault. You groomed me from childhood. You perverted me with sex when I was but a child. You made me and now I'm going to destroy you."

The revelation staggered Rolf. Nira's personality had been forged through sex abuse, her magic warped so that only sex would fuel it. That was a betrayal and a perversion, the realisation making his anger boil. He wanted to strangle the old bastard himself. But who was Nira referring to: Vollos or Rafael or the spirt?

Nira struck out at Rafael with magic. His body jerked, momentarily loosening his grip of Dane. Rolf and Gene pulled on the rope, gaining them an inch or two. Nira struck again and Rafael moaned. More of Dane and Rafael slid through as they pulled again on the rope. "Just a little more," Abbie called out.

Rolf and Gene tugged again. A cackling cry echoed in the room as Nira struck again.

Salvi and the other witches raised their voices. They didn't have much time. Nira screamed as Rafael hit back. A wave of his hand and Nira buckled and fell to her knees. Rolf could see her face. Drool and blood leaked from her beautiful mouth. Her face had red patches and it looked like she was bruised around the eyes. Damn these sorcerers and their magic. How was one ever to feel safe when a wave of a hand could deal out such a blow?

Nira surged to her feet, seeming to act blindly and she hit Rafael with her shoulder. "Now!" Abbie shouted.

With one tug Rolf and Gene brought them through. An outraged cry filled the air as Rolf and Gene let out yells of triumph. They continued to pull until Dane was at the edge of the barrier and slid him through the other side. Salvi and his witches upped the notes on their chant. Rafael bounced against the barrier designed to trap him. Abbie ran forward and freed Dane from the rope and he slid limply to the ground. Dane gasped for breath but didn't appear conscious. Reeva knelt at his side along with Abbie as they tried to rouse him, calling his name, lightly slapping his cheeks.

"Pity he's no longer wolf. He could shapeshift and heal himself," Reeva observed.

On the other side of the barrier, Rafael turned to face Nira. He was enraged now, possibly because Dane was free. "Useless cow." Nira flew back and landed on the floor. Rafael loomed over her, teeth clenched and spittle flying.

The chanting changed key again. The witches must be going for the expulsion now. Rafael's physical body had to be liberated. But what about Nira-Annwyn?

Gene said, "You go to him. I can manage here."

Rolf dropped the rope. "Thank you." It seemed superfluous now that the witches had Rafael trapped. He rushed over to check Dane over. "How is he," he asked Abbie and Reeva.

"Alive," Abbie said. Rolf nodded once then turned his attention to his friend. "Dane?"

There was no response. Dane was still out cold. A scream and he looked up. Nira and Rafael struggled, both trying to strangle the other.

"Nira you have to come back now. We have Dane." Rolf called out, frowning when she ignored him. He was certain that as the circle was designed for Rafael she could walk out of there. "Please, Nira."

With a cry, she leaped and attached herself to Rafael's back, pulling what remained of his hair and cupping his chin as if she was trying to rip his head off.

Through the barrier Rolf saw something like steam rising from his skin. Agony stretched the features of Rafael's face

"Annwyn, it's time to fight back. Come on." It was Abbie calling out.

Nira's face turned into a sneer and she glared at Abbie. "Shut up, bitch!"

Rafael arched his back in agony. His body glowed an opaque yellow and the chanting rose higher. The spell was reaching its apogee. The witches were coming in for the expulsion of spirit. They were going to ram that evil spirit into the afterlife. Rolf licked his lips, not at all sorry, as that evil spirit had tried to kill Abbie on a number of occasions, had irrevocably changed her life, ruining her career.

A scream issued from the sorceress's mouth, so loud and long that it brought goosebumps to his flesh. Nira had been thrown and lay where she fell. With eyes blazing, Rafael focused on them, on the trio that were trying to force the spirit out of his body.

Salvi called out. "We're walking it forward, shrinking it. The evil spirit won't be able to fight that." If not for the barrier, they would have been killed as a large concussion shook the circle. Rafael rose up and remained suspended while the barrier contracted a footstep at a time. Another scream rent the air as the sorcerer collapsed. Wisps of steam-like clouds hissed from his skin. The barrier contracted farther and the mist-like form hovered there. It tried to find a way out, sending tendrils to different parts of the circle. Each time a tendril made contact it drew back as if burnt.

"What about Annwyn?" Abbie called to Rolf.

He shook his head. "There's nothing we can do but hope she will be safe from the expulsion spell."

The semi-opaque dome that was the barrier retracted and retracted until it was just above Annwyn/Nira's body and the cloud of mist that was the evil spirit. The witches lifted their heads, nodded to each other and snapped the barrier closed. The final gasp gave Rolf a shock. It came from Annwyn's prone form. What had happened?

Salvi called out a long spiel of words and made gestures with his ceremonial knife. "It is done. The spirit is banished."

Rafael lay out cold and sprawled on the floor. Jill raced over and knelt by him, checking him over.

"Can I go to her?" Abbie asked Salvi. Rolf looked up and saw the sorceress unconscious near Rafael. He bit his lip as he stared at Dane, worried what it all meant and how his friend would take it.

"Sure, but be careful," Salvi said. He looked exhausted and he and his fellow witches sank to the floor and lay down, whispering to each other with tired voices. Not long after, Salvi stood and went to the circle, starting to erase the markings and all traces of their spell. Rolf grew concerned when Annwyn remained motionless on the floor and non-responsive to Abbie's desperate pleas to wake up.

CHAPTER 15

Abbie crawled forward aiming for Annwyn's inert form. Her face was still as death and Abbie tried to shake that thought away. Now was not the time for catastrophising. There would be plenty of time for that later.

Blonde hair spread across the sorceress's face and one arm lay across her belly while the other lay knuckle down on the floor. Abbie straightened her bent limbs, hoping to make her more comfortable. Reeva came over and draped a thin foil blanket over her. Abbie wondered where they had found it but saw the large first aid kit open on the floor.

"Thank you," Abbie said. "How is Dane?"

"The witch bends to the task of healing him now. He has been badly used—a terrible hex that he is having trouble breaking free from. Also, he needs emotional healing. He trusted Rafael and I fear he thinks his friend betrayed him." Reeva indicated the inert form in front of them "How is the sorceress?"

Abbie bent her knee and rested her chin on it. "I don't know. I can't smell her. It's like there's no one there."

Reeva nodded. "We heard of what happened with her. Rolf reported it to the Council of Australian Werekind. That body was not

Annwyn's but the sorceress Nira's. She stole Annwyn's body when she was just a human. Later when Annwyn had gained power, there was a battle. Annwyn was forced to destroy her own body to save Dane. That is why a bit of Nira lives on in the body that Annwyn wears. I fear the witches' spell casting may have caught them. Who is a spirit and who is real? It is anyone's guess."

Abbie frowned as she studied the slight rise and fall of Annwyn's chest. "You mean the witches might've banished Annwyn to the afterlife and that could be Nira lying there?"

Reeva smiled sadly. "Yes. We won't know until she wakes."

Abbie signed. "If she wakes. Technically they're both spirits. Nira was a partial. Annwyn was whole. Do you think she knew when she went into the circle what danger she was in?"

Reeva's pale eyes glowed in the light as they studied the still form. "I think both of them did. Both of them love Dane."

"I felt sorry for Nira when I heard what was done to her. She was warped by that old man, that disgusting sorcerer. I don't care whether he was possessed by an evil spirit or what. He abused his powers, as well as her."

Reeva squatted next to Abbie and rubbed her back. "All kinds of power corrupts. When people become too powerful, they stop being accountable and that leads them to abuse their power, to think themselves above others. That's why we weres don't belong to the collegium. We are more of a cooperative."

"Do you mean like a community organisation? Egalitarian?"

Reeva scoffed. "I wouldn't go that far. You still have to have people making decisions. Alphas do the day to day, but the council makes the big decisions and there are all kinds on there."

"You?" Abbie asked softly.

"Of course, me. I'm one of the founders."

Abbie brightened up at this comment. "So it's not all macho chest thumping, this world of weres?"

Reeva laughed. "*Oy vey*! Definitely lots of that! But to really get things done you need a woman, and to succeed you need everyone on board. I admit that sometimes we let the males think they are the ones making all the decisions, but often they aren't. Don't give up on that son of mine, Abbie."

Abbie pulled back, shocked that the old woman knew what had been on her mind. "How did you ...?"

"I can read people and I know a bit about Rolf, even though I've kept my distance. You are strong and he needs that. We need that."

"What about Gene?" Abbie asked, just to spice up the conversation. "He made me an offer."

Reeva nodded. "He did and if you can't work it out with Rolf then by all means take him up on it. Gene's shrewd, though." She tapped the side of her head. "Smart. Business smart and people smart. He might be a bit hard to handle."

Abbie burst out laughing. It was what she'd been thinking about Gene. He had looks, dammit, and was probably as built as Rolf, but the Sydney property dealer was harder to pin down, harder to work out. Rolf, though, had something true about him, something sincere.

"I'll keep your recommendations in mind. I may choose my own way. What are my chances of starting my own pack?" she asked the den mother.

Reeva's eyebrows shot up. "Ambitious! It's technically possible, although it's never been done. You would need followers, otherwise you'd be alone." She shook her head. "Weres don't do well on their own. They become unstable, dangerous even, and that's not a good thing."

"Oh, I see," Abbie replied.

"Besides, we're bound together because as a group we are more powerful and we can support each other. Kinship bonds are the fibre of our beings. You take a mate because you want the kinship ties, and children too. Or you stay part of the pack, have sex with anyone in the group if you don't want that commitment, but you still belong. An alpha has to be strategic in taking a mate. He might need kinship ties with another pack, so he makes a strategic alliance. Or he may find a powerful she-wolf that will bring him prestige and boost his pack's standing and give him strong cubs too."

"And love? Doesn't that come into it?"

A sigh leaked out of Reeva's mouth. "Ah, love. Rolf was born out of love. The love didn't last, it only blinded me to Axel's faults. When I became Cohen's mate, that was a different thing. There was passion, of course, because of who and what he was—a great lover and a smart, handsome man. But there was strategy, too. I learned to be more holistic in my choices. There were more variables in my love equation. He was well reasoning, just and shrewd like his son has become. That meant more to me than just a good time. When the passion wanes, there needs to be something else. Respect, honour, duty and affection. Cohen and I were happy."

"What happened to your husband?" Abbie asked.

Reeva's face took on a faraway look. "Ahh. A couple of things. He had a defect in the heart that we didn't know about. He had it in wolf form as well as human, so it wasn't something that would heal like an injury would. And he was betrayed."

"Betrayed?" Abbie asked.

"Yes, in business. He was murdered early last year over a property deal. Gunned down with silver bullets in the driveway of a development site. They knew what he was, hence the bullets. Combined with the heart condition, there was nothing anyone could do. We still haven't gotten to the bottom of it. The human police force has been dragging its feet. Gene is trying to investigate himself, but this changeling curse business set us awry. When this is over, we will find this shmuck and deal with him."

"Den Mother?" Rolf called out. "Can you help me please?"

Reeva nodded to Abbie and went to help. Abbie watched while they laid Dane down. He seemed to be mumbling something and that was a good sign. She gazed down at Annwyn and there was nothing. Not a wisp of magic scent.

Salvi came over and knelt down next to Annwyn's inert form. "I'm sorry she got caught up in this."

"Do you think she'll die?" Abbie asked. "I can't smell anything."

Salvi's eyes widened. "You smell magic?"

"Sorcerer's scent, yes. You too, so I suppose that's smelling magic," she said as she picked up Annwyn's flaccid hand. "Yes."

"What do I smell like to you?" Salvi asked.

Abbie breathed deep. "Floral scents mostly. Lavender, lily and basil with a hint of nutmeg."

Salvi didn't laugh. "How every acute your nose is. And it was your nose that identified Rafael and his evil spirit?"

Abbie thought about this. "In the end, yes. I had not met him, you see. He proved elusive and I guess that was because he knew I could scent him. Instead, he tried to kill me. But I suppose I should not hold it against Rafael, as it was the evil spirit who did that."

"Quite right," Salvi replied. "Rafael is really a gentle soul. I'm glad I was able to help." Salvi stood. "Forgive me. I will go back and attend to him."

Jill appeared at her side. The young woman's business suit was crumpled and grimy. She glanced around, her calculating gaze taken in the scene. "I've called for assistance."

As Abbie was the only one paying attention, she replied. "Good. We think Rafael is free of the evil spirit now."

The sorceress frowned. "Rafael is not recovering well. The possession took a toll on him. We can set up an infirmary here."

Rolf stood up and came over. He looked down on the diminutive sorceress. "Jill that would be a great idea. We also need food, because I think this will take time. Bring beds and whatever you think is required here. We're not going to relinquish our friends to strangers."

The sorceress bit her bottom lip and didn't argue. "Very well. I'll see to it. Then I'll return to assist, if that is all right with you?"

Abbie tried to listen for sarcasm and couldn't detect any. Jill was being sincere. She was actually respectful of Rolf and that made Abbie like her. The sorceress spun on her heel and left the room.

Dane was making more noise. Not much sense, but it was something. Of the three, he was the most alert. Rafael continued to lie still. Salvi administered to him. Mar, one of the witches, came over to Abbie, bringing a cup of water. "This is for you. If you need to take a break, I can sit with her. I'll call you if there's any change."

Abbie stood up and eased out the kinks in her legs and back. "Thank you," she said and accepted the water. She needed to take a break, relieve herself and just breathe, so she accepted the offer and went to find a bathroom.

The vision of herself in the mirror was quite a surprise. She had dark shadows under her eyes and her hair was a riot of tangles. After making herself comfortable, she did her best to put some order into her hair. At the end of the row of cubicles was a shower stall so Abbie fell victim to the idea of hot water on her flesh. She hadn't really thought it through; once she was in she wondered how she'd dry off. She'd have to use her clothes. As the water thundered down on her head and shoulders, she revelled in the sensation. It was wonderful and she could feel the tension run out of her tired muscles. The liquid soap in the wall dispenser was lemon scented and she lathered up well and then sluiced off. When she finally turned the water off, she stepped out to find a pile of fresh towels deposited there. She was in a collegium building so perhaps magically appearing linen was par for the course. She wrapped her hair in one and dried off with another.

The door flew open and crashed against the wall. Rolf stood there. It seems he too had had a shower. His body still had a sprinkling of water drops across his chest and, by the looks of his full erection, he was pleased to see her.

Abbie dropped her towel and stood naked before him, inviting him with her eyes, challenging him with her stance. She hadn't even taken a breath when his body covered her, holding her along the length of his body as he buried his face in her neck. Then she knew that this encounter wasn't simply naked lust. Rolf needed her. Wanted comfort.

Raising her left arm, she ran her fingers through his hair and gripped him tightly with the other. He stayed that way for a few minutes, just still. Then he pulled back, his eyelashes wet with tears.

"Dane?" she asked, knowing what he was worried about most and fearing the worst had happened.

"Awake," he said finally, as he ran his fingers through his still damp hair, making it spike up. He visually scanned her body, his lips lifting at the edges as if he liked what he saw. "Thank you for what you've done today."

"Glad I could help," she replied, lowering her gaze, and noticing that Rolf was still ready for sex. A smile of invitation lit her lips.

Without a word, he lifted her around the waist and held her against the wall. His hot mouth found her right breast and nipple and he sucked hard and fast. His other hand massaged her left breast. Abbie had already been hot, now she was almost at boiling point. She moaned as desire leaked through her lips. The suction of his mouth took her to the edge and left her panting. He changed breasts and Abbie was breathing in hard exhalations as her body succumbed to the stimulation Rolf was plying her with. She was wet and ready and still he teased her, aiming for her mouth and kissing her deep, as his hands found her moist folds. She shuddered as the orgasm hit. She was so hot it had taken only a stroke or two of his firm finger to bring her to the edge.

He released her mouth. "Now, fuck me," she demanded, but he wasn't done playing her. His lips moved down her neck, sucking and biting until her whole body was trembling, so close to coming she could scream. He held her hair and pulled slightly and Abbie growled.

"Do you still want to fuck me?" he whispered in her ear, his hot breath teasing her skin, her mind, her sex.

"Yes!" she said, wanting to be fucked and wanting to fuck him and make him come hard. He held her waist firmly and rearranged himself so that he could lower her onto his erection. Except he was doing it so slow, Abbie was writhing and fighting to lower herself onto him. "Come on!" she cried impatiently, but he just studied her face as the tip of his cock brushed against her moist vulva. Then achingly slowly he lowered her down, his strength and restraint amazing. By the time she was fully impaled, she was whimpering and tears streaked her face. She never once stopped looking into his face, nor he hers. It was challenging and beautiful at the same time. Her eyes closed once she was anchored to him. Then he held her waist and she gripped him with her legs. The sheer strength of him as he played her body against his cock moved her deeply, touched her soul. Shouts, cries, begging echoed around that small bathroom. Enough noise to warn any who dared to enter. Abbie didn't care if they did, she was in the moment. The next orgasm hit like an earthquake, shaking her to the bone, but Rolf was not done. He pressed harder, merging their bodies and then he lowered his mouth and bit her on the neck, a nip of possession. Abbie froze her upper body while he pumped his seed into her. A scream, hers, near deafened her. He'd timed that bite just so, enhancing her orgasm and taking her beyond herself.

He rested his sweaty forehead against hers, breath still hard and fast, but slowing. They gripped each other and then after a moment or two, he withdrew from her body and eased her legs down, still enfolding her in his embrace. Abbie couldn't stand. Normal circulation and strength had not returned. Her muscles twitched, her heart thumped. It was not going to be easy to calm down.

"I need you, Abbie," Rolf said in a rough voice.

Abbie's head jerked up, making Rolf lean back. "I ... I don't ... that was amazing," she said, not quite coherent. She didn't know how to respond to the raw need in Rolf. She was afraid to respond to it, because she wanted to and was wary of what that could mean and what she would have to surrender to share his love.

"Later," he said and kissed her on the forehead. "We'll talk later when everything has returned to normal."

He went into the shower cubicle and washed himself down. "Come in," he said, stretching out a hand to her. She joined him under the warm spray, washing the sweat and the lust down the drain.

"What about Annwyn?" she asked as they dried off and pushed their legs and arms into clothes.

Rolf paused, lowered his gaze and shook his head. Then he kissed her on the forehead again. "See you outside in a bit."

Abbie let out a breath. This was not good. How was Dane going to cope with that? How were they even going to tell him?

After Abbie re-dressed, she crept back into the room where their sorcerous patients lay. Dane wasn't sitting up, but appeared to be responding to questions from Leo. Mar sat by Annwyn's still form.

Rafael had Salvi in attendance. Gene was on the phone in the corner and Reeva was going between them offering supplies and support. Jill watched on, offering to get things as required. Abbie didn't know where to go first to see what was happening. After the bad news about Annwyn, she was reluctant to go there. What if she was dead? Abbie didn't know how to deal. She'd seen too much death of late and someone so vibrant and clearly talented as Annwyn ending was more than she could cope with right now.

Abbie went closer to see how Dane was doing. His colour was better, but his eyes were still unfocused. At least he was speaking in a logical matter, if only to answer questions. He was still fighting the aftereffects of the hex.

When Abbie moved over to where Rafael lay, she thought he didn't look so good. His greyish skin sagged and his eyes were sunken, with darker flesh surrounding his eyeballs. Salvi looked up and gave a tight smile. The 'I am doing the best that I can despite the odds' smile. Abbie noticed just how androgynous Salvi looked. Smooth skin, beautiful features, wide, delicious dark brown eyes, an angular nose with high cheek bones and a full, dark red mouth. Abbie smiled and resisted the urge to soothe the hair on their head. They were just the sort of person you wanted to touch, to experience. She backed away before she did something embarrassing.

There was only Annwyn to check on now and Abbie put a hand to her chest to quieten the uptick in her heartbeat. Why was she afraid? What did she fear from Annwyn or for Annwyn? It was Dane and the love Annwyn had shared with him. It was something that Abbie had envied and admired from afar. They were close, sexually and emotionally. They complemented each other. That wasn't something you saw every day. Just seeing it changed Abbie's views on relationships and how they could work. And now they were faced with losing that. Well, Dane was. She didn't know how he'd cope or how they could help him. They? She meant her and Rolf, but what future was there for them? Not with this alpha business. Not with him expecting her to submit to him. To not treat her as an equal.

Instead of standing there doing nothing, she made her way to Annwyn and tried not to react to the thought of the sorceress dead as she approached her motionless body on the floor.

Just as she neared Annwyn, the sorceress's hand moved. Just a jerk of the fingers, but it was something. "Look! she cried out, before getting on all fours to crawl closer.

Mar, who had been sitting on a chair nearby, shot to their feet, big brown eyes glued to the sorceress. There was someone in that body. It was either Nira or Annwyn and she hadn't thought about what might happened if it was Nira who woke in possession of the body.

Abbie sniffed. There was something. A hint of magic that didn't belong to the witch and was coming from Annwyn's body. It wasn't enough to tell who, only that there was someone inhabiting that body.

Mar smiled at her. "Do you care for her?"

Abbie sighed loudly. "Of course. As a person I care for her as someone who is injured."

Mar smiled and covered their mouth with a hand as if hiding a secret smile. Abbie rolled her eyes. There was no point in arguing with the witch.

A groan escaped Annwyn and her mouth opened as if testing it. The scent of magic increased and Abbie put her mind to work in trying to decode what she was smelling. It was a different scent to that she'd detected before. Not Annwyn and not Nira. She shook her head trying to puzzle it out. The eyes opened and looked around the room as the forehead furrowed in puzzlement.

"Where am I?" the voice said.

"Annwyn?" Abbie asked, taking the woman's hand, and squeezing it gently. The head moved toward her.

"Who's Annwyn?" the woman asked.

"Nira?" Abbie replied.

The woman shook her head. "No."

Abbie gestured wildly to Reeva, who had lifted up her head when they had started talking. "What is your name then?" she asked.

The women let her breath pass over her taut lips as if she was reaching far back in time. "Gwendolin. Or just Gwen."

"You just rest there for a bit. There's been a bit of an accident." Abbie got up and Reeva nodded, indicating she'd stay and watch while she went to talk to Salvi.

"What's going on?" she hissed. "Who is that? I thought the spirit was sent to the afterlife."

Salvi frowned. "It was. There was a risk that Annwyn would be sent too, because it was not her native body."

"Well, now there's someone called Gwen in that body," Abbie said as she jabbed a finger in Annwyn's direction.

Salvi's eyes widened. "Gwen? I have no idea who that is, unless ..."

Rolf loomed. "Unless what?" he asked gruffly. His eyes were creased in worry and Abbie didn't blame him. This unexpected complication was just what they didn't need right now.

Salvi pinched their bottom lip, obviously still thinking things through. "Could Nira have stolen the body before swapping with Annwyn? If that is the case, Gwen could be the one who owns the body."

Abbie fell back, shocked; by the look on Rolf's face he too was taken by surprise. The body had three people in it?

"Can you find out for sure?" Abbie asked. "Is there another plausible answer?"

Salvi shifted brown eyes to stare at Abbie. "Yes. I can ascertain the truth of the matter." They shrugged. "Until I do there's not much call for looking for other explanations."

Rolf's lip lifted in an almost snarl. "What am I to tell Dane?" he hissed.

"Nothing for now," Salvi replied shortly.

Rolf grasped Abbie's shoulder to get her attention. "What about your nose?"

Abbie shrugged. "She smells different. There's some magic, but she's not Annwyn or Nira. We just have to wait and see what Salvi determines."

"Fuck!" Rolf said and turned away.

Abbie didn't blame him for his frustration. She put a hand out to Salvi who had turned to walk away. "Can you do anything? Can we reverse it?"

Salvi blanched. "No. It can't be reversed. If the spell expelled her spirit, then she is gone. All I can do is help you find out who is residing in the body now."

Abbie let him go. Rafael was showing more signs of life. She went back and knelt by Gwen and tried to think of what she could do. "Gwen. Tell me a little about yourself. Where were you born?"

Gwen's green eyes flickered and then focused on Abbie. "Sydney."

Abbie nodded. "Good. Do you have family?"

"Yes, a brother and a sister. My father and mother are alive too."

"How old are you?" Abbie asked.

"I'm thirty-five years old. Is Jake here?"

"Who is Jake?"

"My fiancé. We're getting married."

Abbie extracted a few more details. She needed to get on the internet and check out these details in case they were in a very serious shithole.

Jill came back and was able to lead Abbie to an office with a computer. "We have them for research," the sorceress explained.

Abbie sat down and keyed in key words, like Gwen's name, her fiancé's name and so on. She scrolled through the results, discarding the first ten or so and was starting to think it was all hokum when she clicked on a news article with the headline: 'Man's bride disappears on wedding day'. It was dated five years ago.

Abbie swallowed and read on.

The Coogee Bay venue was the scene of a dramatic disappearance. Bride-to-be Gwen Taylor entered her limousine in her full bridal dress. When it arrived at the church the car was empty. Only the bridal bouquet remained to prove the bride had been in the car. The driver could provide no explanation as to the whereabouts of the bride. The drivers of the entourage who followed the vehicle bore witness to the fact that the car did not stop.

She scrolled farther down the page and an image of Gwen appeared. It was Annwyn-Nira, but younger, smiling with innocent happiness. It was the same body. Abbie sat back. It was true then. Annwyn was gone and so was Nira. This woman, Gwen, was the original owner of the body. What if Nira hadn't body swapped, but had stolen the body and pushed Gwen out into some kind of limbo? When Annwyn's and Nira's spirits were banished, Gwen was free to come back. A dark heavy blanket of grief welled up inside. Not so much for her, but for Dane. Annwyn had sacrificed herself for him.

It was with great reluctance that she returned to the room where the others were gathered. Rolf pounced on her as soon as she entered. She pulled him back to the corner with her. "It's true. Annwyn is gone. Gwen Taylor does exist and went missing on her wedding day. I saw a photo with the article. It's definitely her."

"Shit!" Rolf looked over his shoulder. "I'm trying to prepare him for the worst. He's not fully back yet, but he's asking for Annwyn. He's going to see her and think it's her."

"I know," Abbie said. "I think we need to move Ann—Gwen. I'll ask Jill to organise it. Maybe send her back to her family."

"No, not yet. Move her yes, but Dane will want to see, want to know that she's truly gone. Okay?"

"Yes, I'll arrange it. I think we should move Rafael too. Dane looks like he can move under his own steam. Will your friends stay with Rafael?"

"I think so. I'll go check." He flashed a wan smile that didn't reach his eyes. After he walked away Reeva came up and asked for an update. She was too stunned to talk when Abbie related the story.

Jill came and agreed to move Gwen to a private area within the building. It was on the ground floor and easy to find. Gwen seemed calm enough. Rafael was sent deep into the collegium's offices to a healing centre.

Salvi came to say goodbye. "I'm sorry it didn't turn out as expected. No one could've predicted this outcome."

Abbie nodded and Rolf stood behind her. Salvi lifted sad eyes. "I'm sorry for your friend. If there's anything I can do to help, let me know."

"Sure. By the way, Gwen has some magic about her. Not strong, but detectable."

Salvi pulled a face. "Really? That is odd. Maybe keep her under surveillance. And don't be too premature about sending her back to her people."

Abbie gave Rolf a hug. "Hang in there. Give my love to Dane."

Rolf just nodded and squeezed her hand.

She found Gwen easily enough. The woman was sitting up in bed, drinking tea. "I'm glad you're here. This place is very strange." She eyed the ceiling. "I swear we were somewhere else before, but then I ended up here. Have I been drugged or something?"

"I don't know. But we're keeping an eye on you for now." Abbie took a seat. "What was the last thing you remember before you woke up?"

Gwen lay back against the pillows. "It's hard. Sunshine. Blue sky. White clouds maybe. Happiness."

Abbie nodded. She couldn't make anything out of those things—

they sounded rather vague. The date on the article placed Gwen's disappearance nearly five years ago. She'd have to do more searching on the internet to find out what happened to Jake. It's quite possible he'd gotten on with his life. Who knew that the evil sorceress was a body snatcher and the body she was wearing wasn't hers? Poor Annwyn. Abbie couldn't help but be angry at the injustice of it. Of course, Gwen was to be pitied too. She hadn't asked for her body to be stolen.

CHAPTER 16

To Rolf's relief, Dane continued to improve, becoming more and more like his old self. His eyes were better able to focus. The worrying thing was that every chance he got, he asked about Annwyn. Rolf was at a loss to know what to say. At first, he'd tried to say 'don't worry about that, concentrate on getting better'. But his friend would have none of it.

"Tell me where Annwyn is."

Rolf grimaced. He could not lie, but nor could he tell all the truth straight away. He had to dole it out a bit at a time. "Annwyn went into the magic circle to help rescue you. The witches had to banish the evil spirt from Rafael, as the old sorcerer had you in a death grip."

Dane moved a hand to his throat, swallowed and nodded before closing his eyes to rest.

"Where is she?" he said an hour later when he'd gathered enough strength and focus to speak again.

"She hasn't come around yet." Rolf explained.

Dane's face creased with worry. "Not come around yet? So it's not the hex that Raf ... that it put on us?"

Rolf shook his head. "No."

Dane reached out with his hand and Rolf took it. "It's bad? Tell me."

"We don't know yet for sure, but it could be." It was as gentle as Rolf could be as he explained. As it turned out it wasn't gentle at all. Dane's face screwed up and he moaned. "No, no, no. Why did she do that?"

"Because she loves you. You would've risked the same for her."

Dane quietened then. "I'm sorry. I'm still feeling the effects of the hex." He closed his eyes and seemed to sleep. Rolf owed a lot to Abbie for helping in this situation. He wanted to go to her and see how things were with Annwyn, or rather Gwen. With her nose Abbie could detect if Annwyn was still there. Why hadn't he twigged that Annwyn entering the circle would cause her great harm, perhaps even her life? They were trying to banish the spirit. Salvi had tried to warm them, so he couldn't really blame the witch. Because of Annwyn's unusual situation the outcome had been hard to predict.

Rafael had been shifted to a bed in the collegium and Jill sent word that he was stable. No trace of any evil spirits. They had not suspected that an evil spirit had possessed Rafael. None of them had known. The changes had been subtle, as the spirit ate away at Rafael's control, growing stronger as Rafael grew weaker. Rolf couldn't see how things would have played out differently.

Matters could have been worse, if Abbie hadn't survived and hadn't smelt her attacker. There could've been more deaths, and his kin would have been exposed to the world. He had to be grateful for her, and he was. What if it had been Abbie who had been taken? He looked down on Dane, at the trace of tears leaking down his cheeks, and it chilled him to the core. Now that wasn't worth dwelling on.

Reeva came along to relieve him. "Go see how Abbie is doing. Jill brought her a tablet, so she could research further into Gwen's past."

Rolf stood up and Reeva tugged on his hand as he was walking away. "I know it's hard." She reached up to hug him and he leaned down and accepted the embrace. Tears did come then, unexpectedly. This was his mother and for the first time in memory she was holding him and he her in a time of need. She patted his back. "I'm proud of the man you have become. I know it isn't due to anything that I've done. But it warms my heart."

Rolf tried to smile, only he was afraid he might start sobbing. He couldn't deal with this emotion right now. He nodded dumbly and then headed to where Abbie was. Gene came in as he was leaving. Their eyes met as his half-brother moved into the room. He saw kindness there and his lips responded in a slight smile.

Before going to check on Abbie, Rolf went into the street to clear his head. The city was alive around him. Bustling traffic, people shopping, and the air was chillier than at home. Opposite seasons he thought. At least they weren't in the depths of winter here, or he'd be forced to change into his wolf form to get warm. Rolf tried to think and not think at the same time. His gut churned; his emotions were in a whirl. He was close to Annwyn and the thought that he might never see her again pained him. Worse was how his friend was going to cope. He wasn't sure Dane could, or would even try. They had been a strong match, a love match. The only fly in the ointment had been the sorceress Nira. Then again, it was Nira's action that brought them together. Why was it so hard to untangle things, so hard to lay blame or find the cause? Abbie had come to him through the nefarious actions of others. It did not make her bad, though.

Rolf couldn't bear trying to sort things out in this crowd. He had to go for a run, have the wind in his face. Only vigorous exercise was going to clear his head. If he went to Abbie like this, he'd be trying to bury himself inside her on the spot. While that was joyous and wonderful, it did not help him make decisions.

Rolf ran down the street and kept on running. They were on the outskirts of Denver and he could smell wildlife, animals, and they called to him. Soon he saw the entrance to a large wildlife park. He could smell woods and water and it felt like home. The flat prairie opened up around him. There in the distance were some foothills. He ran farther until he found a decent spot to hide from prying eyes, where he stripped off his clothes and transformed. Then he bounded forward, breathing the taste of freedom and ran and ran and ran.

Abbie was not liking what she found on the internet. Gwen's former fiancé had married someone else within three months of Gwen disappearing. Sure, his fiancée disappeared, but three months? He must've had the other one ready and waiting. How was she going to break this to Gwen? She hadn't even told her that it had been five years. She wished Reeva would do it. Or Rolf, or anyone. Rolf had to tell Dane and that was a task she didn't envy. Where the hell was Rolf anyway? She thought he'd be back by now.

Abbie got a faint whiff of magic again and got up to sniff around the sleeping woman. It was definitely coming from the body. None of her research had indicated any magical ability in Gwen. Maybe it was left over from having her body ridden by sorceresses—good or bad.

Abbie put her head out the door and called out. Jill appeared. "Is there a problem?"

"Is Salvi still around?"

"I believe so. Do you wish to speak to the witch?"

"Yes, please. All of them, if the others are there."

Jill nodded and turned away to pull out her phone to make a call.

Abbie turned back and saw that Gwen looked to be sleeping peacefully, her hands atop the cream-coloured blanket. Abbie perched on the uncomfortable, black-metal framed chair next to her. There was a jug of water and Abbie helped herself. They had brought Annwyn's clothes in and hung them over a chair. Abbie went up to them and inhaled. It was definitely Annwyn's scent. Not her magical scent, but her body scent. Returning to the bed, she leaned over Gwen and inhaled. Mixed results, she thought. There was this subtle spice of magic there and the body odour was the same. Chemically Gwen and Annwyn were indistinguishable.

Abbie paced the room, impatiently waiting for Salvi and his witch companions to show up. There came a light tap on the door. "Come in," Abbie called, facing the bed and pondering.

Salvi came in. "You wanted to talk to me?"

His long, thin braids swished with his movement and it made Salvi look even more beautiful. "Yes, please. Did the others come?"

Salvi came in and shut the door. "No, they have returned home. I was about to leave when I got the call that you wanted to talk to me."

Abbie noted that Salvi didn't look at Gwen on the bed and wondered why. "Yes, I'm puzzled about something."

Salvi's fine eyebrows rose above the deep dark of his eyes. "What is that?"

"The presence of magic in Gwen. It shouldn't be there."

"How can you know that?" Salvi asked. "I detect nothing."

"Go closer to her and see. You should be able to detect it."

Salvi pursed his lips and narrowed his eyes. "What am I meant to detect?"

Abbie groaned in frustration. "Magic. It's back, and stronger."

Gwen slept through all this discussion and Abbie was surprised by that too and wondered why.

Salvi closed his eyes and put his hands on Gwen's midsection. He seemed to be meditating and then after a few minutes opened his eyes and nodded. "You're right. There is magic. It's not Gwen's."

"Well, what is it? What's going on?" Abbie asked.

Salvi moved back and stood away from the bed. "I think that although Gwen really did own this body, what we think of as Gwen isn't really her."

Abbie fell back. "What? That's makes no sense." She pushed back the hope the comment stoked in her mind though.

Salvi nodded slowly. "Yes, I think it does. Gwen was thrown out of her body more than five years ago. With nowhere to reside, she faded. Became what you could call a ghost. A thread of her was anchored to her body. During the ritual Nira was banished to the afterlife. Annwyn came close to being sent too, but I think she's still there. Gwen is but a memory. She's not a full spirit. She didn't get banished, because she wasn't in the body, just tied by a fine filament of spirit. All it has done is come to inhabit the body one more time."

"You mean Gwen will die?"

"Gwen is already dead, I'm afraid. That magic you feel is Annwyn trying to come back."

Abbie collapsed onto the chair. "Will she make it?"

"That depends. I think you should get Dane down here. Put them in the same bed if he's not able to sit by her. It's their anchor that will support her."

"And you're sure about this? Because if I tell Rolf this and it doesn't pan out, he'll be really pissed with me. And there's no saying what it would do to Dane. Rolf is up there preparing him for the worst."

"You go then, and I'll stay with Annwyn. I can help Gwen fade now and then Annwyn will have a clear path."

"I feel sorry for the girl, for Gwen. She didn't ask for any of this."

"I guess not. But what was done can't be undone. A spirit alone without a body to nourish it for five years. I'm amazed she has any sense of who she was."

Abbie nodded. "All right then. I'll go talk to Rolf." She leaned down and kissed Gwen on the forehead, suddenly quite emotional. Gwen didn't have a chance, was given no opportunity. Then, she left the room to go find Rolf.

Rolf was hunched over and wringing his hands. Dane was out cold by the looks of him, but his at-rest face held pain and sadness. "Hi," she said. "You're back."

Rolf jerked up, eyes widening. "Yes, just now. What's wrong? Is she ...?"

"No, no one is dead just yet. Here's the thing. Annwyn is not dead. She's not quite alive either. Salvi says Gwen is just a shadow, the remnant of the girl who once owned the body. She came into the body after the banishment because she'd been hanging around. Like a ghost you know."

Rolf surged to his feet. "Then Annwyn isn't ..."

"We don't think so. She just seems to be having trouble coming back. Nira is definitely gone; that's why the magic I smell is different. I must have been able to scent Nira mixed with Annwyn previously."

Rolf ran his fingers through his hair and sighed like he hadn't slept for a year. "I've let Dane down gently. I think he understands she's gone. He hasn't spoken since. I've been worried."

Abbie looked over to where Dane lay. "They have a strong bond. Salvi suggests, and I agree, that we should put them together. We should take him to Annwyn and let them find each other."

Rolf lowered his head and turned to Abbie again. "I'll bring him. Can you help?"

"Sure," Abbie said. She had the she-wolf to call on for extra strength. "Where's Reeva and Gene?"

"They went out to find a restaurant and a hotel. They'll send word and then we can join them."

"You mean sleep in a real bed. Eat real food?" Abbie was exhausted and hungry. The stress and the exertion had taken its toll, but with all that had been going on she hadn't had time to acknowledge how worn out she was.

Rolf chuckled as he went to Dane's head and arranged his limbs for transport. "This is Colorado. You can eat plenty here, big servings."

Abbie went to Dane's feet and together they lifted him. They could've asked for magical transport, but it was better this way. It was important for Rolf, she thought. He needed to be part of this healing. Dane and he were friends and had been a lot longer than Abbie had been around, and Annwyn, too, if she understood correctly. Rolf was a protector and nurturer. He'd performed both roles with Dane when he'd been cursed. And he'd performed them for her, too. Maybe they could have a bond as powerful. A nice little daydream that. Abbie let it slide as they negotiated Dane's bulk down the corridor and into the room. Salvi had been leaning over Annwyn's body and righted himself on their entry. "Oh good. Just in time. Gwen is saying goodbye. She had to understand that she was no longer living and that it was time to go. I'm about to say the last prayer for her release.

They laid Dane on the floor and went to stand by the bed.

Salvi chanted out a verse in a language that Abbie didn't understand, but the tone was soft and assuring. Gwen had her eyes open and they closed slowly and her face relaxed. There was a pause then a rush of magic piled into the body, hot and strong. Abbie gasped.

"What is it?" Rolf asked, face alarmed.

"The magic is stronger."

"Yes, it is. Quick, put her soulmate with her," Salvi said.

They moved Annwyn's body over toward the wall and then lifted Dane beside her. Rolf leaned over to join their hands and said into Dane's ear. "Annwyn is not gone. She's still alive. You need to help her come back, Dane. Hear me. Annwyn is alive. You need to help her."

Then the three of them stood there watching. After a few minutes of nothing happening, Salvi turned to them. "There's nothing more I can do. Rolf, do you mind if I go home now? I'd like to catch up with Leo and Mar to finish a ritual we were enjoying before you called us here."

"Of course. Thank you. We owe you so much."

Salvi grinned. "Why don't you both visit us in Rome? We could show you a good time." Salvi winked at Abbie and she didn't know how to interpret that look.

"I promised that I would, and I keep my word. Any trip will involve a plane, though, so I can't just pop in when the mood takes me.

Salvi chuckled. "Still don't like the magical mode of transport? Oh well, in time you might get used to it. Use that phone of yours to tell me how this works out. I'd like to hear that the sorcerer couple are restored."

Salvi then stepped closer to Rolf and kissed him full on the lips. Not a tongue job, but not a peck either. Salvi then turned to Abbie and did the same thing. Abbie didn't pull away, but wasn't certain how to take the gesture either. Then he was gone.

Abbie lifted an eyebrow at Rolf. He harrumphed in response and folded his arms across his chest. Abbie was feeling done in. She waited a minute or so and then decided enough was enough. Nothing much had happened since they put Dane in the bed. However, Annwyn's magic was definitely there. "Do you mind if I go find Reeva and Gene? I'm hungry and tired."

Rolf turned to her, his gaze assessing. "Yes, by all means. I'll stay here until I know the result. I'll be along later."

"Sure," she said and then quickly gave him a peck on the cheek. His eyes widened and then he nodded. "Catch you later," she said as she shut the door behind her.

⚜

It didn't take long for Abbie to catch up with Reeva and Gene. They were sitting in the lobby of an elegant hotel, not quite five star but, considering the location, the best available. It was a concrete monstrosity that looked like a large capital letter 'A'. It had a nice bar area with modern and interesting decor. Abbie wasn't quite dressed appropriately, but Reeva waved her in. "I've secured rooms for you. I've taken the liberty of getting some clothes for you, too." She handed over a room key. "Go freshen up and we'll meet you in the restaurant. Gene's already gone up to his room."

Reeva did not look like she'd been dragged across the world chasing down rogue sorcerers and Abbie had to admire that talent.

Abbie twirled the room key. "Sure, I'll be back soon. Keep my seat warm. I'm starving."

The room was on the eighth level at the front of the building. She slipped out onto the balcony and saw that they had views across the city, with the snow-capped Rocky Mountains in the distance. On an easy chair was a pile of clothes. Some for Rolf by the looks of it, and some for her. There was even a pile of make-up, all new.

Abbie swung into the bathroom, with its stone-looking tiles and chrome finishes. She stepped under the water and soaped up, snagging some hotel shampoo to give her long hair a thorough clean. She had to rinse it with conditioner twice to get the tangles out. Then she set about leisurely blow-drying her hair, making it bounce with waves. The styling brush Reeva had acquired was pretty good. It seemed like an age since Abbie had had the luxury of just being alone with herself and grooming.

With a towel wrapped around her, she went back into the room to sift through the clothes. Reeva did have a keen sense of style. She chose a lovely dark green cross-over dress, the skirt of which brushed the tops of Abbie's knees. It was dressy enough for dinner in the hotel. There were some rust and green pumps to go with the dress. Then she sat down in front of the mirror and stared at herself. She moisturised, loving the feel of the face cream, and then proceeded to put on make-up. There was two foundations and both matched Abbie's complexion. Reeva had a very good eye. There were several lipsticks to choose from. Abbie tried them all before settling on a neutral pink tone that gave her lips a glossy finish. She almost didn't recognise herself. No magic at work here, like the last time she dressed up. This was all hand administered, including the hair. Abbie posed in front of the mirror, liking what she saw. She felt almost human. Take that she-wolf, she thought, at the beast that lurked under her skin.

In the lift to join the others, she had a flash of guilt. She'd left Rolf to deal with Dane and Annwyn. She saw herself pouting in the mirrored wall of the elevator. Why should she feel guilty? It was going to work out. Dane and Annwyn would come good. Rafael, she shrugged. She didn't really care about him, unless he went rogue again. All that was ahead of her now was her future, her life. Decisions.

Gene was already at the table with Reeva when Abbie strode in. He stood up when she approached the table and Abbie was a bit put off by this old-fashioned courtesy. "Thank you," she said as he helped her to sit by pushing in her chair. She didn't like the attention or trust it.

Reeva had changed her clothes, too, and looked even more elegant. Before she forgot, Abbie expressed her thanks for the clothes and other personal items. Reeva smiled and nodded like a queen. "You look beautiful this evening, doesn't she, Gene?"

Gene had a glass of red wine in his hand, one with a large glass bowl on a thin stem. He paused before taking a sip. "Divine," he replied and let the crimson liquid slip through his lips.

He lowered his glass and picked up the bottle. "Care for some?"

Abbie lifted her glass and smiled. "Yes, that would be great." To Reeva she said. "Anything interesting on the menu?"

Reeva lifted her lips in a half smile. "For a hungry werewolf? A meat platter. It's a share plate that they can do for three or four if you're interested."

Abbie chuckled. "I'll be in for that. And it saves me looking at the menu. I admit to having a very hollow feeling in my middle that nothing but meat will fill."

Gene smiled and lifted his glass to her. Abbie straightened her shoulders, recognising the sexual advance. These weres were always fucking and thought nothing of casual relationships, but Abbie had to be cautious. This was Rolf's half-brother and there was some unresolved business between them. While she thought Gene was attractive, even if he was a mild pain in the ass, she didn't want to risk her relationship with Rolf. Not unless they severed it completely, which was entirely on the cards if she had the nerve for it. She wasn't quite sure which way the future would go and that unnerved her. If the business with the rogue sorcerer was done, then life should take on a new normalcy. That meant dealing with what was between them. So, she acknowledged Gene's admiration and tried to keep her response neutral.

Waiters came and removed the centre piece of the table and the candles to make room for the platter that was teeming with meat. All kinds of meat, beef, pork, chicken, lamb, goat, venison and sausages of all kinds too. Five kinds of sauces were laid on the table too, hot sauce, jus, barbeque and others. And, as a matter of form, a small platter of salad and a basket of fries sat alongside the main course.

The waiters left and Abbie didn't lunge but politely waited for Reeva as hostess to signal. This she did by making eye contact and lowering her head once. Abbie picked up a T-bone steak and bit into it. Then, realising her mistake, put in on her plate, wiped her hands and began cutting into it. It was soft and rare and delicious. She couldn't speak until after she'd eaten that and two pork chops. "It's good," she said grabbing a slice of lamb fillet. It didn't even make the plate but went straight into her mouth. Lamb was a bit of luxury in Colorado. They raised sheep, but it was a rare thing and considered rather gamey. Two big pieces of smoked brisket came into view as the top layer of meat was consumed and she eased one onto her plate. This meat was well done and slid off the bone. Slathered with barbeque sauce and accompanied by fries, she thought it delicious. Her hunger was nearly sated, but there was room for a little bit more and some salad. The wolf inside didn't like the greens, but she thought vitamins were important.

A server came by and added more fries to the basket. Abbie paused to see how her companions were doing. They were eating steadily, too, and the platter had only a few sausages left. She took one, leaving some for the others. Reeva sat back and lifted a hand. A server came over. "The same again please."

The server's widened eyes demonstrated how unusual a request that was. "Right away, madam."

Gene burped loudly and drank more wine, easing back into his chair and grinning. "That was good, mother."

"I'm glad you think so, son. We have reason to celebrate. This nasty business is over for now."

Gene drank deep and then put down his glass. "Until the next crisis."

"Always so negative. I'm sure it's my job to worry about things."

Gene looked around the room. "I need to get home. A few business deals need my input."

"Yes, I know, but I was hoping you would talk to your brother."

Gene refilled his glass and avoided looking at his mother. He looked under lowered eyelids at Abbie and winked. He took a long draft and sat back.

"Well, aren't you going to comment? It's not his fault, you know."

Gene breathed out of his nostrils long and hard and put the wine glass down carefully. "I don't blame him for being my brother. He's not even a bad wolf or alpha. A bit of a prick, but then who isn't? I'm just not ready to play happy families. Besides I need time to process things."

Reeva screwed up her mouth. "Everybody needs time and it is the most precious commodity. It's the thing we lose track of first and regret the most."

"Ah, philosophising too. What has got into you, mother?"

Reeva harrumphed. "Life. It's precious and it goes hand in hand with time. I should have sought Rolf out years ago. Now all that time can never be recaptured.

Gene's gaze flicked to Abbie. "What do you think?"

"Me?" Abbie fell back against her chair, hand on her chest. "Why are you bringing me into this?"

"You have a stake," he said.

"I do? How?"

Gene shared a look with his mother and then returned his gaze to her. "You're Rolf's mate."

"I'm not." Abbie said flatly. She was going to explain further, but another platter was on its way. Just as they set it down, she smelled Rolf approaching and turned in her chair.

He'd showered and changed into fresh clothes. Abbie must have been distracted by the meat to miss him entering the hotel.

Reeva waved and Gene frowned at the tablecloth. Rolf headed to the vacant seat opposite Abbie and between his half-brother and mother. "Thank you for the clothes, Reeva, and for leaving me a key at the desk."

"My pleasure, Rolf."

"Any news?" Abbie asked.

Rolf inclined his head. "Progress. They were in good hands, so I thought it was time to join you."

Abbie sighed slowly and nodded. It was good to hear.

Reeva smiled. "Just in time for some food. We have had the edge taken off our hunger so please go for it." She gestured to the meat platter.

Rolf met her look from across the table and gave Abbie a nod. "May I have some of that wine?" he asked Gene.

Gene grimaced. "Sure." He lifted the bottle and poured a good portion into Rolf's glass. He then started in on the steak.

Abbie slipped another slice of lamb on her plate, along with fries. Reeva and Gene also scooped more food on their plates. There wasn't much conversation. Rolf ate like he hadn't eaten for a week. He barely chewed, just cut and swallowed. Abbie wondered how he'd gotten on with Dane and Annwyn, but her questions would have to wait.

"May we see the dessert menu?" Reeva asked the server who came up to their table to enquire if they needed anything more.

Gene lifted a finger. "Another bottle of the same wine too, please."

"Do you eat dessert, Abbie?" Reeva asked. "I must admit to being partial to sweet things."

The menus were handed around, except for Rolf because he was still focused on eating and not really responding to external stimuli.

The dessert menu was lengthy. "I do like some desserts. Or at least I used to."

Her eyes focused on key lime pie and that sounded like her kind of thing. Reeva settled on a banana split and Gene decided on a cheese platter.

Abbie passed the basket of fries to Rolf, who had stopped sliding meat onto his plate and eating it. He took the basket and upended it on his plate, stopping to adorn the pile with three types of sauces. He took a long pull of the wine and then got right back to eating.

"Did you want dessert, Rolf?" Reeva asked leaning toward him.

"You choose," Rolf said. "I'll eat anything."

The server came over and Reeva ordered for them all. For Rolf she ordered a chocolate torte and a separate serve of ice cream. "Coffee, too, please," Reeva said to the server, "and bill it to my room." She flashed her key. The server inclined his head and backed away.

Rolf burped and then snaffled the remaining morsels of meat from the platter—two bits of chicken. He relaxed a little and sat back in his chair, resembling his half-brother no end. Reeva just beamed at them both. Her two sons. Something she was proud of Abbie supposed. Abbie felt like an outsider just then, but instead of acting on that feeling and leaving she stayed put. She had a part in this. Gene was right on some level. Exactly what, she didn't know but she wanted to hear what Rolf was going to say.

"I take it you know about our blood connection," Rolf said as he angled his head toward Gene.

Gene sniffed. "My mother had spoken of it." He didn't sound happy or friendly.

Rolf leaned forward. "I didn't know my mother lived. Understand? This is as new to me as it is to you." His turned to face his mother. "I'm sorry. I hope you're not offended by anything I say next.

Reeva pursed her lips and shook her head. "I won't be offended. I'm not proud of leaving you behind."

Gene sat back, glanced to his mother and then back at Rolf. "What do you want? Money?"

It was Rolf's turn to look bewildered and he fell back in his seat as if struck. "Money? Why the fuck would I want your money? I like my life. I'm content."

Gene played with the stem of his wine glass, flashed a look at his mother before focusing on Rolf again. "Then what do you want?"

Rolf shrugged. "I don't have anything in mind. I just thought if you were willing, we could get to know each other better."

With his mouth closed. Gene swirled his tongue over his teeth. "I see." He flashed a grin. "Life is pretty hectic with my business and the pack. But I could find some time …"

"Great." Rolf said, not sounding enthusiastic. "You won't mind if I visit our mother from time to time?"

Gene shook his head. "I wouldn't get in the way of my mother's happiness for anything. We've been through a lot together. We have each other's back."

"In that case, I might go to bed." Rolf stood up and put out a hand. "Will you come with me, Abbie?"

Surprised, Abbie's mouth fell open and her skin heated. She was tired and she wanted to talk to Rolf, but the manner of his invitation set her defences on alert. It smacked of ownership and domination and she couldn't let it pass. She smiled. "I'll be up soon. I have dessert coming. I have my key." She waved it so he could see it.

His eyes narrowed and he nodded once. Abbie couldn't help watching as he strode away. There was tension and anger and something else, hurt.

Reeva let out a long sigh. "You have balls, Abbie."

She turned to face the old woman. "I have to do this on my own terms."

Gene leaned over, breathed red wine on her. "You know I'll take you if you need somewhere to go?"

She tossed her head. "I suppose you'll let me be a free agent in your pack? No requirement to submit to you as alpha?"

That got Gene's attention. "Hell no. You would have to acknowledge me as alpha. Besides, I want you. I'll have you as my fuck buddy anytime."

"A compliment, I'm sure."

She was relieved when the desserts arrived.

Abbie took a turn outside the hotel before heading up to the room she shared with Rolf. She wasn't being chicken hearted. She just needed to build all her arguments and all her energy. She loved Rolf so much that she feared she might buckle, and that would do neither of them any good.

The door opened silently and she pushed into the room. She was hoping that Rolf wasn't naked, because that would seriously undermine her resolve. It was time for discussion and not sex. If the talking went well then there would be plenty of sex later. She stepped into the room. Rolf stood by the open window, the curtains fluttering around him. He turned as she kicked off the pumps she was wearing. "Hi," she said. "You all right?"

He stepped closer but, with the room in shadow, she couldn't see his expression. She tried smelling him and that was strange too. He wasn't angry, as far as she could tell, but she had no idea what it was that he was exuding. Tension, fear, sadness and something else.

"I went for a long run today. There's some kind of wilderness park near here. I ran as a wolf and it helped me clear my head, helped me gain perspective."

Abbie said nothing, just stood there, watching, waiting. He took a step closer and his face caught the light, sending the cleft in his chin into darker shadows, his eyes black holes. He was holding himself together, just.

"When Dane lost Annwyn ... I mean when we thought he had, and I had to help him deal with it, I struggled."

"It must have been hard," Annwyn offered.

"It was the hardest thing I've ever done. But not because of Dane. I felt for him, yes. But I suddenly knew what grief was, what my own would be ..."

Abbie lowered her eyebrows trying to understand. "I don't know what you mean."

"When Dane was faced with losing Annwyn, I understood what it would be like to lose you."

"Oh."

He took another step closer. Abbie stayed where she was, even though her knees trembled. "I know you won't submit to me, Abbie. I understand why. I respect it as well. You're strong in your own right and an asset to any pack, any alpha. I've been an idiot all this time not to see who you really are and what your potential is."

A small noise escaped her mouth. She didn't know what to say.

He took another step and she could feel the heat coming off him. "I think we have to do something about this situation. I've been wracking my brains. I spoke to my mother to get her thoughts. And now I come to you, heart bared for you to see. What will you do with me?"

Tears had started to leak down her cheeks. "What will I do with you? I want you Rolf, more than anything. But I need to be your equal. If you can't agree to that, can't see a way to make that work, then we have to say goodbye."

Rolf trembled. "No. There's no goodbye in this. I have a proposition."

"A proposition?"

"Yes, marry me. Be my co-alpha in the pack. I know you have a lot to learn about being a wolf, but you're strong. The pack will accept you as I accept you."

Abbie trembled all over. Excitement, emotion, love and fear all comingled. She was a mess. "Rolf!" She had trouble controlling her emotion. Tears sprung up again.

Closing the gap between them, Rolf engulfed her in his arms. He didn't try to kiss or caress. He just held her. He was trembling as much as she was. After a few minutes of quiet, where she tried to calm down, Rolf asked, "Do you have an answer for me?"

Abbie could not speak. It was too much to process. It was everything she'd hoped for, but she had not allowed herself to even think it was a possibility. Rolf had offered her everything that was in his power to give.

"I love you, Abbie. I think I have from the moment we met in that stupid bar. I was tempted by you even then, but had business to attend to. Then you turn up as a victim of the curse and the only one to survive. I've been hot for you since the moment we met, and you've been under my skin since the first time we fucked. You've got to see that this is destiny, it's fate, it's love. I love you, Abbie. I know I can't live my life without you. I will do anything I can to make you see that, before I ruin it and let you go. Don't go. Don't leave me, Abbie."

"I don't want to leave you. The prospect of leaving you was tearing me apart. I love you, too, but I want to share your burden, not be trodden under by it. If you meant what you said, I'll marry you and be your co-alpha and I'll make our pack respect me and fear me, just as much as they fear you, maybe even more."

Abbie lifted her face to his, draped her arms around his neck and drew him down for a kiss. The heat in that kiss would've melted paintwork. "Do you mind if we just sleep tonight?" Abbie asked. "I'm so done in, and so much has happened, that I can't relax enough for sex. Is that okay?"

Rolf hugged her. "I know exactly what you mean. Let's snuggle for the night. There's a lot of things to think about, to talk about ... to feel."

They stripped off their clothes and climbed into bed. Abbie snuggled into Rolf and he held her along his body. He was aroused, but that wasn't anything new. What was new was that Abbie trusted him to just hold her, until she asked for something more. They had trust, along with the lust. Respect too and mutual understanding. It was a good start.

Come morning, Abbie had digested all that had occurred the night before. She couldn't have said her sleep was restful. But one thing really stood out. When she thought of Rolf and being his wife and co-alpha, it felt right deep in her gut. It felt true, too, true to what she wanted.

Rolf was instantly awake when she turned her body and ran a hand up his arm. Their eyes met and then their lips and then Abbie didn't think much at all. Later, exhausted and sweaty, they staggered to the shower together. Reeva was expecting them at breakfast and then they had to see how Annwyn and Dane were doing. Rolf had entrusted them to the care of the sorcerers from the collegium, as Jill had proved to be trustworthy and efficient.

As they dressed, Abbie experienced a sense of calm and that sense of rightness continued. Rolf gazed at her, his eyes bright. Holding hands, they headed for the lift. Reeva was alone at the table when they arrived. The den mother saw them holding hands and smiled. Her eyes sparkled and crinkled with delight. "So, you have made a decision," she said, gaze shifting between them.

Rolf nodded to Abbie, indicating that she should speak. "Yes, we have. Rolf has made me an offer I can't refuse."

Reeva clapped her hands. "This is splendid. Tell me more."

The took their seats and then Abbie explained what Rolf had proposed.

"A wedding and co-alpha. That is going to be interesting. As the mother of the groom, do I get an invite?"

Abbie sat back. "I hadn't thought about the official part of things, but of course."

They settled down to eat the huge buffet breakfast. Hunger got the better of Abbie and she worked her way through all the courses on offer. With all the excitement and stress of the last few days, food hadn't been a priority.

Reeva said farewell. She and Gene were being transported back to Sydney via magic. Rolf and Abbie headed back to the collegium to check on Dane and Annwyn. Jill greeted them on arrival, her dark skin looking pasty and her brown eyes bloodshot. She hadn't had a chance to sleep yet. Without complaint, the sorceress took them up to where Dane and Annwyn were being cared for. "They're doing remarkably well."

"That's good. After we've visited them, is there any chance we could get a lift back home?" Rolf asked. "We have a few things to arrange."

"Of course, I'll see to it myself. I haven't had much opportunity to visit Australia. It's a bit off the beaten track."

"I though you couldn't do that ..." Abbie snapped her fingers.

"I can't. Not yet. I'll get help, but I want to come with you so I can check out the country. I've always wanted to visit."

Rolf inclined his head. Abbie was certain he was happy they were off the beaten track. There was certainly more supernaturals in the northern hemisphere. After what they'd been through, Abbie was inclined to agree. Maybe once she'd wanted to be famous and important in her field. Now she just wanted to find her feet again and learn what she needed to know to take her rightful place in the pack and the wider were community. She missed her friends, and knew they mourned her because they thought her dead. At least they had some closure and would recover. Abbie would always miss her old life, especially her friends. But she had no control over being cursed. She was the changeling cursed. Yet she wasn't going to let that ruin her life. With her strong will and her gifts, she would make a good life for herself.

Dane was sitting up in bed, looking somewhat normal. He had dark rings around his eyes and lacked energy. He and Rolf hugged and clenched hands. Annwyn was laying in the bed, looking pale. Abbie went up to her and smiled shyly. Her scent was different, lacked some of the deeper spice that permeated it before. That had to be Nira's influence. "How do you feel?" she asked, after giving the sorceress a peck on the cheek.

"Zapped, flat but grateful."

Abbie smiled and clasped her hand. "I can believe that." Annwyn had been to death's door and back again.

Annwyn elbowed up into a higher position on the bed. "Dane told me what he knew. I have to thank you for letting them know I was there. I needed help to get back. If not for you, my body would have died and I would've ended up like poor Gwen."

"I was glad I could help," she replied. "Gwen seemed very real, but she could never have kept your body alive."

Annwyn tried to smile, but tears flowed instead. "I have never been so scared in my life. I'm so grateful to have a life."

"We're glad you're still here, too. Dane is especially grateful. Now, if I'm not being too egotistical, I have some news. Rolf and I are getting married."

Dane's face lit up. "Well done, Rolf!" They high-fived each other. Abbie coughed, catching Dane's attention. He grinned at her. "I'm not sure how to congratulate you. If I had the strength I'd give you a bear hug. I'd hoped that you two would work it out."

Rolf lifted his chin. "She's going to be co-alpha."

Dane's eyes widened and Annwyn laughed. "Of course, she is," Annwyn said. The sorceress leaned forward and put out a hand for Abbie to grasp. This Abbie did and squeezed the other woman's fingers. There was respect in Annwyn's eyes and acceptance. Now that

Nira was gone, Annwyn was different, gentler perhaps. Time would tell.

"Now that you two are on the mend, we've asked to be taken home. I hope that's okay," Rolf said.

Dane nodded. "We may be a while. The collegium is in disarray. Rafael is not fit to lead and Brun was found dead, so Jill tells me. It's time for some change."

Abbie focused on Dane. "Are you going to lead?"

Dane shook his head. "No, not exactly. I've been asked to help reorganise things and oversee the installation of new leadership."

Rolf's head jerked up. "Elections?"

Dane nodded his head. "Yes. Elections and fairer representation. I'll send you word if I don't get to see you before then."

They shook hands. Tears leaked out of Abbie's eyes. She didn't understand all of the political undercurrents, but sensed this was a new and promising opportunity for all of the supernaturals. Abbie hugged Dane and Annwyn once more when Jill arrived with another sorcerer called Brodie.

"Don't worry," Jill said. "They're in good hands."

Young Brodie was a tall, skinny redhead. If not for the heavy scent of magic surrounding him, she would've thought him a teenager who spent way too much time with computer games. "Ready?" he said.

He took Jill's hand and then nodded. Abbie held Rolf's hand and before she knew it the ground was gone from beneath her feet and then she was standing in the drive outside Dane's house.

Brodie bowed. "We'll leave you here. I promised Jill some sightseeing while we're Down Under."

"Thank you," Abbie said.

They winked out of sight. Rolf's heat spread across her back as he put his arms around her. He lowered his head and inhaled the scent of her hair. "It's so good to be back ... with you at my side."

She turned in his arms, reached up to clasped him around his neck. "It is indeed. I suppose we should talk to the pack now."

Rolf grinned. "They can wait an hour or so. I have something I want to show you."

"I'm sure I've seen it before ..."

Rolf snickered. "We should make sure of that don't you think?"

The she-wolf inside her grinned like a loon. "One can never been too sure of the facts ..."

They entered the shed where it had started and locked the door. Not soon after howls echoed in the trees. The pack was complete.

The End

ACKNOWLEDGMENTS

I acknowledge that this book was written on Ngunngawal country and I payday respects to the Ngunnawal people, the traditional custodians of the land, and elders past, present and emerging.

I'd also like to acknowledge that this book is very overdue. I didn't expect it to take this long, truly. A Phd, a pandemic which completely lost me my focus and creativity, contributed to this delay.

I'd like to thank Lily Mulholland, fellow Canberra writer, who beta read the book and whose comments and detailed suggestions inspired me to finish it. Her thoughtful words held my hand as I went through the book fixing the problems she identified and helped me regain my confidence after not writing fiction for so long.

I'd also like to thank Nicole Murphy, fellow writer and friend for her comments and her unfailing support. We've been at this a while now, haven't we?

Many thanks to Debbie Phillips for edits and Cathy Walker for the great cover, which she made five years ago. I'm glad I can finally put the words behind it.

Dani Kristoff

June 2022

ABOUT THE AUTHOR

Dani Kristoff is a Canberra-based author, who delights in reading and writing paranormal romance. She's been writing since late 2000, which means some 22 years, although she's been concentrating her efforts on science fiction, fantasy and horror. Published both traditionally and independently, she's currently waiting for the results of her PhD in creative writing at the University of Canberra. Her research area is feminism and romance. Her partner is also a writer and they get up to geekery whenever possible.

http://danikristoff.wordpress.com